INCURSION: KNIGHTMARE

THE KNIGHT'S BANE TRILOGY - BOOK 1

BRYAN DONIHUE

Edited by
LAURA "L WRAY" HEWITT

Section 28 Publishing

INCURSION: Knightmare
The Knight's Bane Trilogy–Book 1

Send inquiries to:
Section 28 Publishing
Grand Rapids, Mi 49544
e-mail: bryan@s28.us

Edited by Laura "L-Wray" Hewitt

DEDICATION

It may seem unusual for a paranormal action book, but this book is first and foremost dedicated to Jesus, the Christ - the only true Savior who can save us from evil. He is the real source of Hope.

This book is dedicated to my wife, Christina, and my brood of kids. You've put up with many months of my unavailablility. Thank you for putting up with me.

I have three wonderful editors on this project:

- Kathryn Gerard was my first editor. She helped me get this into shape for the original printing.
- Laura Hewitt is my General Editor. She is the one who truly refined my work to make me sound better, and she pushed me to produce the best story possible.
- David Cassiday is my Continuity Editor. He makes sure that I don't screw up all the little details, while also making sure that the story makes sense.

Any and all of the mistakes that are left in this book are solely mine, usually because I didn't listen to Laura or David.

Thank you to my Grand Rapids gaming group, Incursion: Hidden Worlds. They brought this story to life. They are:

- Ryan DeBoer - Burt "Six" Holstein
- David Cassiday - John "Spooky" Smith
- Zachariah Watkins - Jesús "God" Rivera
- Amanda Verburg - Rebekah "Boomer" Callahan
- Eulene Freeland - Noelle "Doc" Sorenson
- Simon Verburg - Jonas "Ghost" Vanhof
- Nate Miller - Arthur "Heavy" Murphy
- Scott Coles - Christian "Do-Right" Folsom
- Matt Poferl - William "Scout" Buckhorn

Based on an original roleplaying game and world created by Bryan Donihue, Troye Gerard, and David Cassiday. The original "Section 28" name idea was from Troye, and he allowed me to twist it to my own particular flavor.

INDIEGOGO SUPPORTERS

For this novel, I ran a crowdfunding campaign to pay for some of the (rather minor) expenses incurred in self-publishing. I ran the campaign on Indiegogo (indiegogo.com), and can't say enough good things about their service.

I had a group of incredible backers in the campaign. Their support made the campaign successful, and I cannot thank them enough!

Campaign Contributors

Esoteric Research
Jeff Jackson
Jeremy Sampsell

Field Agent
David Cassiday
Ryan DeBoer
Paul Donihue

Veteran Hunter
Matthew Eastman

Eulene Freeland
Troye Gerard
Nate Miller

Support Staff
Jeff Donihue

PROLOGUE

Hunger. Pain. Cruel hunger gnawed away at the creature. Forced to hunt. Searching for prey to feed the growing hunger. Cold, dead eyes saw the world around it. Even though it was a dark, moonless night, the creature saw the path and the surrounding woods as if the sun were overhead.

Sounds. The rhythmic pounding of footsteps on the path. As the creature turned toward the sounds, it caught sight of a young woman. Even though the girl was still fifty yards away, the noise of the music on her headphones was apparent to the creature's newly heightened senses.

Blood. Smell the blood. Nostrils flaring, the creature could almost taste the blood pumping through the veins of the girl. Forcing itself to wait for the prey to come closer, the hunger drove the creature to the edge of madness. As the prey neared, the creature hunched into the dark shadows.

Running. The prey noticed the creature and screamed in alarm. She stumbled to a halt, turned, and ran away in a blind panic. Like prey was supposed to do. The creature leapt toward the girl and snarled as it quickly ran down its prey. One hand reached out and savagely grabbed the girl by the scruff of the neck. A heavy jerk and the prey was dangling from the creature's hand. The prey's screams grew more frantic as she came face to face with the creature. Reaching up, the creature hissed at the girl, and then hit her in the head with a mighty swing of its free hand. The girl shuddered, and her screaming abruptly stopped.

Alive. The prey was still breathing. Her head lolled in unconsciousness, and the creature grinned. Sharp fangs glistened in the darkness as the creature salivated at the thought of feeding. The creature threw its prize over its shoulder and ran into the shadows.

THE EYES ARE THE WINDOWS TO THE SOUL. WHEN THE SOUL LEAVES, eyes that were once capable of driving men wild lose their spark and grow cold. Her eyes were a bright blue. And lifeless.

The flashing light of a camera. The red and blue strobe patterns of the police cruiser. The portable work lights around the crime scene. The bright flashlights shone by the detectives. But none of them were bright enough to bring light back to those eyes.

A short, overweight man leaned over the body of the girl in the alley. His identification badge carelessly clipped to his scrubs proclaimed that he was the Medical Examiner. Careful to not disturb the scene, he reached out a gloved hand and gently closed the girl's eyes. "What gorgeous eyes you had," he murmured.

"What did you say, Bill?" The man in the sheriff's uniform leaned closer to the M.E. and peered at the body surrounded by the detritus in the alley.

Bill Stewart looked up at the sheriff. "Sorry, John. Was just muttering to myself. OK. White female. Approximate age... late teens? Maybe twenty? Did you find any ID?"

John Klooster, the sheriff responsible for the safety of nearly 10,000 residents of Trinidad, Colorado, wearily ran a hand through his short, salt-and-peppered hair. "No personal effects. No purse. No phone. We will go through this alley with a fine-toothed comb when we move the body out, but, if it's like the others..." John trailed off and shrugged.

Bill nodded slowly and looked back at the girl. Laid in the middle of the alley under a broken streetlamp, she was clad only in her undergarments. Studying her hands and body, Bill continued his examination. "No apparent defensive wounds. No visible signs of rape, but I'll test her when we get her back to the morgue. No blood, no bodily fluids." Looking up at the sheriff, he said, "Did your guys find any sign of the attack in this alley?"

John slowly shook his head, and Bill continued with his observations. "I'd say she was dumped here, like the others. Weird, though... It looks like she has the same post-mortem animal marks on her that the others had."

A deputy approaching the sheriff interrupted Bill's train of thought. Noticing the deputy, John looked up and said, "What do you have, Morris?"

Deputy Morris handed a copy of a missing persons report to the sheriff. "I thought I recognized the victim. She was reported missing about a week ago by her parents. They had a recent picture, and it looks just like her."

The sheriff turned toward the body and compared the picture on the report to the lifeless body on the ground. It sure looked like her. He bowed his head and sighed. Looking up, he handed the copy of the report to the Medical Examiner and looked back at the waiting deputy. "Good work, Morris. See if Shane needs any help with the evidence."

As the deputy walked toward one of the detectives at the other end of the alley, the sheriff looked at the M.E., "Well, Bill, she's all yours. When can you get to her?"

Bill thought for a moment and replied, "I'll get to her first thing in the morning. I should have a preliminary for you by tomorrow afternoon."

Thinking through his next several hours' worth of work, the sheriff said, "That'll work fine. The detectives will be at this all night anyway, and I've got to start the paperwork."

BY LATE AFTERNOON THE NEXT DAY, THE GIRL'S PARENTS HAD identified their daughter, and the M.E. had filed his preliminary report with the sheriff. The sheriff had entered the initial report into his department's computer system, which was integrated with the Federal Law Enforcement Information Network.

Hidden in the Law Enforcement Information Network, or LEIN, was a small program that reported traffic back to the NSA. Part of ECHELON, the NSA's domestic electronic spying program, this small subroutine forwarded a copy of the information to the data center.

In the ECHELON data center, a tiny data worm sifted through incoming information, looking for a specific set of parameters. The programmers who created and maintained the ECHELON data center did not know that this little data worm was in their system. Even if the legions of technical wizards had any idea that this little worm were present, they would have to torch the whole system to root this little worm out. But the technical wizards running the most secret software in the nation were unaware that their ultra-secure system was infected. It wasn't their fault—the ECHELON system, and every United States Government system like it, had been built with the worm installed.

This little worm found the report from the sheriff of a small town called Trinidad, Colorado. Recognizing specific keywords from a very long and eclectic list, it looked for more reports from this sheriff in Colorado. Then it moved away from the LEIN reports and searched for archived news reports with similar parameters. Gathering enough data to satisfy its programming, it hijacked a small portion of the system and forwarded its findings to a specific secure server, in a specific secure data center just outside Langley, Virginia.

And then it looked for other "interesting" things.

I

ORIGIN

1

SMITH

Section 28, Outside Langley, Virginia.

There was nothing remarkable about the building complex located just outside Langley, Virginia. A high chain-link fence surrounded the property and modest parking lot. Most people supposed it was a commercial or industrial park full of warehouses or service businesses. No signs hung on any of the buildings to indicate the names of the businesses, and the landscaping was minimal. With a simple brick facade and concrete block construction, the squat exterior did little to attract visitors. The only distinguishing feature about the complex was its private hanger and airstrip, though that was often unnoticed by passersby since it was safely hidden in the rear of the complex.

If someone happened to notice that the complex was even there, they would likely pass on by. If anyone stopped at the building, they would be stopped at the gated entrance outside the parking area. With a gated entrance large enough to accommodate tractor trailers, the guard shack at the gate housed one uniformed guard.

If a visitor is welcome and had permission to be on site, the guard would open the steel gates, and the visitor would pull forward and park in the small main lot. Approaching the building's only visible entrance, a visitor would see an electronic key-card access panel, a small push-button call system, and the words "Authorized Personnel Only" on a thick glass door.

If the visitor is expected, they would be buzzed through the door. Inside, they would wait in a small atrium until the second set of doors were unlocked from inside, then they would enter a typical reception area with a receptionist perched behind a high desk. There, the visitor would wait for their party to come and retrieve him or her, getting an RFID encoded "Visitor" badge from the receptionist.

If a visitor is unwelcome, they would not be allowed past the steel gates. At any attempt of forcefully gaining admittance to the facility, the guard would push an alarm button. This would trigger several events. First, the signal would reach the guard room inside the complex, and an armed rapid response team would be activated. That same signal immediately would be transmitted to the FBI Hostage Rescue Team at the FBI Training Academy on nearby Marine Corps Base Quantico, letting them know a high-value government installation needs their assistance.

Next, the steel gates would lock, and pop-up barriers hidden beneath the asphalt would spring out of the surface behind the gates in a rush of pneumatic air. Designed to stop a run-away armored vehicle, these barriers would be capable of ripping through the underside of most vehicles.

Inside the guard shack, a hidden panel on the wall would open, and the guard would have immediate access to an M4 carbine with a supply of armor piercing 5.56mm ammunition. After loading the rifle, the guard would defend the gates behind bullet-resistant windows and walls of the shack.

If this were not enough to deter an unwelcome guest, the similarly armed group of security officers pouring out of the building would deal with the threat. They would arrest this unlucky visitor for trespassing on government property and would spend a long time in a federal penitentiary all the while trying to determine what sort of building it was that he or she found.

For those unwelcome guests with malicious intent: the armed security team carried automatic rifles and are backed up by hidden machine-gun nests and missile launchers on the roof. Any survivors would then be sent to Guantanamo Bay for interrogation.

IN ONE BUILDING IN THE COMPLEX, A MAN SAT AT A NONDESCRIPT DESK in a sparsely furnished office. The man had close-cropped black hair and black eyes hidden behind small reading glasses. His dark gray pinstripe suit, white shirt, and black tie marked him as a middle manager, while his office, battle-scarred surplus desk, and less-than-comfortable visitors' chairs revealed that he was a government functionary.

The man in the office was pouring over intelligence reports from other agencies and situation reports from the teams of agents he supervised. Hearing a knock on his door, he did not even bother to look up as he said, "Come."

A young man opened the office door and leaned in. "The Director wants to see you, when you get free, boss."

"Fine, Timothy. Let me secure these files, and I'll head upstairs. Would you let him know I'm coming?"

Timothy agreed and returned to his desk outside the man's office. The man in the gray suit collected his files into stacks and reached over to put them in his personal safe. As the safe door closed, he placed his hand on the top of the safe, fingers splayed wide. Around the edges of the safe door, a series of odd looking characters appeared, glowing with a soft green light. The characters disappeared when the man removed his hand from the top of the safe.

Securing the files, he reached for a mug of coffee that was cooling rapidly on his desk. The man drained the last few swallows of coffee and left his office, nodding to his secretary as he passed.

He walked down a long, wide corridor, marked only occasionally with other office doors. None of the other doors had administrators in front of them, and the man mused that it was nice to have a secretary. As he got to the elevator, he pushed a button and waited for a chime to indicate the elevator's arrival. When the doors opened, he pressed the button for the Director's office suite. A small panel slid aside, and a fingerprint scanner levered out. Placing his right thumb on the scanner, a small retina-reading device emerged from behind another small panel at eye level. The man obediently removed his glasses and placed his eye over the device.

Three floors below, the server dedicated to internal security compared the RFID tag in the man's ID to the fingerprint and retinal scan on file. Upon receiving a positive match, the server then compared the biometrics to a list of those that had access to the Director's Suite. Confirming again that the man had special access clearance, the elevator gave an almost imperceptible shudder and ascended.

When the elevator stopped, the doors opened onto a plush reception area with an older woman sitting behind a welcoming mahogany desk that had a rich, warm patina that only comes with age and care. Seeing the man, she smiled warmly and picked up the phone and hit a button. "Sir, Agent Smith is here to see you. Shall I send him in?" A brief pause. "Yes, sir."

Motioning toward the man, she said, "He'll see you now, Agent Smith. Coffee today? Your usual?"

The man she called "Agent Smith" graciously smiled as he strode past her. "Thank you, Mary. I'd love some of your coffee. You really do have the best blends in the building."

Mary smiled and said, "Thanks. Go on in, I'll bring it to you." She turned and headed for the small alcove with the coffeemaker.

Agent Smith reflexively glanced at the red "classified meeting" light. Trained long ago to never interrupt a meeting in progress, he was relieved to see that the red light was not illuminated. Opening the heavy wooden door, he walked in to an office that was a stark contrast to his own.

Plush carpet covered the floor and the mahogany from the reception area carried through to the bookshelves, baseboards, and crown molding. A large and uncluttered mahogany desk was bare of a computer monitor or laptop. What little paper on the desk was meticulously arranged in a series of neat piles and file folders. The glow of a monitor through the glass top of the desk was the only concession to the need for a computer. The only piece of electronic equipment sitting on the desk was his office phone.

The two visitor chairs in front of the desk were stuffed-leather extravagance, and a small conference table with four chairs around it was staged for a meeting. At a gesture from the Director, Smith settled into one of the visitor chairs, turning as Mary brought coffee for both men. Mary closed the door on her way out of the room, pausing momentarily to reach over and turn on the meeting light.

Smith smiled as he inhaled the savory aroma wafting from the warm cup in his hands. "I don't know how she does it, but Mary makes the best coffee I've ever had."

Section 28 Director Clifton Day nodded and agreed with Smith. Several years ago, Director Day found Mary working as an administrator for another department, and she impressed him immensely. After pulling a few strings and threatening another Assistant Director, he orchestrated Mary's transfer to his office. After discussing her new benefits and the substantial raise in pay, she readily agreed to work for him. His life was much easier after that. Director Day knew he was a hard taskmaster and often ignored the social niceties when running his department, but Mary seemed to thrive on the job.

"James, I've read your reports and had Esoteric Analysis run your numbers as confirmation." Director Day's voice came out in a low growl. "Frankly, they scare the hell out of me. They couldn't find any fault in your work and came up with the same recommendation that you did. As of today, I've opened Operation Orbweaver, and I'm approving the formation of your third team, Knightmare. Have you selected any candidates?"

Supervising Agent in Charge James Smith thought for a moment and nodded slowly. His cultured voice had a hint of a southern accent. "Yes, sir. I have pre-screened several candidates. I'm only waiting for your approval to recruit and train. I've still got a couple holes in the team, but I should have the rest recruited by next week."

"Good," Director Day's deep voice rumbled. "Let Mary know if you need anything. Go get your new team spun up. If you are right, we will need them soon."

SAC Smith stood and smoothed imaginary wrinkles in his suit pants. Reaching out, he shook the proffered hand from Director Day and headed towards the door. As he walked towards the elevator, he heard Day shout through the open door to his office, "Mary, get DSS Andrews on the line. Schedule a working lunch here."

2

SIX

Baghdad, Iraq.

Commander Burt Holstein rolled up to the U.S. Embassy doors in one of his company's armored Humvee vehicles. His driver was his second-in-command, Robert Guzman. The trip to the embassy was a relatively short one, but it pulled him away from his current assignment, and it grated on him to be called to the embassy like an errant puppy while his team was out protecting some State Department VIPs.

Both he and Guzman had been contacted by his direct boss, the Regional Security Officer for Diplomatic Security Services. Told to grab his second-in-command and report to the embassy "ASAP," his arguments were cut off before they could form. Leaving the VIPs in the hands of his two squad leaders, Burt snagged a Humvee from the motor pool and tossed the keys to Guzman. The short ride to the embassy was filled with questions as neither he nor Guzman could figure out why they were summoned to the RSO's office.

Climbing out of the oversized SUV, the baking heat of Baghdad crashed into him with physical force, the normally oppressive heat compounded by the fifty pounds of armor, gear, and weapons worn by Burt and his driver. Normally, a civilian wearing that much gear and firepower approaching a U.S. Embassy would set alarm bells ringing and precipitate a violent response from local law enforcement.

Fortunately for Burt, he was not a normal citizen, in a normal city, in a normal country. Burt Holstein was the commanding officer of a team of contractors hired by the State Department to provide security for diplomatic VIPs and their families. Holstein was a senior team leader from the company that used to be known as "Blackwater." Now known as "Academi," the company had a multi-million dollar, multi-year contract to provide private security contractors to augment the Diplomatic Security Services agents in Iraq and Afghanistan. And Holstein was one of Academi's best team leaders.

Burt currently led a team of twenty contractors that worked for DSS. Most often, he and his team were charged with guarding high-value VIPs as they traveled around the city and countryside. He and his team were working guard duty for a small contingent of State Department "fact-finders" that were investigating an incident that fortunately did not happen on his watch.

He had his team split into two separate squads of ten, each one shadowing two of the staffers. Burt was leading one squad, while Guzman led the other. When they got the call over their secure radios, both squads were together as all four staffers were meeting with the mayor of one of the outlying villages. Since the command had been to report "ASAP," they did not have the time to go back to their apartments and change or clean up. Burt figured that the RSO would just have to put up with the sour smells and layers of dust on a man who was working in this sandbox.

As he and Guzman approached the building, they slung the M4 carbines on their backs. Drawing official State Department identification from their pockets, they presented the identification to the Marines at the entrance. Carefully studying the identification and comparing the pictures to the men before them, the Marines eventually handed the wallets back, waving them through the doors. As they entered the lobby of the building, both men took off their gloves and hats, storing them in their voluminous cargo pant pockets. As they handed their wallets to the guards working the metal detectors, the contractors were told to disarm.

Holstein looked hard at the guard in question. The contractor growled a terse, "RSO Hernandez just called us in from the field. 'ASAP' was the word he used. Call his office and clear us through,"

The guard muttered something unkind about Holstein's genetic relationship to monkeys and the anatomically impossible act of procreating with himself. He reached for a phone and dialed an internal extension. Keeping his voice low, he read the names and information from Holstein and Guzman's IDs and appeared to argue with someone on the other end. With a sullen "Fine," the guard hung up the phone and handed the IDs back to Holstein and Guzman.

He waived to the guard standing by the metal detector.

"Go on up. Third floor, RSO's office," the guard said as he motioned to the other guard. "Let 'em go, Mike. They're cleared, as is."

Holstein smiled at Guzman and led his partner through the metal detectors, setting off a cacophony of buzzers and sirens. Walking towards the elevators, Holstein watched the guard pick up the phone and report to the security office. With a smirk on his face, Holstein boarded with Guzman only a few steps behind. As the elevator doors were closing, Holstein smiled at the sullen-looking guard and was rewarded with a raised middle finger salute.

Disembarking the elevator on the third floor, Holstein turned right, walking towards an office he had only visited once before. Walking up to the reception desk in front of the RSO's office, Holstein smiled politely and said, "Burt Holstein and Robert Guzman to see RSO Hernandez. I apologize about the commotion."

The raven-haired beauty behind the desk smiled warmly. Her warm Georgian accent rolled over the men.

"No problem. Mr. Hernandez is expecting you gentlemen. Go on in. Would you like something to drink? Water? Iced tea?" asked the receptionist.

Holstein deferred to Guzman first who replied, "Water, thanks!"

"I hate to be a bother, but the iced tea, is it sweetened?" Holstein asked.

Laughing, the receptionist said, "Of course! What other way is there for proper iced tea?"

Smiling, Holstein laughed, too.

"As a west coast boy, I've tasted the non-sweetened variety, but, if forced to choose, I prefer it sweetened. The tea sounds delicious, ma'am," said Holstein.

He turned and walked into the office with Guzman on his heels.

RSO Hernandez was not behind his desk. Instead, a man in a gray pinstripe suit that screamed "Fed" sat behind Hernandez' desk, and the RSO stood beside him. Holstein took all this information in with a quick glance, unconsciously shifted into parade rest, and nodded to Hernandez.

"Holstein and Guzman, reporting as requested, sir."

"Thanks for coming so quickly," Hernandez said as he looked at both men. "Burt Holstein and Robert Guzman, I'd like to introduce you to Agent James Smith. Agent Smith is from Homeland Security and has requested a meeting with you, Holstein. Guzman, if you'd join me outside."

Hernandez motioned and followed Guzman back out the door, leaving Holstein and the federal agent in the room, closing the door as they left.

Smith stood and reached out to shake Holstein's hand. "Mr. Holstein, I appreciate your coming in today. Please have a seat," the Homeland Security agent said as he pointed to one of the visitor's chairs. "I'd like to discuss a job offer with you."

Holstein shook his head and relaxed slightly.

"What kind of job are you talking about?" Holstein continued, "I'm on contract with Academi for three more years. Most likely, I'll be here for that time. I can probably talk to you more as I get closer, but, if I leave my team now, I will lose my bonus. I'm not walking away from all that cash in my bank account."

Smith let a small smile show on his face. "I understand perfectly, and I've already been in touch with your home office in McLean, Virginia. I'm forming a new team at Homeland Security to… deal with a particular kind of domestic threat and would like to have you lead the team."

Smith consulted a thin file in front of him. He read from the file. "Los Angeles native, born to moderately wealthy parents. Father owned a high-end electronics store where your mother helped until a gang shooting took both of their lives."

The federal agent looked directly at Holstein. "Joined LAPD as soon as you could and excelled at the hard stuff. Appointed to SWAT at age 23. Served two years with merit. Left LAPD to join the Marines. Again, excelled at what you do best, and joined Force Recon, serving with distinction in Iraq.

"When your term was up, you left the service to make some real money. Simple security or police work did not cut it for you... you wanted to make real bank. Academi heard you were available, and you scored a contract that gives you the money you want. Working as a contractor here in the sandbox got you exactly what you wanted: you get to play with guns and make a lot of money doing so."

"When you were 12 years old, you saw a UFO while you were camping in the desert. You've been a conspiracy theory nut ever since, convinced that the government is hiding the aliens from the public." Smith looked up at Holstein. Looking the contractor in the eyes, he continued. "It wasn't a UFO that time, not in the classic sense. It was something... something else."

Leafing through the contents of the file once again, Smith continued, "When you have free time, you spend a lot of it searching for proof that what you saw was real. Your contractor's salary allows you to search for answers in areas and places that most folks couldn't afford."

Holstein sat and tried to absorb the dry retelling of his professional and personal life. "What do you mean 'something else'? How do you know so much about me?"

Smith just smiled and ignored the questions. "I know that your contract still has three years left on it. I am authorized to buy out your contract from Academi completely, including your bonus from this posting, and pay you a salary level somewhat higher than you are currently making here in the sandbox. You would become a full Homeland Security agent, with government service accumulation, and time towards your retirement."

The actual job offer sank in past the shock of having his background laid out so openly. Holstein asked a barrage of questions, "What do you mean 'somewhat higher'? Do you have any idea what I make here? And I still get my bonus? I've never seen the Feds throw around this much money. Only the private contractors can afford that kind of salary. What kind of threat do you need me for?"

Smith's smile widened as he realized that Holstein was taking the bait. "Yes, I know exactly what you make here, and we're going to start you at an even higher salary." Smith set the hook as he offered a number that caused Burt's eyes to widen in shock. The contractor thought about how that much money could help him find the answers he was looking for.

Smith continued, "As to your other questions, everything is classified Top Secret, and I cannot tell you any more until after you come on board. So what do you think?"

Holstein was still trying to process the information. And the job offer. And the salary. He wanted the job. He was hooked by the money, and the fact that he might be able to find answers. He asked the Homeland Security Agent, "What about my team? What happens to them? When would I leave and where am I going?"

Smith slowly stood and walked around the desk. "RSO Hernandez is currently telling Guzman that he is now in charge of the team until Academi sends a replacement. We leave immediately. A quick stop by your office and quarters to get any personal items, and then to the airport. I have a jet on standby, and we'll be wheels up in less than an hour. As to the where? You'll just have to wait and see. This is the only time I'm going to offer this job to you. Do you want it?"

Holstein looked down briefly. Looking back up, he reached out to grasp the proffered hand. "I'm glad to be on your team, sir. Where do I sign?"

Smith chuckled dryly. "I've given RSO Hernandez your transfer paperwork from Academi. You'll sign the official government contracts in a few days. For now, let's get moving. I have a schedule to keep. I need to get you back to headquarters so you can get settled. Once we get you settled, I'll need to go collect your new team."

3

SPOOKY

Fort Meade, Maryland.

Rows of numbers and letters filled all six monitors in front him. Formed in two curved rows of three, each monitor was a twenty-three-inch widescreen display with the whole stack wrapping around almost one hundred forty degrees of his vision. Each was filled with multiple windows of text and data, and anyone watching him work would see him shift his eyes and head in an-almost-neurotic way. Looking bird-like, his focus constantly shifted between the monitors, and his fingers rapidly flew between three different keyboards and two customized pointing devices.

John Q. Smith, or "Q," to his geeky friends, sat in his cubicle buried deep in the heart of the server farm for the NSA. Cropped in a short spiky cut, his red hair framed his face, and his brilliant green eyes hid behind small horn-rimmed glasses. Eschewing the standard shirt and tie demanded by the employee handbook, the young man wore geek-interest-related t-shirts and blue jeans. His boss had long ago figured out that Smith would never dress up regularly and only made sure that he was at least dressed in standard attire when management wandered through the cube farm.

Wrapping up for the day, John finished typing the final few lines of his report. He made a couple more references, read it one more time, and sent it to his boss. As the lead analyst for PRISM and ECHELON, the NSA's domestic electronic spying programs, his report would be the first thing his boss would read on Monday morning. The strange reports and seemingly credible intel about "monsters" kept occurring enough that it made John curious. The deeper he dug, the more he found that confused and confounded his searches.

One name kept popping up over the last couple weeks, "Section 28." There were no hints about what or who they were. They seemed to be a governmental agency, but there was no record he could find—and he had clearance to find anything. Using the vast resources of the NSA, as well as CIA, FBI, and Homeland Security sources, he searched every crack in the internet for information. What few references he found were either sketchy "evidence" on conspiracy theory websites or occasional signals intelligence (SIGINT) that pointed to some shadowy group that dealt with... monsters?

Finding this odd, he began compiling the information a couple weeks ago, and finally completed his report for his boss today. John was not only the lead analyst for PRISM and ECHELON, but he was also one of the key liaisons with Homeland Security for those programs. He thought about it for a few seconds and sent a second copy to his DHS supervisor as well. *In for a penny, in for a pound*, he thought to himself.

Making his way out of the labyrinth that was the NSA server farm, he passed all the checkpoints and emerged into the sun for the first time that day. Blinking painfully against the bright sun, he walked to the parking lot and climbed into his "Ghostmobile."

Growing up in Boston, Massachusetts, his Irish blue-collar heritage was painfully clear in his accent. In older Boston, there were plenty of houses that were rumored to be haunted, and he and his friends used to spend their time wandering those halls. As a budding electronics genius, he often made "ghost hunting" gear for himself and his friends.

At the top of his high-school class, he had scored high enough on

SATs and ACTs to receive a full-ride scholarship to MIT. There his computer prowess and electronic savvy had served him well as he moved to the top of his class in crypto-analysis. While in college, the only distraction for "Q" and his friends was his ghost hunting hobby. He and several friends had often spent their off-time searching out the haunted locations and trying their newest custom equipment, searching for the proof they were so desperate to find.

Once he graduated, he received job offers from several government alphabet-soup intelligence agencies, and even more private firms and banks. With his cryptanalysis background, the two most interesting offers came from a bank on the west coast and the NSA in Maryland. With several of his geek friends taking jobs in D.C. and the surrounding area, John opted to work for the National Security Agency in Fort Meade, Maryland. Because he stayed in the area, he was able to continue "ghost hunting" with his friends from college, and that's where he was headed now.

He rolled down the highway towards a farm outside Manassas, Virginia. This farm was on the edge of one of the Revolutionary War battlefields and was supposed to be pretty active with ghost and poltergeist activity. As members of the D.C. Ghost Hunting Society, he and his team had arranged to spend the night inside the farmhouse. "Q" had several new pieces of equipment that he wanted to test tonight, and his teammates were bringing their new equipment as well. His best friend from high school, Billy, was supposed to be bringing their new equipment trailer/mobile base camp as well. As John drove towards the farmhouse, he slowly relaxed and let his mind forget about the report he sent his bosses.

WHEN MONDAY MORNING ROLLED AROUND, JOHN WAS IN A GREAT mood. He and his DCGHS team scored lots of good evidence on Friday night, including what is called a "Class A" EVP in the paranormal world. This Electronic Voice Phenomena is a sound that is recorded on a digital recorder and is not heard by anyone actually present during the recording. Often, these sounds are recorded at a different frequency than normal human voices, yet they seem to have voice patterns and offer recognizable words. To be a "Class A" EVP, the voice must be clear and distinguishable. Their recording had a deep male voice growling, "Soon you will see." Coupled with some other interesting readings, it had been a fairly successful hunt. Before leaving for work, he uploaded the evidence collected to the DCGHS server, where the video and audio would be available for streaming.

John arrived a bit earlier than usual but still parked in his normal spot, on the edge of the lot, about a third of the way down the outer row. As John approached the large black, ominous looking building, he whistled the theme to his favorite ghost-hunting movie. John was in such a good mood that the onerous security procedures for entering the building and then the SIGINT area didn't bother him as much as they usually did.

But John's mood soured quickly when he got to his cubicle. A note posted on his primary monitor said, "See me ASAP. Kenneth." The "Kenneth" was his direct line supervisor, Kenneth McAllister. John's secure mobile phone then received a text, also from his boss, "Come to my office. NOW."

John swore under his breath. Grabbing the spare shirt and tie hanging in his cube for just such an occasion, he hurriedly drew it on, slipped the pre-tied tie over his head, and scurried down the corridor as he tucked in his shirt and straightened his tie.

Arriving at his boss' office, he knocked on the door and heard an immediate, "Come!" Kenneth McAllister looked like John felt. McAllister's tie was askew, his perfectly pressed shirt was stained with sweat, and he looked as if he got caught with his hand in the proverbial cookie jar.

When he got excited or angry, McAllister's original Texan accent crept back into his voice. The accent was almost overbearing as McAllister continued, "Get your butt in here, John. What in the hell were you thinking, sending that report? It's bad enough that you sent it to me, but you decided to send it to Homeland Security? I just had our Director chew me out. Your supervisor at DHS called *HIS* boss. His boss called the Director of Homeland Security, who called *OUR* Director. And he called me. It was strongly suggested to me that I reconsider the idea of putting someone who sees 'monsters and ghosts' in charge of the PRISM and ECHELON programs. Is he right?"

John's high spirits visibly deflated, and he collapsed into one of the visitor chairs. He had a sudden vision of being reassigned to the IT maintenance department. John tried to defend his work. "Did you even read the report? All I did was correlate data from the programs. It all got flagged, and I just analyzed the data. It's not my fault that these programs compiled this data. And I don't 'see' ghosts. Ghost hunting is a hobby, but it has never interfered with my job here. What's going to happen, Ken?"

McAllister stared at John with a probing look. He seemed to find the genuine innocence that he was searching for. "Listen, John," he began. His voice became much softer and the Texas 'twang dropped away. "This will blow over pretty soon, but you need to step back for a few days. Go hide under a rock. Keep your head down. I'm going to give you a couple of days off work, paid, of course. Heck, take a week. Take some time to relax. Get this out of your system. Come back in next Monday. We'll see what happens then."

John looked defeated. "So am I gonna' be pulled from my current job? What about Liaison to DHS? Am I even going to have a job when I come back?"

McAllister smiled wistfully. "You'll have a job. You're a great analyst. You're a freakin' genius with ECHELON. I'll do everything I can to keep you on this assignment, but you need to keep your head down for the rest of the week. Officially, your report never happened. This so-called 'Section 28' doesn't exist. And the only monsters out there are the ones that bomb malls and hijack airplanes... the human kind of monsters. Got it?"

John absorbed the keywords and nodded slowly. "Got it." He stood and walked out of the office. As he reached his cubicle, he grabbed his messenger bag with his laptop and left the facility.

It was a long ride home. His thoughts kept mulling all the data over in his head. Section 28 has to exist, doesn't it? There's too much data. Distracted, he drove past his exit on the highway and had to backtrack. Pulling into the driveway of his small rental, he grabbed his bag and walked up to the front door. It wasn't until he began to put his key into the lock that he realized the front door was cracked open. Looking around, he belatedly realized that there was a black sedan parked in front of his house that might as well have had a sign posted on it stating, "I am a federal agent." Fear filtered quickly through his mind. *What had he done wrong? Who was waiting for him?* The fear slowly changed to anger. This was his house that they busted into. It didn't matter that they were Feds. They broke into HIS house. With the stress of the morning, this was the last straw. Not caring if the "men in black" were in his living room, he threw open the door, spoiling for a fight.

Sitting in his favorite recliner was an average-sized man in a gray pinstripe suit. His black hair and eyes gave a hint to Native American or Latino descent, but his cultured voice spoke of a gentrified southern upbringing.

"Good morning, Mr. Smith. I am Agent James Smith from Homeland Security. And I'd like to discuss a report that you filed with your boss on Friday."

John was livid. "Get *OUT*," he roared. "Get out of my house. My boss already read me the riot act. I got the message. 'Section 28' doesn't exist. There are no monsters. This conversation never 'officially' happened, and I don't frakkin' know *YOU*! Now, get out!"

Agent Smith raised his hands as if to deflect the words, "I'm not here to, as you say, 'read you the riot act'. I'm here to offer you a job." Agent Smith withdrew his credentials from his inside pocket. "You see, I'm from Section 28. The monsters are real, and we could use your help."

4

GOD

Grand Rapids, Michigan.

The sniper carefully extended the bipod on the front of his rifle. Setting the bipod on the rest in front of him, the man visually inspected the five-round magazine for his rifle then inserted it into the receiver. Grasping the bolt handle, he twisted and shoved it forward, feeling the secure "click" as it locked into place with a round in the chamber. The sniper lifted the cap from his head, brushed his black hair out of his eyes, and put the hat back on backwards.

Next to the sniper, his spotter carefully unfolded the tripod that supported his spotting scope and placed the scope on the ground. With his gear set up, he reached over and tapped the sniper on the shoulder twice in a pre-arranged signal. He then reached to his side and withdrew a pair of binoculars to survey the scene just over a hundred yards in front of him.

Having spotted his target, the spotter carefully placed his binoculars in their case, laid back down, and switched to the spotting scope. He looked in through the windows of the large building in front of him. Keeping his voice low, he began a running commentary for his partner.

"Primary target, one hundred twenty-five yards. Wind speed..." he said as he glanced at the small instrument package set up in front of him. "Fifteen knots, three-two-zero degrees. Gusting to twenty-five."

The spotter performed the necessary calculations on a small computer attached to his wrist. Next to him, the sniper was doing the same calculations in his head. It was a private test to see if his instincts were still sharp.

The spotter received his answers from the computer, and murmured, "One and a quarter clicks up, three and a quarter left should put you spot on. You're good to go, Rivera."

Jesús Rivera made the adjustments to the scope, smiling because he was correct again, and he had the corrections planned before his spotter ever spoke. He brought his eye to the scope in front of him. Caressing the stock of his M24-A3 rifle subconsciously, Rivera looked through the scope and sighted in on the top floor of the Gerald R. Ford Federal Building in Grand Rapids, Michigan.

Home to many federal offices and a U.S. District Court, gunmen had barged past security checkpoints, shooting people and causing terror all the way to the top floor, taking a judge and several court workers hostage. They coldly shot the guards at the entrance on the way into the building and had fired at and wounded or killed every federal law enforcement officer they encountered. Early reports from witnesses said there were three of them. Claiming to be from the Islamic State of Iraq and Syria (ISIS), the jihadists were making demands that certain prisoners be released from Guantanamo Bay and that Sharia Law be officially adopted in the state of Michigan, as it had virtually been in Dearborn, Michigan.

As soon as local law enforcement knew who was holding the hostages, the FBI's Hostage Rescue Team was immediately deployed. They were on the plane and in the air from the FBI Academy in Quantico in twenty minutes and on the scene in Grand Rapids in three hours. Once on site, the local law enforcement responders deferred to the HRT for the resolution.

As the team arrived, their on-site liaison told them that the ISIS jihadists had killed one of their hostages. One of the gunmen stated that if their demands were not met, and if they did not have a helicopter on the roof within an hour, another hostage would be executed.

Thirty minutes before the deadline, the takedown order had been given. Rivera and his spotter, Stuart Duncan, were quickly ordered to post on top of one of the buildings close to the federal building. A position on the roof of the Grand Rapids City Hall would put them on the same level as the hostage takers, and they would be in a great position to guide the entry team.

Rivera activated the microphone around his throat. "Alpha lead, Overwatch. Eyes on target."

The HRT team leader replied, "Overwatch, Alpha lead. Sit Rep."

Rivera counted bodies through the scope, then heard his spotter mutter, "Three bad guys. Eleven hostages."

Since the count agreed with his, he relayed it to the team leader. "Three tangos. Eleven civilians. Tango one, by the entry door, with a mirror to see the corridor. Tango two, five feet from tango one, along north wall. Tango three, looking out the windows."

"Copy Overwatch. Alpha lead to all Alpha. We will execute in three minutes... mark," answered the leader.

Rivera heard Duncan mutter a curse under his breath. "Tango three has eyes. Looks like we're spotted."

Rivera switched to look at the terrorist by the window and watched as he scanned the city hall roofline with a pair of binoculars. He seemed to be directly looking at them and started waving his hands, gesturing wildly.

Rivera uttered the same curse and keyed his mic. "Alpha lead, Overwatch. Caution! Caution! Caution! Tango three has eyes and has spotted our position."

The team leader responded immediately. "Overwatch, Alpha lead. Priority target, Tango one. Take the shot. Alpha team, execute in 15 seconds."

Jesús agreed with the team leader. If the sniper shot the target by the door with the mirror, the other bad guys would have no idea when the entry team would come through the door, or where. Shifting the crosshairs back to the designated tango one, he paused, inhaled his breath, and then exhaled slowly. When he let about half of it out, his trigger finger moved just under a half inch. Easily taking up the slack and breaking at a crisp one-and-a-half pounds of pressure, the rifle fired.

The firing pin struck the primer on the .338 Lapua Magnum round in the chamber. The primer ignited and lit the gunpowder inside the casing, propelling the projectile down the barrel and out towards the target. Approximately twelve hundredths of a second later, the bullet ripped through the window glass, missing one terrorist by six inches. The large projectile slammed into the head of the terrorist by the door approximately five thousandths of a second later. The explosive force of almost 4,900 ft/lbs of energy imparted on the skull of the terrorist, and the head virtually vanished.

As the terrorist by the window heard the crack of the high-powered rifle, Rivera had already cycled the bolt-action and switched targets, centering his sights on the forehead of the troublesome third terrorist. Another breath, another twitch, and another twelve-thousandths of a second later, this bullet did not miss the terrorist at the window. As Rivera cycled the bolt-action again, he shifted the crosshairs again, this time covering the second terrorist, the only one still standing. As the sniper stabilized, he watched the rest of Alpha team break through the door. The first agent through the door pointed his M4 carbine at the terrorist and pulled the trigger. Twice. Six rounds stitched through the terrorist, and he jerked and dropped.

After a few seconds, Rivera watched the all-clear hand signal being given across the team. Alpha lead rasped in his ear, "Alpha lead, Overwatch. All Clear. Good shooting. Wrap it up."

Rivera cleared his rifle and put it away.

Rivera and Duncan sat up, carefully putting their gear in the various pouches and cases. They stood, grabbed their gear, and headed toward the roof access door. This time around, they relaxed and took the elevator to the ground floor. Walking through the building and out the doors, they had stowed most of their gear when the rest of the team returned to the mobile command center.

A giant of an African American named Alton Lynch strode up to Rivera and Duncan. The leader of the FBI's HRT Team Alpha gave a thumb's up to the pair.

"Great shooting, Rivera," Lynch said as he turned to the rest of the team. "All right. Great outcome. Let's get everything stowed. I want to be wheels up in one hour."

AFTER A GOOD NIGHT'S REST, RIVERA ARRIVED AT THE QUANTICO Marine Corps Base training facility for debrief and training. Rivera thought the debrief went well enough, and Lynch only handed out minor criticism about being spotted by the lookout. Walking out of the debriefing room, the team headed towards the mess hall for lunch before their afternoon training. Rivera walked out, deep in discussion with Lynch about other tactics they could have used. They were stopped by one of the administrators for the group.

"SSA Lynch? Special Agent Rivera? There is a visitor here from Homeland Security. He is requesting a meeting with both of you directly. I have him in Conference Room 201, but he requested that I contact you as soon as you finished your debrief. Shall I let him know you are coming?" The administrator waited for an answer.

"Thanks, Krista. Rivera and I can walk with you," Lynch responded.

As they walked, Lynch turned to Rivera. "Any idea why Homeland Security wants you? Did you apply for a new job without telling me?"

"No, sir," Rivera said as he shook his head. "I'm happy here. Did we screw something up in Michigan?"

Lynch just shrugged. "Not to my knowledge. If this guy is recruiting, just say no. Any time one of these interdepartmental headhunters show up, it's never good for the head they are hunting."

Rivera agreed as they reached the conference room. Opening the door, he let Lynch go in first, and followed closely on his heels. Sitting in the room at the head of the conference table was a rather average sized man in a gray pinstripe suit. He had two folders in front of him, both closed. Rivera could see that the front of one folder displayed the FBI agency seal. The other folder was emblazoned with the Department of Homeland Security seal, and Rivera could just make out his name on the tab.

Without standing up, the man greeted the two agents. In a softly cultured voice he said, "Good morning, gentlemen. My name is Agent James Smith, and I work for Homeland Security."

Picking up the folder with the FBI seal on it, he opened the folder and continued. "Great job in Michigan yesterday. Sounds like it was a bad one. Do we have a final casualty count yet?"

Neither man sat down. Rivera could see Lynch stiffen and clench his jaw out of the corner of his eye. The sniper knew that meant his commander was about to shout. Lynch roared at the Homeland Security agent, "How did you get a copy of that preliminary report? That is HRT Eyes Only until the final report is ready. No one outside the Director or the Attorney General in cleared for that file. How did you get it?"

Agent Smith held up his hands as if to ward off the attack. "Relax, Agent Lynch. I have access to far more information than even the AG. Well-written report... really backs up your sniper here. It's good to see that you are watching out for your people."

But Lynch refused to be placated. "Who are you? Where is your ID? Why are you here? Did we trample on DHS' private playground in Michigan?"

Agent Smith reached into his jacket for his credentials, and opening them, he slid them across the table towards Lynch. "As much as I'd like to answer all your questions, Agent Lynch, I don't have the time, and, more importantly, you don't have the clearance for that. Instead, I'd like to spend a few minutes talking with Agent Rivera here. Alone. Don't worry, I won't keep him from lunch." Smith smiled and nodded towards the door.

Lynch carefully scrutinized the credentials and grudgingly concluded they were genuine. He looked at Rivera knowingly. "Remember what I told you. I'll wait outside for you." He then looked at Agent Smith and warned him, "Leave him alone. I back my team, AND I protect my team. He's mine." Lynch left and closed the door.

Agent Smith looked at Rivera and said, "Sit down, Jesús. I'm going to get a crick in my neck staring up at you like that." He glanced down and reached for the file with Rivera's name on it.

Opening the file, he summarized what was there.

"You grew up just outside Denver, Colorado, in a good Hispanic home to first-generation immigrants. Mother Maria and father Ramon, you were their only child. Your father started taking you hunting around the age of eight, and, from all accounts you were pretty good. You originally wanted to be a Catholic Priest, having grown up in the church."

As he read, the agent flipped through the pages, picking out the highlights. Smith continued, "Your family loved the outdoors life. You went camping, fishing, and hunting with your family all the time. During the summer of the year you turned fifteen, your family went camping in the remote wilderness. About two days in, there was a bright full moon. Unfortunately, for you, there was also a rabid wolf in the area. While you were down by the creek doing some midnight fishing, your parents were horrifically killed, torn apart by a wolf according to the local medical examiner."

"Being the good Catholic, you turned to the church to help you with answers. Unfortunately, the priest in your parish was more interested in the altar boys than in helping you find answers. So you ran from the church, never to return."

"You lived well with your aunt and uncle, and your inheritance paid for your admittance to Harvard. Graduated in the top two percent in Pre-Law and had a spot waiting for you at Harvard Law School. You chose the FBI, instead. You are a standout agent. Quickly making the selection for the HRT. Your hunting days in Colorado really helped you become a sniper. And now I want you to come work for me. I am building a highly specialized team that will deal with rather... unique threats."

Rivera felt like he had been sucker punched. Hearing his life story laid out in front of him like a deer on the butcher block, he could barely think. Smith's delivery was perfectly dry, with no emotion. He simply read out of the personnel file. *Wait... How do they have my personnel file?*

Rivera was in such a state of shock that he almost missed the job offer. In fact, it was a few moments later when he finally figured out how to talk again. "What do you mean job offer? I'm happy here at

HRT, despite you dragging my past back to me. What could you offer me that I don't have here?"

"I'm offering answers and a chance to make a difference," Smith said with a smile. "There is a threat facing this country that even your elite HRT is not prepared for. That's why you joined the FBI—to make a difference. You wanted to protect families. I'm offering you an opportunity to do that on a scale you have not seen before."

Rivera asked, "So... Terrorists? Islamists? Nukes? What is the threat?"

Smith paused. "I cannot tell you the threat—it's classified higher than you're cleared for. But I can answer a question that you've had for a long time. It was not a rabid wolf that killed your parents. It was a werewolf. She was pack-less, and had recently been turned. We put her down when we caught her, but she killed your parents and several others before we got her."

Rivera looked at Smith and thought for a few seconds. *Did he really say 'werewolf'? What else is he hiding? Lynch is gonna' think I'm insane!*

"Now, I am behind schedule already, and my next interview is on the other side of the world," said Smith. "I'm only going to ask you this question once. Do you want the job?"

Rivera looked up at Smith and extended his hand across the table. "When do I start?"

5

BOOMER

Pacific Ocean, Off the Coast of Japan.

"What do you mean I've 'been transferred'?" The angry woman wearing standard issue Navy working coveralls was standing in her Division Office on the USS Ronald Reagan, a U.S. Navy aircraft carrier in the Pacific Ocean. The woman with close-cropped hair cursed enough that some of the shipmates hanging around were learning new, creative combinations.

Chief Warrant Officer Harold Goodwin stood and let the young sailor vent for a little bit. He was being a little indulgent, realizing that this transfer would probably kill the career of a very promising sailor.

Having let her rant enough, he cleared his throat.

"Petty Officer Callahan." Goodwin's voice was cold and quiet.

Callahan stopped ranting. Realizing that she had just yelled at, and then cussed out, her boss, she quickly composed herself. "I apologize for my outburst, sir. I was caught totally off guard."

Chief Warrant Officer Goodwin nodded and then said, "I understand. Did you get that out of your system?"

"Yes, sir," Callahan said as she blushed. "Permission to speak freely?"

Goodwin nodded. "As if I could stop you, Callahan."

Callahan continued, "Any idea why I was transferred out, sir? Have I... screwed up lately?"

Smiling at her restraint, Goodwin replied, "No, Callahan. You've been great out in the field... But you probably should not have reported seeing the Loch Ness Monster while diving in Scotland. And then giving your account to that reality TV show was just stupid."

He looked at her shocked face. "You're a Petty Officer. Training other sailors how to blow stuff up. Do you really think Command wants to have one of their senior non-comms in EOD spouting off about monsters? You should have seen this coming."

"But I never claimed to see the Loch Ness Monster, sir!" The sailor pleaded her case. "I simply claimed to have seen what seemed to be a big creature down there. I never mentioned Loch Ness. How am I gonna' get out of this, sir?"

Goodwin liked the young Petty Officer. She was a fantastic EOD, and he knew her old man as a Chief Petty Officer a long time ago.

"I'm sorry, Callahan. This order came from Norfolk. They want you transferred immediately. You are to report to the mail flight for transport to Yokosuka Naval Base. From there, you fly out to San Diego NAS, and then on to Norfolk. You'll catch your new assignment there."

Rebekah Callahan fought back tears as she made her way to her rack. Taking a few moments to change into her dress uniform, she gathered her uniforms, gear, and personal items, which she stuffed into a canvas sea bag. She had just enough time to tell her teammates goodbye, and then she ran to get on the delivery airplane.

Goodwin met her on the stairs up to the flight deck. He looked her up and down with pride as she saluted him—ramrod straight, a perfect salute from the Academy. He returned her salute and caught her eye.

"Callahan, you're great at what you do. I'll see what I can find out, I will try to get you back here. Your father would be proud of you, even with 'Nessie.' You'll come out of this on top."

Callahan fought harder to hold back her tears.

"Thank you, sir," Callahan said, her voice choking with emotion. "I'll make them realize what kind of crappy mistake they made when they sent me to the beach."

Goodwin laughed. "That's the Callahan that I know. You'd better hurry to catch the COD. Dismissed."

Callahan threw one last salute and ran up the final stairs to the flight deck. As she appeared on deck, one crewman escorted her to the large, unusual looking plane. Having just begun service in Carrier Onboard Delivery services, the V-22 Osprey tilt-rotor aircraft had the nose, body, and wings of an airplane, but it also had two huge propellers, one on the end of each wing. These engines rotated through a full ninety degrees. This allowed the plane to take off vertically, like a helicopter. Once it reached the proper altitude, it transitioned and rotated the propellers forward, using the turboprops to act as a normal airplane propeller. This unique method of propulsion made the aircraft a perfect replacement for the aging C-2 aircraft the Navy had been using since the 1960s.

Once she stowed her seabag and strapped herself in, she was told they had a couple minutes while they waited for another passenger. Callahan waited impatiently, fidgeting and trying not to cry until the other passenger finally arrived and boarded.

As he was strapping in to the webbed jump seats, she realized he was not in uniform. Instead, he was in a gray pinstripe suit that looked out of place on the military aircraft. Nodding politely, any greeting was abruptly cutoff as the rear cargo hydraulics whined as the ramp drew back up into the fuselage.

The whine of the ramp was replaced by a louder, deeper whine of the propellers beginning to rotate. This quickly turned into a roar as the first one, then the other engine started and began rotating. Callahan gave up any thought of conversation as the engines roared and watched out the window as they slowly lifted into the air. The noise only slightly diminished as they reached altitude and the engines transitioned to forward flight. Rebekah became lost in her thoughts.

Rebekah's thoughts drifted as she thought about her father who had passed away five, no six, years ago. He was a Chief Petty Officer in the Navy and had been stationed in Norfolk for most of her life. She had grown up on base, and she had fallen in love with the Navy. The only activity that drew her away from the base was racing.

Rebekah Callahan had always loved speed. She loved to be behind the wheel, melting the rubber off her tires on track and off. When her widowed father realized that his little girl was going to go fast whether or not he liked it, he connected her with a local racing club. Sponsoring her first go-kart, Rebekah's father had watched her win her first-ever race. She had never looked back. Gradually working up to dirt-track racing, while dabbling in speedboats, the only thing that made Rebekah Callahan quit racing was joining the Navy.

As soon as she had graduated from high school, Rebekah had been in the recruiter's office to sign the paperwork. With her grades, background, and enthusiasm, Rebekah was one of the few women accepted to the Explosive Ordinance Disposal. She excelled at the training, earning her diving certifications, passing the EOD training, and even earning her jump wings. After five years of service, she earned her Senior EOD badge when she made Petty Officer First Class. Then she took that trip to Scotland.

The changing pitch of the engines brought Rebekah out of her reverie. Shaking her head slightly, she realized they were landing on the helicopter pad at Yokosuka Naval Base. As the V-22 landed, the crew chief came back and dropped the cargo ramp. He yelled loud enough to be heard over the noise. "All right, you passengers, this is your stop. Up and out. The sailor at the end of the ramp will direct you."

Rebekah grabbed her duffle and walked down the ramp. She was followed closely by the civilian. They both walked away from the plane and followed the E-5 into the building at the end of the pier. As they walked through the doors, the V-22 lifted off, heading inland toward the air base.

Rebekah asked the E-5 where processing was, and he gave her directions. As she walked toward the office, she realized the civilian was following her. She slowed her pace then stopped and looked at him. "Excuse me, sir. Are you lost?"

He smiled and replied, "No, Petty Officer Callahan. Actually, I'm headed to the same office that you are."

She frowned as she realized he must have read her name and service rank off her uniform during the flight. "Are you sure you need the processing offices, sir? Transportation is the other direction."

He smiled and a hint of southern charm was in his voice. "No, Petty Officer. I'm definitely headed to the correct office. Shall we?" And he gestured with his arm toward the offices.

When they reached the office doors, the strange man opened the door for Rebekah and let her enter first. Somehow, she expected no less—he had that "gentleman" vibe to him. As she walked up to the desk, Rebekah presented her orders to the clerk. "Petty Officer First Class Rebekah Callahan. Reporting as ordered to arrange transportation to NAS North Island, with an eventual destination of Naval Station Norfolk."

The clerk read through the orders before responding. "If you'll have a seat, Petty Officer, I'll begin working on your transportation. I should have something for you soon." The clerk then looked at the gentleman behind Rebekah, and she knew that she had been dismissed.

The strange man smiled wide for the clerk. "Hello, Cheryl. Back from the Reagan. She's a beautiful ship. Do you have a conference room I can use?"

The clerk returned the smile. "Certainly, Agent Smith. I've held Conference Room 1, as you requested. Commander Douglas is waiting for you in his office."

"Thank you, Cheryl. I'll be using that conference room when I'm done meeting with Commander Douglas."

Thirty minutes later, Rebekah watched the apparently important "Agent Smith" emerge from the Commander's office with a briefcase in his hand, and the Commander followed him out to the waiting area. As they approached her, Rebekah jumped to her feet and threw a smart salute.

Answering the salute, the Commander looked at Agent Smith

then at Rebekah. "Petty Officer Callahan. I'll be talking to you in a little bit. In the meantime, please accompany Agent Smith to the conference room. He'd like to talk to you about an important matter."

Agent Smith smiled at Rebekah and then turned back to Commander Douglas and shook his hand. The Commander gestured for Rebekah to follow Smith, and she numbly followed the federal agent. As they entered the conference room, Smith took the seat farthest from the door, with his back to a wall. He motioned for Rebekah to sit down, and Smith opened his case, removing a rather thick file folder with the Department of Homeland Security seal on it. Rebekah was close enough to see her name on the tab.

The man then withdrew a set of credentials from his inner pocket and opened it, handing it across the table to Rebekah. "We got off on the wrong foot. I'm Agent James Smith from Homeland Security, and I came all the way here to talk to you specifically."

Smith opened the file and read the highlights. "Petty Officer First Class Rebekah Callahan. Senior EOD Technician. Raised in Norfolk, Virginia. Race car and race boat driver. You chose EOD because you got to blow stuff up, jump from airplanes, dive in the ocean, and work with Special Forces. But mostly to blow things up."

"You recently took a trip to Scotland to dive in Loch Ness. On the dive, you saw some sort of large underwater creature, and you decided to tell others." He looked up and caught her eye. "Oh, you did actually see Nessie, well, one of her descendants anyway. But that doesn't change the fact that CWO Goodwin thinks you were suffering from hypoxia. The skipper of the Reagan was worried about having a senior EOD tech that sees monsters. And your Command doesn't like that you went on TV."

Smith made sure that she was paying attention. "If you stay in the Navy, you are currently as high up the ladder as you'll go. You've been scheduled to begin training new EOD recruits. You're going to be stuck teaching new puppies how not to crap on the carpet. If you keep your nose clean and stick it out, you will retire with your twenty years in as a Petty Officer First Class. No more adventures for you."

The federal agent closed and began to put the personnel folder back into his briefcase. "On the other hand, you can come work for me. I'm putting together a rather special team to handle a rather special kind of threat to the United States. You have the skills I am looking for, and I don't care that you saw Nessie. At least she doesn't bother people too much. But I will need an answer. What do you say?"

6

DOC

Vatican City.

T he middle-aged woman in a rather severe business pantsuit with her light brown hair pulled back into a tight bun was walking among the ancient stacks of books and scrolls in the Vatican Library. The section of the library that she was in was normally off-limits. Only a select few were ever given access, and this woman had received her unlimited clearance earlier that day.

As she carefully re-shelved the book, she glanced over and saw a title that caught her eye, *Monstra et Animalia, Of Monsters and Creatures*. Her gloved hands carefully drew the book from its resting place, and she examined the cover. Gold leaf inlay on what felt like leather. As she opened the front cover, she saw the author's name and smiled. Of course, this would be Gustaf Van Helsing's work.

She turned and walked toward the exit. The library itself was in a climate-controlled series of sub-basements with sections like this one having their own specially carved out rooms. As she passed through the archway, she nodded at the Vatican Guard standing at attention. Speaking Italian, she said, "I'm finished, Martin. I'm only removing this one item for study. Go ahead and close the gate."

The guard smiled at her and then closed and locked the gate securely. As she watched the gate close and lock, Doctor Noelle Sorenson, newly minted priest in the Catholic Church, signed her name on the entry log and noted which manuscript she had in her possession. She also noted that she would be taking it for an extended period, in her personal possession. She then turned and left, heading for the small apartment in Vatican City that she had called home for the last year.

Doctor Sorenson had never intended to work for the Catholic Church and had never expected to be ordained into the priesthood, especially since the church officially only ordains men into the Priesthood. How she had ended up in the Vatican was a long and unusual tale.

NOELLE HAD GROWN UP IN THE UNITED METHODIST CHURCH IN Grand Rapids, Michigan. Raised as a "good Christian girl," she had been active in her local church and youth group. As she left to attend an out-of-state university, she had opted for Notre Dame for their history program.

At Notre Dame, she had started learning about the Catholic Church and attending Mass on campus. All of her professors were Priests or lay leaders, and they seemed to have the answers to her questions. After months of attending campus mass, she had begun attending and getting involved in a local parish. Noelle graduated with honors in European History and searched for a Master's program. After completing her degree, she had decided that she wanted to work with people. This had led her back into school where she had started her new major, Sociology. Again graduating with honors, she had once again looked at the job market and did not like her prospects in her chosen field.

Her wealthy parents had offered to support one more degree, and Noelle chose pre-med. The medical field had suited Noelle well, and she had thrived in the classwork. After she had graduated at the top of her class, she had applied and was accepted to the University of Michigan Medical School. With glowing recommendations from her professors, she had moved to Ann Arbor and quickly found a local parish to attend. Her graduation with honors and her completion of the Rite of Christian Initiation of Adults to become a full member of the Catholic Church had been celebrated the same week. Noelle had soon interned and quickly found a residency at a hospital in the Emergency/Trauma center.

The newly minted Doctor Sorenson had found that she thrived in the trauma environment. Where most doctors tried to avoid the ER, she had gladly worked with the emergency cases. During her residency, she had explored other options and had thought about Doctors Without Borders, an organization that brought trained medical staff to third world countries where they were needed. When her residency was finished, she had applied for a position. Seeking extra funds to support her service, her local parish had raised support money to allow her to go help in third world countries.

While posted in Nigeria, Noelle had begun to see an interesting pattern in certain wounds on the people she was treating. Being told that they were so-called-monster attacks, she had grown more curious. When she had asked her supervisor, she had been told that the translator had mistakenly translated the Nigerian word for "animal" or "creature" into "monster." Not satisfied, she relayed the strange stories to her bishop back in Ann Arbor in her weekly correspondence.

When her tour was up and she moved back to Michigan, her bishop had asked more questions about the strange "monster" wounds. What she had thought was going to be a light conversation about an interesting story turned into a very surreal conversation.

The bishop had told Noelle that the wounds she saw and treated were caused by a form of shapeshifter, similar to a werewolf. During her care, she had inadvertently cured one patient from getting the "disease." Furthermore, the Vatican was interested in her story, and in her specifically. The bishop wondered if she would take time and fly to the Vatican to talk to one of the Cardinals there. The bishop had assured her that the Church would pay for the entire trip to Rome. Having always wanted to visit Rome and the Vatican, she gladly agreed.

When she had arrived in Rome, she was ushered into a meeting with two Cardinals and her bishop. Noelle was introduced to the Prefect, Cardinal Gerhard Ludwig Müller, and the Secretary, Archbishop Luis Ladaria Ferrer of the Congregation for the Doctrine of the Faith. After making introductions all around, Cardinal Müller began in a heavily accented English.

"Doctor Sorenson, we asked you to travel thousands of miles because we would like to hear first-hand your stories from Nigeria about the wounds from these monsters."

Noelle nodded and had begun to re-tell the now familiar story. Not embellishing, and not leaving any detail out, she had recounted all of her impressions and actions. As she was talking, the two Cardinals would occasionally mutter back and forth in what sounded like Italian, and one or the other would ask a question to clarify her story. When she had finished, the Cardinals began talking amongst themselves in low Italian again, often switching to what sounded like Latin.

After what had seemed like an eternity, Cardinal Müller had turned to Noelle and said, "As Bishop Roberts has already informed you, you were actually seeing the results of shapeshifter attacks. Not quite what you would call 'werewolves', but close enough for your story. When a person bitten by these creatures survives the initial attack, they are infected with the virus that causes the affliction. You have seemingly done the impossible. Three out of the twenty, or so, victims you treated were somehow cured of their disease."

The Cardinal then seemed to shift the direction of the conversation. "Doctor Sorenson, do you happen to know the history of the Congregation of for the Doctrine of the Faith? No? I didn't think so. Our main purpose is to oversee and help facilitate Church Doctrine. We are here to help His Holiness in the task of making sure that Church Doctrine withstands the tests of time and scrutiny."

The Cardinal continued, "Originally, we were founded as the

Supreme Sacred Congregation of the Roman and Universal Inquisition. I see by your response that you recognize the name of the Holy Inquisition. We were originally established with two missions. First to oversee the creation and implementation of Church Doctrine. Secondly, we were created to help oversee the enforcement of Church Doctrine. The Crusades and the Inquisition were part of that mission."

"One of the... hidden... missions of this Congregation is to search out, and destroy, monsters that threaten the Church. Even most of the Cardinals and Ordained do not realized that we are Monster Hunters. We have a special order called the '*Protectionem Dei Adversus Malum.*' Roughly translated, this order's name is 'God's Protection From Evil.' I would like to formally invite you to join this order."

"Before you give an answer, I would advise you that this order is staffed only by the ordained, or those who are in the process of being raised up. Full members of the order are always ordained Priests with missions to various countries.

"Yes, I can see your question before you even ask it. 'How can you be ordained if you are a woman?' Yes? This order, and this order alone, has a special dispensation from the Holy See to ordain women into this priesthood. With special stipulations, you would train and be raised up as a Priest to fight monsters. Would you serve God by joining the Priesthood?"

Noelle had been stunned. She had looked at Cardinal Müller, then at her bishop, Bishop Roberts, who had nodded solemnly. She had looked back at the Cardinals and took a deep breath, "Cardinal Müller, Archbishop Ferrer, I do believe that I will have to search out God's Will on this matter. May I have some time to think about it and pray for some guidance?"

"Absolutely," Cardinal Müller had responded. "I shifted your worldview. Certainly, take some time to decide. If you have any questions about what the service or training entails, please feel free to ask Bishop Roberts, who is an inactive member of the order."

He had continued, "Your room is reserved for you through the end of this week. If you need more time, we can give that to you as well.

We do ask that the information we provided be kept in the strictest confidence."

"Certainly, Cardinal Müller. It was... interesting talking to you today," said Noelle. "I do believe I need to retire to my room to consider this matter."

As she had stood, the Cardinals and the Bishop stood as well. She had been led out of the labyrinth of corridors and back to her lavishly appointed room.

The very next day, Doctor Noelle Sorenson had informed the Cardinal that she was glad to accept appointment and training into the order. The following two weeks in Ann Arbor had been a whirlwind as she packed for a year-long training in the Vatican. Unable to take everything with her to the Vatican, she had arranged for a storage locker maintained by the local parish. Saying her goodbyes, Noelle had flown out of Detroit and into her new life.

———

THE YEAR HAD BEEN A FRENETIC BLUR OF TRAINING AND STUDY. Between intensive courses in Italian and Latin, Noelle had spent time learning the Church Doctrine, and how to apply and interpret it. She had also spent time on physical training, including basic hand-to-hand combat and work with sharp and pointed weapons. Her favorite courses were those dedicated to the discussion of monsters and the special tools used to fight them effectively.

Noelle had become an expert in banishing the classic forms of the undead such as vampires and zombies. While she learned about other monster types that the church had a history with, her faith and skills fighting the undead quickly brought her to the attention of her instructors.

After about a year of training, Noelle was brought before the Prefect, the Secretary, and several other Bishops and Priests of the Order. The assembled men openly evaluated Noelle's performance and discussed whether her faith and training made her worthy of being lifted up into the priesthood. Throughout the discussion, Noelle knelt on the small cushion placed before the vaunted assembly and kept her face calm and down turned. Even while her thoughts raced, and she reacted internally to the discussion about some of her failures and shortcomings, she was very careful to use her training to keep all of her emotions from showing on her face.

The discussion took well over an hour, and Noelle was beginning to worry, as her legs were starting to cramp. Finally, Cardinal Müller raised a hand to end the discussion. As the conversation stopped, the Cardinal began speaking in Italian, "Rise, my child."

Noelle slowly rose to her feet, and the Cardinal continued, "Doctor Noelle Sorenson. It is the will of this Congregation, and the desire of this Order that you be raised and ordained into the Priesthood. Please step forward and kneel."

Noelle reverently stepped forward to the spot just in front of the Prefect. The Cardinal stepped forward and laid his hand on her head briefly, offering a silent consecration. Then, one-by-one, the other officials present stepped in front of the woman and followed the Prefect's lead. After the last priest had stepped away, Cardinal Müller again stepped toward Noelle and began the traditional consecratory prayer. He then took a stole from a waiting priest and draped it over the back of her neck. It would fall almost to her knees while she stood.

Made of deep black silk and inlaid with spun silver thread, the stole was decorated with a large cross on each end with a very peculiar design connecting the crosses. As she looked closer, she recognized a few Latin phrases in the design. She had also noticed what appeared to be another, even older language woven throughout. As this stole was placed over her head and shoulders, it emitted a faint blue glow from parts of the design. Cardinal Müller muttered a few phrases in a language that Noelle did not recognize.

As the glow had faded, Cardinal Müller reached for a chasuble. Looking like a cross between a renaissance jerkin and a poncho, the vestment had a hole for the priest's head, and then loosely hung over the shoulders and back, with no fastenings at the sides. This particular design had originated in the 16th century and had much shorter sleeves, and the garment ended just below the shoulders on the side, leaving the priest's arms free.

This chasuble was a white, heavy silk with a spun gold thread inlay. A large cross was embroidered on the front and back of the garment, and the design that connected the two was very similar to the one on the stole. As the chasuble was laid on her shoulders, Noelle again noticed a faint blue glow originating from the threads. Cardinal Müller again muttered an invocation in a strange language.

The Prefect stepped back and said, "Rise child." Noelle rose to her feet, and Cardinal Müller continued, "I would like to congratulate the newest member of the *Protectionem Dei Adversus Malum*, Doctor Noelle Sorenson." The assembled men clapped and shook her hand.

As the convocation ended, Archbishop Ferrer, the Secretary for the Congregation, approached Noelle and asked to meet with her afterwards in his office. A short time later, Noelle accompanied the Archbishop to his office just outside the training quarters for her Order. As she was instructed prior to the ordination, she removed her vestments and hung them carefully in her quarters before she walked with the aging Archbishop.

Sitting behind his desk, the Archbishop gestured for Noelle to sit as well. Sitting in the comfortable chair, Noelle leaned back and patiently waited.

The Archbishop began, "Doctor Sorenson, I want to congratulate you again, and welcome you to our order. I have high hopes for you as you go fight the evil in the world. I wanted to meet with you to cover some final matters before you leave the Vatican."

"As you know, the Holy Church does not officially ordain women. Our order has a special, secret dispensation for the practice because there are certain rites that must be performed by an ordained priest for them to work. As such, you are only the third woman, and the only one currently serving, in the history of the order."

"Because of this, you will work to keep your status as an ordained Priest of the Holy Church confidential. While it is acceptable for the people to know that you work for the Church, very rarely will they ever know that you are ordained." The Archbishop looked at Noelle.

"To this end, you will be issued identification and paperwork that shows the Papal Seal. These credentials will gain you access to any of the Church's activities or locations in the United States. They will also enforce cooperation with you from those who also work for the Church."

Archbishop Ferrer drew an identification folder from his desk drawer. Bound in black leather, it was about four inches by five inches, and opened to show a strange identification card inside. The Vatican Special Services ID had Noelle's picture on it, along with her name, and the name and address of the diocese in Ann Arbor. In Latin and English, the card directed that Noelle was a direct representative of the Vatican and, as such, was expected the full cooperation of the person reading the card. Underneath that verbiage was more of the weird unknown script that was on her vestments.

As she accepted the folio, the script and ID had both glowed a faint blue, and then the glow faded. As she examined the folio, the other half contained a document that showed Noelle was a direct representative of Vatican City and was a registered Diplomat and qualified for immunity under the host nation's laws.

Noelle was stunned. *Diplomatic immunity? And what was that strange language?* "Archbishop Ferrer? What is this strange script that is on the credentials and my vestments?"

Archbishop Ferrer chuckled drily. "I wondered when you would get to that. God is all powerful, and your faith in him will help you battle the monsters. The Church also knows that there is other, less powerful authority out there. Sometimes it is useful to invoke that authority when a specific application of Faith does not work as specifically desired. As you will soon learn anyway, the language is an ancient tongue called Enochian, believed last spoken by Enoch. I will let you research and find out where it is from."

The Archbishop made sure to catch her eye as he continued, "One last thing. You are being assigned immediately. You will report to a specific office in the United States Homeland Security, no later than Sunday. There, you will be reporting to an Agent James Smith. You will work on one of his teams to fight these monsters and protect the flock. You will have a dual role. You will be under Agent Smith's authority, operating on his team. You will also continue working for the Vatican. You will report to my office directly. If you have any trouble with any American Church, have them call my office.

"For now, pack your personal belongings for this trip. It is a long-term assignment. Then see Cardinal Giancarlo in the travel office. He will arrange your travel as well as have your contact information and a secure smartphone for you. Go with God."

Noelle stood, shook the Archbishop's hand and went to pack her gear. Next stop, America.

7

WAITING

Section 28, Langley, Virginia.

It had been two days of waiting for Burt Holstein. He had been brought to the Section 28 complex and admitted to the barracks that would be home to him and his new team. Attached to the barracks was a full gym with an Olympic-size swimming pool and a mess hall. The main living area of the barracks had a fully equipped galley, a dining area, and a large recreation area. The recreation area contained a pool table and ping pong table, a massive ultra-high definition screen with theater seating and access to any television channel imaginable, and a server full of movies and television shows to stream at will. One wall was lined with books ranging from popular fiction to classic literature, and reference and nonfiction works. Around the barracks facilities, there seemed to be ten different apartments with adjoining doors to the main living area.

When Burt Holstein had arrived, Agent Smith had handed him the keycard to one of the small apartments and had then explained to him that he was still assembling the team. Burt had been told that he had full access to the current building, but that his keycard would not allow him to exit the building or enter any of the other apartments. Smith had then told Burt that the meals and grocery stocks would be provided but that the delivery staff would not be able to answer any questions. When Burt had asked how long he would be confined to these quarters, Smith had shrugged and said, "I hope less than a week. As it is Saturday, the offices are closed, except for support staff. "

Entering his apartment, Burt had found that it was fully furnished with a small living space, a large bedroom, a small kitchenette, and his own private full bathroom with shower. In the living area, there was a small high-definition television mounted on the wall, a leather loveseat, and an elegant metal and glass desk with a videophone and network cabling ready for a computer or laptop. Finding ample space for his personal effects in the bedroom, Burt had lain back on the bed and just sighed. He stared at the white institutional ceiling. *Great. I'm a thirty-six-year-old man who's just been sent to my room. Indefinitely.* Burt had closed his eyes and had fallen asleep almost instantly, sleeping for nine hours before waking up refreshed.

On Monday morning, Agent Smith brought another gentleman into the living quarters and handed him a keycard for one of the apartments. "Burt Holstein, this is John Smith. John has signed on to work SIGINT and electronics for your team," said Smith as he introduced the two men.

Burt surveyed the man in front of him. Looking about thirty, the six-foot-tall man was skinny to the point of gaunt. His disheveled red hair and green eyes betrayed the man's Irish heritage as much as his pasty white complexion, his boyish-looks, and thin, circular glasses were the epitome of geek chic. The man wore a t-shirt that announced, "There are 10 kinds of people. Those who get Binary, and those who don't." Burt didn't understand the shirt.

Turning to John, Agent Smith said, "Burt is going to be the team leader in the field."

John took his time as he studied his new team leader. Burt was older than John and in his mid-thirties. At five feet nine inches tall, Burt was shorter than John, but he was much stockier. His buzz-cut brown hair matched his brown eyes, and the deep tan told of some time spent in the sun. Looking at the tight t-shirt and cargo pants, John could see that all the weight was muscle. The rugged face, marred by scars, and hard looks told John that Burt was a warrior, and he was used to combat.

Smith turned toward each of them and said, "Well, I'm off to collect your next team member."

After Agent Smith left, Burt showed John the facilities, and John took his personal effects into his apartment. As the mess hall staff dropped off the food for the galley, Burt and John put together cold cut sandwiches and grabbed bags of potato chips and sat at the large table in the middle of the dining area. As John took his first bite, he chuckled to himself. "This sandwich is incredible. I'll have to admit, when I saw that we had a mess hall and galley, I figured we were getting government food. I was starting to regret signing up."

Gradually, Burt and John got to know each other. While they were both very guarded about their youth, they talked about their backgrounds before coming to Section 28 and about their hobbies. They discovered that they both enjoyed really bad sci-fi movies. Realizing that they shared some common ground, each man dropped his guard little by little. They sat back to watch a couple favorite movies in ultra-high definition splendor.

Late Tuesday afternoon, Agent Smith brought another gentleman to what Burt was beginning to call "the barracks." As Jesús Rivera was introduced as the team's sniper, Burt looked over his new teammate.

Jesús was a tall Latino man in his late twenties. His black hair and brown eyes showed his heritage, and the lean, muscular body told of a man who worked out and ate right. Wearing a black tactical shirt and black BDUs usually showed that someone was a "wannabe" or "tacti-cool" operator. On this man, however, the BDUs looked natural and hinted that this man was authentic... the kind of operator that Burt had worked with and got along well with.

The three men sat in the lounge area and slowly began to talk together. Reluctance and wariness stifled conversation. When Burt pointed out that they needed to begin to trust each other as they would soon be working as a team, both men became a little more forthcoming.

Jesús was the first one to cautiously bring up monsters. Recounting what Agent Smith had said about the lone werewolf, he asked the others if they had any similar stories. Burt admitted that he had seen what he thought was a UFO, although Agent Smith had said it was something else. And then John talked about ghosts. When Burt snorted in disbelief, John just looked at him.

John's voice dripped with sarcasm. "Sure. Werewolves and UFOs exist, but ghosts are crazy? Think about this. Just what the heck is Section 28 hiding? If I had my laptop, I could start climbing inside this network."

Jesús and Burt looked at each other and burst out laughing. Burt clapped John on the back, almost bending him over and said, "Point taken, John. Save the hacking for after we're officially sworn in. I'm sure we'll get a chance then."

It was three days later, on Friday afternoon, when Agent Smith brought in their final team members. "Rebekah Callahan, Explosives, and Doctor Noelle Sorenson, Vampire Hunter," said Agent Smith as he introduced the two women to the team.

Everyone gave a slight start at the word "Vampire," wondering if it was a joke. As the team members exchanged bewildered stares, Doctor Sorenson knowingly smiled and said, "I hunt all monsters. But vampires are my specialty."

Agent Smith said, "All right, team. Take the weekend to get to know each other." The DHS agent looked around at the new team. "Monday morning, you'll get sworn in and begin training together. Team meeting is at 0800 Monday. I'll have a staff member come for you then." He then walked out the door.

Burt looked at the two newcomers. Rebekah was a pretty 26-year-old with close-cropped black hair and piercing, bright blue eyes. She was about five inches shorter than his five-foot-nine-inch frame and had a slim, athletic frame. She was a beautiful young woman with a very pretty, pixie-like face. The way she carried herself and the Navy BDUs and white t-shirt told Burt that she was fresh from the Navy.

Doctor Sorenson, on the other hand, did not look like the someone who was used to active field work. Likely in her early forties, she wore a gray pantsuit and was very prim and proper. Her light brown hair was wrapped in a very tight bun, setting off her unusual gray eyes. Just a couple inches shorter than Burt's own five feet and nine inches, she looked more like a manager or business owner, not like the combat-trained "operator" Burt normally worked with. She did not look like someone who could fight a monster. *So how did she hunt vampires?* Burt asked himself. *Wait! Now I'm supposed to believe in vampires? What in the heck did I get myself into?*

Later, the newly formed team gathered their meals and sat at a long table together. Conversation ranged from personal backgrounds to speculation about what they were doing there and soon shifted to a raging debate about whether they were watching a sci-fi movie or the latest romantic comedy. The argument was finally settled by watching a reality TV show about storage locker auctions.

AS AGENT SMITH WALKED THROUGH THE COMPLEX TOWARD HIS OWN living quarters, he received a message on his secure phone. Looking at the message, Smith turned and walked briskly toward the operations room.

As he walked through the doors, the analyst who had sent him the message waived him over to her station. After a brief glance at her data, Smith motioned to the analyst to follow him to the planning center. He unlocked his phone and sent a pre-coded message to both Timothy, his secretary, and his boss, Director Day. The message to Timothy was simple: it instructed Timothy to call a list of staff and have them assembled in the planning center. Timothy was also to arrange with the kitchen staff for delivery of food, coffee, and other snacks.

The message to Director Day told his boss that there was a developing Incursion, and that the planning staff was being assembled. Smith knew Director Day would want a report first thing on Monday morning.

Smith reached the planning center to find that Timothy was already there, deciding which food the kitchen staff would bring to the planning center. As Smith reached his seat at the head of the table, the other staffers trickled in. A mix of analysts, planning strategists, and logistics experts, this staff was trained and assembled for this kind of meeting.

The lead analyst showed Smith a thumb drive, and he plugged it into a receptacle built into the table in front of Smith. As the computer spooled up the drive, the analyst grabbed the remote, and the last staffer came through the door. Closing the soundproof door and engaging the red meeting light, the final staffer took her seat. Smith nodded to the analyst and said, "Go ahead, Joan. What do you have for us?"

Joan looked around the room and made sure that every staff person in the room was ready. Seeing the staff staring at her, she fumbled with the remote. The analyst took a breath to calm her nerves and began the presentation.

Joan began by displaying a map of Colorado with a dot fixed near the southern border of the state, almost directly south of Pueblo. "Trinidad, Colorado. Population, just under eighty-five hundred. An hour and a half south of Pueblo. The search algorithms popped a hit, with an Incursion probability of eighty-nine percent."

"According to the data, there have been five deaths in the last month and a half. Last one happened a couple days ago. Average murder rate prior to this? Zero. The algorithms have also found ten missing people in the area in the last two months." Joan referred to some handwritten notes.

"Every death has shown signs of feeding at the normal locations. Local M.E. is signing off as post-mortem animal activity, but that's only because he isn't that good. The bad news is that the FBI has been alerted, and they are trying to decide if they want to send the BAU."

Smith frowned. He knew the FBI's Behavioral Analysis Unit would impede whichever team they sent. He asked the analyst, "Sounds like Incursion activity. Recommendations?"

Joan looked at her notes. "Team Alpha believes that this is likely a single creature. Most likely a vampire. Team Beta concurs on vampire activity but believes that there may be two. Both Alpha and Beta recommend priority Red."

Section 28 had a priority system set up to triage Incursion events.

The highest priority is Black. Next is Ultra-Red, and then Red, Orange, Yellow, White, and Blue, in descending order.

Smith agreed with the Red priority. Vampires needed attention, but one or two fresh ones were not enough to classify and event as Ultra-Red.

Smith looked around the room. "OK. Priority Red in Trinidad, Colorado. Who do we have available to handle this?"

A woman next to Smith spoke up. "Knightfall is closest, but they're still recovering from their Priority Black," she said. "They are down to twenty percent capable, and their team leader is in rehab for her leg for another month. We also need to replace the casualties from that team."

Another analyst consulted his notes and spoke up. "Knightsdawn is still on location with their Ultra-Red. They are hunting down the 'fae' that came through in Oregon."

Smith thought for a moment and then began, "As most of you know, I've recently recruited the new team, Knightmare. They will swear in Monday morning. They are brand new, but there is a vampire specialist from the Vatican on the team, and most of them are from some sort of federal service. They should be able to handle one or two new vamps. This will be a great field test for them."

Having made his decision, Smith started issuing directions. "Logistics, prepare for the team's departure at 1000, Monday morning. Make sure you have proper ground transport available at the airport for them. Let the Armory know that they will be coming. Oh, and let Norbert know that the new team is coming to him. Send him their files."

"Intel, get everything you can on the town of... Trinidad, Colorado. We need to know who the local government and law enforcement is. Also, find out who is currently the SAC in the Denver office. We may need to give them a 'head's up.'"

"Operations, get the ball rolling. Good catch on the Incursion. Let's make sure this new team has all the support they need. Dismissed."

8

GEAS

By seven o'clock Monday morning, the block of apartments was frenetic with activity as the new teammates prepared themselves for the day. Each person performed their morning routine with a touch of nervous energy as no one had any idea what to expect that day. As the dining crew delivered breakfast at seven thirty in the morning, everyone was out in the lounge area waiting, except for John. He came stumbling out of his apartment about five minutes later with large, dark rings under his eyes attesting to another late night of watching bad science fiction movies.

As the dining crew was leaving, several staffers wheeled large wardrobes through the halls of the apartment block. As the team gathered round, one of the staff said, "All right guys. Welcome aboard. I am Agent Timothy Wilson, but you folks can call me 'Tim.' I am Agent Smith's assistant, so we'll be talking quite a bit." Wilson shook each team member's hand.

Burt appraised the assistant. Timothy Wilson was in his late twenties and looked like the stereotypical "preppy" college frat boy. Standing at five feet eight inches, Tim was blond with blue eyes and very fit and looked like he weighed in just over one hundred fifty pounds. Dressed in an immaculately pressed shirt and tie, Tim looked like he could be on the recruiting poster for any of the federal law enforcement agencies. Burt noticed that Tim was the first staffer that he had seen in the complex who was carrying a pistol. The agent had what looked like one of the Glock handgun models carried in a shoulder holster under his left arm.

Burt realized that Tim had continued speaking. "Today was scheduled to be an orientation day for you guys; however, your team will be going to work earlier than expected. I'll let Agent Smith handle all the details with you, but I wanted to stop by this morning for two reasons. First, I wanted to help drop off your training gear and your official tactical uniforms to be used while on a mission. There are multiple sets of each outfit in here for each of you. If you haven't discovered it yet, we do offer a complete laundry service for you. Just use the bags in your closets, put any special instructions on the form, and drop it off in the laundry area just inside the doorway to your team quarters. They will be returned, folded and pressed, to your individual rooms within twenty-four hours."

"Other than that, I really wanted to introduce myself. I know a lot of details from your file, but that does not mean I know you. When you receive your phones today, my contact information will be preprogrammed. You ladies and gentlemen can feel free to contact me about anything your team liaison cannot handle. Anyone have any questions?"

Burt cleared his throat, "So, we'll be able to leave our quarters today?"

Tim nodded, offering a good-natured smile. "I really apologize about that. Unfortunately, until you have officially been sworn in and signed your contracts, the vast majority of this complex is classified way above any of your former clearance levels. When we brought you here, we didn't anticipate having you in here this long. We really appreciate how patient you have been, especially you, Mr. Holstein."

"We ask that you not stray at all between here and the conference room where you will swear in. Once you are sworn in, you will have access to the vast majority of this complex, and your room keys will act as your access cards to the complex. Any other questions?"

When no one spoke up, Tim made a final request. "Agent Smith would like you to finish your preparations and then be ready at oh seven fifty-five. Your new team liaison will be coming down here to take you to the conference room then. I'll see you guys later."

After Tim left, Burt reached into the wardrobe marked "Training" and grabbed a large bundle of hung clothes wrapped in plastic. Reading the name on the tag, he said, "Rebekah," and handed her the bundle. He then repeated the process until the wardrobe was clean, and everyone had a bundle in his or her arms.

While Burt was passing out the training gear, Jesús opened the wardrobe labeled as "Duty." He continued the process started by Burt and passed out similarly marked bundles to almost everyone on the team. Looking in the now empty wardrobe, he looked puzzled. Jesús turned to Noelle and said, "Sorry, Doc. It looks like they forgot to add a bundle of clothes for you."

Noelle laughed lightly. "I'm sure they didn't forget me, Jesús. My action gear is a little more specialized. And customized. Trust me, I won't look like one of you guys when we go into action."

Jesús thought about it for a moment, nodded, and smiled. "I never thought about it like that."

"I recommend that we put our new gear away before we have to leave," Burt said as he looked at his teammates. "It sounds like we won't be needing the training gear today."

The others nodded their assent and took their clothing into their respective apartments to change.

As they met in the lounge a few minutes later, they all remarked that the training BDU uniforms seemed to be the perfect size. It was almost as if each set were tailored for each person. While they were speculating, there was a slight knock on the door, and a staffer opened the door to the apartment block.

Standing at the door was a young African American woman. She was just over five feet tall, her naturally curly black hair was gathered loosely in the back to form a ponytail, giving her a very youthful appearance. Her brown eyes perfectly complemented her mocha skin. The business pantsuit she wore accented her athletic build. As Burt welcomed her, he spotted a tell-tale bulge as her loose suit jacket flipped open slightly, revealing the butt of a handgun. *Another DHS agent?*

"Ladies and gentlemen, I am Agent Gretchen Massey. Please call me Gretchen. I am your team's direct administrative assistant; my official title is Team Liaison. It is my job to coordinate your life here at the Complex." Burt could almost hear the capital letter she placed on the word. She continued her introduction. "I help coordinate everything from meals to laundry, to entertainment so that you can concentrate on our mission. If you have any issues with the quarters, with your apartment block, or any services we're providing, please let me know. My number will be programmed into your SSP. That's the official designation of the secure smart phone equipment that you will be assigned."

She made a gesture. "Now, if you will follow me, I'll take you to the conference room. Agent Smith is waiting for you."

As the team walked through the warren of hallways and buildings, Burt noticed that there were several identifying marks at every corner that he could not decipher. While there were never any maps he could see, Burt guessed that a simple glance at a corner to read the markings would tell a knowledgeable employee exactly where they were in the complex. As they turned down a corridor mysteriously labeled "Ex1.3.NE," there was a subtle shift in atmosphere. The hall got quieter, as if the very sounds were dampened, and the staffers seemed to be in less of a hurry to move along. Burt noticed that the carpeting in the hallway went from standard industrial to a higher quality carpeting, and the plain metal doors became interspersed with wood doors and the occasional set of windows in the hallway. None of these windows ever showed an outside view. Instead, they always showed the interior of an office or conference room.

Gretchen led them to a door marked "Conference Room Ex.1.A." She opened the door and ushered the team into a large, beautifully furnished conference room. With wood paneling, a large wooden table, and comfortable seating, this room would have been fit for a boardroom for a Fortune 500 company. The large plasma screen at the end of the room nearest the door and the recessed speakers in the ceiling bespoke of fully integrated media. The only thing missing was an executive speakerphone in the middle of the table. At the far end of the table stood Agent Smith.

As the team filed in, Agent Smith motioned for them to sit down. This morning he was wearing the same gray pinstripe suit, immaculately pressed, with the jacket fastened. Agent Smith opened his arms in an expansive gesture and said, "Good morning, ladies and gentlemen. I am so glad we can finally get all of you officially sworn in to Section 28. I know that some of you have been puttering around in your apartment complex for several days now, and I thank you for your patience. As Timothy explained earlier, after this morning, you will not be confined to the apartment complex. In fact, you will not even be confined to this operations complex. Although you will be busy with training and missions, your downtime is your own to do with as you please. Timothy will arrange for any transportation needs that you might have. We'll talk about a lot of that later. I'd like to begin with the formal contracts and swearing in."

Agent Smith reached over and put on a pair of white gloves, the same ones that art and antiquities dealers use to handle rare or fragile items. He then reached over to a closed file lockbox at his right side and opened the lid. One by one, he reached into the lockbox and withdrew a heavy, white envelope. Each one looked like it was made of leather and had a wax seal over the flap on the back. Reading the name embossed on each envelope, he walked around the table, handing out the appropriate envelope to each team member. After watching intently, Burt realized that Agent Smith was careful to never make contact with the person to whom he handed the envelope and that he distributed each envelope individually, never holding more than one at a time.

As John took his pouch, he noticed a weird language written on the seal. As he looked closer, he realized that it looked like the Enochian language he had read about. Called "Celestial" or "Angelical" by the sixteenth century mathematician and occult philosopher John Dee, it was said to be the first language spoken, and the language of angels. They later called it Enochian because the last person on earth to speak it was the biblical figure Enoch.

Pulling a glasses case out of his pocket, John opened the case and replaced his normal glasses with the ones found in the case. The "glasses" that he put on looked like a weird mechanical contraption with multiple spindly arms that held different lenses and could be flipped up and down as needed. John flipped a particular set of lenses down and observed that the wax seal itself had a faint blue glow to it. Pushing that set of lenses out of the way and flipping another one down, he detected a faint green energy glow on the envelope itself.

Whistling softly, John looked at Agent Smith who was once again standing at the head of the conference table and remarked, "Can I get one without the glowing letters and spooky green glow?"

Agent Smith smiled. "No, Mr. Smith. I'm afraid that the paperwork comes standard with that 'spooky green glow' that you mentioned." Addressing the rest of the team, he continued. "Before you open the pouches in front of you, I want you to be very clear about a couple things that will happen when you do so. You might experience a wave of energy or a slight tingling sensation on your fingertips and in your hair. Some have also reported other strange sensory phenomena. I assure you: that is normal.

"This is your last and final chance to not join this team. If you choose to stop now, you will go back to where you were when I recruited you. No harm. No foul. No Take-backs. Does anyone want to exercise that option now?" Smith paused to see if anyone would take the deal.

When no one responded, he continued. "If you would now open your envelopes, taking care not to touch any of the materials from another teammate. Inside you will find a contract and a pen. Please pull both of those items out and begin reading the contract. This spells out your terms of service, and it details our agreement with you. A large part of this contract explains that this agreement will bar you from mentioning Section 28, what you do, or what you are hunting, except under certain, very explicit, circumstances. Even the existence of Section 28 is classified as 'Top Secret - Black,' and is on a need-to-know basis."

"On the back page, there is a spot to sign your name and date it. When you pick up the pen and begin to write with it, you may feel a slight pinch in one of your fingers. This is supposed to happen. At that time, your blood will be taken and mixed with the ink when you sign the contract. Each of your contract agreements is exactly the same, except for Doctor Sorenson's. Hers is slightly different due to her position with the Vatican. At this time, please read through the agreement and sign where indicated."

The teammates all opened their envelopes and began to read their contracts. As John read through the contract, certain phrases seemed to leap out and implant themselves in his brain: "...Secrecy *Geas* will be enforced...." "...Limited license to kill paranormal...." "...Incursion-level events...." "Housing, weapons, and esoteric research..."

More of these phrases rattled through his vision, and John was filled with a mixture of fear and excitement. Along the edges of the agreement, John noticed more of the Enochian markings, both along the sides and across the top and bottom of each page. The further along he read in the contract, he realized that the lettering on the sides of the agreement actually started to glow a faint neon green. For every page he turned, the markings became a bit more prominent and the glow went a bit lower on the next page. When he reached the end, all of the ancient script except the bottom of the page glowed. John held the pen and put the old-fashioned nib to the line to sign his name. As he signed, he felt a pinch and a tingle in his fingers, and the black ink from the pen changed to a deep maroon. As he placed the final stroke and dated the agreement, the script across the bottom of the page flared to life, and then the glow on the entire agreement faded.

John put down the pen and looked at his hands. He could not see any wounds caused by the pen. As he looked up, he noticed everyone else examining their hands as well. One by one, they looked around at each other as they exchanged deeply disturbed expressions. The questions and surprise floating around the room were almost tangible, and Agent Smith cleared his throat to get everyone's attention.

"Now that you have signed your agreements, please place the contract back into the carrier pouch with the pen. Then simply press the flap to the seal and it will close."

A series of blue flashes around the table confirmed that all of the team members' pouches were sealed. In an orderly and meticulous fashion, Agent Smith walked to each team member, one at a time, to retrieve the pouches. After he had gathered all the pouches with the same care that he had shown when he handed them out, he placed the pouches inside the box, closed the lid of the file carrier, and muttered a few words in a strange language. A small blue flash from the locking mechanism indicated that the box was sealed with the same energy as the pouches. At this, Agent Smith peeled his gloves off and turned back to the assembled team.

"Ladies and gentlemen, I would like to formally welcome you to the Department of Homeland Security, Section 28. As of now, you are officially agents assigned to Team Knightmare."

9

KNIGHTMARE

Section 28 Conference Room , Langley, Virginia.

Agent Smith reached to his left and grabbed a stack of identification holders that was sitting on the table. Opening the top set of credentials, he read the name and began passing them out. "Special Agent Burt Holstein. Your new radio call sign will be 'Six.' As team leader, you will coordinate and lead the team while on assignment."

Turning to John, Agent Smith handed him his credentials. "Special Agent John Q. Smith," Agent Smith said with a smile. "Your new call sign is 'Spooky.' Use your electronics wizardry to find the monsters for your team to kill."

As he handed out the next set of credentials, he said, "Special Agent Rebekah Callahan. You like to blow things up, I think 'Boomer' is rather appropriate for your call sign."

The next set of credentials went to Jesús. "Special Agent Jesús H. Rivera. Your job will be sniper and overwatch, making sure your team doesn't get bushwhacked. I do believe that tradition says you should be called 'God.'"

Noelle smiled at Jesús and said, "Little 'g.' Don't forget it."

Agent Smith turned to Noelle. "And, Doctor Sorenson, that leaves us with you. Special Agent Noelle Sorenson. Not only are you the team's resident vampire hunter and esoteric specialist with Vatican training, you are also a trained trauma doctor. I do believe that 'Doc' would suit you well on the radio."

"The credentials I just gave you prove your identity with Homeland Security," said Smith as he addressed the whole team. "If anyone questions the validity or authority of your credentials, have them call Homeland Security with your badge/ID number. They will be transferred to this office, and we will let them know that they are stepping into a pile of crap. Also, tucked into the credential wallet is a government credit card with your name on it. Use it for anything you need. Just make sure you bring back receipts for the Auditors.

"When you are on assignment, your authority trumps local law enforcement, the local FBI field office, and even the Secret Service, if it escalates to that point. You have the full authority to do your job and to protect America, and humanity, from the scary monsters that others simply cannot deal with. When you are not on assignment, you are to use your discretion on exercising that authority. If you suspect that we have a monster around, then use your authority to get the help you need. Do not abuse the authority just because you can. If you do, the 'geas' that you just signed in blood will make your life miserable if you abuse it."

John spoke up, a smile forming as he talked. "So, this is kinda like psychic paper, only it actually has something on it? Cool."

Agent Smith returned the smile, a bit bemused at the reference. "With the exception that you are not, nor will you ever be, a Time Lord. And you, John, would not look nearly as good in a trench coat and scarf."

Rebekah and Burt started laughing, and John sheepishly turned red. Noelle and Jesús looked at the team, and then at each other and shrugged, clearly not getting the reference.

After several moments, Agent Smith cleared his throat to regain the focus of the group. "Now that you all know who you are, I'd like to tell you why you are here." He paused briefly, looking at each team member, and then continued. "All of this briefing is classified."

Smith began as if he was addressing a college lecture hall.

"Throughout history, there have been stories and reports of strange animals, evil creatures, and unexplained phenomena. While most people believe these are just tales, we have found out that the tales have at least some basis in fact. As best we can tell, there are certain locations where the boundary between our reality and another reality, another plane of existence, or another place, grows thin and weak. This weakening is rarely permanent and often appears in locations where it has not previously occurred. Sometimes, this makes the boundary thin enough that something from the other side can pass through the barrier. At other times, the barrier thins, and the fears and dreams of the people nearby allow their deepest fears to manifest in our reality. We call these crossings 'Incursions.'"

Smith could tell that he had his agents' attention. Their expressions ranged from rapt concentration to disbelief to an amused nodding. The one nodding and smiling was John, and Smith knew that he would have his hands full trying to keep John in check. Smith would have to keep the young intel specialist busy.

Smith continued with his explanation. "It is a relatively well-known fact that Adolf Hitler had a fascination with the paranormal. From collecting religious artifacts believed useful for gaining power, trying to communicate with the dead, or somehow using this thinning reality to help conquer the world, Hitler was a growing threat on the esoteric and paranormal front."

"On June 13, 1942, the Office of Strategic Services was formed as an intelligence agency during World War II. One of the smaller, but still substantial, concerns that affected the formation of this new agency was the threat represented by Hitler's esoteric research. Between Section 27 and Section 29 of the Presidential military order that formed the OSS was a small redacted notation labeled 'Section 28 - Top Secret (Black)'. Only a handful of people knew about the formation of Section 28 and to even reveal the existence of this program was considered High Treason. During wartime, a treason charge like this would have meant a swift trial and execution."

"In that original Section 28, this office and complex was formed and began hiring agents and training those agents to fight monsters. When the OSS was dissolved in 1945 for the creation of the CIA, the small redacted notation about Section 28 was again added to the charter. While it was technically no longer 'Section 28' of the new charter, the name and reference remained."

"When the Homeland Security Act of 2002 was passed on November 25, 2002, there was once again a redacted Top Secret (Black) notation that reassigned the offices and personnel of Section 28 to the Department of Homeland Security. Our credentials switched from the CIA to DHS, but nothing else really changed."

"Our mission is to hunt down and either manage these incursion monsters, destroy the incursion monsters, or send them back through the Incursion. There are some creatures who come through, with whom we, and other governments, have certain agreements. Those we work with to protect our citizens. Other creatures come through, we call them monsters. These are the ones that we have to hunt down. We either kill them, or we send them back through the Incursion. This is now your mission."

"To that end, you have virtually carte blanche access to equipment, tools, weapons, and research. Each Incursion is assigned a priority color, from no priority 'Blue,' then 'White,' 'Yellow,' 'Orange,' 'Red,' 'Ultra-Red,' and 'Black,' in ascending order. A priority Black means that the world is actually going to end if we don't get the call right."

Smith paused to catch the eye of every team member around the table. He wanted to make sure that they understood this next part very clearly.

The senior agent continued, "To help protect America from the very teams designed to save her, the contract you signed has a *geas* on it that will tear you apart from the inside out if you intentionally betray your team or Section 28. I watched one former agent turn a gun on the team as soon as he learned the truth. The fire that immolated him after he pulled that trigger for the first shot left nothing except ash."

Agent Smith was melancholy for a moment, and then seemed to visibly shake himself out of it. "As much as I'd like to begin your training this morning, I'm afraid that you are going to have to do some on-the-job training. Last night, we received a Priority Red Incursion. The target area is Trinidad, Colorado. With a population of just under nine thousand, this small town sits about an hour and a half south of Pueblo."

"They have had five murders in the last month and a half. No commonality among the victims except they were drained of fluids and had 'animal marks' on their ankles, wrists, neck, and inner thighs. There have also been ten people reported missing within that same timeframe. The local sheriff has not connected the murders to the disappearances yet, but he has called in the FBI Behavior Analysis Unit to profile the killer. Thoughts?"

Noelle immediately spoke up. "You obviously think that it's vampires. Any idea how many?" she questioned.

Agent Smith smiled and then answered, "Frankly, Doctor Sorenson, I would have been disappointed if you had not come up with that option. Yes, we are thinking vampires, and the analyst team believes that there are only one or two vamps, and that they are fairly new vamps, possibly turned by an Incursion."

"You will have access to records and Section 28 information on your flight to Trinidad. I really want to give you more time to train and prepare for this job, but I cannot let a Priority Red go while you guys are active. Your fire team has all seen combat of one sort or another. This should be a fairly simple run for you. Watch your backs, take care of these monsters, and try not to get your face on TV."

Smith motioned for the team to rise.

"OK, first stop is back to your quarters to grab your tactical BDUs and pack a small bag for clothing and essentials. We've provided duffle bags for your deployments. This should only last a couple days. When you have your bags, drop them in the area outside the entrance to your barracks marked 'Deployment' and head to the warehouse for outfitting."

"Once you have your gear, head to the airfield out back. The jet should be fueled and waiting for you. You need to be 'wheels up' in one hour. Gretchen is waiting outside to guide you back to your quarters and then on to the plane. Any questions?"

The abrupt reality of their impending deployment stifled any questions that were forming from the briefing. Seeing no questions,

Smith dismissed them. "All right then, welcome to Section 28. Go kill some monsters."

The walk back was quiet as each team member tried to absorb his or her new reality. When the team returned to their barracks, they found several boxes waiting for them. Stacked in the commons area, each box had a name on it. Burt stepped forward and started passing them out to the team members.

When John opened his box, he found all the customized electronics that had been confiscated from him when he had first arrived. Sitting in the carefully packed box was his laptop, all of his electronics tools, several thumb drives, and a special wristband. Handcrafted over the course of a year, John's wristband covered most of his forearm and looked similar to plastic sleeves that college quarterbacks wear to keep track of plays and strategy. Inspired by those wristbands, John had designed and built the wristband as a full-capability touch-screen computer. And it was faster and more powerful than the desktops sitting in most homes. Gathering his gear, he ran into his room to pack a bag.

Jesús opened his rather long box to find a rifle case inside. Opening the case and checking the serial numbers, he confirmed that this was, in fact, his heavily customized personal M24-A3 rifle. Checking the action, he realized that it had been thoroughly and professionally cleaned. Although there was no ammunition or magazines with it, he felt like he had just found a long-lost friend. He packed the rifle back in her case and strode to his apartment to put on his tactical gear.

Rebekah's box contained a small assortment of personal electronics and a small necklace-sized velvet box. Rebekah opened the box and blinked away the tears. There was a small note from her former commanding officer, Chief Warrant Officer Harold Goodwin. The note read, "I fought for this. Orders came through the day after you left. Good luck." Underneath the note was a small collar pin of an eagle clutching a fouled anchor. A certificate inside the box announced that she was (then) Chief Petty Officer Rebekah Callahan. She placed the items back in her box and went into her room to pack.

Noelle opened her small box and found a package addressed to her from the Vatican. Opening the small package, she found a note from the Prefect. "Dr. Sorenson, I've enclosed one of the books from the Library. I believe that this will help you in your assignment. Go with God." Looking at the book, she felt the worn leather binding and saw the title *Cum Praeliorum Creaturae.* Noelle translated the title, *Of Battles with Creatures.* Noelle said a silent prayer of thanks, for the book she was holding was written by one of the Order's most prolific monster hunters. It was his battle diary. Noelle wandered toward her room lost in thought.

When Burt was finally able to open his box, he immediately smiled. Sitting inside was a complex holster rig and two pistol boxes. Opening the boxes, Burt caressed the gun inside each box. While they appeared to be normal Beretta 92FS series pistols, Burt knew these were his. A quick check of the serial numbers verified that they were his, and a function inspection verified that the custom-tuned guns were immaculately cleaned. Grabbing the gear, he headed toward his room.

The team met together in the commons area when they were finished dressing and packing. Gretchen led them out the door and to the warehouse. As they were leaving the block of apartments, Gretchen pointed out the spot reserved for "go bags" for assignments. As the team members dropped their go bags, a series of lights lit up along the wall. Gretchen explained that this summoned the staff to take care of their bags.

Walking to the warehouse, they went through another warren of corridors. Eventually the corridors widened out, and the team came to a large vault door that stood open and towered over twenty feet tall. It was about three feet thick. A small sign stenciled on the wall said "Logistics." When Burt remarked about the thickness of the door, Gretchen quietly pointed out that the weapons, gear, and equipment stored in the warehouse could actually affect the course of a nation.

The warehouse was impossibly large inside. Easily thirty feet high, the large space opened up into three distinct areas. Gretchen offered a running commentary for the introduction. "On your right is 'Equipment.' All of your tactical equipment and gear is here... secure radios, armor, electronics, and virtually anything you could want for the mission. If they don't currently have it, they can procure it within twenty-four hours. Normally, you are given more prep time for a mission and can have a list ready for the Equipment team."

Standing behind the equipment staffer was an enormous series of racks and bins. All of which was neatly labeled and ready to supply a mission deployment.

Gretchen continued her tour. "On your left is the 'Armory.' We stole Master Sergeant Russell Garner from the Army, and he is the one who will give you anything that goes bang or boom and anything that makes critters dead. Almost any type of weapon or ammunition is available, and what he doesn't have, he can get. Russell is also a master armorer. If your gun is broken or needs tuned, he can make it shoot better than it ever has. Once you've decided on a normal load out, Russell will have it ready for you on deployment."

Russell Garner was a large, burly man with a rough, blocky face and a salt-and-pepper buzzcut. Looking every inch the former Army sergeant, Russell was wearing a polo shirt and cargo pants, and the distinctive grip of a Colt M1911 stuck out of the holster on his waist. The man appeared to be old enough to have used the same type of weapon while in the military before they switched to a smaller 9mm round. Behind the armorer was a cage of steel that contained a series of racks that held everything from pistols to rifles and shotguns. There were sections where bins of grenades were stacked, and even a section that contained anti-tank rockets. Along the wall to the armorer's right was a series of bins with names, including the names of the team members.

Gretchen led the team to the final area, straight ahead. "And last, but certainly not least, is 'Esoteric Research and Logistics.' Because of what you do, we have an entire staff dedicated to researching how to effectively find, track, and kill monsters. Think of them as the Section 28 'Q' branch. And the head of this rather eccentric group is Norbert Guffy. If you look up 'mad scientist' in the dictionary, I do believe Norbert's picture is shown. On the other hand, if you need to figure out how to kill a particular incursion monster, Norbert will have the equipment for you. From holy water to silver ammunition, and stakes to wolfsbane, if you know what you are hunting, Norbert probably has something to kill it."

Norbert Guffy was a wiry little man around five feet tall. Seated behind a simple wooden desk, his unkempt hair and stained, disheveled shirt suggested a distinct lack of sleep and hygiene. The shirt was barely covered by the worn and frayed lab coat that used to be white, but now tinged gray. His thick, black-framed glasses gave him a slightly bug-eyed appearance. The strange, mechanical keyboard on a metal stand to Norbert's right was connected to a vast machine behind him. The machine was composed of large racks separated and entangled with a confusing nest of rails. Both large and small containers traveled along rails to be stored on the racks. Manipulating the boxes was a complex series of mechanical arms, using pulleys, wires, and bits of copper. John was fascinated by the complex mechanism in front of him and stared in wonder.

Gretchen turned to the team and watched them gaze in amazement as they looked around the Logistics warehouse. She cleared her throat to get their attention. "I know this is short notice, but requisition your gear, weapons, and any esoteric gear. We have about fifteen minutes to get to the plane outside." She then stepped back as the team members dispersed to gather their equipment.

10

LOGISTICS

Section 28 Warehouse, Langley, Virginia.

Burt, Jesús, and Rebekah immediately headed for the Armory. Nodding to the armorer, Burt reached out his hand and grasped the former sergeant's. "Mr. Garner, it's nice to meet you. I'm guessing it was you who cleaned up my Berettas."

"Yes, Agent Holstein," Russell responded. "And please, call me Russell. I think you'll like shooting them even more now. Would you like ammo for them for the mission? What else can I get for you?"

Burt laughed and responded, "Ok, Russell, I'm Burt. Let's go with four magazines for the Berettas and two boxes of additional ammo. I'd like to make the Beretta M9 the standard load out for each member of the team, unless they have a different preference, except for our priest. Also, I'd like an M4, select-fire, with a foregrip and an ACOG on top for the sights. I'll trust your judgement for the setup. Four full magazines and a hundred rounds of extra ammo."

The Beretta M9 was a classic semi-automatic handgun chambered in 9mm. The pistol had been the standard U.S. military sidearm since 1985, and the civilian variants were often used in law enforcement from the mid-1980s through the 1990s. The M4 carbine was the shorter, adjustable stock variation of the venerable M16 rifle that had been in service since the Vietnam Conflict. Updated for modern usage, the M4 had an adjustable stock for individual shooters, a shorter sixteen-inch barrel, and was capable of semi-automatic shots or firing three-round bursts, selectable with the flick of a switch.

Burt turned to Rebekah and asked, "Any experience with a rifle?"

"Some. But I'm better with a shotgun," Rebekah said. "I preferred the Mossberg we used on the ship."

Burt turned back to the waiting armorer. "So, Mossberg twelve gauge. Thirty rounds, split between buckshot, slug, breeching round, dragon fire, and rubber."

Russell went to a rack and grabbed a black Mossberg 590A1 Tactical shotgun. The jet black, pump-action shotgun held five rounds in the tube, a pistol grip, and a collapsible stock like the M4 carbine. By racking the pump, the shotgun would strip out an expended shell and replace it with a fresh round that was nearly a half an inch in diameter. While not great for long distance targets, the shotgun was devastating at shorter ranges.

Rebekah spoke up. "Nice to meet you Russell; I'm Rebekah. What do you have that will make stuff go bang?"

Russell smiled and accepted her handshake. "You must be the EOD Tech. I like how you think. I have everything from Semtex to C4, and even dynamite, available. Anything more exotic will have to meet you on-site. What do you want?"

Both Semtex and C4 were considered "plastic explosives." Unlike dynamite, plastic explosives are an inert, moldable clay-like material that will only explode when the proper trigger is used. Safe to transport and mold, this type of explosive needs the concussive shock of a detonator or blasting cap to start the explosive reaction. Due to its energy potential, it only takes a little to generate the explosive energy of the kinetically slower dynamite.

"I might just fall in love with you, Sarge," Rebekah said as she smiled. "How about two pounds of C4. And an assortment of detonators, you know... motion, timed, remote? The fun stuff. I'll also take four flashbang grenades and four fragmentation, if you've got them."

Russell nodded, and Burt chimed in, "I'll take the same grenade load."

Russell said, "OK, give me five minutes to gather and crate it. I'll send it out to the plane for you."

As Burt and Rebekah walked toward the area marked, "Equipment," Jesús stepped up, placed his rifle kit on the bench, and shook Russell's hand, "I'm Jesús. Great job on my rifle. She hasn't been that smooth in a while."

Russell grinned. "I'm glad you liked it. I was going to leave it for you, but we got notice you were being assigned immediately, so I thought I'd help. Can I ask you something? Why did you choose .338 Lapua? I would think that a .308 would allow for a more selective application. Your magnum is going to shoot through a lot of things a .308 wouldn't."

Jesús nodded. "It might seem that way, but I was on the HRT. Most of the time, if I was pulling the trigger, I was shooting through glass, a wall, or even a car door. I had to have the long distance and heavy penetration. Besides, if you hit a bad guy with the magnum round, they don't survive for trial."

Russell nodded again. "You'll need that penetration for some of the critters that you guys are going to tackle. By the way, I tweaked the scope mount and mounted a new scope of my own design. With a simple click, your scope goes from regular to night vision to thermal. I sighted it in at one hundred yards, but you'll want to verify in the field." Russell reached down and grabbed a small hand-held electronic device that looked like a calculator. "Here's a new ballistics computer. I've pre-programmed it for all the commercially available rounds, as well as the custom rounds we make here. I've even included the fun rounds that the guys in Esoteric come up with. Since you don't have a spotter, you'll need the computer."

The sniper nodded. He paused to consider, and continued, "Instead of the M9, I'd like a good 1911," Jesús said. "It's what I carried for the HRT, and I know the gun inside and out."

Russell's grin grew wide. "Damn. I'm glad at least one of you likes to play with the 1911. I've got a custom built one that you can use, decked out with all the bells and whistles. She shoots through one ragged hole at 25 yards."

"That sounds great. At least four extra magazines, if you will," said Jesús.

Jesús thanked Russell and wandered toward the Equipment section. There, Burt had already ordered Level III flak jacket armor for all the team except the priest and the whiz kid. For those team members, he had requisitioned level IIIA armor they could wear under their clothing. Full battle helmets, night vision and thermal goggles, and secure radios with self-activating throat mikes rounded out the tactical requisitions. The three teammates wandered toward the other team members at Esoteric Research.

When the three combat specialists walked toward the armory, Noelle and John looked at each other and immediately went to talk to the man behind the Esoteric desk. On the plain wooden desk sat a nameplate that read "Esoteric Research–Guffy." Behind the desk the man looked at them quizzically. Realizing that they were waiting for him, he started enthusiastically talking in a running stream-of-consciousness.

"Oooh, you must be the new team. It's nice to finally meet you. I've been waiting hours or maybe minutes." Looking at Noelle, he glanced at her collar and clothing and said, "You must be the priest. Of course you are the priest. Only the priest would wear that collar. Right? Let's see. I know I had a box for you." Bending over his keyboard, he began hesitantly typing letters. "Let's see, that was 'P' for priest, no... 'V' for Vatican? No... Ah. 'B' for box. B-01-DF-6."

Behind the desk, the worrisome contraption of arms, pulleys, tracks, and boxes whirred into life. After a few minutes, a pair of arms brought a medium-sized box right to the desk. Opening the lid, Norbert pulled out a small box, what looked like a cross and a rather full pouch. "OK. Let's see. You have a crucifix, silver, with a wooden stake carved into the end... a box of, hmmm, what was that... something your Vatican recommended... oh, a dead man's blood. And a full pouch of consecrated salt. You guys must be going after vampires! Sounds like fun!"

Noelle accepted the items and asked, "Do you have anything else that might help? Like a way to deliver the blood?"

Norbert's face lit up, and he furiously pecked away at the

keyboard, muttering to himself. A few moments later, the same arms whisked the box away and brought another one. Opening the lid, Norbert lifted out a rather strange looking handgun. He smiled and proffered it to Noelle. "Tranquilizer gun. My design." His face fell momentarily, and he began digging in the box again. Crying out triumphantly, he handed a small box to Noelle. "And here are the darts. Hypodermic. You should be able to figure it out. I hope so anyway... I lost the instruction book. Anything else?"

Noelle shook her head and stepped aside for John. John looked at Norbert and said, "OK, so what kind of gear do you have for me?"

Norbert looked him up and down and suddenly gasped. Muttering and punching furiously at the keys, he had another box brought to him. Inside were two small black pouches. Unrolling one, Norbert looked at John and said, "Let me see your glasses. Come on, come on, you don't have all day."

Reluctantly, John handed Norbert his glasses and cringed as Norbert's deft fingers disassembled his prized glasses effortlessly. The researcher's fingers moved way too fast for John to follow, and it seemed like the glasses almost reassembled themselves. Handing them back to John, Norbert smiled. "Try 'em on. I think you'll like them!"

John placed his glasses back on the bridge of his nose and was instantly amazed. Not only was the world around him sharper and crisper, but he noticed that by simply scrunching his nose a certain way he could switch between the various lenses. John started laughing and thanking Norbert.

Norbert handed John one of the tool pouches that was before him. "Amazing creatures, gremlins. Their stuff is always fun to play with." Norbert's eyes got wide as a thought struck him. He turned back to his keyboard and started muttering again. "Oooooh. One more thing. Let's see, was that 'B' for bullet? No... 'P' for pistol? No... Aha! 'G' for ghoul. GX-3-D-414-Z."

Again the boxes whirled around, and the mechanical arms brought a small but armored box down from the racks. The excitable Norbert gingerly pulled out a small padded carrying case with an explosives symbol on the side. Setting it on his desk, Norbert opened the airtight case. Inside the case, John could see a small box of ammunition nestled deep into thick foam padding. Norbert smiled at John while he closed the lid and secured the box.

Handing the box to John, Norbert said, "OK, a special surprise for you. Use on a vampire. Be VERY careful. Don't shoot anything you want to keep around. Have fun!"

Norbert turned to the team members coming up behind John. "And what can I get for you?"

Burt, Rebekah, and Jesús had walked over to the Esoteric Research area and were listening to the conversation between Norbert and John. Burt smiled at Norbert's greeting and said, "Do you have anything that we can use? It looks like we're vampire hunting this trip."

Norbert nodded and smiled, and then said, "Yes, yes. Let me see what I have here. What calibers are you carrying?"

As Norbert started typing on the keyboard, Burt answered, "Nine millimeter, and five-five-six. And Rebekah has a twelve gauge. And Jesús has three-three-eight Lapua, and apparently a forty-five auto." Burt looked at the holstered pistol strapped to Jesús's waist.

A fair amount of clicking and clacking sent the arms scurrying through the racks. Norbert muttered, "Only two vampires. Newbies. Calculate one hundred rounds of nine. Ninety rounds of rifle ammo. Twenty for the pretty girl with the shotgun. Thirty for the scary sniper..."

Eventually, the arms retrieved four of the containers, and the researcher dug into them. He began placing boxes of ammunition on the desk. "Two hundred rounds of nine millimeter. One hundred rounds of forty-five. Ninety rounds for the rifle. Twenty shotgun rounds. And thirty for the sniper. My own design. Brand new. Should work." Norbert shrugged. "Should, anyway."

Burt and Jesús opened their respective boxes and compared rounds. The rounds inside looked like a standard jacketed hollow-point design with a couple major distinctions. The outer coating of the jacket appeared to be silver, and Burt expected that it would test as silver as well. Inside this actual hollow cavity sat a piece of wood. Noelle leaned over and looked at the round. Nodding appreciatively, she turned back to Norbert. "You've combined silver shot with a wooden stake in a form that can be delivered from a distance. How ingenious. I'm going to enjoy working with you."

The researcher blushed crimson. "Thank you. It just sounded like it should work," Norbert said as he shrugged. The researcher looked up and saw Gretchen pointing to her watch across the hall. He said, "You guys need to get going. Vampires waiting. Have fun hunting!" And he began sending the cargo boxes back to their proper places.

The team turned and saw Gretchen waiving them forward. As they reached her, she said, "Your gear is on the plane. It's time to get 'wheels up.'"

The team followed their administrator through a couple short corridors and out into the bright Virginia sunlight. On the tarmac before them was a beautiful white jet. As the engines began to spool up, John emitted a sound that was very close to a squeal. "That's a Cessna Citation X. They are super rare, way expensive, and we get to fly in one?"

Noelle turned to the young computer wizard and said, "So? It's a plane. What's so special about this one?"

The pure fanboy adulation instantly made Noelle regret her question. John began speaking rapidly, "It is literally the fastest private jet in existence. It has a top speed of over point-nine Mach, or nine-tenths the speed of sound. We should be in Colorado in less than three hours with this thing cranking up..."

John continued excitedly pointing out technical details, but Noelle tuned him out. Instead, she walked a bit closer to Gretchen and asked her a question. "So, Gretchen. How does a government agency afford all these nifty toys and privileges? I can't imagine Congress approving this budget extravagance."

Gretchen smiled at Noelle as they approached the stairs into the plane. She replied, "Because of our classification, we cannot really be expected to publish a budget now, can we? As part of Homeland Security, we have certain discretionary funds available, and you are all correctly identified as Special Agents of Homeland Security. But we also hold the patent on several items through dummy corporations and holding companies. Add those lucrative royalties to the appropriations, and we can fund you enough to do your job.

"Very few agents ever retire from active service. You guys will live a rough life, so the Director believes that you should be taken care of while you are here. He looks out for everyone in Section 28, but he pampers the Incursion teams, and those of us who look out for you."

One by one, the team members climbed the stairs and boarded the jet. Each one gazed in amazement at the plush leather seating and chrome and glass furnishings inside the plane. Each found a leather recliner and sank into its comfort. As Gretchen climbed aboard last, she leaned into the cockpit and said, "All right Captain. We're all aboard, and the gear is stowed. Take off, please."

As Gretchen sat in her seat and fastened her seatbelt, the noise from the engines shifted from a high-pitched whine to a roar, and the plane began to move. As it taxied to the end of the runway, the sleek jet paused momentarily as the captain received clearance from air traffic control. Given the priority code, the air controller cleared the traffic around the field and gave permission to the captain to take off. Both the captain and the copilot placed their hands on the throttle controls, and the captain pushed the throttle forward to its limit. Holding the brakes for a short second as the engines built thrust, the pilot released the brakes, and the jet leapt forward, clawing for the sky.

The jet lifted off the runway. The pilot pulled the stick back toward him, and the plane climbed rapidly in a steep ascent. The copilot picked up his microphone and announced to their passengers that they would land in Pueblo, Colorado, in just under two-and-a-half hours.

Agent Smith watched the jet until it disappeared from his sight. The senior agent turned from the bay windows in the mess hall and walked back to his office. Before he got there, his aide approached him and handed him a folder. Looking at the name on the folder, Smith looked at his assistant. "Has this been verified, Timothy? Do they really have him locked up?"

"Yes, sir. Norfolk Police Department has him in jail awaiting trial. I don't know how we missed it, but he's been there for two months.

I've had Logistics get a vehicle, and it's waiting outside. I've also arranged to have him transferred to a holding cell at the sheriff's office so you can talk to him."

Smith smiled at Timothy. "Do you have anything stopping you from being my driver today?" Timothy shook his head, and Smith continued, "Then let's go catch a ghost."

11

GHOST

Norfolk, Virginia.

J onas Vanhof sat in the holding cell at the Norfolk Sheriff's Office. He had been in custody for over two months and expected to spend the rest of his relatively short life in prison, at least until the Commonwealth of Virginia could execute him. It was all his fault that he had been caught. He had forgotten the first rule: don't be a hero. He should have left at the first screams, but he didn't. He had to play the hero.

The police officers and sheriff deputies had found him with a body, freshly murdered. Jonas had been cleaning up his gear and getting ready to leave when the officers kicked in the door to the couple's house. As Jonas had run for the backyard, the sound of crashing glass announced more officers were waiting for him there. Trapped like a rat, he had fought back, using his considerable hand-to-hand combat skills. While no officers had been permanently disabled, several had to go to the hospital. It had taken three tasers to finally drop Jonas to the ground.

Having been quickly denied bail, Jonas had waited to be assigned a public defender. His public defender had been frustrated when Jonas would not give her any answers about why he was there or give her any defense that she could use. She could not even get Jonas to plead temporary insanity as a defense. They were now just waiting for the trial.

After two months in a jail cell, Jonas was dragged out, put in shackles and leg irons, and transported to the sheriff's office. There he was placed in a holding cell and told to wait. None of his guards would give him any explanation, and Jonas just accepted it as his life. Sitting with his head down on his knees, Jonas heard the guard approach his cell, and then he heard the electronic lock disengage.

At twenty-seven years old, this was not his first time in a cell. While awaiting trial, many of his fellow prisoners had thought his six-foot-four-inch lanky frame meant he was weak and vulnerable. He didn't have mass, or obvious muscle tone; Jonas looked scrawny, as any easy target should. He only had to give a severe beating to two other prisoners for the rest to leave him alone. His long blond hair was usually up in a loose ponytail, and his blue eyes told those who looked that he was far older than his years.

"Hey, inmate. Wake up, or I'll wake you up." Jonas felt the tip of a baton touch the back of his head. He looked up into the guard's face. The guard continued, "Get up, scumbag. Someone wants to talk to you."

As they walked out of the jail cell, the guard leaned in close and whispered, "I know the guys you hurt. They're good guys." When they approached the edge of the cell, the guard shoved Jonas face first into the edge of the doorframe. "Oops, you should be more careful there, pal."

Jonas felt a small trickle of blood run down his forehead and blinked to keep it out of his eyes. The guard at the gate blatantly ignored the cut on Jonas' forehead and let them through. His guard led him to a room with only one door, no windows, and cameras in two of the corners. The table in the center of the room was bolted down and had a steel ring in the middle of it and a large red button on one side. The guard took him into the room and unshackled his hands long enough to run the chain through the loop in the table.

The guard said, "Sit down. Your visitor will be with you in a moment."

Jonas did not have to wait long. A medium-sized gentleman in an impeccably tailored gray pinstripe suit walked through the door, closing it behind him. Jonas could see that the man was carrying a file folder with the Homeland Security Seal on the jacket. As the gentleman walked in, he withdrew a small cylindrical object from his inner pocket and walked toward the camera closest to him. He pressed a button built into the base of the object and waived the cylinder within a couple feet of the camera. He then walked over to the other camera in the room and waived it near that one as well. Replacing the object in his suit pocket, he walked around to sit down across from Jonas. The man smiled, and Jonas could think of nothing other than a shark circling its prey.

"Now we can actually talk," said the man in the suit. He opened the file in front of him and began skimming through the contents. As he worked his way through, he began speaking calmly, in a tone that suggested he was reading out of a dry history report. "Jonas Vanhof. Twenty-seven years old. You were caught in the house of a middle-aged bank manager, having recently killed the banker and his wife.

"The evidence gathered by the police shows that you were in the process of cleaning up after yourself. They found customized knives covered in the couple's blood. The wife was found upstairs in the bedroom, naked. There were vicious bite marks on her arms, and her head was found three feet away from her body. The man was found on the first floor, in the living room, naked. While there were no bite marks on this one, the man's head was found behind a chair across the room, approximately eight feet away. And there were signs that you had struggled with both of them pretty violently."

"Forensics also determined that it was you who kicked in the front door. Your boots matched the prints around the house, as well as the large impression left on the door itself. All in all, the evidence left around the house and all over the scene point to you as some sort of sick, sadistic killer." The man looked up at Jonas over the rims of his glasses. "Are you, Jonas Vanhof, a 'sick sadistic serial killer?'"

Jonas thought the man sounded like he was asking something as casual as what flavor of ice cream he wanted. Jonas leaned back and shook his head.

Jonas began counting off facts awkwardly on the fingers of his manacled hands. "Your suit is way too nice for the detectives around here. You disabled the cameras. And you didn't threaten to beat me up. Are you a Fed? A spook?"

The man smiled and responded with a question of his own. "What actually happened in that house, Mr. Vanhof?"

Jonas considered the options. Believing the man may be from the secret government agency his uncle had told him about, he decided to lay it all out. Jonas sat up and said, "You want to know what happened? I'll tell you, but you won't believe me." He recounted the tale.

NORFOLK, VIRGINIA. TWO MONTHS AGO.

It was a dark night. Jonas specifically chose tonight because it was a new moon. The moon was nowhere in the night sky. The night was darker, the shadows were deeper, and things that relied on the moon for part of their power would have just a little less.

Jonas parked his car three blocks away from his target's house and walked casually until he was about three houses away. Because of his earlier recon, Jonas knew that the next couple houses would be quiet and the inhabitants asleep long before his two-o'clock-in-the-morning activity. *Got to love the suburbs*, Jonas thought to himself. *At least everyone goes to bed at a decent hour.*

As Jonas approached the front porch, he looked around one last time to make sure that he was not being watched. Carefully moving as silently as possible, he was worried that the monster he was hunting would hear him coming. Intimately aware of the heightened hearing and sense of smell, Jonas was careful to walk only on the soft grass. To avoid alerting the monster with his scent, he was in freshly laundered and bleached clothing that had been rolled on the yard outside the target's house.

Tonight's target was a rather surly bank manager. This manager had a reputation for being short with customers and outright hostile with his employees. Treating everyone else as if they were simply not worthy of his time, he had callously rejected a customer's loan application and made inappropriate derogatory comments comparing the customer's manhood to his creditworthiness. The desperate customer had lost control, attacking the manager viciously. Before the security guards could pull the irate customer off him, the manager had suffered severe bruising, a broken collarbone, and even some bites on his arms.

That was a month ago. The recovering bank manager had never realized anything was wrong until that first full moon. Fortunately for his wife, the manager had been out of the house the first time he changed. When the new werewolf had changed that first time, his instincts had pulled him to the forest to run and hunt. The following morning, a local farmer had found three of his cattle slaughtered and half-eaten in the field. The manager had woken up, naked, alone, and cover in dried, congealed blood.

Putting two and two together to get an impossible four, the manager had figured out that, against all the odds, he was a werewolf, a mythological creature. He had hidden his new affliction from his family, but he could not hide the reports from the eyes of Jonas. When his sources had traced the wolf to the bank manager, Jonas had traveled to Virginia to kill the wolf before he could kill a human.

Jonas stepped up on the porch, carefully avoiding the loose step his earlier reconnaissance had discovered. Approaching the door, he withdrew a lock-pick set from his inner coat pocket. He reached for the knob to unlock the door and heard a loud, terrified scream from inside the residence.

Jonas had two options: leave now, before the neighborhood woke up, or go help whoever was shrieking. Even as lights in the surrounding houses lit up, the monster hunter drew back his leg and kicked hard at the door, landing a solid blow right beside the lock and breaking the frame. The door swung open, and Jonas moved inside. Hearing the shrieks turn to moans, he raced up the stairs, his long overcoat trailing behind him.

Rounding the corner on the landing, he was met by a large furry mass that crashed into him. The collision was enough to shake them both, and they tumbled over the side of the railing onto the floor below. Vicious snarls and growls sounded from the large wolf-like creature as it tried desperately to sink its teeth into Jonas' face. Jonas could see the gleaming fangs and smell the fetid breath of the creature as its jaws snapped closed mere inches from his nose.

As the creature drew back again to bite, Jonas brought his forearm up into the path of those powerful jaws. The teeth clenched shut on his limb, and he cried out as his arm was crushed. The specially prepared abilities of his overcoat worked with the thick leather of the sleeves to stop the razor-sharp canine teeth from penetrating. In a small corner in the back of his mind, Jonas realized he'd be lucky if his arm was not broken from the bite.

While the creature gnawed on the monster hunter's forearm, Jonas slipped his free hand down and grabbed the hilt of a knife sheathed on his side. With the creature on top, the hunter was just able to draw the knife and thrust upward toward the heart of the wolf. The honed blade sunk in to the hilt, parting the skin and slipping between ribs in its quest for the heart. The creature howled in sudden, overwhelming pain as it was forced to release his forearm and to try to scramble away from Jonas.

Wrapping his legs around the creature, the wiry hunter heaved and flipped over, putting the wolf on its back on the ground. Jonas continued to drive the knife inwards, working the blade back and forth to wreak havoc on the creature. His other arm was now free of the wolf's mouth, and, with that one, he reached behind his back to withdraw the large machete from its sheath.

Raising the machete in a high swing, he abruptly brought it down on the neck of the creature. On the first swing, he made it most of the way through the neck, but stopped against the spine itself. The wolf suddenly went rigid and began reaching for its throat. With paws that were changing into human hands as he watched, the wolf creature tried to stem the flow of its lifeblood from its severed arteries.

The second swing of the machete cleaved through the spinal column and severed the head from the body. As it rolled away, the shape changed and the facial features became human. Jonas reached down and pulled his knife from the now-human torso it was buried in. Standing, he glanced up the stairs and heard small movements.

Covered in the creature's blood, Jonas climbed the stairs. Walking into the bedroom, he saw the wife of the banker in bed. She was nude and lying on the bed with her hands covering her face. The massive bite marks on her shoulder were no longer bleeding, and she appeared to have fainted.

Knowing that it was too late for her, the weary hunter grimly walked to the side of the bed and raised the machete. When he moved her arms away from her face and neck, the woman stirred. Incoherent, she saw a man with a large machete in his hand standing over her bed where her husband had just attacked her. She began sobbing and repeating the words, "No, please, no," as she begged for her life.

Jonas looked down at her and raised the machete to deliver a blow. "I'm sorry," he whispered as he brought the machete down.

"THE POLICE SHOWED UP AS I WAS CLEANING UP TRACE FROM THE house. When they busted in, I tried to go out the back. There were four of them out there, and I guess I put a couple of them in the hospital. Sometimes I forget to pull my punches with mere humans. And for the past two months, I've been dealing with a public defender that is clueless and wants me to take a plea bargain, a jail crew that wants to make me suffer for beating up those cops, and fellow inmates that finally have learned not to pick on me, or else they suffer a beating." Jonas finished his story and looked at the man in front of him.

The man consulted the file he held and looked at Jonas over his glasses. "As strange as it may seem, Mr. Vanhof, I believe your story. That is why I'm here.

"You are originally from the Pacific Northwest, and you believe that you are the last in your family's bloodline. You were trained to hunt monsters since you were little. And you've been on your own since your uncle was killed. You are good at what you do. Unfortunately, you got caught this time."

Jonas smiled wearily. "So which secret government organization are you from? CIA? NSA? Ghostbusters?"

The man chuckled. "Mr. Vanhof, my name is Agent Smith, and I work for the Department of Homeland Security. I have a team that could use your particular... expertise. This is a onetime offer. If you come to work for me, this little problem goes away."

"As you know, Virginia is a death penalty state, and I hear that the prosecutor is going to try to make you dance that chemical dance. Your prosecutor has political aspirations, and he's been waiting for a juicy case like yours to come along. If you choose to work for me, the prosecutor will have to find another case to hang his political hat on. So what do you say? Do you want to take my 'Get out of jail free' card?"

Jonas started laughing at the absurdity of Smith's offer. Tears flowed down his face as the stress and fear of the last couple months fed the near-hysteria. After he had composed himself, he was wiping away the tears when he spoke again. "So let me get this straight. I can either come with you, and get paid to do what I was doing before, or I can rot and wait to die. I think that's a pretty easy choice to make for me. Where do I sign?"

"We'll get you signed up as soon as we get out of here," Agent Smith said as he smiled and shook the proffered hand. As Agent Smith stood and walked to the door he said, "The paperwork is waiting for my signature. You will be out in less than an hour." Agent Smith knocked on the door to let the guard know that he was done. "By the way, it's good to have a member of your family on one of my teams again."

12

HEAVY

Norfolk, Virginia.

I t was closer to two hours later when Jonas and Agent Smith walked out the front of the Norfolk Correctional Facility. It had taken less than an hour to get Jonas released into Agent Smith's custody. The sheriff had complained to the prosecutor, and the prosecutor had called a local judge to get the transfer halted. Before the ink was dry on the injunction, he had received a call from the Virginia Attorney General and from the Governor's office, letting the judge know that enforcing the injunction would start an avalanche of trouble. The judge nullified his own injunction.

With that roadblock out of the way, the prosecutor could not stop the prisoner custody transfer. But when Agent Smith had demanded the personal effects, including the murder weapons, the sheriff had thrown every obstacle he had into the fray. From administrative "delays" to "missing documents," it had taken Agent Smith over an hour to retrieve the personal effects from the sheriff's office. In the end, it had required a threat from Agent Smith to bring in a team from both the Attorney General's office and the Department of Homeland Security to perform a complete audit and civil rights check on the sheriff's department, all the members of the department, and the correctional facility.

When Jonas finally received his clothing and gear, he stepped into a restroom to change. As he emerged fully clothed and equipped, Agent Smith was forced to calm the sheriff again just to avoid a near riot from the law enforcement present. As they stepped outside, the local press moved en masse toward them, shouting a cacophony of questions. Both Agent Smith and Jonas stayed silent as they moved through the crowd. The reporters quickly lost interest on the pair as the sheriff and prosecutor stepped out of the doors and announced a press conference.

Agent Smith and Jonas climbed into the back of the blacked-out Chevy Suburban. Timothy turned around and smiled at the two men, extending his hand to Jonas. "It's good to meet you, Mr. Vanhof. My name is Timothy." He turned toward his boss and said, "Sir, we have a developing situation in D.C. I forwarded a summary to your phone, but it is something we should move on quickly. I do believe you'll be interested."

Agent Smith nodded at Timothy and said, "I'll trust your judgement. I'll read up as we head that direction. Mr. Vanhof, I fear we may be a little delayed before we get you started in your new life."

Timothy nodded and turned around. He put the truck in drive and pulled out. Reaching down, he flipped a series of switches on the dashboard. At the front and back of the truck, red and blue emergency lights strobed. Under the hood, a very special box sent out a signal ahead of the vehicle. As the modified truck neared an intersection, the box changed the lights at the intersection to green as they were about to cross through it, clearing the path for the vehicle. As traffic began to clear out of their way, Timothy sped up. As they reached the top of the entrance ramp on I-64, the roar of the big V-8 filled the air as Timothy reached a cruising speed well above the posted limits.

IN A NEIGHBORHOOD JUST OUTSIDE GEORGETOWN UNIVERSITY STOOD A historic brownstone. Outside that brownstone a line of police cars and a SWAT van blocked the street. Both ends of the block were cordoned off with police barricades and officers, and media crews waited impatiently just outside the barricades.

The blacked out SUV rolled to a stop, the vehicle's lights still flashing, and Agent Smith and Jonas both got out of the truck, leaving Timothy to wait. The pair walked up to the nearest officer, and Agent Smith drew out his credentials.

"Excuse me, officer. Department of Homeland Security. Who is the officer in charge right now?"

The officer glanced at the badge and then at Agent Smith. "What do you guys want with this one? Just some nut job that whacked his parents." When he received no answer, the officer nodded, "Lieutenant Porter is in charge; he's over there by the SWAT van."

Agent Smith thanked him and strode purposefully toward the SWAT van. On the trip from Norfolk, Agent Smith had called up the initial reports and found something very interesting. A direct Incursion alarm had tripped the sensors in D.C., indicating that at least one creature had stepped directly through into the heart of the city. Signature types had indicated that it was some form of a vampire. The alert had been quickly corroborated with a 911 call from the location in question. The massive array of sensors in the area noted shortly after the arrival that the creature or creatures had been terminated. That level of prowess had interested Agent Smith immensely.

Arriving at the SWAT van, Agent Smith again flashed his credentials. "Agents Smith and Vanhof, Department of Homeland Security. What happened, Lieutenant?"

The lieutenant looked long and hard at Smith. "This has nothing to do with Homeland Security. This was a Vet who went nuts and killed his parents. Caught him with those freaky looking knives in his hands, just sitting and sobbing on the couch. I had to call SWAT in to talk him down."

"This guy is a Vet, Spec Ops. According to his jacket, he's a staff sergeant in the Eighty-Second Airborne. It sounds like he was home visiting his family, and he just kinda went nuts. He'll probably claim some sort of PTSD. Sick son-of-a-bitch killed his parents, his little sister, and apparently a couple other guys whose heads we found. He then starts spewing some BS cockamamie crap about monsters and bodies disappearing. I think he got a hold of some bad drugs and just lost it. I went ahead and notified the Army, but like I said, this isn't Homeland Security's business here."

Agent Smith listened intently, thought for a moment, and calmly and politely said, "I'll be the judge of that. Where is the suspect now?"

The lieutenant shook his head. "You Feds are all the same. The guy's still inside, but it's an active crime scene. You guys can talk to him at the precinct."

Agent Smith frowned, and his words turned quiet and cold. "No, lieutenant. As I explained, we'll speak to him here. We will maintain the integrity of your scene, but we will talk to him."

Agent Smith walked toward the house, and Jonas quickly followed. The lieutenant waived to the officer standing in front of the door, "It's OK, Sam. Let them through." The lieutenant muttered under his breath, questioning the human parentage of the agents as they walked out of earshot.

Agent Smith and Jonas walked into the house. Noting the narrow rooms and corridors common to brownstone houses, they walked to the living room, breaking up a cluster of officers and medics, all hovering around an African American man that was handcuffed and sitting on the couch. Even sitting down, the man's bulk was imposing, and the handcuffs seemed tiny and fragile around his wrists.

Flashing his badge again, Smith announced, "I'm Agent Smith, and this is Agent Vanhof. Department of Homeland Security. I need to speak with this suspect. Alone. Please clear the area."

Despite a buzz of murmuring in the room, the officers and medics slowly filed out of the room, with one of the SWAT members remaining behind to stand in the open doorway of the house. As they were leaving, Jonas noticed that one officer had an evidence bag containing two large curved knives. Reaching out, he said, "Excuse me, officer. Can I have those for a moment? Don't worry. Chain of Custody is still intact."

The officer handed Jonas the weapons, and Agent Smith nodded approvingly. Agent Smith turned back to the man on the couch and spoke while he consulted information on his phone.

"As you heard, I'm Agent Smith, and this is Agent Vanhof. Could you tell me what happened?"

"I think I'd like my lawyer now," the large man's voice rumbled.

As Smith was talking to the suspect, Jonas looked around the room. Noticing evidence markers laid out, he knelt by a severed head that was laying on its side. Jonas reached down and slowly lifted the lips apart, baring the teeth. Not surprised, he revealed a set of large, pointed teeth that would look more at home on an animal than on a human. Looking around, he saw a small pool of fluid that looked like it was disappearing as he watched. The thick black ichor seemed to be melting and drifting away like smoke. Nodding, he stood up and walked over to Smith. He leaned in close and whispered a few words in Smith's ear. Smith nodded and Jonas sat down and began to examine the knives.

Smith turned back to the suspect on the couch. "Are you Staff Sergeant Arthur Murphy? Currently assigned to the Eighty-Second Airborne Division?" When the big man nodded, Smith continued. "Despite your troubled past, you excelled in the Army. You are a natural leader, and your CO thinks very highly of you."

"The police seem to think that you went stark-raving mad and that you will take the weasel way out and claim it was some sort of PTSD. They say you came home hopped up on drugs–probably crack. You then butchered your family and those two headless guys. Are they right? Are you just another lunatic Vet with PTSD?"

The man stared at Agent Smith intensely. The anger in the man's voice was palpable, and he appeared to barely keep it under control. Through gritted teeth, the man spat the words out, "No, sir. I am not suffering PTSD. Nor did I kill my family. In fact, I found these two guys attacking my family. I was so mad I guess I killed them. But I never killed my family."

Smith looked at the man as he tried desperately to hold himself together. He knelt down in front of the suspect and gently, quietly said, "I believe you. In fact, I have a different theory. I believe that the two headless men savagely attacked your family. You fought with them, one at a time. It looks like you sent one of them through the wall over there and somehow found those special knives. Once you had those knives in your hand, I would say that you got the first one and then the second one. In the end, I bet you had to decapitate them to stop them. In fact, I would bet that when you decapitated them, the bodies just sort of... dissolved into the goo that is over there. Since then, it's been slowly evaporating. Am I right?"

The man looked at Smith incredulously. "That's almost exactly how it happened. I don't know why I decapitated them... I just did. How did you know?"

Smith was about to answer when the other agent spoke up.

"Agent Smith, I think you should see this." Jonas held up the knives he had removed from the evidence bag.

Smith walked over and looked at each blade carefully. Jonas pointed out faded script that looked like it was a combination of Chinese and another, much more ancient script. He then handed them back to Jonas. "Great eyes," Smith said. "I'm not sure I would have seen that myself."

Smith walked back over to Arthur. "Sergeant Murphy, where did you get the knives?"

Arthur looked up, questions fluttering across his face. "They were given to me personally by a Nepalese tribal leader that we worked with. I filed all the correct import paperwork with the Army. In fact, I have the declarations around here somewhere."

"I believe you," Smith said. "You have no idea how lucky you were to have those blades today. I would bet that these khukuris are probably what helped you kill your parents' killers. Actually, if it was a tribal leader, chances are he knew that you would need to have the pair of blades available."

Smith stood and continued talking. "Staff Sergeant Murphy, I'm going to make this offer only once..."

LIEUTENANT PORTER WAS JUST WALKING UP TO THE HOUSE TO KICK OUT the Feds when they began to leave. Between the two Feds walked the suspect who was not in handcuffs. Porter slammed to a halt and yelled at the men to stop where they were. Drawing his sidearm, Porter yelled for the tactical team. Jonas felt Staff Sergeant Murphy tense up.

Porter barked at Agent Smith, "Stop right there. That man is in the custody of the Metropolitan Police Department. You have no authority to release him or to remove him."

By now, the tactical team and several officers had come running to the lieutenant's aid. Smith, Jonas, and Arthur were quickly surrounded by officers with their sidearms drawn. While none were directly pointed at the Homeland Security Agents, the implied threat of the drawn weapons made the tension palpable.

Agent Smith held up a hand and calmly addressed Lieutenant Porter. "This man is now under the supervision and jurisdiction of the Department of Homeland Security. If you have any doubts about my authority in this matter, you can call Homeland Security with my badge number. Let's all calm down. Make the call, Lieutenant."

Porter reached out and took the agent's credentials. He grabbed his cellphone and called his Captain. Quickly and succinctly summarizing the situation, he asked his superior to contact his Homeland Security liaison. After what seemed like an eternity later for the lieutenant, he received a call on his cell from the Captain.

"Lieutenant Porter. This is Captain Meyers. Homeland Security has control and jurisdiction of that scene. Follow their lead. Agent Smith is the SAC on this one. If Smith tells you the suspect is leaving with him, escort him to his car."

"But, Captain," the lieutenant stammered. "How can they get away with this? This isn't federal. It's a nutcase Vet. This one should be ours. Have we heard from the Army yet?"

The captain cut him off. "Listen, Bill. I hate this as much as you do, but I have the Chief breathing down my neck on this one. The Director of Homeland Security answered the call on this one directly. Just suck it up and deal with it... they're Feds."

Lieutenant Porter hung up from his call and holstered his sidearm. "All right, guys, stand down," he announced to all who were present. "It's official. Homeland Security is the lead on this one; we're just cleanup."

Approaching Smith, Porter continued, "Sorry about that, Agent Smith. This is just so... irregular."

"I understand, Lieutenant Porter," said Agent Smith as he smiled graciously. "I'd be just as upset as you are right now. If you would have your people continue processing the scene, I would appreciate it. Have your forensic people work the house. Also, if you would have your M.E. perform the initial autopsy, my office will be in touch with your department for the findings. Have all reports forwarded to my office at this number." Smith handed Porter a business card.

"I'll be taking charge of Staff Sergeant Murphy here, as well as taking the weapons into my possession. Is there anything else you need from me?"

"No, sir," Porter said as he shook his head. "I'll have the reports forwarded as soon as they get filed."

With Arthur and Jonas trailing, Agent Smith walked toward the Suburban. Jonas climbed into the front passenger seat by Timothy while Smith and Arthur took seats in the back. Porter watched with a mixture of disgust and relief as the truck left the scene. He was glad to be rid of the Feds. He hated it when they interfered; it always caused him more headaches and paperwork.

Signaling for the forensics team to join him, Porter began assigning tasks as he heard the roar of the big V8 engine take the Feds away.

II

MISSION

13

PIECES

51,000 Feet Over Indiana.

Gretchen Massey, the Knightmare Team Liaison, grabbed a silver briefcase from the storage compartment in the back of the Citation X and returned to her seat at the small conference table. Flying just under the speed of sound, the plane was much faster than a larger commercial airliner, and the trip to Pueblo, Colorado, was nearly half-way over.

After the flight attendant had seen to meals and the comfort of the passengers, the team had gathered around the active surface conference table for the mission briefing and planning. John "Spooky" Smith brought up the maps of the area on the electronic surface of the table and pointed out various land features and points of reference. He then posted all the medical examiner's reports and police files alongside the maps.

Spooky looked across to the team leader and said, "All right, boss. What's the plan?"

Burt "Six" Holstein studied the maps and information laid out in front of the team. After paging quickly through the maps, he seemed to find what he was looking for. Looking at Gretchen, Six asked,

"Gretchen, what kind of transportation will we have? Will it be equipped as a command post?"

Gretchen consulted the notes on her secure phone and said, "Yes, sir. I have an armored command transport waiting for our arrival. Full mobile communications and control."

The team leader nodded at the information and looked at the rest of the team. "Ok, team. Here's what I'm thinking. We will stay at this little motel on the outskirts of town. Gretchen, can you arrange that?"

Gretchen nodded and drew out her phone to make the call. Six continued, "We'll set up our staging and command center at a building owned by a non-governmental community organization. We have the exclusive use of the building as we've asked that they close operations from that building while we are in town. The building should have enough rooms and is located across from the only hospital in town. From what I understand, the forensic labs and the M.E.'s office are in that hospital. This will be our 'ops center.'

"When we arrive, we'll meet with the sheriff and the mayor at the ops center. While there, I want you, God, up on the rooftop with your rifle. You are on overwatch until I need you on an entry team."

Jesús "God" Rivera smiled and nodded. Turning to the team priest, he asked, "Doc, any clue what the best way to spot these guys is? Will they show up on night vision? Or thermal?"

Noelle "Doc" Sorenson thought for a moment and consulted the leather-bound book in front of her. "I don't believe night vision will work. Thermal should work, instead. Vampires run colder than normal, and often colder than the surrounding climate. According to our records, the only time that they radiate any measurable heat is just after they have fed. This goes away quickly, and they soon return to their normal temps—usually around forty-five or fifty degrees."

Six smiled at the information and turned to his electronics specialist. "Spooky, when we are set, launch the UAV and use the thermal to search for cold spots as well. Maybe we'll get lucky."

Turning to Doc and Boomer, Six said, "Doc, I want you to go chat with the coroner. See if he's on the level and see what he has to say. Boomer, I want you with her as backup."

Doc nodded, and Rebekah "Boomer" Callahan asked a question,

"Do you want me armed with the twelve gauge? Or with only my sidearm?"

"Take your shotgun," Six responded. "Better safe than sorry. Your badge should clear up any authority issues. That goes for all of you. Everyone carries their primary rifle with them. I would rather get nasty looks than be defenseless against the monsters."

Gretchen indicated that she had something to say, and Six nodded in her direction, "Gretchen?"

Gretchen glanced at her phone and then back up at the team. Addressing the entire team, she said, "Ground transportation is waiting, as is your block of rooms at the motel. I also just received word from headquarters that the FBI has dispatched a Behavioral Analysis Unit team to Trinidad to assist the locals with the case. The BAU knows DHS is en route, and they will be informed that you have jurisdiction. They are going to be focused on profiling the criminals based on human psychoses. You are not hunting humans, and their profiles don't apply. They should touch down just before we do."

The team leader nodded grimly. "It seems it's going to be up to me to meet with the sheriff, mayor, and this FBI team. I'll try to keep them distracted while gathering information from the locals," Six stated.

Gretchen pulled out the aluminum equipment briefcase and set it on the table. The latches responded to her thumbprints, and the airtight case hissed slightly as the top opened. When the case laid flat, the team could see five brand new smartphones. Each smartphone had a case and holster packed in the foam below it, and mounted above each was a team member's call sign.

As she handed them out, Gretchen turned on each device to let it go through its power process. As the little white fruit appeared on the screen, a grayed-out Department of Homeland Security seal replaced it, and she handed the phone to its new owner. She talked as she handed them out.

"These are your new Secure Smart Phones, or SSPs as they are called around the office. Each one is synced to its own user, and each one can only be operated by its owner, or someone on this team. As they fire up, you will see a list of somewhat standard apps, as well as a few new icons. There are several contacts already programmed into the phone, such as myself, Timothy, and Agent Smith, and you have full access to voice, video, text, or email—all secured.

"There is a folder of apps on your phone you really should not mess with until you get back from this mission. The apps are esoteric in nature, and you could do great harm to your teammates unless you know what you are doing. Other than that, have fun exploring. Also, you do not have access to the application store, as the software on the phones is somewhat... non-standard. And, Spooky, don't open it up until you get back to the labs at Section 28. I know you want to, but just trust me. The anti-tampering protections are a bit more vicious than your standard protocols. I wouldn't want you to be eaten. Questions?"

Spooky raised his hand. "Any way I can get this to sync with my wrist computer?"

Gretchen gave a soft laugh. "Actually, Norbert already synced the two devices. He asked me to tell you he was quite impressed by your, how did he put it, 'fun little device.' He said he would have recommendations when you get back. Any other questions?"

The various team members shook their heads, and Gretchen continued, "Ok. We should be about an hour out. Take the time to rest and relax. You won't have much time when you are on the ground." She turned her chair around and stood up, walking to the cockpit to talk to the pilots.

———

JUST UNDER AN HOUR LATER, GRETCHEN RETURNED TO THE PASSENGER compartment and said they would land soon. The team quickly stowed their loose equipment and buckled their safety belts.

In the cockpit, the pilot contacted the tower controller for Pueblo Memorial Airport. "Pueblo Memorial. This is DHS Special Zero Three. Requesting direct clearance."

The traffic controller looked at his displays and saw the special Homeland Security notes attached to the flight plan. Noting the flight time, he wondered what kind of plane they were on. It looked like a small business jet, but it had traveled just under the speed of sound. "DHS Special, Pueblo Tower. Direct clearance to runway Two-Six Left. Winds are west-northwest at five knots. Nearest traffic at ten miles, fifteen thousand feet and climbing."

"Pueblo Tower, DHS Special. Roger Two-Six Left."

The pilot concentrated on landing the plane gently on the assigned runway. Despite the slight crosswinds, the touchdown was textbook perfect. As the plane rolled out towards the end of the runway, ground control contacted the DHS pilot and guided him to his designated parking spot. He also informed ground control he needed fuel "ASAP" and clearance for a rapid departure.

As the plane came to a halt, the team members stood and stretched. Grabbing their gear, they approached the door, and waited for the attendant to drop the stairs.

Six stepped into the bright sunshine and immediately put his sunglasses on. The clear air and beautiful sunshine allowed him to see the mountains rising to the west, past the city of Pueblo. Stepping down onto the tarmac, he was met by a woman in sunglasses and a suit that announced "Fed." She stretched out her hand toward him.

"Agent Holstein? I'm Sonja Hart, the DHS SAC for this region. I've got your ground transportation waiting for you, as requested. Will you need any backup or assistance for your deployment?"

He shook Agent Hart's proffered hand and introduced himself. "Please, call me Burt. Except for transportation, I believe we have everything we need for the deployment. If I need anything, I'll let you know." He released her hand.

Agent Hart evaluated the rest of the unusual team as they filed off the plane. Her eyes widened as Doc stepped off the plane in her gray business suit, with a weird sidearm in a holster on her hip. She looked back at Six and asked, "What's the deployment about? I wasn't given any information other than to bring you the truck. What's going on out here?"

The team leader shook his head. "I'm sorry Agent Hart. You're not cleared for that information. We'll take it from here. Are the keys in the truck?"

Agent Hart nodded, and her voice grew cold. "The keys are in there. I don't like being in the dark about what's going on in my region. It usually means I have to clean up someone else's mess. Do not make me clean up your mess, Agent Holstein." With that statement, she spun on her heal and stormed off toward the waiting vehicles.

Six looked at the truck waiting for his team. *Subtlety is not on the menu*, he thought to himself. The truck was a jet-black Golan Mine Resistant Ambush Protected truck, called an MRAP, manufactured by an Israeli firm. Six was familiar with the truck, with the angled front end, and the steel cage surrounding the bullet resistant glass, having driven one while in Iraq. Unlike the MRAPs from Iraq, this one had emergency lights mounted on top and in the grill and was marked with "Police" and "Rescue" on the front and rear bumpers. The only other markings were the Homeland Security seals plastered across the sides. Sitting over two feet off the road, the truck stood over seven-and-a-half feet tall. Almost eight feet wide, the truck was an enormous nineteen feet long. There was not one detail about this truck that was subtle or understated. He loved it!

He turned to his team and barked, "All right team, let's get our gear. Our transportation awaits."

As the team lugged their bags toward the truck, a fuel service truck pulled up to the waiting Citation jet. Gretchen arranged for the fueling and then climbed back aboard. As the fuel truck departed, the attendant closed that hatch, and the pilot restarted the engines for the flight back to Langley.

Inside the truck, Boomer climbed up in the driver's seat. Six looked at her and raised his eyebrows.

"Trust me, boss. I'm the one you want driving this heap," she said in her most innocent voice as possible. The former racer car driver continued, "For the rest of you, I really recommend that you strap yourselves in. We'll be in Trinidad soon."

AFTER A BRIEF STOP AT A STORAGE FACILITY OUTSIDE NORFOLK TO retrieve the majority of Jonas' gear, Timothy had driven the agents back to Section 28. Once they had arrived, Agent Smith had left them in the care of Timothy, with a planned regrouping in three hours. Smith had a busy couple hours ahead of him. He had needed to prepare the contracts and credentials, remove Staff Sergeant Murphy from the Army, and clean up a few police reports. He would be busy.

Timothy had escorted Jonas and Arthur to the Knightmare apartment block and had taken the time to give them a brief tour of the facility on the way. As they had walked, Timothy had answered all the questions he could, and had explained more about the mission and drive of the team. Leaving out the "Incursion" background, Timothy had studiously given non-answers about that, and other classified information.

After a meal and a brief rest, Timothy finally arrived to escort Jonas and Arthur to the conference room. There Agent Smith greeted them and told them to sit down.

The DHS agent started, "Gentlemen, I'm glad that both of you chose to join our team. As Timothy informed you earlier, it is your job to kill monsters—something each of you has done before. You will be joining as a member of a larger team that is currently deployed. In fact, you will leave tonight to join them on their current deployment. But before we can do that, you need to sign some paperwork."

Jonas watched as Agent Smith put on a pair of white cotton gloves. He then reached over to a closed lockbox at his right side and opened the lid. Smith reached into the lockbox and withdrew two heavy envelopes, one at a time. Made of white leather, each envelope had a wax seal over the flap and a name embossed above the seal.

Jonas looked at the envelope in front of him and saw a weird script written on and around the edges. Although he could not read what the script said, he recognized the symbols of the ancient Enochian tongue. Agent Smith continued, "Before you open the pouches in front of you, I want you to be very clear about a couple things that will happen when you do so. You might experience a wave of energy or a slight tingling sensation on your fingertips and in your hair. Some have also reported other strange sensory phenomena. I assure you: that is normal."

"This is your last and final chance to step down from this team. If you choose to decline, you will go back to where you were when I recruited you. Granted, that would be police custody for both of you, but you certainly wouldn't be in nearly as much danger as I'm going to throw at you. Do either of you want to exercise that option now?" Smith paused to see if either would take the deal.

When it was clear that neither man wanted to leave, Smith continued, "If you would now open your envelopes, taking care not to touch any of the materials from your other teammate. Inside, you will find a contract and a pen. Please pull out both of the items and begin reading the contract. This contract shows that you are freely offering to join the team and will be bound by the terms of this contract. This contract is also your formal work contract for the Department of Homeland Security, assigned to Section 28. A large part of this contract explains that this agreement will bar you from mentioning Section 28, what you do, or what you are hunting, except under certain, very explicit circumstances. Even the existence of Section 28 is classified as Top Secret - Black and is on a need-to-know basis."

"On the back page, there is a spot to sign your name and then put the date. When you pick up the pen and begin to write, you may feel a slight pinch in one of your fingers. This is by design. At that time, your blood will be taken, and mixed with the ink when you sign the contract. Each of your contract agreements is exactly the same. At this time, please read through the agreement carefully and sign where indicated."

It took over an hour for both men to carefully read through the lengthy documents. Once Jonas and Arthur signed the contracts, Smith directed them to carefully place them into the envelopes, and then he collected and stored the files. Reaching for the two credential holders on his left, he smiled and said, "Welcome to the Department of Homeland Security, Section 28. Here are your credentials."

He handed the first folio to Jonas. "Special Agent Jonas Vanhof. Your new call sign is 'Ghost' while on missions. Your role on the team is two-fold. First, you are the second in command of the team. You will support your team leader, Burt Holstein, in that role, assisting with planning, as well as media relations and liaison with local law enforcement. Your secondary role will draw on your unique background. You are tasked with esoteric R&D in the field. You have the resources to know what it takes to kill most of the nasties you come across, and you have the experience to rig up any supplies or materials to be effective."

He handed the second folio to Arthur. "Special Agent Arthur Murphy. You are the heavy weapons specialist for the team. Primarily fire support, you will augment the standard firepower with something bigger. Your mission call sign is 'Heavy.'"

Agent Smith then said to both team members, "I would love to give you much more time to learn and work, but I need to fly you out tonight. So, I will have Timothy take you to the Section 28 Warehouse. Draw whatever gear you need. Gretchen, your Team Liaison, should be back in about an hour. I want you ready for your trip in two hours. You can sleep on the flight."

As the new agents left the conference room, Agent Smith compiled all the records and prepared the pertinent information to be sent to their new team leader, Six. He had now officially closed the recruiting for Team Knightmare.

Jonas and Arthur followed Timothy to the Warehouse. Jonas spent most of his time while in the Warehouse, talking with Norbert. Afterwards, he drew ammo for his revolver from the armorer and a Kevlar vest from the Equipment section. Arthur, however, spent a great deal of time talking with Russell. Reminiscing about their time in the service, Arthur eventually drew a sidearm and his favorite weapon of all time: the M249 Squad Automatic Weapon. The SAW was a belt-fed machine gun that used the same rifle cartridges as the M4 carbines that the rest of the team carried, and could even use M4 magazines in a pinch. Holding one in his hands again, Arthur couldn't wait to get to his new team. He then walked over to the Equipment section to draw a heavy flak vest and the rest of his kit.

As Jonas and Arthur were stowing their gear into their bags, Gretchen walked into the Warehouse and introduced herself. Looking a little frayed around the edges from the last seven hours of traveling, she held a travel mug of coffee in her left hand. As they talked, she led the two new agents toward the airfield where the Citation was again being fueled and prepped. The flight attendant greeted that agents on the ground and let them know they were still waiting for the replacement flight crew.

Within a few minutes, the fresh flight crew emerged from the complex and walked toward the plane. After a quick, but thorough, pre-flight inspection, they told the attendant and the team they could board the plane. Within moments, the plane was making its second flight that day to Pueblo, Colorado.

14

TRINIDAD

Trinidad, Colorado.

As the blacked-out MRAP screeched to a halt in the parking lot of a building owned by a community organization, the passengers inside all had different reactions. The monster Cummins turbo-diesel rumbled and died away. Boomer turned around from the driver's seat and smiled. "Everyone still alive?" she asked.

A general chorus of moans and groans greeted her query. Six managed to find his voice and asked, "Where on earth did you learn to drive like that? I thought we were going to die... several times!"

The driver smiled and blushed at the same time. "I used to race cars and boats growing up. That's why I'm the driver. Besides, we made it in record time."

God groaned from the back, "Yes, but that was normally a ninety-minute drive. I know. I grew up around here. I'm not sure I could have made it in an hour in my car, let alone an armored truck. I don't even want to know how fast you were going."

Boomer laughed. "That's good because I couldn't tell you. I buried the speedometer when we left Pueblo. The important thing is that we made it." As she finished, a sheriff's car came roaring up, lights and siren blazing. The siren abruptly shut off, and a man in a sport coat and Stetson hat stepped out of the passenger side.

The explosives expert looked sheepish and said, "Heads up, boss. Looks like the locals know we're here."

The team leader sighed and shakily climbed down out of the rear hatch. Pausing to catch his breath and calm his nerves, he straightened and walked toward the lawman. Drawing his badge from his pocket, Six held it up so the sheriff could see it. "Special Agent Burt Holstein, Department of Homeland Security. Are you Sheriff Klooster?"

The sheriff nodded and looked the Fed up and down. He reached out his own hand. "Yes, Agent Holstein. Sheriff John Klooster. I didn't expect you guys for another hour. They told me your plane only landed an hour ago."

The man laughed weakly. "If you get any reports of low-flying aircraft shaped like a truck, or possibly UFOs, you might want to talk to our driver." Boomer smiled and waved as she climbed out of the truck.

Sheriff Klooster shook his head. "Well, that's a first for Feds, actually admitting to something. So, what brings Homeland Security to our humble little town?"

Six looked at the sheriff and said, "Can we find someplace to talk privately? And you may want to get the mayor involved."

Thirty minutes later, the mayor, the sheriff and undersheriff, and the Trinidad police chief and assistant chief were assembled in a conference room in the team's ops building. While the rest of the team was checking the gear and preparing to hunt the creatures, their team leader was holding the initial briefing.

As the assistant police chief walked in, Six began his prepared speech. "Good afternoon, ladies and gentlemen. For those of you I have not met, I am Special Agent Burt Holstein from the Department of Homeland Security. I would introduce the rest of my team, but they are preparing for our deployment. Everything I tell you in this meeting is Confidential and Need-to-Know. You do not have the authority to determine who needs to know."

Ignoring the questioning looks, Six continued, "We are the advanced team for a unit that specializes in a particular kind of terrorism campaign. We have very specific, credible intelligence that the five murders you experienced over the last month and a half are tied to a very specific type of foreign operative. I know that the FBI is sending a Behavioral Analysis Unit to help profile what you, and they, believe is a serial killer. They will work the situation from that angle while we work it from our own direction. At this time, that is all that I can tell you; however, I will expect full cooperation while we are here. I expect to wrap up this in a couple days at the most. Does anyone have questions?"

The police chief slightly raised his hand. "I believe your victim intel is wrong. We had another body show up this morning, same 'M.O.,' same weird animal marks. I believe the coroner's got the body now, doesn't he John?"

The sheriff nodded slowly and looked at Six. "Bill, our M.E., should be opening the victim up now."

Six nodded his thanks to the sheriff and looked around the room. "All right, does anyone else have any questions?"

When he realized that no one was going to ask another question, he dismissed the impromptu meeting and walked out to the MRAP. As the rest of the town's officials filed out, he asked the sheriff to wait for a moment.

"Sheriff? Any chance I can get an escort out to the latest crime scene? I'd like my team to look at it. I will have a few of them head over to the hospital to talk to your coroner, as well."

The sheriff nodded and radioed for a deputy to come to the building. "I've got one of our rookies on the way over here to escort you guys," he explained to Six. "Bill, our coroner, is over in the hospital. The morgue is in the basement."

The sheriff's eyes narrowed and became serious. "Are you going to level with us, or will you just piss all over this town and wait for the next victim to be snatched and killed?"

Six paused for a moment and looked at the sheriff, carefully considering what he could say. "Sheriff, I cannot divulge any classified information about the threat; however, my team is here to handle it. I do honestly expect to wrap up this in just a couple days." Six reassured the sheriff.

The sheriff looked at the crew in and around the truck. He then looked back at the DHS agent and asked, "Just what kind of special team are you running? I don't believe I've ever seen a stranger advanced team."

The leader of this rather odd crew followed his gaze. "Officially? We are here to investigate and verify the threat and resolve the matter to keep the community safe. Unofficially? Our team is tasked with neutralizing a very particular terrorist subset. And as per our charter, we expect to file this case under 'Case Closed. Suspect Deceased.'"

A patrol car pulled up in the parking lot, and a young deputy got out. The rookie walked over to the sheriff and said, "Sheriff? Dispatch said you wanted me for escort duty?"

The sheriff nodded and replied, "Deputy Folsom, I want you to escort this Homeland Security team to the last crime scene. I'm sure they'll take their truck. Guide them over and make sure that our folks help them out." The sheriff turned to Six and continued, "Agent Holstein, this is Deputy Folsom. He'll be your guide today."

Six nodded and shook the young deputy's hand. Slightly taller than the DHS agent, the deputy was very young and had that clean cut, all-American, blond-hair-and-blue-eyed look that was made for a recruiting poster. He looked the deputy up and down before he spoke. "Good to meet you, Deputy. I need to talk to my team briefly, and then we can get going. If you want to get your car ready?"

The deputy was smart enough to take the hint and walked over to his car. Six spun on his heel and walked toward the truck. Upon reaching the truck, Six gathered everyone around into a small group to discuss his new information. The rest of the team had already checked their equipment, put on their armor, and donned the throat microphones and secure radios.

Six began his briefing. "All right. New intel. Yet another victim last night. The feedings are getting closer together, so we need to set up shop and take care of this thing quick. God, I want you on the roof of the hospital, as we discussed in the briefing. It's the tallest building in this area, and you'll be able to see most of town, and provide over-watch for this location. This building is our new command post."

The team leader turned to address everyone else as he continued, "Spooky, I want you to launch the drone. Look for cold spots. Help God with overwatch duties. Doc, Boomer, go talk to the coroner. His name is Bill. Doc, it's your specialty. Find out what we're hunting."

"Spooky, once you launch the drone, you and I will follow the deputy in this war wagon to the latest crime scene."

Spooky grinned and started laughing. "Ooh. I like that. This big bad MRAP is now officially 'The War Wagon.'" The others chuckled along as they could hear the capital letters that Spooky used.

"Everyone clear on their job?" Six saw nods all around. "Ok. We all have radio communications. If anything pops up, call it out. Don't worry about using 'military' language or 'tactical' signals. Use plain English. These are scrambled and secure enough to use."

God grabbed his rifle bag, Boomer slung her shotgun over her shoulder, and the two accompanied Doc as they walked across the parking lot toward the hospital's main entrance.

As they walked away, Spooky climbed back into the newly chris-tened War Wagon and emerged with a large remote controlled drone. The young analyst started the small engine and threw it in the air, and the drone took off, climbing into the sky. Reaching down, Spooky grabbed a controller and piloted it in a perimeter over the town. The electronics expert climbed back into the truck, sitting in front of two screens set up where he could monitor the drone's flight. The team leader climbed into the driver's seat, started the engine, and waived the waiting deputy onward. As the deputy pulled out, Six pulled out behind him, the War Wagon dwarfing the police cruiser like a hunter on horseback following a hound.

The vehicles rolled away while the three remaining agents all walked toward the hospital. Walking through the main entrance, they made quite an imposing sight: two figures wearing SWAT armor and a woman wearing a cassock and a clerical collar. The older security guard at the main desk stared in shock for a couple seconds, then rose to his feet as he stammered, "Can I help you?"

Doc opened her credentials and showed them to the guard.

"Homeland Security. Can you please point us in the direction of the morgue?"

The guard shakily pointed in the proper direction and then weakly raised a hand in protest when the two women went in that direction. The larger gentleman in armor and toting a rifle case looked around, seemed to find what he was looking for, and headed for the stairs. The guard reached down and grabbed the phone. He knew the sheriff's cell phone number, and he was sure he should probably check on the strange trio.

After a couple of rings, the sheriff answered his phone. "What is it, Uncle Ron? I'm kind of in the middle of something here."

The security guard's reply was bemused. "I think part of whatever you stepped in just walked in my doors, heading for the morgue. What's going on, John? Have we been invaded?"

"I'm sorry, Ron," the sheriff began. He sounded slightly abashed. "I forgot to call you and warn you. We're stuck with Homeland Security for a couple days while they figure out that our murders aren't terrorist related. Just let them go about their business."

"All right," the older man conceded. "Heck, I only have a few minutes 'till I go home, anyway. I'll let the kid deal with them tonight."

The two women walked down the hall to the bank of elevators. Seeing the signage that declared the morgue was in the basement, they boarded the elevator and descended. When the doors opened, they followed the hall until they were in a cold, sterile entryway.

With cold remains storage, two autopsy bays, and a viewing area, the morgue occupied almost the entire basement. Walking through the first set of doors, the two women found an office door that proclaimed, "William Stewart, M.D., Chief Medical Examiner." Doc knocked on the door and heard a muffled "Come!" from inside.

The priest entered first, while Boomer followed, closing the door behind her. Before them was a short, overweight man who was balding on top and smelled like cigarette smoke. An unlit cigarette was perched between his lips as he bent over paperwork behind his clean, orderly desk.

"Doctor Stewart?" Doc spoke up first.

"Yes? What do you want? You can tell the sheriff that he'll get the paperwork as soon as I get it done," the annoyed man snarled without looking up from his handwritten notes and partially filled forms.

Doc looked at her partner and frowned. "Doctor Stewart, I'm Doctor Noelle Sorenson from the Department of Homeland Security. This is my partner, Special Agent Rebekah Callahan. We have some questions we would like you to answer."

Stiffening, the rude retort on Doctor Stewart's lips died out when he looked up at the two agents darkening his doorway. Seeing one in a collar and cassock, and the other carrying a shotgun and dressed in a flak jacket, made him lose track of what he was going to say. The pause became uncomfortable, and the coroner recovered his voice. "I'm sorry about that. What can I do for you ladies today?"

"We're here investigating the recent series of deaths," the priest said. "I understand you had one last night as well? Have you already performed the autopsy?"

Doctor Stewart switched to an ingratiating smile. "Yes, I've done the post-mortem. I believe the sheriff has all the files, except for the one I'm literally finishing right now."

Doc nodded. "I've read the reports. I would still like to see the remains myself. I'm not questioning your work, Doctor, but I am a medical doctor and would like to see the bodies and evidence first-hand." Doc's voice seemed to chill the air. "Do you have a problem with me looking at the remains?"

Dr. Stewart visibly blanched. "No. Of course I don't have any problem with that. However, all but the last two have been buried or cremated, according to family wishes. We'll have to get a court order to disinter the bodies..."

"That's fine," Doc said as she nodded. "If we need to see the other bodies, I'll get the order. In the meantime, let's pull out the other two." She and Boomer turned to leave the office. The doctor quickly followed them.

The three people walked into the cold storage room. They prepared two gurneys, and then Doc and Dr. Stewart moved the two bodies on to the gurneys, one by one. As they wheeled the bodies into the autopsy room, Boomer shivered in the cool temperatures.

Watching from the other side of the room, the explosives expert winced as each body was laid bare on an autopsy table.

The priest grabbed a mask and face shield and bent over the first body. This was the newest victim. A male, in his early twenties. He looked empty. Glancing at the incision on the chest, she turned to the doctor. "So, you've completed post-mortem. What was the cause of death?"

The doctor looked at her and said, "Organ failure, due to exsanguination. I have no real cause for the blood loss. The wounds on the arms, thighs, and throat all are from predators indigenous to the area —probably wolf or mountain lion. All the wounds are post-mortem."

Doc looked even closer at the wounds. She pulled out a small spiral-bound notepad and began recording her findings. Seeing the doctor trying to interfere with her partner, Boomer walked over to the doctor and asked him some basic questions.

She noticed that the doctor was glancing back and forth between the clock and Doc. She saw beads of sweat form on the man's forehead, despite the chilly room temperature. She wondered what he was hiding.

Boomer sought his attention. "So, Doctor... Stewart, was it? Did all the bodies have these kinds of markings?"

Dr. Stewart turned to face Boomer, who was encroaching on his personal space. Putting on his best clinical voice, he said, "Of course. All the markings were the same. Wherever they are hiding the bodies, there are some pretty fierce predators. Some have come in chewed up worse than this kid."

The demolitions expert looked straight at the M.E. "What's got you so nervous, doc? Anything else we should know?"

Boomer saw a momentary flash of panic in the man's eyes. "No, Agent Callahan. Why would I have to hide anything? Why am I nervous? On top of some crazy killer running around town, I have two Homeland Security agents on my doorstop, questioning my work. I'm about done for the day, and I would like to finish up."

Doc suddenly looked up from the second corpse. "That's ok, doctor. I'm done here. I thank you for your time, and I look forward to helping you out on this case." The priest peeled off her gown, mask, and gloves and strode toward the door. "Come on, Rebekah. Let's go tell the boss what we saw."

As they walked out, the doctor stood there glaring at the backs of the ladies' heads. He wondered who was going to help him put away these bodies. Then he wondered what he would tell Zachariah.

15

CONTACT

Trinidad, Colorado.

The deputy's cruiser and the large black truck pulled up to the curb in downtown Trinidad. Police cars lined both sides of the street, and a forensics van sat at the end of an alley that was blocked off with crime scene tape. Six nodded to Spooky and jumped out, following the deputy toward the alley. The DHS agent pulled his credentials from his inner pocket and showed them to the officers near the edge of the tape.

The team leader spoke up. "Special Agent Burt Holstein, Department of Homeland Security. Who's in charge here?"

A man and a woman, both wearing suits, came to the edge of the crime scene tape. The man was tall and thin, dressed in a wrinkled suit, with a stained tie and mussed hair. The bags under his eyes and the stubble on his face told the agent that it had been some time since he had seen a shower or a bed. His partner was about six inches shorter than the man, despite her two-inch heels. As a contrast, her suit looked pressed and clean, and she looked more composed. "Detectives Young and Toursier," she said as she introduced herself and her partner. "What is Homeland Security doing down here?" she quickly inquired.

Six ducked under the crime scene tape and extended his hand to shake hers. "Detective Young, we're here to make sure that this isn't some case of a deeper threat against the nation. What can you tell me about this scene?"

Eyeing the large black armored truck and eschewing the proffered hand, Young stepped in front of him and looked him over. "Since when is DHS interested in serial killers? We've got the FBI's BAU on the way to help us. Frankly, it looks like you will screw things up."

Six smiled and said, "Hey look, we're all on the same team. I promise: we're not going to interfere with your investigation. Our job is to help solve the problem." The agent stepped around the detective and continued toward the alley.

Young's frosty tone drove the warmth from the area. She began rattling off facts from her notes. "Same routine as last time. Pick an alley without cameras, knock out the street lamps, and then drop off the body. In. Out. Done. Clean and simple."

Six looked up at the detective and asked, "So they are not killed here? Hmm. Any clues about who might be going a little nuts in your town?"

The detective looked at the brusque agent with a mixture of hostility and disgust. "I'm sorry we're not omniscient. This is my sixth crime scene in as many weeks. Of course we don't have any idea who is doing this. Do you and your mighty DHS?"

Six looked a bit chastened. He softened his tone as he replied, "We have a couple good guesses, but nothing I can point you to. But that's what we're here for." He turned as he heard another large vehicle pull up behind him.

Climbing out of a black Suburban were three men and a woman. With nearly identical dark gray "power" suits, sunglasses, and attitudes, the FBI had arrived. The leader of the team walked up to Six and held up his badge. "Special Agent Grant Taylor, FBI. Who are you and why is Homeland Security here?"

Six smiled and pulled out his own badge. He could see the hostility on the agent's face and tried to calm the situation. "Special Agent Burt Holstein. We're here because we believe this is one of our cases. Although you and your team are working the serial killer angle, we'll be working another. And before you ask—it's classified above your pay grade."

Agent Taylor angrily shook his head and stalked past the agent and toward the detectives. Six approached the War Wagon; he glanced back and saw the BAU team congregating around the lead detectives. Keying his secure radio, he subvocalized, "God, this is Six. Any signs of our targets?" The radio attached around his throat picked up the minute vibrations and sent them out over the radio.

A few seconds later, there was a reply. "Six, God. Negative on targets."

The team leader climbed up into the truck and glanced back at the young man who was mesmerized by the screens in front of him. "Any signs of our targets, Spooky?" Six's voice was hopeful.

Without looking up, the young man shook his head as his gaze passed from screen to screen.

The older gentleman sighed and keyed his radio again. "Knight-mare, this is Six. Let's regroup at ops center in ten minutes. I'll run and get us some food on the way back. I want to figure out our next move." Six received a chorus of affirmatives.

The team leader climbed into the driver's seat and glanced back at his electronics specialist. "Spooky, contact the mayor, and the sheriff. Have them meet us at the ops center in an hour. And have them contact the press. We'll have a press conference in two hours." Spooky gave him a thumbs up as his other hand reached for his phone.

ELEVEN MINUTES LATER, SIX PULLED THE WAR WAGON INTO A PARKING spot in front of the building they were using as an operations center. As he climbed out, he saw the same three agents who had been at the hospital walking across the parking lot, the two women in a very animated conversation. His hands full with the bags of food, he told Spooky to grab the city map and walked inside the community center and into the conference room he had appropriated.

Laying out the fast food, Six accepted the map from Spooky and tacked it up on the large corkboard. He then grabbed a sandwich and coffee and started to eat. As the rest of the team filed in, they each took their food and drinks and began to eat.

"All right. Let's get this party started," Six said as soon as he finished swallowing his last mouthful. "Quick review. I visited the crime scene and talked to the lead detectives. Basically, it's the same M.O. every time. Killed somewhere else and dumped in an alley with broken lights and no cameras. These newbies are being smarter than the average killer. Doc?"

Doc nodded and finished chewing the bite she had just taken. She cleared her throat and began, "The coroner was... off. There were two bodies that hadn't been buried or cremated yet, and they were both the same. Feeding marks on the thighs, wrists, and necks. It looks like a garden variety vampire feeding."

The DHS team leader looked at the priest and asked, "What are some of the characteristics of this 'garden variety' vampire? Is there more than one kind?"

The team's priest nodded and took a breath. "In a short—answer: yes. But if you want to know what you are fighting, you need to understand a little more background. First off, forget almost every-thing you have ever seen from movies, TV, or books. Very few points are correct and most of the big 'facts' are wrong."

"The traditional vampire, what I referred to as the 'garden variety vampire,' is not a suave, debonair creature of the night who seduces by looks. They do not have the gothic sense of dress. And they abso-lutely do not sparkle. Unless you roast them with a flamethrower, then their ashes glow a little." The chuckles around the table rose to nervous laughter.

Doc continued, "When a vampire is created or appears from an incursion event, they are monstrous in shape and form. Very animal-istic with sharp teeth, not just the canines, filling their mouths. They can quickly grow long, razor sharp fingernails and use their enor-mous strength and speed to hunt, capture, and feed on their prey."

"When they feed, they do not poke two little holes in the neck. Instead, they rip open places where the major arteries are closest to the skin. They will rip open the throat, gnaw on the wrists, and shred the inner thighs. They need the oxygen-rich living blood to circulate in their bodies. Their own blood is cold, black, and sluggish. They can survive off animals, but most prefer the taste of human." The slightly queasy expressions around the table offset Doc's calm, cool delivery. Boomer, in particular, was really regretting her choice of hamburger.

"So how do we stop or kill them? Garlic? A cross? What?" Six questioned.

The priest shook her head. "Again, ignore Hollywood. Garlic does absolutely nothing against a traditional vampire... except give it bad breath. A cross that is wielded by someone who has faith in that cross will drive a vampire away or make them cower on the ground. And that applies to any religious symbol. As long as the symbol represents the faith of the bearer and the bearer believes in the faith, it will be effective. I've read reports of the Star of David being wielded by Jews and even pentacles wielded by Wiccans."

"The most effective way to kill a vampire is to stop blood flow to its head. This stops the regeneration from happening, and the creature will die. Either separate the head from the shoulders or do enough damage to the heart that it can no longer function—although this takes far longer for the vamp to stop attacking you."

Boomer looked up and asked, "What about stakes? What does a wooden stake do?"

Doc shrugged. "The stake has a very weird effect. As best as we can determine, the most effective use of the stake is to use it as a 'grounding rod.' A wooden stake to the body, other than the heart or head, has no effect. A stake to the brainpan will interrupt the function of the brain and end the vampire's life—as long as the stake stays in there long enough to effect true brain death. If you stake a vamp through the heart, it seems to basically interrupt the function of the heart, as long as the stake is there. However, if you can stake the vampire through the heart and into the ground, it completely paralyzes them."

Spooky spoke up, "Can they be cured?"

"Great question!" Doc responded. "A vampire that was recently turned can be cured by killing its sire, the creature that made it. Although it's never a guaranteed cure, we have reports of two victims from the same sire, one being cured upon the death of the sire, and the other staying inflicted with the virus. The death of the sire must occur sometime within the couple days after it was turned, and the timing is different for every turned creature. I've never seen any reports for a successful cure after three sunrises."

God looked thoughtful. He thought about the vampire movies he'd seen and asked, "What about sunlight or ultraviolet light? Does that hurt them?"

The priest answered him, "This is one that Hollywood gets partially right, Little G. The ultraviolet rays in natural sunlight and artificial UV rays will burn and blister a vampire. Their skin is about a hundred times more sensitive than ours is, and they have a built-in psychological condition. The net effect is that if they could build up the willpower to completely cover themselves, and if they wore some really strong sunblock, they might be able to walk around during the day, but if sunlight hits their skin, they receive a third-degree burn within a few seconds."

"Silver is also really effective at slowing down the regeneration rates of vampires, and it physically causes a severe allergic reaction when it touches a vampire's open wound. This causes them to feel a severe burning sensation. It's not quite as strong as the lycanthrope's reaction to silver, but it hurts them."

Doc opened the small, leather-bound book in front of her and flipped through a couple of pages, taking care with the parchment. She read a few of the notes from the book aloud: "This type of vampire gains power as it grows older and as it feeds. New vampires are fairly easy to kill, with the right equipment; however, some the older masters were notoriously difficult to dispatch. Most masters will have a place where they stay during the day, a 'nest,' if you will. Typically, they have their newbies guard the nest, occasionally having familiars or revenants standing guard."

Sensing that questions were coming, the vampire expert continued, "Familiars are humans who have willingly offered their service to the vampire. While they may occasionally be bled for food, typically, they are simply controlled through will, fear, or mind control. It is difficult to tell who a familiar is as they rarely wear any outer sign."

"Revenants are basically a cross between a zombie and a familiar.

They are a ravenous beast that feeds on living flesh. They retain some of their intelligence when they are turned but are completely loyal to their master."

Doc looked around. "That pretty much sums up what we know about typical vampires. Headquarters believes we are facing a couple recently turned traditional vamps here. There are technically two other types, called the 'vampyre' and the 'dhampir.' The vampyre is a creature that is typically classed as a 'psychic vampire.' They feed on the emotional energy of the humans around them, thriving on intense emotions such as fear, hatred, and even love. They are very intense and have different weaknesses. In fact, this is probably where the legends of the vampire's power of seduction come from. Current records are fairly sparse as this type is very rare."

"The other type, called the 'dhampir,' is the offspring of a vampire and a human. While they do not inherit many of the more animalistic traits of their sire, they also are not affected by many of the same weapons. Dhampir are mortal and are not necessarily evil. In fact, there are records of some becoming great monster hunters."

The team sat in stunned silence at the wealth of information that Doc had provided. They looked around at each other, many of them again wondering why they had joined the team. Doc returned to her seat, and Six recovered from his momentary lapse.

Six looked around the table at his team. He cleared his throat and gave orders. "Now that we have intel on these critters, let's hunt them down and kill them. I will be meeting with the mayor, the city council, and the sheriff tonight, and I'm sure the FBI will be there. Because the activity is speeding up, we will be instituting a town-wide curfew. Hopefully, we'll be the only humans hunting tonight."

"As before, I want God up on the hospital roof on overwatch. Spooky, get the UAV up in the air. Doc and Boomer, I want you ready to respond here in the truck. I'm going to go meet with the mayor and then we'll have the press conference. After that, I'll be back out to the truck to be able to go hunting." As the team stood and headed for the War Wagon, the team leader went to meet with the mayor and sheriff.

THE TEAM COMMANDER WRAPPED UP THE PRESS CONFERENCE AND announcement of the impending curfew. Ignoring all the reporters' questions, he grabbed his notes and headed out to the MRAP. As he reached the truck, Boomer was coming out of the rear hatch.

"Hey, boss man. Spooky just got a couple of weird cold blobs moving down an alley about a block from here. I was coming to get you."

Six nodded, reached for his rifle, and activated his radio. "God, this is Six. Spooky picked up movement. We're going to go get this critter. You stay here and cover the VIPs in the city center. Doc, Boomer, you're with me. Spooky, you cover from above."

Spooky waved from inside the truck as Doc climbed out. Draped over her normally demure suit jacket, the Catholic Priest wore a pure white stole with many intricate designs woven throughout. Around her neck hung a cross on a long chain, and Doc carried a very large cross that was ornately inlaid with an intricate silver design and mounted on a sharpened piece of wood.

Six activated his radio as he closed and secured the truck doors. "Spooky. Direction and range to target. What do you have?"

Spooky came back quickly. "Northeast of this location. There is an access drive behind this building. It leads to a neighborhood. About two hundred and fifty yards. Satellite and directional sent to your phone."

Six responded. "Roger. Northwest, about two hundred and fifty yards. Access drive behind city center. God, watch the VIPs and Spooky."

The sniper replied with a simple, "Copy."

Six grabbed his rifle with both hands and then turned toward the two women. "Boomer. Doc. Let's go get a nightcrawler."

He then turned, and they walked at a relatively fast pace down the access road toward the area where Spooky had seen the suspicious cold spots.

Rounding a slight bend, they came to a road. Across the street was a row of houses, with a church across and to the right. Six looked at Doc.

She shook her head. "No way. They can't go on consecrated ground."

Six nodded and moved across the road, carefully walking down the cross street.

From three stories up, God tracked the team as they walked. He shifted and moved his gaze back to the command center. Picking up binoculars, he scanned the area around the buildings and the truck. As he swept past the unlit sides, a dark shadow caught his attention. Moving slowly, the shadow appeared to study the side of the truck and the front of the building. The sniper saw another dark shadow slink out of the brush and move toward the back of the building.

Clicking his binoculars into thermal mode, he saw that the moving shadows were colder than the surrounding areas. Subvocalizing into his radio, he called out, "Six, this is God."

"Go for Six."

"Six, I have three cold shadows back here at the ops center. One is going around the back, make that two going around the back. One is heading toward the War Wagon. Spooky, heads up. One is coming your way."

Six looked at the other two team members. "Copy, God. We're on our way. Once the target is verified, you are cleared to engage. Repeat. Weapons free."

Even as the sniper acknowledged his leader's orders, he was putting the binoculars down and shouldering the rifle. Calculating for wind and drop, and flipping the scope to a thermal setting, he looked for a target. He barely caught sight of one as it broke around the building. God soon heard the screams from inside the building.

Six and Boomer sprinted toward the building, hoping they were not too late. Doc was a touch slower; her modest flats were definitely not combat-ready.

Six waved to Boomer as they approached the building. The screams inside were dying out as they reached the back door. Seeing the door already ajar, Six shouldered through the door, moving into the room and raising his rifle to his shoulder in a practiced move.

Outside, Spooky heard a terrible screech and howl as something slammed against the rear hatch to the War Wagon. The electronics wizard was quivering as the truck physically shook under the repeated blows of a creature trying to get to him. Raising the gun in one shaky hand, the young agent leaned over and waited for his opportunity.

Earlier, Spooky had carefully pulled the special ammunition that Norbert had given him from its padded case and cautiously loaded two of the bullets into the magazine for his Beretta. As the howling intensified, he could see that the thick armored door was moving against its frame. Spooky reached out and timed his actions with the pulls from whatever was trying to get to him.

As the creature gave a fantastic heave, the analyst popped the latch on the door. The creature flew back, stunned, and landed on its back in the parking lot. Spooky saw the terrible visage of a small girl turned feral animal. The rows of sharp teeth gleamed as she snarled and rose. The young agent pointed the gun and pulled the trigger twice.

The once-young girl howled in pain as a blinding flash lit the area. There was a thunderclap, and Spooky saw the monster's arm fly away from her body. Wrecked and in severe pain, the creature howled and bolted into the night. The electronics specialist slammed and locked the truck's back door. He then began to shake.

Dimly registering the gunshots from outside the building, the DHS leader paused at the carnage staining the walls and floor around him. Blood spatters stained the walls of the room and body parts were scattered around the space. That moment of shock wore off as he finally glimpsed a feral creature with a half-gnawed arm in its mouth. The creature paused a moment too long to stare at the agent's sudden entrance. As it turned to run out the front of the room, Six pulled the trigger on his rifle.

Calmly walking rounds up the creatures back, Six shot as fast as he could, while still maintaining control. As the fourth round hit the creature at the top of the spine, Boomer burst through the door and raised her shotgun.

The demolition expert's Mossberg roared, and the vampire fell to the ground with a large hole where its spine and heart once were. Cycling the action, her shotgun roared again, this time taking off the top half of the creature's deformed head.

As Six began shooting the vampire inside the building, God watched another creature burst out of the front door. The thing paused momentarily to look back into the building and howl. That pause was long enough to center the reticle on the creature's head and squeeze the trigger. Less than a tenth of a second later, the large silver hollow-point bullet with a pure wood core entered the forehead of the creature. The former HRT sniper had just enough time to register that the vampire used to be a teenage girl before the head disappeared in a spray of black goo. *Huh. I guess dipping them in Holy Water makes them even nastier,* God thought to himself. A grin worked its way across his face.

Inside the building, Six and Boomer quickly made sure the rest of the building was empty, and then Six announced, "Six to all team. Building is clear." He nodded as Doc crossed the threshold.

"God to Six. Exterior clear. One Tango. One Body."

"Spooky to Six. Truck is clear, although I might need to change my underwear."

16

COVER-UP

Ops Base. Trinidad, Colorado.

Doc stood in the doorway and blanched at the carnage. Even her worst experiences working for Doctors Without Borders did not prepare her for this. The vampires had not tried to feed. They had simply slaughtered everyone inside. Using their tremendous strength and near-invulnerability as powerful weapons, they had butchered everyone in the main hall. The priest could see enough parts to piece together several bodies, and she estimated that there must have been ten or fifteen people here when they were massacred.

She walked toward a corpse that was quickly becoming a pile of what could only be described as goo. She looked at Six and asked, "So, is this what's left of the one you guys took down?"

Six looked up and said, "Yep. Is this a vampire?"

Doc knelt down and carefully turned what was left of the head around so she could see the mouth. Seeing the telltale rows of razor-sharp teeth, she nodded. "This one's a bloodsucker. Help me clear out the rest of this room. Where is the other one?"

The DHS leader nodded toward the front of the building. "God said he got one outside," he said, distracted by the gore and remains around him.

The vampire specialist stood and walked toward the front door. Stepping outside, she immediately saw the black slimy ooze that covered the area around the broken front door. She looked around but could not find any remains large enough to be a head. As she watched, the black slime evaporated into thin air, as if it was ecto-plasm from a ghost.

Keying her radio, the priest called for the sniper on the roof, "Little 'G,' this is Doc. Where are the remains of the one you shot? Am I missing something?"

Doc could hear the smirk as God answered through the tactical radio, "Negative, Doc. Apparently, when you hit the head with one of these rounds doused in Holy Water, the critters do their best to explode into little pieces of goo."

Six cut in. "God, knock out the commentary. I need you to spot for us. We need to clean this one up. Spooky, keep the drone up. Let me know if any humans are coming. We should have law enforce-ment in moments. We'll keep them outside for now. Also, Spooky, prep a report so I can send it to Agent Smith. We're going to need more cleanup on this one. Doc, come back inside and make sure nothing will be found of the creature. Boomer will help."

A chorus of acknowledgements sounded over the radio while Doc walked back inside to collect the remaining vampire's head. Six passed the priest on his way out to greet the approaching sirens.

IT HAD BEEN A LONG NIGHT FOR THE TEAM. BY THE TIME THE FIRST LAW enforcement officers arrived, all trace evidence of the vampires had evaporated like water droplets on a hot summer sidewalk. Doc placed the head in an evidence bag, sealed it, and took it to the truck. Six then arranged for the medical examiner to take care of the victims and had talked to the undersheriff and the deputy chief of the police department for a few hours. It took some time, but he finally convinced them that his team was in charge of the operation and that DHS would handle the entire investigation.

The medical examiner had retrieved all of the body parts and was in the middle of the gruesome task of piecing together the bodies and accounting for any missing parts. It took threats of physical arrest and detention in Guantanamo Bay to get the coroner to ignore that there were no bodies of the attackers. Only repeated reminders that this was a national security matter kept the coroner from complaining to the press.

It was the press who had been the most difficult to handle. The DHS team leader enlisted the help of the sheriff's department and the police department to set up a quarantine with a one hundred fifty foot perimeter from the building. The press were relentless, hounding the police and the team about the deaths inside. It had driven them into a frenzy knowing members of the press were slaughtered at the same time.

While the press were difficult to handle, the worst phone call Six made was to Agent Smith at Section 28. Agent Smith critiqued the actions of the team, pointing out where they had done well, and where they needed improvement. Smith also informed the team leader that there were two more new agents on the way and that one of them would handle media relations and function well as the team leader's second-in-command.

Smith informed Six that he would send their dossiers to him electronically and that the new agents were already on the ground in Pueblo, waiting on a DHS Black Hawk tasked to transport the new agents to Trinidad within the hour. After confirming the landing spot, Smith assured Six that he would have all the support he needed to go after the remaining vampire, the young girl who got away.

After ending his phone call with Smith, Six ordered God down from his perch on the roof of the hospital and call the team together, briefing them on the new team members. As they were stowing their gear in the War Wagon, they heard the distinctive sounds of an incoming helicopter. Six looked up as a jet black military helicopter slowed to a hover over the hospital helipad. The Sikorsky UH-60 Black Hawk touched down and two men climbed out of the open helicopter side door. As soon as their feet hit the pavement, the men pulled four large duffel bags and two long gun cases from the open door and placed on the ground.

The larger man on the left from Six's point of view slung a rifle case over his back, reached down and grabbed two of the duffels, and walked toward the team as he hunched over to avoid a possible rotor mishap. The second man also placed a rifle bag over his back and visibly strained to lift the two remaining duffels. He did the same hunched duck-walk toward the team. The engine noise increased, and the helicopter lifted off with a roar from its twin turbines. Once the helicopter was in the air, the men straightened up and headed for the team. As they approached, Six was amazed when the mass of the man on the left seemed to keep getting larger and larger.

Arthur "Heavy" Murphy was a mountain of a man. His dossier said the man was six feet seven inches and weighed in just a hair under three hundred pounds. The DHS team leader could tell that all the weight was muscle. The width of his shoulders barely fit inside his armor, and he had ripped off the sleeves of his uniform. The large, bald African American man smiled as he dropped one of the bags and raised his hand in a crisp salute.

"Special Agent Art Murphy. Reporting for duty, sir. So, what do you want dead?" The large agent's deep voice boomed.

Dragging the two duffels behind Heavy, the other man stopped and dropped the handles of the bags. While not quite as tall as the walking giant, the slender Jonas "Ghost" Vanhof seemed to disappear inside his voluminous leather overcoat. Between the black leather duster and the worn, black gaucho hat perched atop his head, Ghost looked about as far from a DHS agent as Doc did. Slender to the point of gaunt, Six didn't believe the reported weight of 190 pounds, it must include the weight of the leather duster. Ghost reached inside his coat and withdrew his identification.

Flipping the ID open, Ghost grinned and announced, "Special Agent Jonas Vanhof. I hear you have a vampire problem?"

Six just shook his head at the levity as he introduced himself and the team. Reaching out his hand to shake the hands of both new team members, the team leader said, "Special Agent Burt Holstein. I'm your boss. And this is the rest of your team." Six pointed to each one as he introduced the team members by names and call signs. Turning to the new team members, he continued, "Team, this is Arthur 'Heavy' Murphy and Jonas 'Ghost' Vanhof. Heavy is our heavy weapons specialist, and Ghost is my second-in-command... and apparently he is an esoteric research prodigy."

Old and new team members exchanged handshakes and greetings. After a few minutes, Six quickly reigned the team back in. "Let's head back to the conference room. We don't want to give the press anything to waggle about."

Once the team walked back into the building and settled around the conference table, the lead agent looked up and said, "Ok. We have a major situation here. We've got at least one vamp still on the loose. We have a media feeding frenzy because of the latest attack, which we need to address A-S-A-F'in-P. The national media is now paying attention, and our faces will probably be on the news, if they aren't already. We will hold a press conference shortly. What are our options?" Six briefly looked at his secure phone to read a message from Agent Smith. "As if things aren't enough, the FBI has dispatched a Hostage Rescue Team to this area. We are still in charge... barely. We need answers."

Ghost spoke up almost immediately. "Simple: terrorism. Blame the attack on some crazy terrorists and say that there is still a danger to the public. The media will draw that conclusion anyway because of the arrival of the HRT. Hold the press conference and institute a curfew from sundown until sunup. During the day, we can sleep and prep, and we'll hunt tomorrow night. If you want me to, I can be the spokesperson for this conference. I even have a suit with me for the occasion."

The team leader thought for a bit and nodded his assent. He looked around the table and asked, "Are there any risks, or anything we're missing?"

The team's priest spoke up softly, "What if someone talks to the media? What is our contingency?"

Six looked at Ghost and then back at Doc. His face was grim when he spoke, "Our contingency is simple. We do what DHS does best.

Stall. Obfuscate. And if nothing else works, ship 'em to Gitmo. This entire operation is classified as 'Top Secret, Need-To-Know.' We just need to remind the couple of players who know something that they face federal prison time. Will that work?"

The priest nodded and said, "That will have to do."

"All right. Ghost, you go do the press conference," said Six. "I'll go with you, but I won't answer any questions. I will take the time to talk to the locals. They will be in charge of the perimeter around this building. Absolutely no admittance to this. After Ghost does his song and dance, we'll catch some rack time. Any questions?"

When nobody raised any questions, the team leader stood up, signaling the end of the meeting. The lanky new second-in command stood up, grabbed one of his duffel bags, and headed for the bathroom to change. A few minutes later, a very different agent emerged from the restroom. Dressed in a suit and tie, he looked like a respectable bureaucrat, exactly like the public information officer he should look like.

Six and Ghost walked toward the waiting mob of reporters, more of whom were arriving by the minute. Ghost noted news vans from Denver and Pueblo, as well as the large national cable news outlets. Stepping forward, Ghost nodded to the undersheriff and raised his hands for quiet. He addressed the assembled crowd.

"I am Special Agent Jonas Vanhof. That is V-A-N-H-O-F for those of you who can't keep up. I am the press liaison for this operation, and I will be issuing a short statement tonight. I will not be taking questions during or after the statement."

"At approximately nine o'clock last night, a special Department of Homeland Security action team was notified of suspicious activity at on East Main Street. As the team responded to the reported activity, an unknown number of suspected terrorists entered the back door of this location. There they attacked and killed Sheriff John Klooster, Mayor Scott Jennings, four agents from the FBI's Behavioral Analysis Unit, and three members of the press. This attack was pre-planned, and the distraction was designed to draw the DHS team from the building."

Ghost ignored the rising murmurs from the crowd and continued,

"When the DHS team realized that this building was the intended target, they responded as quickly as possible. When they responded, they were able to take down two of the terrorists. At least one of these terrorists got away. We do not know which group these terrorists represent, nor do we know how many remain in the area. Until we capture the rest of the terrorists, we will continue the curfew from sundown until sunup. This curfew applies to all citizens of Trinidad. The only exceptions are on-duty law enforcement personnel and on-duty emergency responders."

"If you notice someone who appears suspicious or who acts irregularly, please contact your local law enforcement agency. These suspects are considered heavily armed and very dangerous. Do NOT attempt to apprehend them by yourself."

"As I mentioned. I will not be taking questions today. Good day." Ghost walked away from the press to the wild cacophony of shouted questions and accusations—real and implied.

Six joined him as they walked back to the ops center. His admiration for his new second-in-command was evident in his voice, "Great statement. You're already worth your weight out here. So how did you become an expert in chasing monsters? Your file says you got busted for killing a werewolf. Just a hobby?"

The esoteric specialist shook his head. "That was not my first," he said in a low voice. "You could say that this is a family curse to hunt creatures."

When he realized that the gaunt man was not going to elaborate, Six looked questioningly at his second. "And?"

Ghost shook his head. "Let's leave it at that for now." His grim tone brooked no argument.

The lead agent slowly nodded. He could wait for a better time. As they approached the War Wagon, they could see the entire team lounging on, or in, the truck. Six climbed up into the truck and sat in the jump seat next to Boomer, and Ghost took a seat in the back. As soon as the back door was closed, Boomer fired up the engine and dropped it in gear.

The hotel arrangements were made at a small motel just off the interstate, close to the team's ops center. The exterior of the single-story motel was white against the glare of the sun. The motel was shaped in a right angle like the letter "L", roughly splitting the rooms along each axis, with access to the rooms along the outside from the parking lot. There were only a handful of rooms in this hotel, and they chose it for access to the interstate and its location close to town. Taking up one entire side of the motel, they quickly divided up into pairs for security on Six's order. The two female agents, Doc and Boomer, took one of the rooms. Six and God decided to share a room, which left Heavy and Ghost in the last room.

Directly outside the block of rooms, the War Wagon sat, occupying multiple parking spaces. Nestled inside the truck, Spooky had refused to sleep anywhere that was not surrounded by heavy armor. Six had only acquiesced when the young agent brought up that he was the only one who knew how to use all the sensors and defensive perimeter gear in the War Wagon. That made him the logical choice to sleep there.

The team had been up for over twenty-four hours by the time the lead DHS agent had requested a pair of officers in a patrol car to watch their rooms so they would be undisturbed. Other than running off the occasional reporter, the police officers had a very quiet day watching the sleeping DHS team.

17

HUNTING

Ave Maria Shrine, Trinidad, Colorado.

On a hill just south of the hospital stood a two-story white structure, a shrine. From its inception in 1934, the shrine had seen the ebb and flow of the area for nearly one hundred years. A black armored truck was parking in the shrine's parking lot. And around the back of that truck stood four gentlemen wearing black tactical armor and carrying military rifles.

Inside the truck, Six leaned over the projected landscape that Spooky was showing on his displays. "According to the UAV, we've got four cold spots just a half kilometer due south of here, on the other side of this ridge. We'll be silent from this point on."

He looked at each of the men as he assigned the marching order. "God, you're behind me. Heavy, you're behind God, and Ghost, you've got the rear guard."

All of them nodded, and Ghost pulled at the collar of his armor vest. "You know, boss, I'd rather be in my duster than this armor stuff. It's way too restrictive for my movements. And I guarantee that I'd be better armored."

Six shook his head and sighed. "Not tonight. Take the armor. We'll discuss it after this strike."

The team leader looked at his team. "Let's move out. Spooky, you've got eyes on the targets?"

Spooky looked back at him. "Yeah, boss. Still being stupid."

Six shook his head. It felt like a trap, but he had no other choice than to spring it. He flipped his night-vision goggles down and began to walk due south. One by one, the others followed him into the rapidly darkening night.

He made his way slowly and carefully through the scrub brush that carpeted the area. As team lead, Six was constantly scanning all around him, but he could not shake the feeling of walking into a trap. The men behind him were nearly silent, attesting to their care and training. Reaching the spot marked on his navigational display, Six raised a closed fist to halt the team and spoke softly into his throat mic, "Spooky, this is Six. Target status?"

The agent replied almost immediately. "They're still sitting dumb and happy. You're all clear."

"Copy." Six raised his hand and waived it forward. God moved up on his right, walking parallel and about two yards away from the team leader. Heavy moved forward to Six's left, opening up the same spacing to the team lead. Ghost drew closer to his leader, still on rear watch, constantly looking around the team for danger. As they got close to the summit of the ridge, Six raised his fist again and motioned for a halt. Stepping tentatively closer, his head just barely cleared the summit. Switching to his thermal optics, he scanned the area in front of him where the creatures should be, and came up empty.

Scanning all around on that side of the summit, his thermal optics failed to detect any unnatural thermal cold spots. Stepping back, Six again subvocalized, "Spooky, Six. Negative contact. Where are they?"

"They're right there, Six. I'm seeing them on the drone. Wait one second."

The wait seemed interminable for the team in the field. In the truck, Spooky was typing furiously and watching his screens. Suddenly, he saw five cold spots moving to surround the team on the ridge.

Spooky keyed his microphone to warn the team. "Alpha team,

Spooky. Those were a decoy. Five, repeat five, cold spots closing rapidly. Look around you."

Six jerked and swept his gun all around him as he looked through his optics. He quickly picked up two cold spots almost directly to his left, and they were closing in fast. Bringing his sights up and on target, Six keyed his mic again. "Alpha team, weapons free. Kill the SOBs." He released the microphone and grabbed the forward grip on his carbine and squeezed the trigger twice.

The muzzle flash from his rifle lit the night as the high velocity rounds entered the chest of the creature. The two silver slugs with their wooden payload caused the vampire to stumble, and it let out a fierce cry. Six silenced the screams with two more 5.56mm tumblers between the eyes and out the back of the creature's skull, along with the rotting meat in the brainpan.

Six pivoted to the next creature on his left as he barely registered God's rifle barking on his right. Four quick rounds through the creature's chest caused it to stop in its tracks. Six again took advantage of the pause to pull the trigger three more times. At least one of the three entered the howling creature's head, exploding violently out the back of the creature's skull.

To the lead agent's right, his sniper's first two shots hit the creature in the elbow and shoulder. God noticed that the vampire now had a stump of an arm. It ended where the specialized rounds chewed through the flesh. Mentally cursing, God took careful aim and began pulling the trigger. He casually walked the rounds right up the torso and into the cranium of the vampire, instantly killing it. The former HRT operator swung to his right to seek out more targets.

On Six's left, Heavy opened up with the Squad Automatic Weapon. Holding and aiming the large machine gun as if it were a rifle, he centered the sights over one of the remaining vampires, and then he pulled the trigger for a relatively short burst. Using the same rifle rounds as the rest of the team, the heavy gunner smiled as the rounds seemed to make the vampire dance. With a final burst to the head, the vampire's body tumbled to the ground.

The vampire that ran toward Ghost was suddenly surprised to see his target drop to his knees in a crouch. Smiling a horrible smile with those razor-sharp teeth, the vampire lunged at Ghost. With a speed that belied his build, a wooden stake appeared in the hunter's left hand while he drew his Webley Mark IV service revolver with his right. As the vampire loomed over him, Ghost shoved the wooden stake right through the chest cavity and into the heart. As the vampire collapsed onto the esoteric hunter, the weight of the body made it difficult for him to get out from underneath the stunned, but still dangerous, creature.

Ghost found enough strength to grab his revolver and point it at the forehead of the vampire on top of him. He squeezed the heavy double action trigger and was rewarded with a loud "bang" from the revolver. The 200 grain .38 caliber bullet split the forehead of the vampire open. Feeling the creature go limp, he fired again for good measure.

Suddenly the weight was lifted off him. Looking up, Ghost saw Heavy holding the rapidly decomposing body over him and then fling it off into the brush. Heavy extended his hand. Accepting the hand up, the lanky agent thanked the big man profusely.

Six stood and surveyed the area for the firefight. "I knew this was a trap. Someone is setting us up. Notice we're up over eight vampires so far, not just the one or two they said there were. We need to talk to Smith." He barked out orders, "Tag and Bag anything that didn't disappear, and then back to the truck."

Doc and Boomer were again interviewing the medical examiner as he sorted through the remains from the prior night's attack. The pile of unidentifiable parts grew steadily, and the bodies that were pieced together were incomplete.

The explosives expert wandered around the lab and offices while her partner kept the coroner busy with questions and suggestions. Doc noticed that the local doctor was getting more and more distracted as her partner passed around the labs. She wondered if it was a territorial thing or if the doctor had something to hide. She looked for any signs that the doctor was a familiar for a vampire, but there was nothing outwardly noticeable.

The chatter of the other team members' conversations was background noise for the team's medic, and she was only half-listening to the transmissions. She wanted to see if this coroner caught the unusual wounds or if he was incompetent. So far, he had passed over the wounds, but he had not made any big deal out of them. So either he must be incompetent or he is dirty.

Boomer stormed back into the labs from the direction of the offices. "Did you hear that? We need to go. They will want us to meet them at the ops center. They may need your help."

Doc started to respond, but her team leader's voice spoke in her ear. "All team. Meet at ops center immediately. Six out."

Boomer keyed her mic. "Copy, Six. Beta Team en route. Do you require medical?"

"Negative," Six replied. "New critical intel."

"Copy, Six. On our way." Boomer looked at her partner. "Time to go."

Doc nodded and followed her partner out of the labs and out of the hospital. They walked across the parking lot and arrived barely before the War Wagon slammed to a halt, rocking on its formidable springs.

Six climbed out of the truck and said, "Conference room. One minute."

Forty-eight seconds later, the team was assembled in the conference room. The lead agent filled them in on the details of the ambush

"This means that we are fighting something more than a couple newbies. That's at least eight vampires, including the one that Spooky nearly blew up. I've talked to Agent Smith, and he is tasking greater resources our way. Officially, our mission has been upgraded to Ultra-Red. Any recommendations?"

At that moment, there was a knock on the conference room door. Opening the door, Six found a pale young female deputy almost in tears. She choked out, "There's been another attack... just now. It's at one of our deputy's houses. You can follow me."

Six looked at the team. They were already standing and heading toward the door. "Ok, deputy. We'll be right behind you. Just wait for us to mount up."

Thirty seconds later, the War Wagon was loaded and following behind the deputy's patrol car in a mad dash across town. Three minutes later, the War Wagon came to a halt on a residential block. Multiple cruisers and ambulances lined the road.

As the team climbed out of the truck, two black Chevy Suburbans squealed to a stop. Suddenly eight men wearing green tactical armor and carrying automatic weapons piled out of the new trucks. God recognized his former team. He leaned over to Six and pointed, "HRT is here. You better step up if you want to stop them from taking over," the sniper recommended.

The lead DHS agent told the rest of the team to enter the house where the attack had occurred and to begin the investigation while he went to talk to the HRT commander. As he walked, he noticed a distraught young deputy being consoled by his peers. He paused momentarily when he realized it was same deputy that had been their guide around town the day before. *Nice kid. Shame. What was his name, Fuller? Fulton?*

He stepped up to the commander of the FBI's Hostage Rescue Team and flashed his badge. "Special Agent Burt Holstein, Homeland Security. Did you get the message from Washington? We're primary on this case."

The commander looked at him coldly before he replied, "Believe me, I got the memo." The commander's gravely voice sounded harsh to the DHS agent's ears. "Where do you want us?"

Six put up a hand to shake the commander's hand. The HRT commander accepted Six's handshake and the DHS team leader spoke, "We're going to secure the scene. Canvas the neighborhood. This is supposed to be real fresh. It is possible that the bad guys are still in the area. We believe they're armed with blades and high on a new PCP variant."

The commander dispersed his men. When the senior DHS agent turned to walk toward the house, his radio sounded in his ear, "Six, God. House is clear. It's a freakin' slaughterhouse in here. Looks like a trail out the back."

Six keyed his mike as he quickened his pace. "Copy, God. On my way. Spooky, get our UAV up and out looking for cold spots. Let's see if this is more vamps."

Moving in through the front door, Six crashed to a halt. Someone had splashed what appeared to be dark red paint all over the inside of the living room. The walls and furniture were covered with the mess. The team leader surveyed the room and saw a crime scene technician's flag by a hunk of meat that looked like it could be part of an arm. And then Six realized the "paint" around him was the drying and congealing blood of the victims. The scene at the Government Center had rattled him, but this was even worse. This attack was more vicious, more terrible, and there seemed to be fewer body parts lying around.

Walking through the front room, he joined the rest of his team in the kitchen. Looking around, he realized that this calm, cool, professional fire team was on the verge of breaking down. They had all seen horrific death before, but this was a level they had never encountered. He saw fear and pain in the eyes around him, and he wondered what they saw in his.

"Ok, team. What do we know?" The team leader's voice was coarse.

God spoke first. "Looks like there were at least two creatures. The wife was in the living room; there are two little girls upstairs. At least what little remains of them. The deputy was the first on the scene at his own house. He didn't see anything other than the slaughter before he called for backup. Other members of his department found the girls upstairs."

Six turned to his team priest. "This doesn't look like the vampire scenes we've found before. Is this normal, or is this another creature?"

Doc shook her head, fighting to hold back her tears for the family. She choked out her words, "If I had to guess, I'd say this was a zombie. But they would still be here. They are actually pretty slow in real life. Messy and voracious, but slow."

Six looked around and swore. "Whatever they are, they die tonight. Ghost, can you follow their trail?"

Ghost looked at the back door and shrugged. "I think so."

Six nodded and keyed his radio. "Spooky, this is Six. Any sign of creatures?"

"Negative, boss," the electronics specialist was quick to respond.

The lead agent pointed to the door and continued, "All right. Let's head out. Ghost, you're up."

The tall, lanky agent led the way out of the back door of the house, following blood trails left behind by the other creatures. As they walked out the back, Ghost could see the trail of blood and guts leading them to the left and over a fence. The esoteric specialist led the way, and the rest of the team followed, rifles ready. Doc had a little trouble scaling the short fence and brought up the rear.

As they approached the house next to the crime scene, they all heard screaming and growls from the house just over the next fence. The team turned to Six, and he quickly made a decision. "God, Ghost, and Boomer, you are Team 'B' on the front door. I'll bring Heavy and Doc with me through the back. Team B, you come through when you hear the gunfire. Watch the exits. Go. Go. Go!"

God, Ghost, and Boomer raced around the front of the house, just two houses south of the original scene. Six, Heavy, and Doc ran toward the screened-in back porch of the target house. As they ran, the lead agent keyed his radio. "Spooky. Activity in the house two south of the scene. Focus the UAV here."

As Six heard the confirmation from Spooky, the trio slammed through the back door to the porch. The screams inside faded to a gurgle as Six paused at the threshold of the back door. He jerked his head to Heavy, and the large man raised his enormous boot. A single kick tore the door jamb off the wall, and Six rushed through with his rifle raised. The small kitchen was strewn with overturned furniture and ripped open cabinets, but the sounds were coming from the room ahead.

As he moved through the doorway, the lead agent saw two creatures ravenously ripping an older man and woman apart with their bare hands. The creatures used to be human, but no trace of humanity remained. Their pale gray skin had a rough texture and was drawn tight where it was visible. The ripped and shredded remains of clothing hung loosely from their gaunt frames. Their fingers ended in long, dagger-like claws, and rows of sharpened teeth filled mouths that seemed to open wider than was possible. Coal-black eyes stared from hollow faces at their prey.

The blood and carnage were sprayed everywhere in the feeding frenzy. Six didn't hesitate. He pulled the trigger, aiming at the creature closest to him. Round after round hit the creature, and it jerked from each impact. Six noticed quickly that the creature wasn't reacting to the silver bullets. Even as it howled in pain, it stayed on its feet. At his left elbow, Heavy stepped up and stroked the trigger on his machine gun. The creature jerked more as the bursts all landed on target—the creature's chest. With a final burst that climbed its way up to the creature's head, the final two rounds blew open the top half of the creature's head.

When they heard Six's team burst through the door, God raised a booted foot and kicked the front door. It shuddered but remained shut. Rearing back again with all of his might, he kicked the door just below the knob. The second kick sent the door crashing inward on its hinges.

Boomer stepped into the front hallway of the small house. Pivoting left, she had less than a second to realize that there was a creature coming at her, and that it was dripping with gore. Instead of raising her shotgun to her shoulder, she simply swiveled and pulled the trigger, firing the big 12GA from her hip. She was too close to miss.

The large silver and wooden slug entered creature's diaphragm. The shot was a powerful enough blow that the creature stopped its lunge. As the creature howled in rage and pain, the young woman racked the pump on her scattergun, and pulled the trigger again. And again. The third shot opened a very large hole in its chest, dissolving the heart and the edges of the lungs into a fine spray of black ichor. The creature fell backwards in shock, and Boomer raised the Mossberg to her shoulder and stroked the trigger, sending the one-inch diameter piece of silver and wood through the front of the skull. The kinetic energy from the slug removed the entire back half of the head, and the corpse slumped over.

God and Ghost rushed past, and the sniper called out, "Coming into the room."

The demolitions specialist rejoined the rest of her team just as Six told his team, "Heavy, take the front door. God, take the back. HRT and SWAT will be coming quickly at the screams and gunfire. DO NOT let them see the bodies. Keep them outside. Boomer, help me clear the rest of the house."

The small, single-story house was confirmed clear of any other monsters thirty seconds later. As the team leader walked into the living room, his heavy weapons specialist motioned to him from the front door. Six walked up to the door and was greeted by an irate Las Animas County SWAT captain.

"If you don't let me and my men in here, I will arrest you and your team. This was our own. I want to see the bodies of the bastards who did this!" He was getting angrier by the minute.

Six held up his hands, palm out, to calm the captain. "Captain Jackson, it IS your own deputy's scene. If you and your men investigate, you will taint the evidence for anyone we missed. We are the perfect third party to investigate this one. You have to see reason. Just know this: two suspects down. And this is still our call. If you have any questions, please call my department. You have my badge number."

"In the meantime. I will have the HRT guard the scene until your lab techs get here. I'll talk to you in the morning when I have a better grasp of what's happening."

Six turned and walked back into the house. The lead agent found his sniper on the back porch talking with the HRT guys.

"No, seriously. I'm glad I joined this team," God was saying. "I know all the secrecy crap is annoying, but I'm doing important stuff. Even better, I'm finding answers to questions that I've had for a long time."

The HRT team leader clasped his former teammate on the shoulder. "If you ever want out of the 'secret club' and want to come back to the real world, give me a call. I'll have you back anytime. And if you ever need backup, we'll be there to pull your butts from the fire."

God laughed. He noticed Six standing there and motioned him

closer. "Hey, Boss. This is Special Agent Alton Lynch, HRT command. He was my team leader before I joined this team."

Six nodded at the large man. "We've met. And I believe he's still a little mad that we are here. Agent Lynch, I can honestly say thank you for giving us Agent Rivera here. Even if it wasn't voluntary. Jesús is a great testament to you and your team. If I ever get done with him, I'll send him back." The team leader stretched out his hand.

Lynch took the proffered hand and squeezed. "You better treat him right and send him back whole. Or I'll hunt you down myself."

Six nodded solemnly. "I make sure all my guys and gals come home whole... if it's in my power."

Six looked at Lynch. "While I've got you here, I would like to have a couple of your team detailed for a few hours to guard this crime scene and the other one. Just until the techs get done. Not only is this part of our original case, but keeping this in our jurisdiction removes any potential conflict of interest from the sheriff. Can you do that?"

Lynch nodded and called four of his team over. "Pearson. Sanders. No one but DHS and the lab techs come in or out of this house. Williams. Jones. You guys cover the other house." The HRT commander ordered, "Stay outside. This is a DHS scene, and we are seconding to them for this duration."

Lynch turned to Six and asked, "Can we get a briefing in the morning?"

Six nodded. "Absolutely. I'll brief you when I brief Captain Jackson and the undersheriff. Unfortunately, I don't think we're done here yet."

18

DAYLIGHT

Ops Base, Trinidad, Colorado.

I t was a beautiful sunny afternoon in Trinidad, Colorado, when the black MRAP rumbled to a halt outside the building they were using as a base. The back hatch opened, and a weary group of individuals exited the vehicle. As they wandered into the conference room, the five men and two women sat heavily in their respective seats.

Six looked around the table. "Let's regroup what we know, and what we don't," said Six as he began the briefing. "I'm going to bring Agent Smith in on this meeting with a conference call."

The DHS team leader dialed a number on his SSP and hit the speaker toggle on the touchscreen. Agent Smith answered on the second ring. Six said, "Agent Smith, I've got you on speakerphone for this briefing. I think you need to be in on this one."

"Thank you for including me on this meeting, Agent Holstein." The cultured voice of the senior agent was clear over the phone speakers. "I've read through all your reports. Any mistakes so far are solely caused by your lack of specific training here at HQ. I'm noting those only so we can correct that deficiency when you and your team get back.

"Overall, though, I have to commend you on an excellent operation so far. You guys have handled way more than any of us thought you should be thrown into. This was supposed to be a fairly light training mission. We have upgraded this mission to 'Ultra-Red,' which means you will be granted access to virtually unlimited assets. Burt, this is your mission, so I'll turn it over to you."

Six smiled. "First up: Doc. You handled the autopsies last night? How did those go?"

Doc stood wearily. "We learned several things from the corpses themselves, and even more from the hospital," she said.

WHEN THE ASSISTANT CORONER AND CRIME SCENE TECHNICIANS HAD arrived, Six had ordered Doc to ride with the corpses and had informed her that she would handle the autopsies herself. He had sent Boomer along as a backup, in case any was needed.

Doc had supervised the handling of the two deceased creatures and had stood with the bodies until they had been packed into the ambulance for the short ride to the morgue in the basement of the hospital. Boomer had climbed into the passenger seat with the driver while her partner had ridden with the techs in the back of the transport.

When they had reached the hospital, the body bags had been wheeled down into the morgue, and the bags had been placed on the exam tables in preparation of the coroner's autopsy. When Bill, dressed in an exam gown and a surgical mask, had approached the tables, Doc had held out a hand to stop him.

"Bill, I am officially relieving you of the autopsy of these remains," Doc had insisted. "Unfortunately, you don't have the Top Secret Clearance required to perform the autopsies. As you know, I'm a board-certified medical doctor, and I will handle the post-mortem. In fact, I cannot even have you in the room with me while I do the autopsies," she had said.

"Are you kidding me?" Doctor Stewart had let the outrage seep into his voice. "You can't keep me out of my own lab! State law says that you have to be a certified Medical Examiner to perform an autopsy. You don't have the qualifications."

Doc had withdrawn her credentials from an inner pocket. She had opened them up and shoved them into Stewart's face. Her voice was cold and calm as she had said, "This is my authorization. This is officially a Department of Homeland Security operation and is currently classified Top Secret. You do not have the clearance. Period. Now get out before I throw you out."

Doctor Stewart had sneered and stepped closer, his bulk menacing the agent. "You couldn't throw me out if you tried," he had growled.

There had been a loud mechanical "snick-snack" of the slide on a pump shotgun racking that had echoed in the room. Bill had turned to see Doc's partner. Her shotgun had been raised, but not quite pointed, in Stewart's direction.

"Doctor Stewart. You will leave the labs to Doctor Sorenson," Boomer's voice had come out cold and hard. "Right now you are treading on very thin ice. If I think that you are actually threatening my partner with physical violence, I will end you. Are we clear?"

Stewart had gulped audibly. He had nervously rung his hands and had started stuttering and stammering an apology. Turning quickly, he went to his office to grab his jacket and phone and then left the lab.

Doc had looked at her partner and said, "I do believe we no longer have a friend in this office. Thanks for the back-up."

Boomer had smiled and put the shotgun on safe, slinging it across her shoulder. "No problem. Guy was a creep before this started. I'm going to go wander through his office," she had replied.

He partner had nodded in agreement. "Before you go, can you help me drag the bodies out of these bags? I want to work on these creatures."

The two women had wrestled the cadavers out of their body bags and had prepped them on the exam tables. As Doc had begun to slice into them with her scalpel, her partner had wandered into the office to snoop around.

About four hours later, the weary priest had removed the mask from her face and called for Boomer. "Can you come help me?" She had asked. "I want to bag these things up and get them over to the crematorium before our good doctor gets wise."

They had placed the bodies back into the body bags, and each had grabbed a gurney, wheeling them around the corner to the crematory. As they had entered the section, there was a lone technician waiting behind a desk. He had looked up, puzzled at the unexpected intrusion.

Doc, still dressed in her surgical cover gown, had been the first to speak. "I've got two here that need your services ASAP."

The technician had shaken his head. "No ma'am. There is nothing scheduled. Do you have the correct paperwork? I don't think I've ever seen you around here before."

Doc had shaken her head, and the two agents had pulled out their credentials. The team's priest had spoken up. "Special Agent Noelle Sorenson, Department of Homeland Security. This credential here is my authorization. I will sign any paperwork you need me to sign, but you will fire up the furnaces. Now."

The face of the technician had gone pale, and the eyes had become slightly glassy for a moment. Then his eyes cleared, and he had said, "I don't like it, and you will need to fill out all kinds of paperwork. But you can do that while the furnace is working."

As the technician had walked away, Doc had seen a faint blue glow rising from her credentials in the dimly lit lab. It was so faint that she would never have noticed it in a well-lit room, and the glow had faded to nothing as she watched. *I must ask Agent Smith about this later,* she thought.

The technician had sat behind his console and had typed a series of instructions into the computer. Doc and Boomer had stacked both bodies onto the conveyor belt that fed into the furnace and had closed the massive door.

They both had heard a "click" and a "whoosh" as the natural gas furnace inside lit fully. Soon the furnace itself was at 1800 degrees, and the inner chamber door had opened, allowing the bodies to be shifted into the furnace. Ninety minutes later, with the monstrous bodies turned to ash, the female agents had walked out of the hospital and had hitched a ride in a police cruiser to head back over to the hotel.

———

As Doc finished her recounting, Ghost spoke up. "Revenants. They were revenants, weren't they?"

She nodded at Ghost, then turned to Six. "Ghost is right. They were revenants."

The team leader spoke up. "Ok, so, other than having to put a ton of bullets into them, how do we kill these... revenants?"

Doc sighed and opened up her small leather book. "As I mentioned before," she began. "Revenants are basically a cross between a familiar and a zombie with some vampire speed and strength built in. Revenants have been traditionally used to guard the vampire nests during the day as well as enforcers to keep those in its nest in line. They are fast, hungry, vicious, and fiercely loyal to their master."

"When a traditional vampire 'turns' or infects a human, they can either turn them into a vampire or into a revenant. When a recently infected vampire tries to turn someone else, the result is almost always a revenant. Newly minted bloodsuckers don't have the control and willpower to create a true vampire yet."

Spooky raised his hand, and the priest nodded at him. "Doc, if these things are as loyal and obedient as you say, then they were set loose by the vampire to purposely terrorize the town, correct?"

Doc wearily nodded, her exhaustion was evident. "That would be my guess. It is the explanation that makes the most sense."

"So again, Doc. How do we kill 'em?" Six chimed in. "And can they be cured?"

The vampire specialist consulted the pages of her book.

"No, they cannot be cured." Doc continued to read from the little book. "Unlike vampires, the changes are irreversible. As for killing them? They are designed to take a lot of punishment. Like zombies, hits to the head will work and explosives will work as well. Like zombies, they do not receive pain from the nerve endings in their skin, so burning them, or using a baseball bat, will not work."

"On the up side, they are not technically undead, so they are mortal. Do enough damage to the heart or brain, and they will die. Think of them as if they were doped up on extreme PCP. Hard to stop, but they still have to have a heart and brain to live. They are also not 'contagious;' a bite will hurt, but you will not become a revenant. Although their saliva tends to be teeming with filth and decay, so you will probably get a nasty infection. Any other questions?"

Heavy looked up. "Will the special ammo do anything to them?" he asked.

Doc shook her head. "No, Heavy. Other than normal bullet damage, the silver ammunition is designed specifically for vampires." The priest looked around.

Agent Smith's voice rose from the phone in the center of the table. "Thank you, Doctor Sorenson. We'll add this information to our database. Would you be so kind as to forward your autopsy notes when you get a chance?"

"I'll send them as soon as I can," Doc replied. "If you need any more information about revenants, you might want to contact the Vatican as well; they have better records available."

Agent Smith paused momentarily. "Thank you, Doctor," he continued. "I'll have Timothy make the call. Back to the problem at hand. It's obvious that there are at least a few more vampires and some of their minions in the area. I've sent a re-supply of ammo for you. The helicopter should be there shortly. So what is your next step, Agent Holstein?"

Six looked around the table. He sighed and said, "At this point, sir, we're going to be combing through our data for any patterns. I've got Spooky working on the UAV and any other sensors we've got. Can you task us a satellite or two for extra coverage? Is there any way we can get some reinforcements for this?"

Agent Smith paused and then spoke again. "I've already tasked one of the NSA's KH-12 satellites to you. Spooky, you... now have access to the satellite in real time. It should be in geosyncronous orbit overhead in about ninety minutes. Unfortunately, I don't have any reinforcements to send you. This is code-word Top Secret, and you need to do your best to keep your actual mission and targets under wraps. You've already raised a big enough stink that we're working overtime to keep the President from noticing. So you can't get any of the locals to help, either."

Spooky spoke up. "Agent Smith? Any response to the requested vehicle specs that I sent? Any chance we can get that before the op is over?" he asked.

Six looked at his youngest agent and mouthed, *Vehicle specs?*

"Yes, John," Smith replied. "I approved the load out. Norbert's currently working on the specs now, and we should have it ready in a couple of days. I'll have it flown out to you, if you are still there when it's done. If there's nothing else, I'll let you get back to work. Keep up the good work."

As Agent Smith broke the connection, Six looked at Spooky. "What did you order?" he asked.

The young agent looked too smug for anyone's comfort. He could not keep the mischievous tone out of his voice. "I thought about ways to upgrade the War Wagon. Sounds like version two will be here soon."

Six turned his head as someone knocked on the door, and the team leader asked them to enter.

The assistant police chief of Trinidad was standing in the doorway. "Agent Holstein? We have a really weird situation, and I think it should be brought to your attention."

The lead DHS agent nodded and motioned for the man to come into the room fully.. "Come on in. What's up?"

"Trinidad only has two pharmacies in town, one in the hospital, and one new chain across town," the assistant chief explained. "The head pharmacist at the hospital has not showed up for work for almost two weeks. I've known Virgil for twenty years, and he almost missed his kid's birth because he was at work."

"Originally, he asked for a week off for vacation. At the end of that week, he began calling in 'sick.' Every day, for the last six days, he has called in sick at 8:45am on the dot. Today, he failed to call in."

The agents exchanged questioning glances as Six took notes.

The assistant chief continued, "The hospital's HR gal said she called him today when he did not show up or call. She said he answered the phone, but when she asked him if he was coming in to work, he started 'giggling.' That was the word she used, 'giggling.' Virgil hasn't giggled since he was three. Instead of sending one of my men up to his house, I thought I might give this to you guys. Is this something you want to check out?"

Six looked around at the team, then back to the officer. "Absolutely. This sounds like something I'd rather have us handle. What's the doctor's name and address?"

The assistant chief consulted his notebook. "Virgil Templeton." He rattled off the address. "Virgil lives at the top of one of the low foothills. He's the only one on the crest. It's a large hacienda-style ranch with an inner courtyard. He's a shorter guy, about five foot two, and is real skinny. He is sixty-three, according to records, and is bald on top with a white mustache. Are you going to want any of my people or sheriff deputies to go with you?"

"No thanks, chief," Six shook his head and replied. "We'll handle this one solo. Just keep the perimeter to this building secure as we instructed. The HRT will check around here in town, and we'll follow up with Mr. Templeton. I'll let you know how it goes."

As the assistant chief left, Six looked at the team. "It looks like we've caught a break. Doc, any idea what's going on with the pharmacist?"

The priest thought for a moment and then said, "Either he's now a familiar or he's been turned. No telling until we see him."

"All right." Six was planning and making decisions on the fly. "We will assume that there is a nest up there. Full combat gear. Spooky, when we get satellite coverage, point it at the house. Until then, get the UAV up and overhead. We've got ninety minutes until satellite coverage, so Doc and Boomer, you guys hit the sack. Take a power nap."

They all turned as they heard the loud rotors of a very large helicopter. Six motioned for Heavy and God to go meet the chopper for the resupply. He then turned to Ghost. "All right, monster hunter. What else can you tell me to help us prepare?"

Heavy and God ran outside and looked up. Instead of a Black Hawk helicopter, they saw a large airplane with rotors on the wingtips and an extended ramp down the back. As the aircraft settled on its landing wheels, the two agents ducked and ran toward the plane. The cargo master was placing the last of four large duffels on the end of the ramp.

Each of the agents grabbed two and hurried back toward the ops center. As they walked, they both heard the roar of the propellers increasing. Turning, they watched the V-22 Osprey virtually leap into the air and climb quickly into the clouds. Walking toward the War Wagon, they saw that the rear hatch was down, and Spooky was inside at the controls of the ever-present drone.

The two men set the bags down and opened them. Inside were multiple cans of linked ammunition for Heavy's machine gun and forty loaded magazines for the team's M4s and multiple magazines for the team's pistols. Digging, God was happy to also find several magazines of ammunition for his sniper rifle and several boxes of Norbert's special 12GA ammunition for Boomer's shotgun.

The heavy gunner was grinning and laughing. "Gee, it seems like Christmas came early this year! Now we can go hunting!" he exclaimed.

"Seems more like Halloween to me, but whatever." The sniper flashed a grin.

Ninety-three minutes later, the team finally got complete satellite coverage over the area. They gathered around the electronics specialist's screens as the agent pointed out the layout of the house.

"Can you show us thermal on this thing?" Six asked.

"Not for this house," Spooky replied. "It has a clay tile roof. That clay has absorbed the sun all day and is radiating that heat right now."

Six studied the house and the surrounding area intently. "Ok, team, here is the plan..."

19

GIGGLES

Foothills East of Trinidad, Colorado.

T he War Wagon sat idling on the side of the road in the late afternoon sun. Just around the next hill was the half-mile long, winding driveway that led to the pharmacist's house. Six was reviewing the plan with his team.

The team leader pointed to the various members of his team. "Spooky, you are going to drive us up to the front drive. God, you're up through the roof hatch; I recommend the M4 this time... I want you in on close support with the team. Doc, you and Boomer are in the back, waiting to jump out as soon as Spooky stops. Heavy, Ghost, and I will be on the outside rails, hanging on and providing cover."

"When we get to the house, we are all going to rapidly dismount and go through the front doors. Heavy has the ram. God, you are still up on the MRAP until we're inside and then I want you on the roof."

"Once the doors are breached, Heavy, Boomer, and Doc cover right, Ghost and I cover left, and we assess what we have. Do not engage if it's just a crazy old man. If there are any creatures, weapons are hot. Anyone have questions?"

Everyone shook their heads. Six nodded and said, "All right then, let's mount up."

God popped the roof hatch and stood up through the hatch. Six, Heavy, and Ghost all climbed out the rear hatch and up onto the side mounts of the massive truck. Boomer closed the back hatch and keyed her mic. "Six, Boomer. All set inside."

Six's reply was immediate: "Spooky, proceed."

As the War Wagon approached the pharmacist's driveway at the bottom of the hill, Spooky looked back and noticed one of the sheriff department's cruisers with no lights on following them at a distance..

Spooky keyed his mic. "Six, Spooky. We have a local sheriff following us. What do you want me to do?"

Six turned around and looked toward the road behind them and saw the cruiser hanging back about five hundred feet, traveling as slowly as the MRAP.

"Spooky, Six. Stop the truck in the driveway's entrance. I'll deal with the occupants. Heavy, Ghost, watch around us. This may be a distraction. God, you cover me as I approach."

Spooky stopped the truck at the end of the driveway. Six hopped off and waved the police car forward while God provided cover.

The sheriff's car pulled up, and a young deputy got out. The team leader realized it was the same young deputy whose family had been killed the night before. Even though it had been less than twelve hours since their investigation, the kid looked like he hadn't slept in days. The bags under his eyes and his rumpled uniform told the tale of his loss and suffering.

Raising his fist to halt everyone, Six carefully walked toward the deputy. In a low voice, the veteran leader growled, "What are you doing here, deputy? You need to leave right now. You are interfering with a federal investigation, and I'm not in the mood to deal with any shit."

The young deputy defiantly raised his chin. "If the SOBs that killed my wife are holed up here, I want in on the raid. I deserve that."

Six muttered under his breath about foolish sacrifices and shook his head. "Look, I'm sorry about your family, but you deserve to live. Let us handle this. Get out of here while you still can."

"I have nothing left. I'm going in there with you, or behind you. Your choice," the deputy said as he crossed his arms and stood tall.

Six changed tactics. The DHS leader looked at the deputy and glanced pointedly at his pistol. "What are you going to use? Just your sidearm?"

The deputy walked around and popped the trunk of his cruiser. He reached in and pulled out an AR-15, the civilian model of the M4 carbine that Six was carrying. He loaded a magazine and pulled the charging handle to chamber a round.

Realizing the deputy would cause trouble on his own, Six reached into his pocket for his credentials. "I tried to warn you, kid." He flashed his credentials in the deputy's face. "I am Agent Burt Holstein from the Department of Homeland Security. This is a Top Secret-code word operation. You are hereby seconded to the operation and must forever keep your damn mouth shut. Do you understand?"

The deputy's eyes glazed over for a second, then cleared. "I understand," the deputy said. A look of confusion briefly crossed the deputy's face, and he shook his head slowly. "What did you just do to me?"

Six ignored the question, and instead, said, "Hand me your AR." The slightly confused deputy gave it to the federal agent.

The veteran agent released the magazine and pulled the charging chamber as he cycled the round out of the chamber. He reached into the pouch on his side and grabbed three magazines. One of them went into the magazine well of the deputy's AR. Six then pulled the handle again as he loaded a new round. He handed the two spare magazines to the deputy. "Your ammunition was worthless. This new ammo will actually work on the target."

Accepting the rifle back from the DHS leader, the deputy asked, "What are we doing at Virgil's house, sir?" The young deputy was curious about all the firepower needed to take down a kindly old pharmacist.

"We're actually not sure yet, Deputy... Folsom is it?" The deputy nodded. "In fact, I think I can use your help with this. I want you to knock on the doctor's door. See if you can get him to come to the front door so we don't have to kick it in."

"Now park your car across the driveway to block access. Once you are done, climb up next to Heavy there. You'll ride with us up the hill.

You follow my orders. You do what you're told. And maybe, just maybe, you get to keep your soul."

The young deputy smiled at the words, then realized that the dour agent was not kidding. He quickly pulled his car forward to block the end of the driveway. The deputy turned on his overhead light bar, locked the patrol car, and clipped the keys to his belt.

Folsom looked shaken as he clambered up the side of the MRAP. He tightened his grip on his rifle. No matter what happened to him, as long as he took out the monsters that took his wife and children, he was sure he would find peace.

Six climbed aboard and told Spooky to move out. Spooky slowly maneuvered the massive armored vehicle up the winding drive. When they pulled to a halt at the house, they all dismounted and staged by the door.

Six keyed his mic again. "Spooky, Six. Any change in the house or courtyard?"

"Negative, bossman. Looks like we're clear," answered Spooky.

"Great. Launch the drone and keep an eye on the satellite feed. You're our eyes tonight, Spooky. Back us up."

Six motioned toward the front of the house, and the deputy nodded. He walked toward the front doors. The rest of the team looked at their leader as if he were stupid for letting the deputy, of all people, simply stroll up to the house. Six shrugged, "He's now one of us, at least temporarily. Try not to let him get killed."

The deputy rang the doorbell. A deep booming gong sounded throughout the house. He then knocked on the door and heard his loud raps echo throughout the seemingly empty house. Two more cycles of the doorbell and knocking finally brought a voice to the door.

An old man's weak and sickly voice spoke softly through the doors, and a short shadow of a man could be seen through the frosted glass inserts. "Yes? Who is it? What do you want?"

"Virgil? It's me, Christian Folsom," the deputy responded. "You've known me all my life. Can you come out here and talk to me please?"

The old man's voice seemed even shakier now. "Christian? Why are you up visiting me? Is something wrong at the hospital?"

"Yes, Virgil. It's Deputy Folsom. I would really appreciate it if you would come out to talk to me. Can you open the door a little so I can see that you are ok? Some of us are getting worried about you, Virgil."

But then the voice behind the door suddenly changed.

"Hee, hee." Virgil childishly giggled. "Why would I come out there? I don't think your 'friends' want to talk to me… I think they want to hurt me."

The voice erupted in a fit of giggles.

"Virgil! Open up," Folsom demanded as he pounded on the door. "I don't want to have to come in there! Just come out and talk to us. Please?"

The giggling grew maniacal and then slightly calmed.

When the voice spoke again, it was deeper than it had been in years. "Why don't you come in, boy? Invite your friends, too. I think they'll enjoy it here."

God looked down from the roof of the MRAP and spotted shadows moving behind the windows across the front of the house. "Six, God. I've got movement behind the doors. Multiple shadows. And I see movement in many of the windows. He's not alone in there."

Six reached out and grabbed the back of Deputy Folsom's vest, yanking him back off the porch. Six nodded to Heavy, and the big man lifted the battering ram. All the team members raised their weapons as Heavy brought the ram forward and smashed open the front doors, right at the jamb. Glass and wood splintered and flew inward, closely followed by the front doors themselves. Standing in the doorway was a creature who used to be Virgil Templeton, giggling hysterically and holding a beautiful, old, double-barrel shotgun whose barrels looked like cannons to Six as he stared straight down the bores.

Six and Virgil opened fire at the same time; the rest of the team followed closely their shots. Six placed two shots dead center of the chest, and the muzzle of his gun began to climb toward Virgil's head. The twin loads of double-ought buckshot scattered as they left the ends of the barrel. Unfortunately for Virgil, the old man's aim wasn't quite so perfect, sending both loads of shot right between Heavy and

Six. One of the pellets hit the armor on Six's shoulder and bounced away, slightly rocking the DHS leader on his heels. The rest entirely missed their targets.

Behind Six, Ghost brought his rifle up to his shoulder and pulled the trigger twice. Both of the shots scored solid hits in the torso before his follow-up shots climbed over Virgil's head. Boomer stroked the trigger of her shotgun, sending the three-quarters-of-an-inch-wide slug of silver and wood into the heart cavity. All the metal flying through the chest of Virgil ripped through and tore larger holes out of his back. The second shot from Boomer's shotgun put the silver and wood slug through Virgil's face.

As Heavy brought his SAW up to aim ahead of him, Deputy Folsom stood there, open-mouthed, with shock while he tried to comprehend the violence he had just witnessed. The team moved past him, fanning out left and right to cover their entrance. The deputy gave a strangled cry when the body of the man he had known all his life began to dissolve into wisps of smoke.

"God, Six. Go to the roof," Six said after keying his mic.

The area to Six's left opened into a very large living area with a fireplace. He barely had time to notice the fine leather furniture as a revenant screamed around the corner. Following the screaming creature was what appeared to be a human wielding a fireplace poker.

Six and Ghost targeted the gray-skinned revenant at the same time, squeezing off rounds in the chaos. Multiple rounds walked up his torso with the final four missing their marks over the creature's shoulders. The creature stopped and looked down, screamed, and ran again. Boomer stepped between the two men and raised her shotgun. She stroked the trigger twice, pumping the slide on her shotgun between shots.

Her first shot hit the revenant in the upper chest, leaving a very large hole, and momentarily stunning the creature. The second hit the creature's nose. The corpse fell as if poleaxed as the contents of its skull hit the wall with a sickening "plop."

Six shifted his aim and squeezed the trigger. He fired two rounds into the chest of the familiar, causing the target to explode. Ghost squeezed the trigger once; his M4 shot a three-round burst of bullets.

He watched as two of the rounds went wide with the third finally connecting with the man's head. The round exited the man's skull in a furious explosion as it plastered gore on the furniture scattered around the living room.

Deputy Folsom had watched in horror as the DHS agents calmly shot and killed an old pharmacist that he had known his entire life. He had watched a body disappear into thin air. And he had even watched the leader and two of the other team members open fire on a creature that seemed straight out of a horror movie. *It took two rifles and a shotgun to bring down just the one creature!* He marveled to himself. But when he tried to wrap his head around how the team had gunned down Stevie Nelson, a man whom he played football with in high school, it was too much to comprehend. Deputy Folsom froze, waiting for his brain to come up with a logical explanation of what his senses were telling him.

Six and Ghost moved toward the open living room area according to their plan, and Heavy, Boomer, and Doc shifted the opposite direction. They entered a modern marble and granite kitchen wrapped around the corner toward the back of the house. Scrambling over the island was another revenant with crazed hunger in its eyes and screams of defiance oozing from its mouth. Behind the creature, another revenant with the rough gray skin and a human familiar scrambled toward the team.

Heavy and Boomer pulled the trigger at the same time. The shotgun and the burp of the machine gun mingled in the air as the revenant was thrown back across the granite island, disappearing out of sight behind the island. Heavy shifted his aim toward the other revenant. Pulling the trigger twice, the heavy gunner braced himself as his machine gun spat two bursts of fire. Each burst chewed over the chest area, leaving many gaping wounds in the revenants shredded torso and causing it to stop momentarily. Before the beast could recover completely, Heavy twitched his finger twice more, sending two more bursts into the figure. The final burst climbed through the creature's shoulder, with the final two rounds striking the head and ending the creature's miserable life.

Boomer was suddenly aware that the human familiar running

toward her was a young teenage girl, maybe fifteen or sixteen years old. Her black hair and olive skin spoke of her Native American heritage, but her wild eyes and unintelligible howls spoke of her status as their next target. She hesitated long enough to have the girl close the distance before Boomer could pull the trigger.

The demolitions expert regained her bearings in time to raise her shotgun across her body to stop the young girl's thrust with the carving knife she was wielding. As the girl tried to slash and stab Boomer, the agent was driven backwards. Boomer collided with the stainless steel doors of the refrigerator. While the teenager had the ferocity granted by her insanity and devotion to her master, Boomer had sheer physical muscle mass coupled with panic-driven reactions. Heaving forward, the explosives expert used her momentum and threw the girl across the kitchen to collide with the island in the middle. The familiar bounded to her feet, and as the girl came at her again, Boomer treated her shotgun as a short club and knocked the teenager across the head with the butt of the stock. The girl crashed to the floor, sliding into the cabinet base hard enough to elicit a "crack" as her head connected to the hardwoods. Judging from the angle of the girl's neck, Boomer was certain that the familiar would never fight again.

Doc approached the kitchen and knelt at the girl's side to feel for a pulse. Shaking her head at Boomer, her sorrow turned to surprise as she yelled out a warning. Boomer and Heavy spun around and watched the revenant they first shot climb up over the island and spring toward them again. Although the creature was much slower this time, it was still growling and angrily snapping at them. Boomer casually raised her shotgun and stroked the trigger. The three-quarter-inch slug took the creatures head off, with the fragmented skull disappearing just above the eye sockets. As Boomer reloaded her shotgun, the three agents looked at the ceiling. They heard footsteps running across the roof, and then they heard gunfire.

God leapt from the top of the War Wagon and landed on the roof, rolling with the jump and coming to his knees easily. He carefully looked across the flat, tiled roof, only detecting roof vents and tiles. He noticed an open-air courtyard in the middle. Walking to the edge, he looked down into an overgrown courtyard and spied a large pair of cellar doors in the middle. Across the courtyard, he could see windows and glass doors on the other three sides of the courtyard. Looking through one set of doors, he could see two men armed with shotguns standing and waiting in ambush for his teammates.

He quickly raised his rifle to his shoulder and aimed through the scope at the first one and paused to steady his aim. He settled the crosshairs over the front man's head and squeezed the trigger. His rifle barked, and the window's pane spidered from a neat hole near the gentleman's head. As the man crumpled, the sniper swung to the second man, who was looking at his partner and the large pool of blood forming around the body. God watched as the man began to turn toward the window, and the agent pulled the trigger again. Just like the hunter who leads the moving deer to make his shot, the sniper gave a brief lead on where he believed the target's head would end up, and he was correct. The man's head intersected with the trajectory of the bullet in mid-flight, and the second ambusher crumpled to the ground as the glass door exploded inward.

Six leaned around the corner just in time to see the glass door disintegrate and the second lifeless body crumple to the ground.

"Thanks, God. Good shooting," Six said after he keyed his mic.

"That's why I'm here," the sniper quipped back.

Six motioned for Ghost to move forward as they carefully walked through the living room toward a long hallway with several doors. He watched as his sniper dropped into the courtyard and then brought his attention back toward the hallway. Motioning for Ghost to cover him, Six opened the door and swung around the corner as he rapidly scanned the bedroom for hostile targets. "Clear" he muttered so that Ghost could hear him.

He moved to the next door. Again, the bedroom was clear.

Across from that bedroom was another room, used as an office, and it, too, was clear.

The next door revealed a very large and luxurious bathroom with a second exit door. Moving through the bathroom, the two federal agents approached the door. Throwing open the door, they moved into the very spacious master bedroom. When they heard a slight noise behind a door straight ahead, they both raised their guns. Six motioned for his second-in-command to open the door as he covered it with his rifle.

As Ghost reached for the knob, the door slammed outward and a piercing screech filled the room as a small creature virtually flew out of the closet. The little girl looked to be no more than ten or eleven, but the rows of vicious teeth and the blood red eyes said she was no longer human. Six pulled the trigger, catching the creature in mid-air as it leapt toward his face. The two rounds in the chest burned the creature severely as her face twisted into a contortion of pain. The third round ended the creature's suffering as it traveled through the bridge of her nose and into the creature's brain. Her body crashed to the ground just short of Six. Ghost stepped forward and drew his machete. The silver inlaid runes on the blade glowed a bright white as he brought the large knife down across the creature's neck and severed the head of the young vamp.

Ghost flicked the black ichor from the blade and sheathed his machete, grabbing his rifle again. Both men walked back through the bedroom and hallway and made their way carefully to the other side of the house to meet with their team.

Heavy, Boomer, and Doc worked their way toward the back of the house. As they walked through the dining room, they heard another howl. They quickly spun around in time to see a creature with bright red eyes leaping at them. The creature was faster than the revenants, and it was between the agents before they could fire. The vampire backhanded Boomer, and she flew across the dining room and crashed into the wall with a thud. The creature then grabbed Heavy's machine gun and smacked at it, ripping it from the agent's hands.

A bright blue glow suddenly lit the air as Doc spoke in Latin and held her cross in front of her. The light was blinding to the creature, and it cringed away from the priest, covering its eyes with its forearms. Heavy reached up and drew the massive fighting blades from the sheaths on his back. As they cleared the leather, both blades glowed a ghostly green along their razor-sharp edges. The heavy weapons specialist swung mightily, bringing the blades toward each other. Unerringly, the blades sought the vampire's neck. The blades came together in a mighty clash, cleaving through the upraised shoulders and arms meant to ward off the light from the cross, and completely severing the head of the vamp. The head dropped to the floor alongside the severed arms, which were already beginning to dissolve into mist.

Heavy stared down at the ancient khukuri as the glow began to fade from their clean edges. Transfixed, he muttered, "Huh. I didn't know they did that."

Doc looked up at his hulking form. "What, nobody ever told you they were enchanted? Come on. We've got the rest of the house to clear."

The priest walked over to Boomer as she slowly got to her feet. "Anything broken, any injuries? You good to move on?"

The demolitions specialist looked back. "No problem, Doc. Just knocked the wind out of me. Damn things are fast." Boomer bent down to pick up her shotgun.

The three agents worked together and cleared the bathroom and hallway leading to the back porch.

Heavy clicked his mic. "Six, Heavy. This side is clear, we're coming back to the front of the house."

"Roger, Heavy. We'll meet you on the porch," replied Six.

The team gathered at the front entrance where the deputy was still standing. He was finally coming to his senses and was realizing that he was in way over his head. Six walked up to him and said, "You ok? You just kind of freaked out on us. Are you sure you don't want out?"

Deputy Folsom shook his head. "Sorry. I'm still having trouble dealing with monsters in town. I knew these people." He pointed to the first familiar that the DHS leader and his second had killed. "I played football with Stevie in high school. What the hell do you people do?"

Six chuckled at the inadvertent joke. "Yeah. That about sums it up. We still have a cellar to clear, are you with us?"

The deputy nodded his agreement.

Six keyed his radio and said, "Spooky, we're all clear in here. Anything coming out of that cellar?"

20

UNDERGROUND

Templeton House, Trinidad, Colorado.

"Ok, guys, I have a little thermal leakage from around the doors. That means that they are not sealed tightly. Nothing else on the satellite." Spooky announced over the radio.

"Copy that, Spooky," Six replied. He turned to address the team. "Ok, we have myself and Ghost on one side. Heavy and Boomer, pull on the other door. God and Doc should be at the opening so that they can shoot, or dispel, anything that comes out."

"This should be just a cellar, but it would make a perfect hiding place for any creatures during the day. We have not found the master yet, so we should expect him to be here. Any questions?"

No one had any questions.

The team leader continued his impromptu planning session. "If we go down in there, I will be on point. Doc will be next, flanked by Heavy and Ghost. Boomer and God, bring up the rear. Let's move out."

The team assembled in their assigned positions around the massive set of double doors, and the members on either side reached out to grab the handles. Each door was about nine feet tall, just over three feet wide, and seemed to be about two inches thick and made of solid steel. On "three," the teams pulled their assigned doors, straining with the effort that the solid doors appeared to require. Both doors flew open and sent all four team members sprawling. As Six looked up from the ground, he saw a system of pulleys and counterweights for the doors, and it looked as if one person could have lifted the doors easily. *We probably should've tried the doors first.*

With the doors now open, the team could see stairs descending into a dark cellar. These were no ordinary stairs; they were stone stairs cut into the bedrock beneath the doors. These stairs were worn and extended down into the earth about fifteen feet before they curved around a corner and led out of sight.

"Stairs," God called out to his teammates. "They go down and around a corner. Visible light. Clear." He stood with his rifle poised at his shoulder, waiting for the others to get in position.

The rest of the team scrambled back to their feet, each of them nursing bumps and bruises from the fall. They shouldered their weapons, and Six led the fire team into the cellar. About fifteen feet down, the worn stone stairs became broken stone stairs and curved around the corner. At the corner, the leader leaned around the angle, letting his rifle barrel lead the way. The stone walls became rough-hewn stone. The stairs eventually ended at a well-worn dirt floor, and the walls of the stairwell opened up to reveal a dark cavern.

Strung across the ceiling of the cavern was a series of wires, with a bare bulb hanging down about every twenty feet. The rough cavern walls ended about five feet to the left of the stairs, and the wall across was just over twenty feet away. To Six's right, the cavern stretched about thirty feet before curving out of sight to the left. The floor was relatively even and free of obstacles or debris; however, thin stalactites tightly clung to the ceiling approximately ten feet overhead. The floor was packed hard from what could only be years of use, and bare bedrock rose up through the hard earth, creating small pockets of stone flooring.

As the team maneuvered through the cave, they spread out behind Six. They rounded the corner, and the corridor opened up into another cavern. Across from the team, Six noticed a smaller passage leading off into darkness. To the left the cavern was deep and had a large stone formation that blocked his view of the end of the cavern.

Six, Boomer, and the rest of the team heard melodic plops and drips of water at the other end of the dimly lit cavern. They froze when a growl interrupted their footsteps. With a raised fist, Six signaled the team to halt. The growling appeared to be coming from the other side of the rock formation. As Six stepped to his left, Ghost and Heavy stepped to the right and aimed around the large block of bedrock. The others stepped out from the passage and took their positions.

Around the formation roared three revenants, their jaws open in eager anticipation. The creatures had almost reached the agents when the team opened fire. Six fired at the creature on the far left, in between the rock formation and the wall of the cavern. Boomer joined in; she pulled the trigger on her shotgun and worked the pump as fast as she could. A combination of high-powered rifle rounds and shotgun slugs nearly tore the creature in two. The revenant was still vainly trying to crawl toward them when the team leader aimed and shot the creature between the eyes.

Ghost and God opened up on the revenant on the other side of the rock formation. As the sniper calmly and methodically walked his rounds up from chest to head, the esoteric hunter peppered the creature with rounds to its chest and abdomen. When God finally put his fourth round into the head of the creature, Ghost ran his rifle empty and switched to a full magazine. The lifeless creature fell at the feet of the two shooters.

The former HRT operator looked at the hunter and said, "Next time, try aiming."

Ghost sheepishly returned God's grin.

The remaining revenant leapt for the heavy gunner. Two bursts of machine gun fire drove the creature back and left it dazed. Deputy Folsom aimed his rifle at the creature and squeezed the trigger twice. The first shot took the creature in the chest; the second shot hit the creature between its eyes. In the back of his mind, he thought he recognized the contorted features of Mrs. Marshall, his high school English teacher. He could not help but to take in the crazed eyes and the mouthful of sharp teeth for later... he knew he'd see them again in his nightmares. He thought he saw the body stir one more time, and he resolutely walked over and shot a point-blank round through the Mrs. Marshall's forehead.

The cavern echoed with the sound of automatic gunfire.

"Well, they know we're coming now," Six said as the echoes subsided. "Everyone be prepared."

As they moved into the center of the cavern, they noticed a pool of water at the far. As they got closer to the pool, they could see that it was very shallow and crystal clear.

After studying the pool for a few moments, Six concluded that the pool of water must be coming from underneath the wall.

He looked at Doc curiously. "Do you think you could summon up enough prayer to make that puddle Holy Water?"

She pondered the small pond briefly and then shrugged. "I can try."

She walked forward, and the others moved to create a defensive perimeter around her. She bent down and slowly began a chant in Latin. Closing her eyes, Doc prayed, asking the Spirit of Christ to bless the water and to make it Holy.

"That should do it," she responded a short time later.

Six nodded and smiled. "Let's move on," he said.

The agent led the team toward the smaller passage Six spotted earlier. A short led them into another cavern. Approximately the same size as the previous cavern, the walls were rougher. They had almost a hand-carved look, and there were two other exits from this cavern. As the team entered, Six noticed a large misshapen hole in the cavern floor. Large enough to fit a compact car into, the hole was pitch black just below the surface of the hole, and all of them felt waves of malevolence coming from it.

God positioned himself over the small three-foot passage that led into the base of the cavern wall opposite from where they had entered. Heavy trained his machine gun on the passage at the other end of the cavern. Six, Doc, and Ghost walked closer to the dark hole in the floor. When Six shined his flashlight across the surface, he could not see any deeper than the edge as the light seemed to be absorbed at the very surface of the darkness. Ghost took a chemlight from his vest pocket and broke it to mix the chemicals. He tossed it into the middle of the darkness, and the inky black seemed to swallow the fluorescent tube whole. The darkness rippled where the chemstick had entered the surface.

Six looked at Doc and asked, "Is it me, or did that darkness actually... ripple?" The team leader was at a loss. "What the hell is that stuff?"

The priest calmly looked at her boss. "To paraphrase your answer to Deputy Folsom earlier, I believe you have answered your own question." After a pause, she continued, "It is Evil." The team heard the capital "E" in Doc's voice. "I believe this is a hellgate, and it is something that we do not have the ability or desire to deal with now."

Just then, the sniper behind them let out a yelp. They turned to look and saw him backing away from the hole he was guarding. A low growl could be heard coming from the hole.

Moments later, a large, bloated head and upper torso pulled itself out of the hole and clawed its way toward God. Trailing torn and bloody entrails behind as it crawled, the torso reached its desiccated hand for the team's sniper. God shook his head to clear it and aimed his rifle down at the creature's head. A single shot rang out, and the bloated head exploded, showering the area around the creature with gore. The agent wiped the tread of his boots on the rock to remove bits of brain matter from his shoes. He looked at the priest and raised an eyebrow.

Doc shrugged and said, "Zombie."

God shuddered. "Shall we toss a grenade in there to make sure nothing else is coming?"

Six shook his head. "We're in a cavern. It could collapse the whole thing. We'll let Boomer prep explosives and set a timer for our exit. All right, let's get moving."

At the far end of the cavern, the wide passageway sloped down and around to the right. There was a small pool of water on the left. Six looked at the water, and then at Doc, and cocked his eyebrows.

She leaned over the pool for a few seconds to study the water.

"It must be connected to the other," Doc announced. "This is already Holy."

Six nodded and led the team around the corner of the passageway. After a short passageway, they stepped out into a larger cavern. The wall across from them was almost thirty feet away, and the cavern stretched half again that from sidewall to sidewall. At the far end there was another pool of water, and this one looked deeper and murkier. It also ran through the passage that was the only other exit to the cavern. The team spread out and approached the shore of the pond. As the team leader looked through the narrow passageway across from him, Six noticed that the water continued through the passage and that he could see another cavern at the end of the passage.

In what had become her routine, Doc stepped up and prayed in Latin over the pond of water. The team spread out around her, making sure she stayed safe during the ritual. Six noticed that her garments began to glow blue, and he suddenly realized that they hadn't checked the water beforehand.

The water exploded outward, and two creatures leapt out from the water. The vampires were smoldering and smoking, with parts of their flesh melting away as the pool of Holy Water began to take its toll. A screaming vampire landed on each side of the priest.

As Six shouted a warning, one of the creatures struck Boomer, knocking her twenty feet away and into the cavern wall. The other creature struck Heavy and sent his bulk flying.

Both creatures turned to look at Doc and hissed, "Priesssssssssst!"

She grabbed her crucifix and thrust it toward the vampire on her left. The ornate cross flared to life, its pure light driving the shadows from the cavern and pinning the vampire to the cavern floor. She shouted in Latin at the vampires, and both screamed in agony and pure hatred.

Six, God, and Ghost opened fire on the vampire on Doc's right. Through the melting, acid-burned features, the creature snarled as the men poured a stream of silver and wood bullets into its flesh. The creature's torso nearly split in two, and the barely connected lower half landed in the Holy Water pool. New agony hit the vampire until rounds from Six and God found its misshapen skull to end its agony.

The other vampire was pinned in place with the power of Doc's faith while the Holy Water melted and desiccated its flesh.

Deputy Folsom stepped up and took aim at the creature. His first two shots hit the chest dead center, tearing through the vampire and knocking it flat. His final shot was a carefully aimed shot through the skull. Black blood and gore exploded out and fell into the Holy Water, sizzling and melting into nothingness.

Boomer and Heavy climbed to their feet.

The big man winced and held his right arm tight to his chest. "I think it dislocated my shoulder. I can't lift it at all."

The priest stepped up to the Heavy and said, "Take off your armor. I need to feel your shoulder."

The giant man stripped his armor off while the rest of the team took up positions around the two, with Six, God, and Ghost watching the cavern through the next passage, and Boomer and Folsom watching the area behind them.

The team leader tried his radio. "Spooky, Six. Do you copy?"

When there was no response from Spooky, he tried again, "Spooky, come in. This is Six. Do you copy?"

Again, no response.

"Must be this cavern mucking up the signal," Six muttered out loud.

Doc looked at Heavy and said, "Brace yourself. This is going to suck."

She gave a yank and a twist, sliding the shoulder back into its natural socket with an audible "pop."

The heavy gunner let out a string of curses.

"Sorry, Doc. I try not to curse around you," Heavy said after the pain had subsided. "Arm feels right. I should be good to go."

"Don't worry about it," replied Doc. "We'll x-ray your shoulder when we get back to town."

Six looked at his gunner and said, "You and I need to talk. You taught me a few new choice invectives I've never heard before. All set?"

Heavy flexed and moved his arm. "I'm a bit stiff, but I should be good." He picked up and cradled his machine gun to prove the point.

Everyone took the time to change their magazines and prep for the next passage.

"Alright, boys and girls, it looks like we have to get wet. God, you are up for point; Ghost will follow. You guys go through first and provide cover while we come through."

The sniper looked at the water in front of him. He tentatively stepped into the cold water and waded forward. As he got about six feet from the water's edge, the water level stopped rising, and the water leveled out to about thigh-deep. The monster hunter walked in after him, keeping his rifle up and out of the water. As they walked through the passage, the cavern on the other side seemed smaller.

God keyed his mic. "This cavern's about twenty-five by thirty. Has one other exit. Standby while we look around the corner."

The two men approached the bend and slowly moved around it. The passage narrowed and doubled back and opened into a small six-by-ten cavern. Looking around the small cavern, the men concluded that there were no other exits and that the cavern was obviously empty.

God keyed his mic again. "Dead end boss. Nothing back here but a small cavern. We're at the end."

"Copy that," Six responded. "Come on back through. We'll bug out."

He leaned over to his demolitions specialist. "Boomer, make a small charge on a timer that we can toss into the zombie hole. Key word: small."

Boomer pouted her lips and said, "Sure. I finally get to blow something up and you make me be reasonable." She grumbled as she assembled the charge.

The two agents waded back across to the vampire cavern. The team slowly walked back the way they had come. When they reached the zombie hole, Boomer set the timer for two minutes and tossed a small charge into the hole.

"Do you want me to toss a charge into the evil pit, boss?" The explosives expert looked pleadingly at her boss.

"How about we not pick a fight with a hellspawn right now," Doc interjected. "We have a bad enough time with vampires."

After a brief pause to really comprehend what the priest had said, Six nodded. "Good call. Negative on the bomb into the pit, Boomer. Alright, let's keep moving back up top."

The team cautiously wound their way back to the surface. Carefully maneuvering through the passages, each team member was alert and looking for trouble. They double checked every nook and hidden corner carefully to make sure they were not leaving any creatures alive down there—neither living nor unliving.

As they reached the first cavern, they all heard a frantic radio call from a rather panicked young agent.

"... Calling Six. Come in, Six. Repeat. Spooky calling Six. Come in, Six."

"Spooky, this is Six," the DHS leader broke in. "We're back. There is an underground cave system here, and we lost communication. We're all fine. We're coming back up now."

"Copy that, Six." The team could hear the relief in their electronics specialist's voice. "Everything is still clear up here."

Heavy was the last man to leave the cave system. As he mounted the last couple of stairs, he heard a rather loud muffled roar. The rumble came through his combat boots.

"Did you all feel that?" he asked as he looked at the others. "Just how much C4 did you use, Boomer?"

"I swear. I only used a small amount," Boomer promised. "Unless something else in there exploded, we should not have been able to hear it."

A waft of dust rose from the cavern stairs.

The heavy gunner pointed to it and said, "We might want to talk about how much is 'a little'." He chuckled as he climbed the stairs.

Six closed the doors and keyed his mic again. "Spooky, do we have any chain and locks in the War Wagon?"

There was a slight pause before Spooky responded. "Have a little chain. I also have a small welding torch. Would that work?"

Ten minutes later, the team met by the back hatch of the MRAP. Heavy returned from the house carrying a small torch in his hand.

"That door is chained shut, boss. I also welded the doors to each other and tack welded the outside seams. It would take a lot of work to get back down that hole."

"Great, Heavy. Sit down and rest your arm." Six looked at everyone else, including Spooky. "Ok, we need to tear this house apart. If it looks like a pertinent record, grab it. Spooky, you're on electronics. Don't worry about figuring out what's on them tonight. Just take the whole device, computer, etcetera. Check the garage. Check every nook and cranny thoroughly. I want every record. We need to find out what's going on in town."

"We will not be coming back to this location. We will burn the house down, and then DHS is seizing the land and everything on it. So grab every scrap, every note, and every bit of information. Pile it in the truck, and we'll sort it tomorrow."

Just over one hour later, the team had gathered every electronic device and bit of information in the house. From the deceased familiars' cell phones to the pharmacist's computer and tablet, everything that contained a microchip was stored carefully in the back of the truck. All the doctor's paper files were sorted in stacks on the ground outside. By the time the team had collected all of the information, the contents filled the back of the MRAP. There was only room inside for the driver and one passenger.

Spooky climbed up into the driver's seat, and Doc rode shotgun in the passenger's seat. The sniper climbed through the turret hatch on top and sat in what was becoming his usual perch. Boomer spread accelerant around the house to ensure a hot and fierce burning. After she set a small detonator, she climbed up on the truck. The rest of the team climbed onto the running boards outside of the MRAP for the short trip down the winding driveway. Spooky drove to the bottom of the hill and parked across the driveway to completely block access to the property.

Boomer's face lit up when she pressed the detonator. The sparkle in her eyes was soon reflected from the hillside as flames lapped at the interior of the house on the hill. Within thirty seconds, the entire structure was ablaze and Six could hear sirens coming from town. When the fire engines arrived, the DHS agent waved his badge and informed the trucks that they were only allowed to go up the drive to make sure that a wildfire did not result from the intense flames that had set the house ablaze. They were not, under any circumstance, allowed to extinguish the house fire.

Six sent Heavy and God up to the house with the firemen just to make sure the emergency crews let the blaze fully consume the house.

By three o'clock in the morning, the flames were out. The team rode back to the hotel to get some sleep before they would begin to tackle the mountain of information that was in the back of their War Wagon.

21

DO-RIGHT

Hotel, Trinidad, Colorado.

I t was a cold, foggy morning when Spooky woke up to pounding on the ramp door. He stiffly climbed out of his chair in the War Wagon and walked to the back. As he looked out the gun port, he saw Six holding two cups of coffee in a cardboard drink carrier. The young agent unlocked the ramp and dropped it to the parking lot, raising dust as the ramp hit the pavement.

The lead agent climbed up the ramp and handed the coffee to the junior analyst. "Have you started working on anything yet?" Six inquired.

Spooky took a long drink of coffee. He finally spoke, "Ahh, the nectar of the gods. Normally, I'm an energy drink guy, but this is perfect. No, I haven't worked on anything we got last night."

He looked down at his wrist computer and said, "It looks like we've got some other information, though. When we found out that the pharmacist was involved, I asked HQ to run a telephone records dump and to correlate it to major activity, known friends, and a couple other parameters. It looks like they sent me a file."

Spooky walked over and dropped into his workstation seat. After only a few moments of typing, he soon brought up a document and displayed it on his main screen. The analyst looked it over carefully and pointed out interesting facts.

"Look there," Spooky said as he pointed to a telephone number in his document. "Our giggling vamp had never contacted this particular phone number until after the slaughter of the sheriff, mayor, and FBI guys." He gestured to another number and continued, "He also kept frequent contact with this hospital number."

Spooky bent over and typed furiously, muttering as he went. "Let's see... If we cross populate here... What if we looked at it this way? Oh, that's interesting!" Six could not keep up with whatever his specialist was doing between his dual monitors. The team leader finally gave up and sat back to savor his coffee. He figured that Spooky would let him know when he found something interesting. Six closed his eyes.

"That's IT!" Spooky's shout startled Six, and he spilled now-cold coffee over his hand. The agent was looking at him expectantly.

Six looked back at his electronics genius and said, "What do you have, Spooky?"

He turned and pointed at three phone numbers buried amidst the multitude of screens and windows. "This top one is the deputy mayor's number—her private office line. He's been making several calls a day to her since the massacre. According to her private schedule, he's also been in to see the now-acting Mayor Desiree Marshall three times. There isn't any reason for him to be talking to her quite that much, especially with no other history within the last three years."

He pointed at the other two highlighted numbers on his screen. "This top one goes to a specific line in the hospital. It just so happens that this one is the private office line of the county coroner, Bill Stewart. They talked occasionally before, but it ramped up all of a sudden after we took out that ambush."

Spooky sipped his now-cold coffee and then looked at the cup in disgust. He set the cup down and continued. "This one was harder to run down. It seems to be one of those burn phones. Unfortunately, for our quisling coroner, he didn't, in fact, throw it away. In fact, it's on and still broadcasting. We've traced it to the hospital, and it's most likely in the morgue with him. How stupid can you be to buy a throwaway phone and keep it? It seems like these are the only two people that are connected to the drug guy's vamp side."

The lead agent nodded and smiled. He clasped Spooky on the shoulder hard enough to make him wince. "Great work, Spooky," Six said. "We still need to process the rest of the information just to make sure we don't miss anything. We'll do that at the base ops. Until then, go take a shower and wake up. We'll need you in top form, and it's been a while since you've left that seat. I'll stay put until someone else comes out."

"Will do, boss," Spooky replied with a sheepish grin.

The young agent peeled himself back out of his chair and grabbed his clothing bag and opened the ramp. He walked down the ramp and brushed past Boomer as she headed toward the War Wagon to speak to Six.

TWO HOURS LATER, MOST OF THE TEAM WAS IN THE CONFERENCE ROOM sorting through the mountains of paper and electronic data they had collected the night before. Spooky had his forensic computer tools running overtime and was merrily mining all the electronic data he could retrieve from the former pharmacist's phone and computer. Ghost, assisted by Heavy and Boomer, led the effort to gather any usable data from the paper files. Doc was on the phone with her Vatican contacts in an effort to hunt down research of a more esoteric nature.

About a mile down the road, Six walked into the acting sheriff's office with Deputy Christian Folsom in tow. Six reached out to shake the sheriff's hand while the deputy stood at attention. The deputy looked like had not slept for two full days, and the two days' growth of beard and tousled hair was far from the clean, professional looks he normally wore. His wrinkled and smudged uniform attested to his sleepless night. The acting sheriff looked almost as bad as her deputy. The dark circles under her eyes and wrinkled uniform showed that her past couple days had been rough as well. She motioned for the two men to sit in the seats across from her as she sat behind her desk.

She looked at her deputy with care in her eyes. "How are you doing, Deputy?" she asked with a tone of concern in her voice. "I'm so sorry for your loss. We'll do everything we can to help you get through this... that's what your Trinidad family is here for."

Christian wearily nodded and then spoke. "Honestly? I'm numb. I don't think I've hit the full impact yet."

The sheriff nodded. She kept her voice smooth, but it grew cold and hard. "You should be off work now. What are you doing in uniform? What is this about you responding to the scene last night at Virgil's house? Have you completely lost it?"

The DHS agent took this opportunity to speak up, earning a grateful smile from Christian and a cold glare from the sheriff. "Sheriff Sweeney, I believe I can answer all of your questions. Your deputy was a great help to us last night as we ran down some local sources that seem to have been involved in the original murders that brought us here, as well as the murders of the sheriff, mayor, and FBI agents. Those sources were also involved in the murders of the deputy's family and the older couple that night. Deputy Folsom offered his services, and I made the choice to bring him on board in our investigation."

The sheriff turned her glare on her deputy and then returned to the agent. "You caught the suspects in the death of his family. In fact, you told me that you have been able to track down several of the people that are turning my city into a slaughterhouse. How can a junior deputy, just out of POST training help you?"

Six shook his head and said, "I'm sorry, sheriff. I cannot give you specific information, as it is classified way above your pay grade. But I am here to tell you that as of last night, and for the foreseeable future, he needs to be officially seconded to my team." Six continued, "Deputy Folsom will act on our authority, and I expect that he will be temporarily removed from his duty shifts until he is no longer working with my team. I realize that you would normally provide compassionate leave, but he is not currently taking it. He will be working for me."

The sheriff stood and shook her finger at Six. Her voice rose to a shout. "How dare you come into my town, into my office, and treat me and my department like this? You do NOT have the authority to unilaterally second one of my deputies. You sure as hell do not have the authority to keep him from compassionate leave after his family was slaughtered by the guys you are chasing. I'm about done with you and your team using my town for a shooting range. Get out of my office. And get out of my county."

The federal agent calmly stood and reached into the breast pocket of his fatigues. He withdrew his credentials and slowly opened them in the sheriff's line of sight. "I assure you, Sheriff Sweeney. I have the full authority to do what I am doing. You do not want the shit storm I can rain down on your county. I, Special Agent Burt Holstein, of the Department of Homeland Security, formally require you to assist me and my team to accomplish our mission. You are to help us within your legal and lawful power, and you will not interfere with, or retaliate for, the work that Deputy Christian Folsom will be performing for my team. Do you understand?"

Six was glad to see the faint greenish glow emanating from his credentials. He was getting a handle on this esoteric-hero stuff. The sheriff's eyes glazed over briefly, and then her face re-animated. The anger and resentment visibly drained from her. She was calm, but her posture still seemed tense.

The sheriff nodded and gritted her teeth. After a few moments, she responded, "I understand. And I can't wait until you are out of my county."

The agent's tight smile never reached his eyes. "Believe me, I can't wait either," he said. He motioned for the deputy to stand and then turned and walked toward the door.

As they walked out of her office, he looked at the deputy and said, "Let's stop by your supply room to get you a couple new uniforms, and then we'll drive by your house to pick up some clothes and toiletries."

AN HOUR LATER, THE TWO MEN ARRIVED AT THE BASE OPS IN THE deputy's pickup truck. Six and Christian walked into the conference room and were met with a massive pile of paperwork that threatened to collapse and bury those around the table under old records. The lead agent looked around and said, "All right team, the good deputy is officially ours, at least for the time being. What do we have?"

Ghost spoke up first, "We've confirmed our earlier suspicions, bossman. Acting Mayor Desiree Marshall is one of the vampire's creatures, most likely a familiar. Spooky also traced down the other phone. It belongs to our twitchy friend, Bill Stewart, the coroner. He's likely another familiar. We confirmed both of these connections through the electronics we confiscated."

"Great job," Six said with a smile. "So what do we know about familiars? Doc? Ghost?"

The priest looked down as she read from her notes, "My researchers at the Vatican tell me that familiars are typically humans who are enthralled by the vampire through a psychic hold, or who willingly give themselves to the vamp. The stronger the vamp, the stronger the connection and hold. If this master is the one who made them familiars, then they should be well connected."

"Great, but how do we break them? Silver? Stake?" questioned Six.

Doc shook her head. "No. These are actual, unmodified humans. Their one weakness is that they get real twitchy and cannot help but react when someone presses too far about their master. Indirect questions make them act as if they are in the throes of drug with-drawal. They get nervous ticks and even have a hard time talking. Direct questions seem to just set them off, so ask them questions."

Ghost asked a question. "Can familiars be cured? Can the vampire's hold be broken?"

Again, the priest shook her head and continued, "No. The only way they can be 'cured' is to kill the master they are connected to. Unfortunately, this often drives them insane. This mental break has been permanent for every subject the Vatican has seen. But some-times, it's the best way to make them talk."

Six looked at the team and said, "Let's get this party started. We can either wait until the vamps attack again, or we can have a chat with their pet familiars, and step up the action. Anyone favor wait-ing?" He looked around to see his team shaking their heads.

"Pre-emptive strike it is. We need a location and plan of attack for the two pets. We'll have to hit them simultaneously, or they will get spooked. Do we know where they currently are?"

Spooky waved to get the team leader's attention. "Yeah, boss. The mayor is in her office at city hall, and according to her calendar, she is scheduled to be there all day. The quisling coroner is also in his office. This should be a simple divide-and-conquer."

Six divided the team. "Ghost and Heavy, you guys and Do-Right are Alpha Team, with me. We'll be talking to the Mayor. Spooky, you'll be driving the War Wagon and monitoring status while we are inside." Spooky started laughing, trying to keep quiet, but failing.

Six tried to ignore the young genius and continued with his assignments. "Doc and Boomer, take God with you. You guys are Beta Team. You go have a chat with the creepy coroner. Everyone be on their guard. We need to find out where the master vampire is, and what he's planning."

"Be ready to move out quickly. We may have to act on information faster than we had planned. Questions?"

Ghost raised a hand. "Yeah, boss. What is our load out for this?" he asked. "I'm not sure the full tac gear is appropriate for these interviews."

Six nodded in agreement with Ghost. "Good call," Six said. "Load out is the following: no rifles; no machine gun, Heavy; pistols only. This means no tactical armor. Simple fatigues. And make sure you take your credentials and your sidearm. Anything else?"

After not hearing a response, their leader continued. "Let's load 'em up, then. Stow your heavy gear in the 'Wagon, and Beta can head out across the parking lot."

The young agent was still laughing as tears streamed down his face. The senior agent glared at him. "What in the hell are you laughing at?" the agent demanded.

Spooky barely wheezed his answer: "Do-Right. The Canadian Mountie who rides his horse backwards." He devolved into even more laughter.

By this time, the rest of the team began to chuckle. Doc broke into outright laughter and exclaimed, "I used to love that show!"

Six looked at Christian. "Sorry, kid. I didn't think they'd catch the reference. Should've known Spooky would pick it up."

Christian smiled with everyone else. He knew that this laughter was not directed at him. The team needed something to laugh about, and a silly nickname seemed to fit the bill.

"That's ok, boss. I kind of like it," said Christian. "Frankly, it's how I feel right now."

The laughter eventually died down and the oppressive weight in the room seemed to have been lifted. With all the death and horror that the team had seen over the last couple of days, they needed a laugh. Christian felt himself give a small smile for the first time in what felt like days. He realized that he desperately wanted to be on this team when they left Trinidad. He only hoped that they saw his value.

Beta Team walked across the now familiar parking lot as they made their way to the hospital. Waving to the security guard as they passed, they walked down the stairs to the basement. Las Animas County Medical Examiner Bill Stewart was sitting behind his desk, writing notes and working on the unceasing paperwork that his job demanded.

Doc knocked on the frame of his door. Her voice was warm as she asked, "Hey, Doctor Stewart? Do you have a few minutes to talk?"

Across town, Spooky pulled the enormous War Wagon across three parking spaces in front of the city/county building. When he noticed his boss's questioning look, the agent smiled and said, "What are they going to do, to me? I'd like to see them try."

Six shook his head as the crew popped the hatch and scrambled out of the truck. When they had dismounted, Spooky closed the hatch from inside and sealed the vehicle so he could begin to monitor his electronics.

The rest of Alpha Team walked through the front doors of the building.

Six heard his electronics expert in his ear proclaim, "I'm into the camera system. I've got eyes on you."

The DHS agent subvocalized a brief "Copy" as the team walked toward the stairs to the second floor. As they approached the mayor's office, Six noticed the mayor's administrator at the desk and two plainclothes police officers wearing suits who were standing at attention outside the door to the mayor's inner sanctum.

The federal agent smiled his most polite smile and drew his badge. Flashing the credentials at the administrator, he said, "Special Agent Burt Holstein, Department of Homeland Security. I would like to meet with the mayor, please."

The raven-haired administrator seemed unfazed by the credentials. "I'm sorry, Agent Holstein," she replied. "The mayor is very busy right now and is getting ready to leave for a meeting in the next few minutes. I could maybe work you in... tomorrow?"

Six continued to smile, but his tone grew colder and harder. "You don't seem to understand. I'm being polite right now, but I'm losing my patience. I will need to see the mayor right now. Not tomorrow. Not later. Now. You can either clear us through the doors, or we will go through the doors, anyway. It is your choice."

The two bodyguards next to the door tensed and took a step toward the agent. Heavy calmly stepped in between the two officers and his boss. Smiling, he crossed his massive arms over his chest. His sleeveless t-shirt and BDU pants only accentuated the mountain of muscle that the bodybuilder was carrying. The big man's deep voice was soft and warning. "You fellas need to calm down right now. You know we're federal agents. Do not start something that you don't me want to finish."

The administrator swallowed nervously as she glanced back and forth between the stand-off in front of the door and the agent in front of her. Six made the decision for her and continued, "Listen, Miss Adams. I'm going to go in there now. Please feel free to let her know I'm here."

Six, Ghost, and Christian all walked past the guards. The DHS agent opened the doors, and they filed into the inner office as the administrator frantically called her boss.

"I'm going to wait out here, boss," Heavy said as he stared at the two bodyguards. "Holler if you need me."

Ghost closed the double doors behind the trio as they entered, sealing out the noise of the building. It was a plush office with a large oak desk and comfortable furniture. The mayor was placing the phone on its receiver as Six approached her desk.

Desiree Marshall was a slim African American woman with classical features and long hair that she wore down her back. She had spent her entire life in Trinidad and Las Animas County and had worked her way up the political ladder with grit, determination, and a backbone of solid steel. Capable of listening to her constituents and verbally flaying her opponents, she was used to her enemies underestimating her exactly one time. As acting mayor, Ms. Marshall would not put up with these federal agents barging into her office uninvited.

Six did not get a chance to speak; Mayor Marshall verbally attacked him before he came to a stop.

"Just what do you think you are doing?" she demanded. "Bullying past my administrator and physically threatening my police officers? I don't care what kind of badge you have. I'll have it in my desk before this week is out. I have an entire collection of badges from sanctimonious law enforcement pricks that I've had fired over the years." She smiled a hungry grin. "It will be nice to add a DHS badge to the collection."

The agent held up his hands to ward off the tirade. "Madam Mayor, I'm sorry that I had to barge in on your busy schedule, but I had some very important information that I had to talk to you about. It's about our investigation here in Trinidad. I believe that we're almost wrapped up. Can you spare a couple of minutes?"

The mayor's demeanor changed visibly from overtly hostile to coldly calculating. "If it will get you out of my town faster, I will spare you three minutes—no more."

"Yes, ma'am," the agent replied. "I can honestly say that it won't take more than that. In fact, I actually have one quick question before I tell you what we discovered."

"Well?" the mayor demanded impatiently. "What's your question?"

"Are you a familiar for the vampire master?"

The mayor snapped. Her conservative, calf-length skirt tore as she leapt across the desk at Six. Her eyes were wide with insanity, and she growled as she rushed at him. He was not expecting the direct attack and barely warded off her fists as she aimed punches at his face and throat.

Six grabbed her arms in his powerful hands as he tried to keep the feral woman off of him, all the while yelling for the deputy to grab his handcuffs. The mayor surged, howled and ripped her arms out of the agent's hands. Six responded by with a solid punch that stunned the mayor and a wild haymaker that connected to her jaw. The mayor fell as if pole-axed, thumping to the floor as the doors burst open. The bodyguards ran inside with weapons drawn pointing them at the team.

"Freeze. Police!" yelled the officers.

Six drew his sidearm with lightning speed, countering with, "Federal Agents!"

It quickly became a standoff—until Heavy stepped into the room. The mountainous agent slammed a thick hand across the arms of each police officer hard enough to make them drop their pistols. Grabbing the police officers by the back of their tailored jackets, he hauled them off of their feet and turned them around to face him. He shook them until he was sure he had their attention.

Six paused to take a breath, and then said, "The mayor is under arrest for assaulting a federal agent: me. The deputy will handcuff her, and we will take her with us. Do you understand?"

When the two officers reluctantly nodded, the big agent slowly put them back on their feet. Six nodded to Heavy and motioned for Ghost to help Christian take the mayor out to the truck.

He keyed his radio. "Spooky, Six. Fire up the Wagon. We have a prisoner."

Heavy was the last to leave the office area. He remained behind to make sure that no one interfered. He turned and looked at the still stunned police officers. As he glanced around the posh office area, he muttered under his breath, "I hate politics..."

22

FAMILIARS

Mt. San Rafael Hospital, Trinidad, Colorado.

While the Beta Team talked with Medical Examiner Bill Stewart in his office, God waited outside the cramped office and watched the halls. He noted that the crematorium was shut down and empty.

"Doctor Stewart, do you have those files for the original group of deceased that brought us here?" asked Doc. "I'd like to take another look at the files... and at the bodies," she explained.

The doctor hesitated as he handed over his files. Boomer noticed his hands and forehead were sweaty despite the cool temperature of the lab. He looked guilty of something, and she knew what it was.

After Doc quickly reviewed several files, she looked up at Stewart and asked him for some help. "I want to take another look at the post-mortem wounds," she explained.

"Sure," replied Stewart. "Which one did you want to start with?"

After the priest looked at the folders she said, "Let's start with that last one. The remains will be freshest."

Stewart nodded, and they all left the office.

Doc and Stewart donned surgical gowns and gloves and retrieved the remains from the cooler. Boomer stood near Stewart, subtly boxing him in against a wall.

The DHS medic began pointing out the various slashing and tearing wounds.

"What did you determine did these wounds? Was it some sort of big cat?" Doc questioned as she poked and prodded the injuries.

Stewart nodded fitfully. "Y-Y-Yes," he stammered. "A big cat, maybe a mountain lion. Why do you ask?"

Doc looked at him and then back to the corpse. She continued, "Because these bites have the same characteristics as human bites, albeit bites made by sharper teeth. Where did you get your degree from, Doctor?"

"Princeton," the doctor angrily replied. "I graduated with honors forty-four years ago. What of it?"

The priest looked quizzically at the man before her. "Because I don't understand how someone with your experience and time can mistake an obviously human series of bites for big cat bites," she continued. "They look nothing alike. Can you explain that?"

The doctor raised his voice shrilly and caught the attention of the sniper in the hallway. "I've got more experience with big cat mauling than you ever will! I'm telling you, this is a big cat. Post mortem."

Hearing the rising voices, God approached the lab, and placed his hand lightly on his sidearm. He reached for the door leading into the lab.

Doc looked at Doctor Stewart and calmly explained, "That's another thing. These wounds were not post mortem. These wounds were the cause of death. I'm really not sure how you missed that. There are two choices: either you are hugely incompetent, or you are covering up something. Which is it?"

The doctor paled at her words. He tried to choke out an answer, but Doc cut him off again.

"If I had to guess, I'd guess that no one can be this incompetent and hold a Medical Examiner position in this day and age, which leaves me with one real option: you are covering up for someone... possibly the real murderers?"

The coroner was ashen and trembled at the accusation.

Doc's voice took on a light, conversational tone as she continued. "Although I do have to admit one thing: the monsters that did this to these victims are technically more creature than human."

She looked Dr. Stewart straight in the eye. Her voice grew quiet as she continued. "How long have you been a familiar, Bill?" she questioned.

The priest was not sure what to expect, but the suddenness and target of Dr. Stewart's attack took her off-guard. In one frantic movement, the coroner grabbed a scalpel from the instrument tray and swung wildly at Boomer who was standing next to him. The scalpel missed the explosives expert's throat by less than an inch. The doctor overbalanced on the swing, and the agent's instinctive kick caught him in the gut. The kick drove the air from his lungs, doubled him over, and left him struggling to breathe.

When he saw the attack, God burst through lab door, running to help his teammates. Doc stepped back out of the sniper's way as God barreled into the fray, knocking aside the scalpel still clutched in Dr. Stewart's hand. A hard punch to the forearm made the doctor's hand go numb, and he dropped the improvised weapon. Boomer delivered another kick to the M.E., and her combat boot connected squarely between the doctor's legs, driving the man to the floor in agony.

God grabbed and twisted the doctor's wrists behind his torso, roughly hauling him up from the floor, and planted him in a nearby chair. A quick search around the office produced some industrial strength zip-ties. The sniper secured the struggling coroner to his desk chair. The sniper leaned over the doctor and whispered, "Next time, don't attack a woman who is trained in combat. Especially if she's already pissed at you."

He patted the doctor on the head and walked over to where the rest of his team stood.

Doc looked at both of the other agents and chuckled. "Mental note, if you ask a familiar if they are, in fact, a familiar, they get violent. Good to know. So now what?"

God looked at her and said, "Let's see how the other team is doing. See what Six wants us to do." He keyed his radio. "Six, God. What's your status?"

"Six. We have one in custody for interrogation. You?"

The sniper answered, "We've got one as well. Why don't you come to the morgue? It's quiet, and there's a back entrance for privacy."

"That's a great idea, God. We'll be there in five. Six out." The team leader sounded stressed.

The stoic sniper looked at his teammates, "Well, seems like the party is coming to us."

FIVE MINUTES LATER, THE MRAP BACKED UP TO THE MORGUE'S entrance. As the back hatch opened, two police cars and a sheriff's patrol car pulled in and blocked the MRAP.

Six looked at the officers and the sheriff as they got out of their respective vehicles, and he looked back at his team.

"Heavy, you're with me," Six said. "Spooky, stay in the truck. Ghost, Do-Right, you guys escort the mayor inside and secure her with the coroner. I'll take care of these guys."

The lead agent thought for a moment and made a snap decision.

"Spooky. Contact the HRT and get them deployed over here right away. I want about half of them here; the rest should go to the base ops and secure the files."

Six turned, and Heavy climbed down out of the back of the War Wagon to stand beside him. They walked calmly over to the officers who were gathering around the black MRAP. As they approached, the murmurs and talking grew louder and angrier.

Six keyed his radio and subvocalized so the gathering officers could not hear him. "Spooky, ETA on the HRT?"

"Two minutes, boss," Spooky replied.

Six raised his hands up to shoulder level in an effort to calm the growing voices. "Ladies and gentlemen, before you get too angry, let's talk about what's going on."

He nodded to a couple of the people in the group. "Chief. Sheriff. I'm glad you are here as well. Let me explain what happened."

"Your team kidnapped the mayor, Agent Holstein," Sheriff

Sweeney interrupted in a voice as brittle as glass. "What are you doing to this town?"

The federal agent looked over the restless crowd of uniforms, stalling until he saw one of the FBI trucks pull around the corner. As the HRT agents climbed out of the truck, Six addressed the group.

"I understand that there are a lot of questions today. Mayor Marshall is currently in my custody. She is under arrest for attacking a federal law enforcement officer, namely me. Our investigation led us to the acting mayor and the coroner as potential leads in the case."

"As it turns out, both are in custody because we believe they have a connection with the terrorist cell that's been targeting this town. I will update you on our progress, as I can, without revealing classified information in an ongoing investigation. That is all I can tell you at this time."

The grumblings were cut short, and the crowd of officers dispersed when the armed and armored HRT team took up station around the MRAP and in front of the hospital door.

"Thank you for moving so quickly, commander," Six said as he addressed the FBI's team lead. "I'll handle security inside. If we can have you guys on site here for the next couple of hours, and on site over at our ops base during that time as well, we would appreciate it. We are close to wrapping up this mess."

"I hope so, Agent Holstein," the commander said as he looked at Six. "I've done some checking. You and your team are brand new to federal service, and we don't work the same here in the states as you did in Iraq."

The DHS agent chuckled. "Believe me, I know that. I'm just doing the best job I can to take down these bad guys," he said.

Six and Heavy turned to walk through the loading dock doors and left Spooky enclosed in the War Wagon surrounded by HRT.

As the men walked into the morgue, Six observed that both familiars had been securely fastened to chairs and that the chairs were three or four feet apart and faced away from each other. As they sat back-to-back, the two snarling people in front of him could not see or take their cues from each other.

Six smiled and walked into the mayor's line of sight.

"Madam Mayor, this is how this session will go. You can either cooperate and answer my questions or cooperate after we torture you. It is completely your choice. What do you say... want to take the easy route?"

The mayor looked sullen and glared at the agent with her head bowed low and her hair covering part of her face.

"You will not get away with this. He will find you and rip your throat out," the mayor threatened.

"All right, mayor. I'll take that as the obvious 'F-U' that you intended it for. Let's see what the coroner has to say."

Six moved into Doctor Stewart's line of sight. "What do you say, Bill? Easy or hard? Your choice."

The coroner just spat. His phlegm hit the floor by the agent's foot. Six backed away and looked at the rest of the team in disgust.

"The hard way it is then. Let's break these fools."

Doc stepped forward and said, "May I try something first, boss? I have an idea that just might get us some information."

Six nodded to her, and she moved to stand in front of the coroner. The priest leafed through her leather-bound book again and found the page she wanted. She looked up and placed her hand on the coroner's forehead, and then she spoke in Latin.

The effect of her liturgy was instantaneous: Doctor Stewart looked like he had been electrocuted. The energy that ran through his body froze his muscles, and he began to convulse. The lead agent looked at Doc in alarm, but she never stopped reading from her book. Stewart rocked back and forth in his chair.

Drool ran out between his lips as he muttered, "Cannot betray master... Going north... Cannot betray north... Going master..."

The mayor hissed at the coroner. She craned her head around to see him and threatened, "Shut up, fool. Do not betray Zachariah."

The coroner hissed at the name. "No. Mustn't betray him. No."

Six looked between the two prisoners and then approached the mayor.

"So, Zachariah is your master, huh?" he questioned.

"You are not worthy to speak his name. Shut your mouth, interloper," the mayor hissed. "You cannot stop our master. Soon everyone will get their reward."

Six turned to Doc and asked, "Anything ring a bell with this Zachariah character?"

While the priest shook her head, Ghost nodded and said, "I can't believe it. The rumor is true."

The entire team turned to look at the esoteric hunter. He continued, "Look, there have been rumors of an ancient master out here somewhere. He's supposed to be at least a couple hundred years old. If so, he's powerful. Twice in my prior life, I came across a reference to this 'Zachariah.' If he's mixed up in this, he's been here for quite some time."

Ghost turned to the mayor. "How long have you known your master?" he inquired.

Mayor Marshall hissed and squirmed to get free. "I will not tell you anything more."

Doc approached the mayor and laid her hand on the mayor's forehead. Doc spoke in the same Latin that the team heard earlier.

But the mayor did not react as the doctor had—she laughed instead.

"Fool. I have been with the master for a long time, I am immune to your parlor tricks and beliefs in a dead god. That will not work on me."

Six knelt down to look her in the eye.

Calmly and coldly, the agent whispered, "I don't care if you are not afraid of God. You should be afraid of me. I have the authority to do with you as I please. If you do not help me, you will regret it when this is over. After I find and kill Zachariah, I will then personally take you to one of those secret little government holes designed specifically for terrorists. You will disappear. Forever."

The mayor blanched but attempted to put on a brave face. "You cannot. There are enough people in this town that know you took me. The news will be all over this story."

Six smiled coldly. "I have the authority. And you are part of the terrorists that were attacking this town. Your people won't care about you. But none of that matters. You will tell me what I want to know."

The mayor shook her head.

"Never. I would never betray the master."

The agent smiled and tilted his head at the coroner who was regaining some semblance of coherence.

The agent's voice dropped to a whisper as he leaned closer to the mayor's ear. "You don't have to betray Zachariah. Your fellow familiar will. He can't stand the pain. And when I'm done with him, you will be next."

Six pulled a roll of duct tape from his fatigues and placed a strip over the mayor's mouth. He stood, drew his gun, and aimed it at the corpse that was still laying on the examination table. He motioned Boomer out of the firing line and wordlessly cautioned everyone to protect their ears. When his team had all plugged their ears, he pulled the trigger twice. The shots echoed in the small lab, and the corpse twitched at the impact of each bullet.

Six walked around to face the coroner. Doctor Stewart's face was ashen, and he violently twisted his neck to see the mayor.

The lead agent knelt down and stared silently at the coroner. After a brief pause, Six spoke.

"The mayor decided not to cooperate," Six said in a casual, conversational tone. "Do you want the same fate? There is no vampire present, so you will not be coming back. Now, what information do you have for me?"

"Don't kill me, please!" the coroner pleaded almost immediately. "All I know is that Zachariah is the master. He's working with some scientist in some small town north of Trinidad. I swear, I don't know anything more."

Six looked at his second-in-command.

"Do you believe him? Does that sound like Zachariah?" questioned Six.

Ghost shrugged.

"He's always been a legend. It's hard to know which stories are true and which are ones that he made up to scare the humans," explained Ghost. "Best guess? Yeah. It sounds plausible. Although why he is working with a scientist kind of scares the crap out of me."

Six looked at the coroner again. "What do we do with him?" he asked. "We can't turn him loose."

Ghost looked at his boss. "We have two options," Ghost offered. "Take them to Gitmo or kill them. Your choice."

The lead agent nodded.

"Let me think about it," he said. "Tape up the doctor's mouth. I want to have a chat with the mayor again."

As Ghost taped up the doctor's mouth, Six walked out of the lab to retrieve another chair from the office. He placed the straight-backed chair directly in front of the Mayor and sat backwards on the chair, protecting his chest and groin with the chair back.

The agent reached out and roughly ripped off the tape from the mayor's mouth. She gasped as several layers of skin stuck to the tape. He balled up the sticky tape and leaned over.

"Which scientist is Zachariah working with?" he pointedly asked.

Her reply was immediate, "You are not fit to speak his name. I don't know which scientist."

Six smiled and drew his knife from its scabbard at his side. He gazed at the exquisite finish and razor-sharp edge on his favorite Marine Ka-Bar fighting knife. Balancing the heft of the blade on an open palm, he waved the blade in front of the mayor's eyes.

"What are you trying to do, threaten me? You can't touch me," she said with a sneer.

Six smiled, flipped the knife in the air, grabbed the hilt so that the blade was pointing down, and drove the blade into the mayor's left thigh. The razor edge easily sliced through the skirt covering her thigh, through the meat of her thigh, and into the bone itself.

The mayor screamed. A shrieking and wailing cry that was testament to her pain.

Six bore his weight down on the knife. Leaning over, he looked into the mayor's panicked gaze and said, "Do I have your attention yet, Mayor?"

The mayor nodded and stopped screaming. She whimpered in agony.

The agent calmly asked again, "Who is Zachariah working with? Where is this scientist's lab located?"

The mayor shook her head, refusing to speak through the pain.

He wiggled the knife back and forth. Excruciating agony flashed up the mayor's leg, and she let out a new series of howls.

"Feel like talking yet?" Six ask conversationally.

The mayor nodded.

"Doctor Kaine. He has a lab up north in Divide. For god's sake, just take the knife out already," she pleaded.

Six continued to pry. "See, now I'm starting to believe you. How long has he been in the area?"

With tears streaming down her face, she admitted, "About twenty years."

"What is he planning?" questioned Six.

The mayor stopped and shook her head. Six took that as a cue and once again leaned on the knife, grinding the tip into the mayor's femur and ensuring her cooperation.

"All right, I'll tell," she relented. "The doctor is turning the vampire virus into a weapon. That's all I know."

Six looked at the priest and said, "I hate to say this, Doc, but these guys weren't all that tough to break."

The priest calmly regarded her boss. "I'm pretty sure the Vatican would loathe to use that method of information extraction," she said.

Six smiled, "Except for that darn Inquisition." The team leader stood up out of his chair and called Ghost and Doc out of the exam lab and into the coroner's office. The three walked into the office, and the senior agent asked, "Doc, can these guys be restored? Can we break the spell that Zachariah has over them?"

The priest shook her head. "These two are far too gone for them to ever be cured," she said. "Either throw them into a psych ward somewhere dark and dirty or kill them. Those are the only two humane options available. Once we kill the master, they'll be completely insane."

Ghost knew that his boss would want to kill them, and he was becoming increasingly bothered by the growing human body count. He knew he had to say something.

"So let's use that to our advantage," the monster hunter suggested. "Once we kill this master, they should go crazy. Toss 'em in an institution where no one will talk to them. If we kill them, we have to explain how and why they died in our custody. If they go bat-crap crazy, who cares what they say about us, or vampires, or anything?"

Six's smile was cold.

"I like that solution," he said. "Saves the problems. We just need to get them locked up until we kill the bad guy."

He called for Do-Right.

"Deputy, can we drop these two into solitary cells, at least for a day or two?" asked Six.

Christian nodded. "Yes, I think the sheriff will cooperate. I'll contact some deputies that I know so they can keep an eye on them."

Six nodded and said, "Set it up. If you have any problems, let me know. I'll deal with it."

He walked over to the prisoners while the deputy made the phone calls.

The mayor was whimpering in agony as blood seeped slowly from the wound in her thigh. "So, do you believe us? We told you the truth. What are you going to do now?" she pleaded.

Six replied coldly, "Yes, I believe you. I also know that I need to keep you out of the way while we go kill your master. You're going to jail. We'll transport you to Gitmo when we get back."

The mayor screamed in rage and violently jerked at her bindings to get loose.

The senior agent leaned down and said, "Calm down, or I will knock you out. Your choice."

Six looked pointedly at the bleeding wound on the mayor's leg, and the mayor immediately calmed down.

Six looked at his team. "Doc, bandage up the mayor and the coroner so they can sit in a cell. Put the bodies of the original victims into the furnaces and fire up the crematorium. Let's clean up and figure out where we are going next."

Six keyed his radio and spoke, "Spooky, did you get all the particulars?"

"Got 'em, boss," Spooky responded. "In fact, I've got a location on this scientist, and you aren't going to believe where this guy is hiding."

III

INCURSION

23

PLANNING

Pueblo Memorial Airport, Pueblo, Colorado

At the west end of the airplane parking ramp, far away from the terminal of Pueblo Memorial Airport sat a building that looked like an aircraft hanger, its blue and gray exterior large enough to house a military cargo jet. Instead, it was the main fuel office and depot for the airport with rows of fuel pumps and a small office attached to the outside. A large black MRAP marked as "Police/Rescue" and "Department of Homeland Security" eased its way through the security gate mounted in the airport perimeter fence, and the vehicle came to a halt at the end of the parking ramp. After the engine was cut off, the engine tick, tick, ticked as the large Cummins diesel engine cooled. The rear door swung open, and a group of heavily armed agents dropped down out of the truck.

"Seriously, Boomer. Can we keep it under the speed of sound next time? I almost lost my lunch." The tall lanky agent wearing a long leather jacket and a brimmed hat stood shakily against the back of the truck as he tried to keep his knees from wobbling.

"What's your problem, Ghost?" the driver said as she dropped out of the back hatch and stretched her muscular arms. "We got here safely, and we even beat the plane."

A man who exuded command walked over and clasped the complaining agent on the shoulder.

"Forget about it, Ghost," he said. "You won't win this argument with her."

Six glanced down at his secure phone and said, "Gretchen just sent me a message. They're two minutes out."

A deputy sheriff, whose brown and tan uniform contrasted against the black tactical BDUs of the rest of the team, shakily climbed out of the back of the armored vehicle. "Agent Holstein? You never told me I needed to take out a life insurance policy for when Boomer drives. Monsters I can handle, but I'm not so sure about her driving."

Six started laughing and clapped the young deputy on the shoulder, and the others joined in.

Moments later, the team turned toward the runway as they heard the large roar of an arriving jet. Six had expected to see the Citation X aircraft the team had used on their last flight, so when the team leader saw a monster of an aircraft coming in for a landing, he was shocked.

The two large jet engines under each wing roared as the monster cargo plane made a graceful landing at the end of Runway 26L. With a wingspan of almost one hundred seventy feet, the Boeing C-17 Globemaster III was enormous.

As the Air Force jet rolled out at the end of the runway nearest to the team, Ghost looked at Six and asked, "What did Gretchen say she was bringing us?"

The team leader shook his head and turned when he heard laughing behind him. He saw Spooky climb out of the MRAP they were using. Spooky lugged all of his electronic equipment out of the truck and struggled not to drop the precious gear onto the tarmac.

Six looked at the electronics specialist a little closer and asked, "Why are you laughing? Whenever you laugh like that, I have to do more paperwork. What's going on?"

Spooky's reply was drowned out as the mammoth plane reversed the engine thrust to slow down. As the aircraft passed their end of the tarmac, the team felt the rumble and the roar of all four turbines. An airport pickup truck raced toward the team from the terminal and rocked to a halt beside the scattered agents. The team tensed in surprise and reached for their sidearms while the men in the truck ignored them. A three-man ground crew got out of the pickup truck and waited for the plane to taxi to its spot on the ramp.

As the massive jet taxied toward the tarmac, the three waiting ground crew members guided the giant plane to its parking spot. The four turbines wound down, and the noise quickly became more bearable. Just as Six was about to ask Spooky about his laughter again, the door on the side of the fuselage cycled open and dropped, forming into a set of stairs. At the same time, they all could hear the whine of hydraulics as the rear ramp lowered.

Agent Gretchen Massey stepped to the doorway of the plane. She saw the team and walked down the stairs, carrying a small suitcase. Behind her, a man dressed in an impeccable gray pin-stripe suit adjusted his lapels and followed her down the stairs. He joined Gretchen at the bottom of the stairs, and they walked toward the waiting team. As the new arrivals walked to the team, a shuttle bus from the airport approached across the tarmac. Gretchen waved to get the driver's attention, and he pulled to a stop right where the team was standing.

The man in the suit approached the sheriff's deputy who stood beside Six. He reached out his hand and introduced himself.

"Deputy Folsom? I am Agent Smith, of the Department of Homeland Security. I suppose you could say that I'm your new boss," he said. "I'm sorry to hear about your loss, and I want to welcome you to the team. Mr. Holstein has had nothing but good things to report. Do not worry. I'll take care of things with the sheriff for you."

Deputy Folsom wondered just who his new boss was that this guy thought he could "handle" the sheriff.

Agent Smith continued, "We will have to postpone the official swearing in until after this mission, but I wanted to greet you personally."

Smith looked at the rest of the team and said, "It will take a little while to get your new gear offloaded. This bus will take us to a conference room that I've reserved in the terminal. Ms. Massey has arranged food as well so we can go over the new equipment with you."

Agent Smith turned to look at Spooky while the rest of the team climbed aboard. "Grab your projector. I've got intel for your mission," he told the electronics specialist. As they boarded the bus and pulled away from the giant aircraft and headed toward the terminal, Six watched a squad of heavily armed men in tactical uniforms assemble and surround the plane and the MRAP on the tarmac.

DURING THEIR CONFERENCE, AGENT SMITH EXPLAINED THAT HE HAD arrived with the team's new vehicle and that Norbert had loaded it out according to their specifications.

The team leader looked over at his electronics specialist and frowned. He turned back to Agent Smith. "Just what specs did Spooky send you?" he asked.

Smith smiled. "You'll have to ask him," he said. "I know Russell and Norbert were up for almost two days straight getting all the systems integrated. However, this... War Wagon, as you call it, should be outfitted for anything you need while in the field. It will go with you on most direct action missions from now on. And if you find it lacking, work with the warehouse to get it straight."

Spooky leaned over to Ghost and whispered, "We really do have our own 'Q' branch."

Ghost nodded his agreement.

Agent Smith looked right at him and gave a hint of a smile. "Trust me, Mr. Smith, the 'Q' branch isn't nearly as good as Norbert and Russell. Those Brits have been trying to recruit them for years."

Spooky's jaw fell open as he digested what Smith said. Before he could ask a follow-up question, Smith continued his briefing.

"As of right now, I have classified this mission as a Priority: Black. Working with the intel developed by your team, and especially by your very own Mr. Smith, we believe this is far larger than we initially thought. That is why I decided to make the trip out with Ms. Massey."

"The intelligence you were able to recover led you to a Doctor Bishop Kaine."

An image of a thin, brooding scientist in a lab coat filled the screen.

Smith continued, "Doctor Kaine is a brilliant specialist in genetic engineering, and worked for the CDC in Atlanta until about ten years ago. At that point, the scientist's rough demeanor and elitist attitude finally rubbed the wrong person the wrong way, and they fired him. As they escorted him out of the building, he made several threats against the personnel at the facility."

"It was then that he stepped out of the public life and dropped off the grid. We've been able to figure out he raised the funds to buy an abandoned Atlas 'F' ICBM missile silo just north of a town called Divide, Colorado. I've had the exact GPS coordinates loaded into your new truck."

Six looked at Smith and asked, "So why is this now classified as a Priority: Black?"

Agent Smith looked at the team leader, then looked around the table. "Before I answer that, I want to talk about the master that was named by the familiars. This is not a random master vampire who has happened to hang around for a long time. This particular 'Zachariah' is one of the oldest known vampires here on earth. He's also the only one who's been able to stay ahead of this office."

"We have no idea how old this evil creature is, but he has taken out some of our best people. He has caused a lot of havoc in America and around the world. He is powerful."

Ghost spoke up. "Sir, the last information I heard was that he was at least a couple hundred years old... possibly turned during the American Revolution. Our records go back at least that far for him, but my... researchers... couldn't find any more information for him."

Smith nodded. "Thank you, Mr. Vanhof. I trust your research. So this master is at least two hundred years old. If he is working with a disgruntled genetic engineer, then he is probably planning something that will certainly qualify as a Priority: Black."

Agent Smith flipped a small switch on the projector and the flat images shifted. A three-dimensional rendering of the blueprints projected a holographic walk-through of a missile silo, rendering and rotating in the air in front of the team.

Agent Smith continued. "This is the last known configuration of the Atlas F missile silo that Doctor Kaine purchased. There is no telling what the scientist has changed, but this information may be helpful to you, anyway."

After the team reviewed the walk-through twice, Agent Smith outlined the course of action for the mission.

"Team Knightmare, here are your mission parameters," said Smith. "Priority One: Find out what Zachariah and Doctor Kaine have planned and stop it. Priority Two: Avoid destroying any of the scientific equipment or computer equipment or any paper records that the doctor has on his experiments. If his research has released a new threat, we need to have that information to stop it. Priority Three: Destroy the bunker and lab facilities after you have cleaned out the equipment. Make this site go away."

Boomer smiled when she heard the word "destroy."

Smith looked even more serious than normal.

"As a Priority: Black mission, you have almost unlimited resources," he continued. "Unfortunately, the other two Incursion teams are down or busy. Due to the nature of the mission, you are not authorized to bring in more team members. However, your new War Wagon and the equipment I'm bringing you should help with that."

"This new MRAP will be your team's personal truck and will be transported to any site where it is needed. It has been customized and outfitted beyond the standard MRAP to help with your rather unique challenges. In it, we've also packed a large amount of ammunition and some other gadgets that should help you take down this fiend."

"Ladies and gentlemen, this master has haunted our organization for years. This creature is responsible for the deaths of many agents, including my first partner. It is up to you to send him to the hell he has eluded for so long."

Agent Smith looked up as Gretchen walked into the room. "I see that Ms. Massey has indeed brought a light lunch. Let's eat this and then get you on your way."

HALF AN HOUR LATER, THE TEAM WALKED TO THE WAITING SHUTTLE BUS at the entrance of the airport. Before they could climb on, two SUVs with dark, tinted windows pulled up. Special Agent Hart, the SAC from Denver, climbed out followed by a small team. She quickly walked around the truck and came to an abrupt halt when she saw Agent Smith and Gretchen.

"Agent Smith?" The surprise in Hart's voice was evident. "I didn't know this was one of your teams. I should have realized that when I got stonewalled in DC. Next time, if you want to give me some heads up, I won't give your team such a hard time."

"Don't worry about it, Sonja." Agent Smith let a hint of amusement show in his voice. "If it would have been necessary, I'd have had Timothy call you. As it is, I believe you can have your MRAP back today."

Agent Hart's SUV followed the shuttle out on the tarmac toward the hangar where they had parked the War Wagon.

As they approached, Six realized that there was an even bigger armored truck, all in black, parked next to their MRAP. He spun on his heel to face his electronics specialist. "What the hell is that? Just what did you ask for, Spooky?" he asked.

Behind him, Spooky laughed. "Boss, I told you I was requisitioning a new War Wagon. Call it Version 2.0, but this thing should really rock and work for all of our missions. She is not the most subtle beast, and she should be perfectly decked out inside."

A small contingent of armed DHS tactical agents surrounded the vehicles. Two of them also stood by the stairwell to the C-17. The department's Citation X was parked next to the C-17, and it, too, had its own guard.

The shuttle driver dropped them off by the two large MRAPs. His mouth gaped open, but he was smart enough to leave before he asked anything he would later regret.

Hart's SUV pulled up beside them, and she and her team got out of the vehicle as they stared at the second truck.

Hart stammered a little. "When I got the call to come get our truck, I thought you guys were leaving." She pointed to the new truck and asked, "What the hell is this monstrosity?"

The new truck was a larger, beefier, blockier version of their previous truck. Built on an International Harvester platform, the Navistar Maxxpro Plus was one of the most used MRAPs in Iraq and Afghanistan. This model stood ten feet tall and was painted a deep matte black. Outfitted with emergency lights in the grill and on the exterior, the top was also ringed with small lamps that pointed outward. A large floodlight that was capable of rotating 360 degrees was mounted in each corner of the roof. The only markings on it were small decals on each door with the DHS logo and the words "Department of Homeland Security." Perched on the roof was a small cluster of antennas that include radio, satellite, and a few whose use was only known to Spooky.

The front driver and passenger doors and the rear loading stairs made entry and exit easier than their previous truck. Boomer opened the driver's door and climbed up into the massive vehicle with ease. As she looked at the instrument cluster, she noticed a few switches that were cryptically marked, but a toggle switch on the control cluster between Boomer and the front passenger marked "Rear Hatch" caught her eye.

She flipped the switch to the "Down" position.

At the rear of the vehicle, a small hiss the pneumatic seal opening was barely audible. The rear hatch lowered with a hydraulic whine. A thin sliver of light from the back turned into daylight as the rear ramp lowered and turned into a short set of stairs.

Spooky was the first to climb the stairs, lugging his electronics behind him. He quickly walked over to the seat in front of the electronics station. As he sat down, the lights and panels lit up around him. Plugging his laptop into the waiting ports, the electronics specialist put on a headset. A voice prompt echoed in his ear and on the screen and told him to identify himself.

He pulled the microphone close and said, "Identify. Agent Spooky. Alpha One."

The screens around him hummed to life. He glanced down and realized that his forearm computer had also synchronized with the system. He grinned typed away as he whistled a theme that Boomer later recognized as belonging to a show about other federal agents that looked for monsters and aliens.

The team's sniper was the next one to board the new truck. Once he was in the MRAP, he popped the top hatch of the truck, just to get a feel for it. The hatch itself was slightly wider than the one in the roof of their previous truck, and this one added several features that would allow him to be a much more effective shooter from the top of the vehicle. He dropped back down and sat in the surprisingly comfortable seat. He noticed the five-point harness attached to each seat and caught Spooky's eye.

God lifted the seat buckle and asked, "Was this your idea?"

Spooky just grinned.

God nodded and said, "Good thinking." He then reached up and clipped both his sniper rifle and his carbine to the interior of the roof by the turret hatch. The custom brackets would be perfect for his firearms for secure storage and easy access for the sniper.

Heavy climbed inside the cabin of the MRAP and grinned. It was marginally larger inside, and the big man didn't feel quite so compressed. He leaned over and popped the latches on a bin marked "Heavy - Weapons and Ammunition." Inside was his favorite machine gun, the SAW, and nestled next to it was a smaller, futuristic-looking rifle. Unlatching the gun, he pulled it out and laughed. His booming laughter made Ghost stick his head inside the back and look at the big gunner.

The hunter looked at Heavy and said, "What's up, big man?"

Heavy grinned and said, "Christmas came mighty early this year. Looks like I get a new toy."

Heavy held a black rifle that bore a slight resemblance to the other team members' M4 carbines. The black polymer stock and forearm of the Auto Assault-12 belied the weapon's roots as a hunting shot-gun. Capable of feeding from an eight round magazine or a 32-round drum magazine, the fully automatic assault shotgun could spit out 12GA shotgun rounds at the rate of five rounds every second, an effective cyclic rate of 300 rounds per minute. Advanced recoil reduction design meant that the recoil from the full-power shotgun was less than other modern rifles that shot far smaller rounds.

Boomer turned around and noticed the shotgun in Heavy's hands.

"No fair!" she complained. "I want a new shotgun. That one probably has less recoil than my Mossberg."

Heavy looked over and flipped open the latches for the container marked with the name of the EOD specialist. He smiled back at the driver and said, "No worries, Boomer. You have a shiny new toy as well. It looks like Norbert's also loaded us up with lots of mags and drums."

Boomer smiled and turned back around as Ghost climbed up into the MRAP. He found a long bundle placed in his storage bin. The bundle contained with a note from Norbert that read, "This might help you in your hunt this time. I believe it belonged to a relative of yours."

Inside the bundle was a cane that appeared to be made from an ancient wood. The years of handling had soaked oils deep into the gnarled cane and created a patina that only came from time. A silver head extended from the top of the well-worn shaft. There was a silver band on both sides of the joint where the head met the cane. As Ghost placed both of his hands upon the ancient gnarled wood, several runes appeared in glowing white along the cane's form.

Ghost grasped the handle in his right hand and the shaft in his left. With a slight twist and pull, he separated the head from the shaft. Inside this beautiful old cane was a slim, rapier-like blade attached to the handle to form a sword. As he drew the blade partially, the sword recognized that he was family and emitted a soft white glow before it faded to shiny metal.

Outside the new War Wagon, Six talked with the DHS SAC from the Denver office.

"Agent Hart, I hate to leave things for you to clean up, but you need to be aware of two prisoners that we have down in the county jail in Trinidad," explained Six.

Hart looked from Six to Smith and back. "You arrested someone? Who? What do I need to do about it?" Hart asked Six.

Six tried to figure out how much he should tell Hart.

"We have the acting mayor and the county coroner in custody in a holding cell in the county jail," Six began. "They are currently charged with assault on a federal officer. If our mission is successful, we will take care of their final disposition. However, if our mission happens to fail, you will need to coordinate with Agent Smith's office for final disposition. If you could send a couple of agents that you trust down there today and relieve the deputies currently watching them, I would appreciate it."

"Your team will immediately know if we are successful, as the prisoners will probably go absolutely batcrap crazy. If that's the case, we'll be back to take care of them as soon as we can," Six concluded.

Agent Hart looked at the commander of this weird mix of agents that now included a sheriff's deputy from the county they were just in. She nodded and managed to sound inconvenienced and obliging at the same time.

"All right, I'll send some folks down there. You'd better deal with this. I don't want this to wash back on me or my team," said Hart.

Six smiled tightly and then agreed. "We will," he said. "There is also a team from the FBI HRT in town as well. They know DHS is in charge. Have your agents use them if necessary."

Again Hart nodded. "Anything else I need to know?"

Six gave a small laugh. "One last thing. The top speed on your little MRAP is limited to just over ninety-five miles per hour. According to our pilot, er... driver, it gets a little dicey to handle at that speed."

Six turned away as the Denver agent's mouth opened while she processed that news. She couldn't believe anyone would be crazy or dumb enough to go ninety in an MRAP.

Six shook hands with Agent Smith and Gretchen as they walked toward their waiting Citation. Smith motioned for the captain of the airplane to begin the preflight check and turned to the team leader.

"The C-17 stays here until you guys are done. It will transport you and the truck back to the shop when you are done. Keep me appraised. Good luck and kill that creature."

Six saluted as Smith and Gretchen climbed the stairs. He turned and quickly walked back over to the waiting War Wagon, v2. He opened the side door and climbed into the passenger seat. As he fastened his seat belt, he gazed at the laptop station and row of gauges and instruments in front of him. He turned and saw Doc and Do-Right climb into the truck through the rear ramp.

Boomer looked over her shoulder and asked if everyone was present. After she received a chorus of "Here" and "Present"—and a lone "I'm not here," from Spooky—she flipped the switch. The rear hatch whined up and closed with a solid thunk.

As Six closed his door, Boomer reached down and turned the key in the ignition. The massive 435 horsepower Cummins Diesel engine fired up smoothly. Engaging the transmission, she turned to Six and asked, "All right, boss, where are we going?"

24

BREACH

Divide, Colorado.

Approximately twenty-five miles west of Colorado Springs on State Route 24 lies the little town of Divide, Colorado. Settled in the 1880s, the town sits on the north slope of Pike's Peak, and is home to 127 people. The beautiful mountain views and the unique geography that has water run-offs in all cardinal directions draw visitors to, and through, this quiet little town.

Almost an hour and twenty minutes after leaving the Pueblo Memorial Airport, a large black MRAP bearing DHS markings rolled into the parking lot of the lone grocery store in town. The driver found a spot toward the back of the lot and turned off the engine.

Furious typing and the opening of latches in the back broke the silence.

Six turned around from the front passenger's seat and said, "Spooky, do you have eyes on the target yet?"

Spooky nodded without glancing up. "Yeah, boss. The satellite came online about five minutes ago. I'm targeting the area now for visual recon. And mirroring to your laptop... now."

Six looked at the display in front of him and nodded.

"All right folks," Six began. "It's just after 3pm so daylight will keep the vamps inside. And there are no signs of any guards outside. We are about three and a half miles from the turnoff to the silo. This is an abandoned Atlas-F silo. We believe we can get in. You know our objectives. First, figure out what the master and the mad scientist are doing, then stop it. Then kill them. Second, save the equipment because we might need it. Third, take out the bunker and anything in it."

"That second priority means that we have to be very careful of where we shoot and what we shoot it with. Heavy and Boomer," the team leader looked at the two in question, "That means try not to use the pretty little FRAG-12 grenades for your new toys. In fact, be extra careful with your new toys, period."

Ghost nodded at his boss and asked, "What's the protocol? How are we going in?"

Six looked at Spooky and said, "You're not going to like this." Spooky just stared as he got an idea of what his boss was going to say.

He looked at the rest of the team. "Everyone goes in. Ghost, you and I are on point, and Heavy will back us up. Doc and Do-Right will flank Spooky behind us, and Boomer and God will bring up the rear. You guys will watch our back."

Spooky was almost apoplectic when he said, "What the hell, boss? I'm not leaving this truck. I'm your electronics guy, not the shoot-'em-up guy. That's your job."

Six looked directly at the young analyst. "I need you along for your electronics expertise," Six reassured Spooky. "There is no telling when we're going to come across a lock that needs a code or a computer that needs to be cracked. In this case, you are vital to this mission. I'm putting you in the middle to protect you."

Spooky's eyes were wide, and he shook his head, making his wild hair fly. "I don't know anything about breaking codes on locks or anything like that. I won't be of any help."

Six consulted his computer. "According to the stores listed on this truck, in your pouch is something called an 'Electronic Lock Kit' and a special set of cables to use for your wrist computer. Both of them were placed in your bin by Norbert."

Spooky opened the bin at his side. "Frak me. There is a kit in here.

I don't know whether to thank Norbert or to kick his butt when we get back."

Six smiled and asked if everyone understood the mission. He received a chorus of nods.

"If we have to split up," Six continued, "The fire teams will be the following: Alpha Team will be myself, Ghost, Spooky, and Do-Right; Doc will lead Beta Team, consisting of Boomer, God, and Heavy. Load up with plenty of ammo. Take some stun and frag grenades if you're comfortable with them. Keep in mind that this is a giant steel trap. Ricochets and fragments will suck, so watch your fire and choose carefully."

"Because it is a giant steel can, the weapons fire will be deafening. Make sure each of you has your custom earplugs in. They connect to your radio, and will help dampen the gunfire and echoes. Also, use the tactical throat microphones for your radios. That will allow you to talk at a lower voice and still be heard. They can be keyed just by touching the sensor at your throat."

The couple team members who hadn't put in their earplugs quickly did so. Doc handed Do-Right a new pair. While they weren't quite custom fit, they would block out much of the gunfire, while allowing him to hear the radio traffic.

Six continued, "When we reach the end of the access road that leads back to the silo, Boomer will stop and everyone but Doc, God, and Spooky will bail out."

The team leader pointed at his sniper. "God, you are up through the turret for the approach. Heavy, Do-Right, Ghost, and I will ride on the outside for rapid deployment. Boomer will drive us up to the silo and will block the drive leading back to the main road."

The team leader received a round of upraised thumbs, and he nodded to his explosives expert. Boomer fired up the truck and moved down the road until she spotted the small over-grown trail that led off to the left where the GPS said it should. She pulled into the car path and stopped. She flipped the switch to drop the rear hatch as Six climbed out the passenger door. The passenger door slammed shut as the rear ramp dropped fully. Sitting about a foot and a half off the ground, the bottom stair easily cleared the weeds.

God popped open the turret and sat up through the opening, shouldering his M4 carbine. On the passenger's side of the vehicle, Ghost jumped up and grabbed the handhold just behind the front door, his carbine held loosely in his right hand. Having shed the heavy outer armor and BDUs, Ghost had instead opted for his original hunting outfit, including his long black leather duster and hat. Heavy jumped up next to the lanky hunter. The big man grinned as he slammed a drum magazine into his new AA-12 and charged the bolt.

On the driver's side, Six mounted up next to the window, holding his carbine in his left hand. Do-Right climbed up behind his boss and held his own personal AR-15 in his hand. Six looked over the former deputy and noticed that the deputy had taken the time to change into the standard black tactical uniform and armor that Gretchen had brought from headquarters.

Six nodded his approval. "Those BDUs look good on you," he said to the deputy.

He turned and rapped on the glass, giving the signal to his driver to move forward.

Boomer flipped the switch to close the rear hatch as the big vehicle lumbered forward. Careful to maintain an even track and relatively slow speed, the explosives expert was very mindful of her exterior passengers. About three hundred yards down the access path, there was a fenced off clearing amongst the trees to her right with a small, squat building marking the entrance to the silo. Pulling up and blocking the gated entrance, she brought the truck to a halt and shut it down, mindful of taking the keys with her. She flipped the ramp release, and the back ramp dropped, allowing God, Doc, and Spooky to exit the vehicle.

Boomer waited until they had exited, and then she raised the ramp again, sealing the back against intrusion. She climbed in the back and got her new AA-12 out of her weapons bin and grabbed several drums and a couple magazines of Norbert's special ammunition. She purposefully left the mini grenades in the truck. After reaching up to check that the top hatch was shut, the demolitions specialist grabbed her pack containing explosives and grenades and climbed out the driver's door, locking it behind her.

The team moved into formation. They carefully watched all around them as they approached the seemingly abandoned silo entrance in front of them. Ghost opened the gates with a loud creak, and it was only then that he realized that the surrounding forest was absolutely still and quiet. It was unnatural and confirmed to the veteran hunter that there were monsters in this area.

The team cautiously approached the entrance to the silo. The heavy steel door showed few signs of use, but the gleaming oil on the hinges revealed a hint that the "rusty abandoned look" might be just for show.

Six motioned for Ghost to cover him as he gave a tug on the handle of the door. It was solidly locked from the inside.

Six looked at Boomer and said, "You're up. Quiet and small."

The demolitions expert nodded and grabbed a strip of detcord from her pack. Sometimes used to trigger other explosions, Boomer knew that the "detcord" was a small explosive itself, and figured it should be enough to open the armored hinge on the door.

Motioning for the team to stand clear, she attached the leads to the detonator in her hand.

"Fire in the hole," she warned.

A loud ripping sound came from the front of the bunker entrance, followed by the loud "clang" of a heavy metal door falling off of its hinges echoed. The team quickly assembled in the entrance, and they shined their lights down the darkened stairwell. Ghost grabbed two glowsticks and broke them to activate their phosphorescent glow. He tossed each glowstick down the stairwell. The team could see that the stairs went down about two stories and ended on a landing. They could see through the grating on the stairwell, and it looked clear. In formation, the team entered the bunker.

The team carefully made their way down the metal stairs. Each agent watched for signs of rusted or broken stairs before they stepped, and each was looking around them for cameras or hidden obstacles.

Ghost hit the bottom of the stairs first and raised his hand to bring everyone to a halt. Leading away was a long corridor of cement. At the end of the corridor, Ghost's light revealed a corner with a passageway to the left. Other than the weapon lights mounted on the carbines and the ghostly green glow of the chemlights, the tunnel and entrance were pitch black. Ghost scanned the wall and saw that the ceiling was a maze of steel mesh-encased conduit about ten feet overhead. The corridor itself was clean and free of debris or dust.

Ghost motioned his hand forward and led the team down the long corridor as Spooky took one last look at the sunlight filtering through the open doorway. He noticed that he was not the only one to glance back at the sunlight fading away as they pressed forward into the silo.

When the team reached the end of the corridor, the Ghost stopped and covered his boss with his rifle as Six approached the corner cautiously. The team leader peered around and spied a large hardened steel blast door designed to withstand attack and invasion. He tried the door, but it was locked.

Stepping back, Six turned and spoke in a low voice, "Spooky. Locked blast door. You're up."

Spooky nervously stepped forward and pulled a small box with wire leads out of his pack. All the security doors, including this blast door, were originally equipped with 1960s-era electronic locks. As he approached the door, he noticed that the electronic locks had been upgraded to current standards by the new owner. He pushed a key card into the slot waiting for him. Several wire leads ran from the card back to the small computer in his hand. As he watched the digital display, he saw numbers spinning down into a five-digit sequence as the computer used a brute-force attack to hack and find the correct passcode. When it finally stopped, he looked at the team leader and nodded.

Six nodded back and raised his rifle toward the door. The electronics genius keyed 4-9-4-3-6 into the keypad. The blast door hissed as it released its vacuum seal and swung open. The area beyond the door was designed to be an airlock, with another blast door roughly seven feet away. Unfortunately for the mad scientist, he seemed to have forgotten to seal the inner door. When the heavy blast door finally came to a stop in the open position, Six stepped in front of the door, leaning against it to make sure it did not close until his team was past it.

"Ghost, go through to the other door... looks like another blind corner," Six whispered. "Heavy, you follow. Block the open door until we all get through this mantrap."

Ghost and Heavy nodded as they moved past their leader. The area beyond the trap was lit with cold fluorescent light spilling from around the corner. As Heavy braced his back against the open blast door, Ghost cautiously peered around the corner. This corridor dead-ended in a blast door that appeared to have been forcibly opened and then torn from its hinges. Distracted by the massive steel door laying on its side, the hunter almost overlooked the small camera mounted in the upper right corner of the corridor.

He eased back around the corner and walked back to Six. "The next corridor is about twenty-five feet long, with a busted blast door at the end," Ghost reported. "There is also a camera mounted up high. It looks to be a newer model and is probably active. Past that, there appears to be the final blast door that is partially open. I couldn't tell if it was damaged."

Six nodded. "Ideas?"

Ghost's grin turned mischievous. He handed his rifle to his boss and said, "I'm going to stroll down the corridor and kill the camera. Once it's dead, the rest of you can come around the corner without being seen. If he sees me coming, he might think I'm alone."

The team leader thought for a moment and nodded his approval. He said, "I like it. Go for it."

Six turned to ready the rest of the team while the hunter pulled out the silver-inlaid cane and strolled around the corridor as if he belonged there. Once he reached the end of the corridor, he made sure that the area was clear and calmly reached up with the cane tip and smashed the little plastic camera. As he pulled the cane back down, the hunter heard a loud curse echoing from somewhere beyond the partially opened blast door.

Ghost clicked open his mic and warned Six, "Time to move, boss. Someone knows we're here."

He moved back down the corridor to meet the team as they rounded the corner. Grabbing his rifle from Six, Ghost tucked the cane away and raised his rifle to his shoulder. The team moved back toward the end of the hallway that Ghost had just vacated.

When they reached what should be the last blast door on the level according to the plans, Ghost found that the door was partially jammed and would open no wider than three feet. He motioned for Six to cover him, and, with his rifle raised, Ghost squeezed through the door. Quickly stopping to brace against attack, he found himself on a stairwell landing with a flight of stairs leading down.

The stairwell was an open well made of metal lattice and grillwork that was typically used in industrial catwalks. There were three short flights of stairs, each ending at a steel lattice landing. Looking down through the open grill and sides, the monster hunter could see the final flight of stairs ended at the first control level. Ghost stepped to his right as he tried to cover all three flights at once.

Six came through the blast door opening and realized that Ghost needed help. He told Ghost that he would cover him and motioned for the monster hunter to proceed to the next landing. The team leader swung his rifle down to cover the flight below them. Ghost shifted slightly and covered the stairway in the middle while slowly moving down the wire mesh stairs, stopping at the first landing. Heavy stepped through the doorway and immediately covered the stairs below them with his shotgun.

The top landing was getting a little crowded when Six spoke up. "Three stairways leading down to command level one," he said "Heavy, Spooky. When we hit the bottom landing, you guys stay there and cover the stairs down to command two. Everyone else, will clear command one. Watch your targets and look for Doctor Kaine."

Heavy pointed his shotgun down the stairs in the middle. Six and Ghost carefully descended the stair flight and guarded the lower landing with their rifles. They paused on the last landing before the doorway to gather the rest of the team. Doc and Do-Right quickly stepped through the blast door up above and walked down, joining the two lead agents on the landing. Boomer and God also squeezed through the blast door and quickly joined the rest of the team with Heavy and Spooky bringing up the rear. The team made their way down the relatively short flight of stairs and came to a landing across from a six-foot wide opening with a faded sign above the open doorway proclaiming "Command Level One." Nothing living was visible.

As the team knew from the blueprints, the command level was a large circular level, roughly forty feet across with a ceiling approximately fifteen to twenty feet tall. The level was separated into compartments. According to the original plans, the first two doors to the left should be a janitor's closet and restroom, respectively. Beyond the monolithic wiring and ducting conduit in the middle should sit a small kitchenette, and the back of the level should house a mechanical room for HVAC and potable water.

At a silent three-count, Six and Ghost simultaneously burst through the opening. Ghost swung right slightly to cover the open side of the room as his boss stepped forward and opened the janitor's closet. Behind the two men, Boomer and God moved into the room and covered the restroom and the kitchenette entrances. Doc and Do-Right stepped in and to the right. The former deputy concentrated his sights on the mechanical room.

Doc noticed her vestments begin to glow their etheric blue and shouted a warning just as the first vampire burst from the kitchenette, distended jaws open and brimming with teeth. As the vampire charged out of the kitchen, the door to the restroom was flung open, and a human familiar reached for God who stood closest to Doc.

When Six turned to fire on the familiar rushing his sniper, he noticed that two revenants were running out of the mechanical room. He concentrated on his target, but he did not pull the trigger as he realized that Boomer was standing just beyond his target. He mentally switched gears and swung the butt of his gun at the maddened familiar's head, dully noting that the familiar was another teenager like those from the mad pharmacist's house. The butt of his rifle connected with the back of the girl's head just as the butt of God's rifle stroked into her jaw. The force of the two blows violently jerked the girl's head around, and Six heard the bones of her neck snap as the body of the girl collapsed to the floor.

Boomer opened up with her shotgun as the vampire reached for her. The full-auto shotgun spit out a round every fifth of a second, and each three-quarter-inch bullet was one of Norbert's special vampire hunting slugs. The twelve-gauge shotgun roared, and four slugs hit the chest of the vampire, sending it sprawling backwards from shock and energy. The demolitions specialist grinned wildly at the lack of recoil in her new toy. She raised the gun to her shoulder and fired another short burst, thumping three rounds into head of the vampire before it could recover. The head of the vampire disappeared in a mist of ichor.

As she raised the muzzle of her shotgun, she spotted two more vampires coming from the kitchen around the corner. She centered her shotgun on the beast to the right. As she pulled the trigger, Boomer heard at least two rifles open up around her. Both vampires were soon overwhelmed by the firepower as it hit them. Both Boomer and God scored head shots on their respective monsters, and Six contributed to the withering firestorm.

Do-Right and Ghost targeted the two revenants that came howling from the mechanical room. Ghost called, "Right," and began firing at the monster on the right. Do-Right switched targets to the left-most revenant and pulled the trigger on his rifle.

Four holes appeared in the revenant's chest right over its heart. This staggered the creature. The former deputy raised his aim slightly higher and put the reticle right on the bridge of the creature's nose. Do-Right squeezed the trigger three times. He smiled slightly as the rounds all struck, emptying the monster's skull and dropping the creature's body to the ground.

Ghost managed to hit his revenant several times in the chest, but the shots only slowed the creature down as it shook off the effects of the bullets. He pulled the trigger again and again and felt a "click" as the bolt locked open on his carbine. He dropped his rifle to let it swing freely on its sling, and he drew the cane sword from his belt. With a click and a twist, the blade sprang to life and glowed white as it rose out of its sheath. The remaining revenant suddenly forgot the wounds in its chest and cringed back in abject terror. In a classic fencing stance, Ghost advanced on the creature.

The monster quickly tamed its momentary fear and lunged at the hunter. He blocked the creature's claw attack with his sword as sparks danced all along the blade where the beast's claws struck. Ghost smiled as he whirled in a classic riposte, and the blade seemed to leap forward of its own volition and skewered the creature. The beast screamed in pain, and smoke poured from where the sword ran it through.

As he ripped the blade out of the creature, Ghost parried the next claw attack with the shaft of the cane and again swung a masterful riposte. This time the blade met the creature's face and plunged through the eye and into the brain. The creature immediately stopped and dropped to the ground as if it no longer had bones. As he pulled his blade from the creature's corpse, the hunter flicked the blade slightly to remove all the black ichor off the blade.

Ghost sheathed the blade as its glow faded. As he turned around, he saw the rest of the team staring at him.

Six looked at him and said, "We really need to have a chat about your background. I have a feeling I'm being left in the dark."

Ghost shrugged. "I suppose we should talk about it soon," the hunter replied. "After this mission."

Six nodded.

"What was that blade?" questioned Doc. "I've never seen anything like it."

The hunter chuckled drily. "It's designed to burn and damage vampires, or any of their spawn," he said. "It's been in my family for generations. Now I think it's time we go, boss," he said as he turned to his leader.

Six nodded and sent Do-Right, God, and Boomer back to wait with Heavy and Spooky. The rest of the team quickly cleared the remainder of the small floor. In the kitchen, they discovered a young girl, barely alive and fading fast, with feeding marks all along her throat, wrists and thighs.

Doc looked at her boss. Her voice was filled with compassion, "If we don't take care of her, she'll become a revenant as she dies."

Six said, "Wait a minute. I thought they were supposed to be cured if we killed the master that turned them. Why isn't she cured?"

Doc shook her head. "She hadn't turned before her sire was killed. If she had already turned, she might have turned back. Unfortunately, if they're still alive but not fully turned when the master dies, then they turn into a revenant."

She raised her cross and stake. Doc looked at Ghost. "Use your machete," she said. "Take her head once I perform the rites. It's the only merciful option."

The priest prayed over the young girl. The Latin phrases caused the girl to cry out in agony until she mercifully passed out from the pain. With a sharp plunge, Doc drove the silver spiked end of her cross into the girl's chest and straight into her heart. Ghost quickly stepped up and swung his machete and ended her torment.

25

KAINE

Decommissioned Atlas Missile Silo, Divide, Colorado.

The three agents were in a more sober mood as they rejoined the rest of the team. Heavy and Boomer both covered the stairway leading down with their shotguns, and everyone exchanged their partially emptied magazines for full magazines for their firearms.

Repeating the journey to the first command level, the team leapfrogged down the first two landings, pausing before the final set of stairs. Because he knew the command level two should be the same size and shape as the level one, Six decided and stood at the top of the stairway leading down. He called out in a loud voice, "Doctor Bishop Kaine. We are here to talk with you. Come out with your hands raised. I'm giving you ten seconds to surrender peacefully… starting now."

The group heard a howling scream that announced the presence of revenants. Two of the creatures barreled out the doorway below the team and lunged for the agents. Alerted by the screams, Heavy and Boomer both aimed and opened fire with their AA-12s. The deafening roar of the full-auto shotguns quickly drowned out the screams of the revenants. The creatures never realized what happened as their mangled and torn corpses collapsed on the stairs.

Not willing to wait any further, the team moved down the stairs. As they reached the bottom, Six and Ghost again went through the doors first with Ghost covering the right side and his boss the left. Two human familiars, each holding an aluminum baseball bat, stood by the ancient control center equipment on the left side of the room. As the humans surged toward Six, he flipped the selector switch on his M4 to burst mode and pulled the trigger.

A three-round burst chattered from the rifle hitting the chest of the familiar on the right. Six shifted to the left and placed a second burst into the chest of the other familiar and watched as both tumbled to the floor. Flipping the selector switch back to single, Six stroked the trigger twice, once into each familiar's head. He stopped to cover what appeared to be a bedroom to the back and an open sleeping quarters in the center of the room and then motioned for the rest of the team to protect him by watching the other half of the level.

Ghost shifted his aim to the right as another screaming revenant burst around the corner. The deafening clatter of the full-auto shotguns carried by Heavy and Boomer joined his rifle fire. The chest and head of the creature disappeared in a spray of ichor, allowing the bottom half of the body to crumple to the ground.

God and Do-Right stepped over to join their leader in covering and exploring the left half of the level. Protected by the two agents, Six walked toward an open doorway located where an office was originally located on the plans. Six spied an unmade bed and some typical bedroom furniture in the former office. As he approached the room, he carefully looked into the partial gloom and paused. He barely restrained himself from pulling the trigger.

Huddled in the corner was a young girl, no more than eleven or twelve years old. Her disheveled clothing and frightened face marked her as a victim, not a monster, and that made the DHS leader pause. He quickly scanned around the room to make sure that no other monsters were in there, and he muttered over his headset that one victim was alive.

Meanwhile, in the other half of the command level, Ghost slung his rifle and pulled the cane from his belt as Doc's vestments began to glow blue once again. He and Heavy stepped forward, allowing the priest to protect the rear of the party, while Boomer watched out for Spooky.

Another revenant screamed and burst from its hiding place. It was moving so fast that it was still moving forward when it met its end at the tip of Ghost's ancestral blade. Ghost didn't have time to pull the blade from the skull of his latest kill when yet another creature appeared and charged for the hunter. The full-auto burn of Heavy's AA-12 roared as the center torso of the revenant who was attacking Ghost disappeared in a spray of ichor. The hunter yanked his blade free of the skull of the dead revenant and looked at the big machine gunner.

"Thanks, man," Ghost said to Heavy. "Stupid skull on these critters doesn't like releasing blades."

The trio of agents moved further around to see the rest of the level. Ghost, Heavy, and Doc entered what appeared to be a fully functional portable genetics laboratory. Centrifuges and Gene-tracing equipment sat on the counters, with racks of test tubes and computers set between them. At the far back wall, was a man who matched the file photo of Doctor Bishop Kaine. The scientist's white lab coat was absolutely pristine, and he was holding a couple of vials of an unknown liquid material. The tall, gaunt scientist was graying around the temples and wore his long dark hair in a ponytail. Reading glasses were perched on his head.

From his viewpoint, Ghost surveyed the back corner of the lab where three large chairs with straps for the hands and feet of the subjects were arranged. In one of the chairs, what looked like partially human remains were still strapped into the chair. Only half of the remains looked human; the other half looked like some form of a nightmare straight out of Hollywood.

In the only other occupied chair sat a vampire that was straining to break the bonds that held its wrists and feet to the chair. As soon as the vampire saw the blade in the hunter's hands, it recoiled in fear. When Doc entered the room, her vestments glowed bright, and the vampire panicked in its attempt to free itself.

Ghost watched one of the thick synthetic wrist straps stretch and then break, the incredibly dense materials no match for the panicked strength of a vampire. The hunter quickly stepped forward and rammed the blade straight through the creature's eye socket. The vampire's snarling and growling were cut off abruptly as the blade passed into the creature's brain. The smell of burning, rotting flesh filled the room. A quick yank and the blade came free enough for the hunter to swing and decapitate the fiend. All three agents turned to the human scientist as they heard Six's report of finding the victim.

"Six, this is Ghost. This side is clear. We have Kaine."

Ghost, flicked the blade to clean any remaining offal off the blade and sheathed his sword. The glow had left both the sword and Doc's vestments by the time the rest of the team arrived. Heavy remained where he was by the door and pointed his shotgun at the unmoving Doctor.

Ghost noticed Kaine smile when the other part of the team appeared with a survivor in tow. He had just begun to wonder about that satisfied grin when the little girl shrank back and tried to hide behind Boomer.

Later, Six would piece together that several things happened simultaneously. It was when Doc began walking toward the child to check her over for injuries that Doc's vestments once again lit with a brilliant blue glow. The child let out a loud hiss and climbed his explosives expert's back, swiping its now-clawed hand at the back of Boomer's neck.

Boomer immediately bucked hard. The movement broke the child's grip and sent it flying toward the wall. The girl nimbly shifted in the air and gracefully landed on her feet about ten feet away as she hissed and spat. Six noticed that the girl now had extended claws for hands and a mouthful of sharp fangs that were not present before. Rapidly filing that information away for later, he raised his rifle but did not shoot because he was afraid of hitting the equipment behind the creature.

Loud chanting in Latin filled the room, and a power thrummed through the team. Doc's vestments were so bright that it was hard to look at her. She had raised her large wooden cross in front of her and was walking steadily toward the vampire.

The creature hissed and spat, occasionally taking an ineffectual swipe at the priest, but it could not move any further. The vampire was pinned to the spot where it stood by the will and power of God, as called and wielded by the priest. The closer she got to the creature, the more it shrank toward the ground, almost crouching into a position to grovel.

As she stood over the creature, Doc noticed that the girl was wearing some sort of camp uniform. She wore a shirt and shorts embellished with the emblem of some place called Blue Mountain Camp. The vampire looked up with defiance in her eyes. The priest carefully knelt over the creature and forced it all the way down to the ground. A quick turn of the wrist, and the silver end of Doc's cross plunged into the young girl's chest and pinned her to the ground as she screamed in agony and with hatred.

Heavy stepped forward and drew his khukuri blades. The edges glowed green as he stepped up and chopped off the vampire's head. Tears rolled down his cheeks as he sheathed his blades. Doc noticed that the girl's body did not disappear into the ether like a normal vampire's body would. She supposed that this was a different type of vampire, and she made a mental note to record as much information as she could about this new breed.

The rest of the team turned to a still smiling Bishop Kaine.

"Doctor Kaine. You will come with us now," Six said as he stepped toward Kaine.

The scientist gave a slight chuckle. "I don't think so. In fact, if you don't stop killing my people and drop your weapons right now, you will face a nightmare you never dreamed possible."

The DHS agent looked around at his team. Doc was applying bandages to Boomer's neck, a lot of bandages from the look of it. Heavy had stepped back and was now guarding the door to the command level with his shotgun raised and pointed out the door. The rest of the team stood in a loose semi-circle around the mad scientist.

Six looked back at Kaine and said, "From where I stand, you don't have any bargaining chips. It looks like we've won."

Kaine shook his head. The scientist's voice was smarmy as he laid his cards on the table.

"Commander. In my hands I hold two vials of my latest creation," he began. "In fact, you've just experienced the results of the first direct field tests. You see, I've weaponized the vampire virus.

"Not only that, but I've given our new master race back the daylight. This virus infects one in every five humans by turning them into vampires. For those who it turns, they retain their old face and demeanor, unless hunting. They also are able to ignore the effects of sunlight and UV light. In short, they become the master predator that they were destined to be."

"Why do that, Doctor?" began Doc, "Why work with the monsters to enslave the human race? What's in it for you?"

Kaine smiled as he answered, his voice smooth and light. "Money, of course. Power. Wealth. Control. Zachariah has assured me that I will have a place in his dominion over the Earth. I have given him the power to walk in the sun, and I'm going to give him an army to control. And I will be well rewarded."

"Unfortunately, I'm quite immune to the virus. One of the unlucky. However, Zachariah guaranteed my safety and position of power. So I have to settle for 'favorite pet.' I don't mind. At least I will not be left outside to be hunted."

Doc continued her questioning, "How does the virus work? Airborne or fluid contact? Is it a typical pathogen, or is it something else?"

The scientist looked puzzled. "How would a priest know all that to ask the questions? What are you?"

Doc smiled and said, "I'm a board-certified physician. How did you get blood-sucker and human genes to mix?"

Kaine laughed. "Vampires start out human and are changed by the original virus. All I did was deconstruct that virus and made a few, select changes. Zachariah offered plenty of test subjects, and I certainly didn't have to get 'FDA approval.'"

Kaine smiled and continued. "To answer your question, priest.

The initial virus is airborne; however, every one of my new, improved vampires passes on the virus to those they bite or scratch. Your unfortunate team member over there will have to wait a couple of days to find out if she's infected."

The scientist looked at the rest of the team and raised his hands, showing off the vials filled with liquid. "Now put your weapons down and surrender, or I will drop these vials and see how many of you turn into monsters." The scientist smiled and raised the vials. "What will it be? Do you want to chance becoming a vampire here? Or do you want to live another day?"

Six looked at the rest of the team and then back to Kaine.

"What do you want, Kaine?" asked Six.

"It's simple," said Kaine. "I'm going to walk out of here. When I'm clear of the bunker, you can do whatever you want. Until then, you don't get to do anything. If you follow me, I'll drop one of these vials in here. If you follow me outside, I'll drop one outside, and we'll see what happens."

The scientist took a step forward, and the team made a small path. As he cautiously walked amongst the team, Kaine looked at Boomer and shook his head. "I really hope you turn, darling. You could be a fun little vampire for Zachariah."

Boomer's eyes filled with hatred, and she shook with rage. God had to lay a restraining hand on Do-Right's shoulder. He could sense that the deputy wanted to intervene.

Keeping the agents in his sight, Kaine slowly walked backwards and away from the team. His smile grew broader as he crossed the room. As he approached the doorway, he nodded his head at Six and said, "I'll be seeing you, commander…"

The scientist abruptly stopped. His smile turned to a puzzled look and then to anguish. Kaine opened his mouth as if to speak and blood poured out. He half-turned to look behind him and collapsed to the floor.

As the scientist fell, Heavy released his big Ka-Bar knife and reached out to scoop up the delicate vials of the virus. Once he was sure that he had the vials securely in his massive hands, he nodded at his team leader.

"Sorry, boss. I couldn't let that guy leave with this virus," Heavy said. "Where do we want to put them?"

Heavy walked toward the lab area as Six and Ghost scoured the area for a safe vial storage and transportation case. Once they found a suitable vacuform case, Heavy retrieved his knife. Yanking it free, from Dr. Kaine's remains, he calmly wiped the blade off on the corpse's clothing.

"Next time you want to take over the world, watch your back, Moron," he muttered.

Before he stood, Heavy noticed a small card that had partially fallen out of the scientist's lab coat. He grabbed the card and realized it was the electronic access card for the large blast doors. The big man handed the card to Six.

Six nodded his thanks and looked at Spooky. Six waved the electronics specialist over. "Spooky, secure these electronics and download whatever data you can from them."

He continued, "Ghost, help Spooky collect as much of the data and experimental equipment as possible."

"God. Do-Right. You guys cover the doorway. We still have to clear that silo—and we haven't run into Zachariah yet."

The commander walked over to the chair where Boomer was sitting. He looked at Doc, but she answered his unasked question with a slight shrug.

Six leaned over his explosives expert. "How are you feeling, Boomer?" he asked.

The demolitions specialist shook her head. "Those damn claws hurt. Even the fairly shallow cuts I have were bleeding like crazy," she explained. "What's going to happen, boss? What if I change?"

Doc laid her hand on Boomer's shoulder while Six pondered that very question. The team leader looked right into the scared young woman's eyes.

"I don't honestly know, Boomer. If you turn, we'll probably have to put you down. Unfortunately, we can't worry about that right now. We need to take down this silo, and we'll need you to do it. Are you up for the task?"

Boomer nodded her head slowly, wincing as the bandages pulled at her wounds. "I can do it, boss."

Six smiled and stood back up. "All right, people. We have a silo to clean out, and some electronics to salvage. God. Do-Right. You stay here and guard the virus and Spooky while he does his thing. The rest of you: it's time to kill more monsters."

26

SILO

Decommissioned Atlas Missile Silo, Divide, Colorado.

S pooky quickly inventoried all the computer and electronic equipment in the lab. As he sat down in front of the computer, he clicked the mouse to wake it up from hibernation. The computer sprang to life with no requests for a password or verification of any kind. *Smart enough to create a vampire virus, but dumb enough to leave his computer without a password,* Spooky thought to himself. Spooky shook his head and went to work digging through the system.

God and Do-Right took up positions at the doorway to cover their technical specialist while Spooky mined the computers for data. They watched as the rest of the team filed out the doorway and down the short set of stairs to the final landing. At the bottom of the landing was another blast door, and this one was closed and sealed.

Six swiped the card in the access lock. The electronic readout above the keypad blinked to life and then said, "Enter Code."

"Spooky, Six. What is the access code for the blast doors?" he called over the radio to his busy electronics specialist.

Spooky thought for a brief second and then replied, "If I remember right, it was '4-9-4-3-6.'"

The team leader punched in that code and the door hissed open.

"Thanks, Spooky," he said. "Spot on."

Ghost was the first to step through the open door. Having sheathed the cane-sword, he once again held his rifle, muzzle up, ready to shoot monsters. The hallway beyond the door was about six feet wide and almost ten feet tall with the same maze of conduits and cables running along the roof. The access tunnel itself was about thirty feet long and ended in another closed blast door at the far end. Other than that, it was empty.

Ghost waved everyone through and walked toward the other end of the hallway. When he finally reached the end, he approached the closed blast door with Six. The team leader looked at the rest of his team and asked if everyone was ready.

"We have no idea what's in the silo area," said Six. "It could be empty for storage, or it could be Kaine's failed experiments. Make sure you have a full magazine. Watch your cross fire."

"Remember from the blueprints that there is a giant fifteen-foot gap in the middle of each floor. It's the elevator access. If the platform isn't there, it's a long way down to the bottom. The Department of Defense should have cleared out most of the heavy equipment, but there's no telling what Kaine moved in. Everyone ready?"

Ghost said he was ready while Heavy and Boomer gave a thumbs up gesture. Doc just nodded as she mentally prepared herself for more monsters.

Six radioed the others. "God, Six. We're opening the other blast door. If anything comes out of that tunnel that isn't us, kill it."

"Copy," said God.

The DHS team leader reached up and swiped the access card and then keyed in the passcode. The door hissed and began to swing open. Six gripped his rifle a little higher and thought, *Once more into the breach. Literally.*

SPOOKY SAT AT THE SCIENTIST'S COMPUTER AS HE TRIED TO understand the filing system that Dr. Kaine had used. All the folders and documents had labels that contained a series of numbers and letters and were in no order that the electronics specialist could discern. Giving up momentarily, the DHS agent inserted a specially built USB key in the slot on the front of the desktop unit. Wires ran from the USB key back to a small box that contained a power supply, a solid-state hard drive, and a couple of circuit boards. When the USB device was plugged in, a series of small lights flashed down the side of the device. When all the lights were a solid green, Spooky pushed the button on top of the device to initiate a process that would automatically copy every hard drive and storage device attached to the computer.

With the copy process underway, the specialist randomly opened files and folders to see what was available. What little he understood made Spooky realize that this computer likely contained all the data necessary to replicate the process and all the methodology behind it. He idly wondered what new gadgets Norbert could come up with if he got his hands on the data.

One document caught his eye. Labeled "Bu68dk3-668DH," the file was a memo from a youth camp. The document explained their dates and fees and that the good doctor would be welcome to send his son during the session designed for middle-school-age children that summer.

Kaine's son? According to the file, he didn't have any kids, Spooky thought to himself.

The realization that he had seen the camp logo somewhere before suddenly struck him, but he could not quite remember where.

Spooky looked around the lab. His eyes fell on the body of the young vampire, the one created by Kaine's virus. The blue of her shirt and shorts matched the blue of the camp logo. *Was that it?* The agent stood and walked over to the corpse. He nudged her and rolled her onto her back. As he looked down at her body, he realized that the same logo as was on the letter was on her shirt. Spooky softly swore.

The specialist drew looks from the other two agents as he ran back over to the desk and rummaged through the paperwork scattered over its surface. He found what he was looking for only after a few seconds. Raising the document in the air, he turned to the other two agents.

"Uh, guys, I think I know where Kaine tested the virus," said Spooky. "This guy was pure evil."

THE DHS TEAM LEADER HEARD THE SQUELCH AS HIS RADIO ACTIVATED.

"Six, this is Spooky. I think I figured out where Kaine tested his virus."

Six was about to reply when Ghost keyed in the numbers on the keypad for the second blast door. Designed as an airlock at this end of the tunnel, both the outer door between the command bunker and the silo and the inner door leading into the silo itself were locked and sealed. But the team leader was a fraction of a second too late, and the door hissed its release and opened.

Havoc.

Two distended hands with razor-sharp claws wrapped around the door frame and yanked it open. The vampire standing in the doorway disintegrated under the withering hail of vampire-killing rounds from two rifles and two shotguns. The body was already disappearing into smoke before it hit the floor.

Six and Ghost immediately stepped through the doorway and stopped at the edge of the landing. A short span of steel grating led across the two-foot gap to the platform. Massive steel springs supported an octagonal platform about thirty feet across hung over the open space and attached at points around the inside of the silo. In the center of this platform was a square hole, about fifteen feet across and surrounded by a waist-high railing. According to the plans, this was supposed to be the second level in this structure.

Six looked up and saw the steel mesh underside of the level above them, with an elevator waiting in the center of that level. The team leader looked down through the same steel mesh beneath his feet and saw at least one other floor below. The silo was a bit overwhelming. The massive size and construction made Six pause briefly.

When the gunfire echoes died away, the team heard a cacophony of growls and screams, both from above and below. Six looked up and saw the platform above and stairs leading up from across the platform. The team leader spotted the elevator call buttons next to the pit and made a quick decision. He motioned to Ghost to close and secure the blast door. When the door slammed shut and hissed closed, Ghost joined him.

The DHS commander looked around and summed up their predicament succinctly. "Shit," he said.

He pointed to the Doc's glowing vestments and said, "Let's do this, people. Ghost and I will call the elevator. Doc, you help keep my back clear of nasties. Heavy, while we wait for the elevator, you cover the stairs. Boomer, your head is on a swivel—watch all the sides. We clear this out right now."

He reached over and hit the call button for the elevator.

As the elevator groaned and move toward them, the rumbling was overshadowed by a roar from above. Leaping around the edge of the platform, a vampire rebounded off the concrete walls and sprang toward the team. Boomer didn't hesitate as she stroked the trigger on her AA-12. The volley of rounds caught the vampire in midair and tumbled the young creature. The vampire looked like she was maybe fifteen or sixteen before she was turned, and the rounds shook her hard enough that she landed in a heap.

Doc stepped forward as she shouted her Latin blessings, and the creature shrank back. Shaken by the fall and stunned from the priest's incantations, the vampire could not defend itself against Ghost's ancestral blade. The hunter stabbed the creature through the chest, then reversed and swung, striking the creature's neck and shearing the head clean away.

Distracted by the vampire, Heavy almost failed to see the revenant throwing itself down the stairs. When the creature leapt from the stairs, Heavy's burst of shotgun slugs tore into its chest. Thrown off balance, the creature misjudged its landing. It crashed into the railing that surrounded the elevator shaft and bounced over the edge, screaming all the way down. The screams abruptly cut off with a crash from far below that shook the elevator's frame.

Six was watching the area above when the revenant dropped over the edge of the platform and nearly landed on him. As the creature tried to bite him, the commander shoved the barrel of his M4 into the creature's open mouth and pulled the trigger. Ichor sprayed out, and the lifeless body tumbled over the edge.

When the elevator reached eye level with Six, the waiting vampire leapt out. The small boy, maybe eleven or twelve years old, grew fangs and claws and reached for the leader's face. As he quickly backpedaled, Six gave a startled shout, and Ghost swung around. The vampire shied away from the hunter and the priest; instead, he leapt for Heavy.

Heavy dropped his shotgun on its sling to dangle and drew the pair of khukuri blades from the sheaths on his back. Meeting the leap head on, both Heavy and the boy vampire swung at each other. The glowing blades were again unerring and removed the creature's head in one graceful movement. As the glow faded from the blades, Doc pointed and gasped. Heavy looked down and realized that there was blood running down his arm from a long, thin scratch down his forearm.

"Damn. Thing must've scratched me," Heavy said as he flexed his arm and moved around, causing a thin trickle of blood to ooze down.

Doc pulled out a small first aid kit and did a very quick bandage wrap on the wound. She tied the bandage and asked, "How's that feel? Good to go?"

Heavy nodded and picked up his blessed blades. "I think I'm going with these while we're here," he said.

The team stepped onto the platform and pointed their weapons upwards. Six pushed the button marked "Level One," and the lift started to rise.

As they slowly rose above the floor of the top silo level, Six looked around and was glad that there was nothing waiting for them. The team leader locked the controls on the panel and looked around. Boomer swiveled to keep watch over the nearby stairs.

Level one was mostly storage boxes and trash. It looked as if the creatures had been actually living on this level. The stench from the garbage was vile and masked the odor of anything else that was up there.

Six looked at his team and paused while he looked at Heavy.

"Are we ready? We're going to go down, level by level," Six explained. "We'll lock off the elevator on each floor as we reach it. We clear this place out as we go down. Scorched earth. When we get down below, Boomer, you figure out how to bring the house down.

"As we lower, everybody stay as close to the center of the platform as possible. Form a box in the middle with Doc in the center. Boomer, you and I will be on opposite sides. Ghost and Heavy, you guys are on opposite sides. Doc, you stand in the center and keep us alive and keep the really evil stuff back. Questions?"

Everybody shook their heads, and Six reached out to unlock the lift controls. He pushed the button for the third level. The lift descended. As they passed the second level, the team all subconsciously moved closer and thought about what they might find.

As they dropped below the second level, the lift rattled and a pair of taloned hands grasped the edge. As a vampire poked its head over the lip of the lift, the creature found itself staring down the large barrel of Boomer's shotgun. The vampire snarled, and Boomer pulled the trigger. The regular vampire's body started to dissolve before it hit the platform below.

As the lift came to a stop on the third floor, Six stopped it and locked out the controls. There was a large stack of packing boxes in front of Heavy. A scream tore through the air as a form hurled itself over the boxes and at the team. As the second creature bounced over the boxes, the big spec ops machine gunner realized that they were revenants and shifted his stance for the fight.

Boomer shifted to face the screaming creatures when she was startled by hissing from directly above her. She looked up and saw a vampire release its grip on the ceiling of the level and begin to drop to the floor. The fiend pushed off the ceiling and was headed straight for the explosives expert. Boomer knew she wasn't fast enough and prepared herself for the attack.

The glow around the team intensified as the vampire got close to Doc's vestments. An outstretched hand and a shouted phrase drove the creature away, to make it land in a heap in front of Heavy.

The stunned vampire landed right in front of the revenants

caused the lead creature to trip and land sprawling across the vampire's back. Startled momentarily by the fallen vampire, the second one paused.

Heavy spotted the opening and took it. As he stepped forward, both blades whistled through the air and bit deeply. One blade took off the top of the sprawled out revenant's skull, and the other swiped clean through the neck of the vampire.

Boomer recovered quickly and sighted her shotgun down the barrel at the one remaining revenant. She stroked the trigger twice and sent two short bursts into the chest and face of the creature that killed it instantly. Boomer switched out her drum magazine for a fresh one and turned to look for more targets.

Six was watching the stairs when the young child vampire bounded up and over the top. Screaming in defiance, it rushed at the agents. The team leader pulled the trigger and sent a three-round burst of Norbert's ammunition into the chest of the young girl. The blast staggered the creature, but she quickly regained her footing and snarled. With bloodlust in her eyes, she again leapt at the DHS leader.

Ghost lunged forward. He timed his thrust to place the tip of his weapon right through the ribcage and pierce the heart. The vampire screamed in agony and rage as the blade burned its flesh from the inside. The creature raked its claws toward the hunter, raking them across the leather-clad arms and chest of Ghost's duster.

That one act of defiance was to be the creature's last. With the vampire pinned by the sword, Six aimed at the head of the small creature and pulled the trigger. Twice. Ghost pulled the blade free, and the body slumped to the ground.

Six quickly checked on his team. When each member of the team confirmed they were ok, Six engaged the lift. As they passed below the lip of the third level, the team scanned every nook and cranny of the walls and floor. This level was completely empty and was without even boxes or trash. Six didn't even pause the lift.

The fifth and sixth levels were also clear of monsters and debris, but that changed as the lift dropped toward the seventh level. Three sets of talon-tipped hands grasped the edge of the lift on different sides. The coordinated vampire attack struck with precision and speed, and the three vampires were on the platform before the team could react.

One of the vampires struck at Six directly. It reached up and knocked his rifle aside, avoiding the burst of bullets. As the vampire leapt onto the DHS leader, the vampire overbalanced its prey. Six crashed to the lift floor, and he fought for his life underneath the vampire.

Ghost's blade struck the vampire and ran it through the back and into its chest. The vampire howled in pain and reached up to swipe at the hunter. Six used the hunter's distraction to draw one of his M9s from the thigh holster. As he pointed the muzzle into the belly of the beast, the leader pulled the trigger.

By the fourth shot, the vampire rolled off Six and was stunned on the platform. Ghost yanked his blade free and swung it hard. In one swift movement, he cleanly removed the head of the creature. Six looked at the rest of the team to see how they were doing.

One of the vampires had landed in front of Heavy. Prepared for the attack, the big machine gunner raised the blessed blades he still carried and swung to decapitate the creature before him. The blades carried through the vampire's upraised arms and decapitated the creature. The heavy weapons specialist looked to his right and saw the vampire, cowering as it shrank away from the holy wrath of the priest. Boomer lined up the barrel of her shotgun and pulled the trigger, and the head of the cowering vampire exploded.

The team had no time to rest as four revenants attacked the platform. Six paused the platform at the floor of the seventh level, and the revenants leapt out of hiding. This time a concentrated roar of firepower quickly knocked out two of the creatures. Ghost and Heavy danced around the other two creatures as the teammates used their blades to wound the creatures while holding them out of striking distance.

Heavy was the first to get his kill. The two blessed blades bit deep into the neck of the revenant who proved too slow to avoid the big agent. With a simple yank and strike, the head of the revenant dropped to the platform as its body followed behind.

Ghost's revenant got desperate as its only remaining partner was killed. The revenant lunged, attempting to wrap up the hunter in a fatal embrace. Ghost's family blade burned right through the revenant's chest, but, unfortunately for the hunter, the creature used its last remaining strength and smashed its fists into the hunter's shoulder. Ghost felt a "pop" as the revenant died. Sheer agony blinded the hunter with red, and he passed out.

27

MONSTERS

Decommissioned Atlas Missile Silo, Divide, Colorado

Doc rushed over to the fallen hunter. As Six saw the priest bend over and worked on Ghost, he called out, "Cover Doc. Everyone pick an angle."

The medic-turned-priest gently, but quickly assessed the passed-out hunter. She noticed that his shoulder was in an odd angle, but she did not find any other wounds on his body. She rummaged through her field kit and found some smelling salts. She wafted the aromatic spirits of ammonia under his nose. Ghost awoke with a start and then cried out in pain as he clutched his shoulder.

Doc looked down at him and said, "Your shoulder has popped out of socket. This will hurt."

Ghost nodded and grasped her arm as she pulled and twisted. The pain flared and threatened to drag him unconscious again until the joint popped back into place. The pain dulled to a low ache, and Ghost flexed his hand and arm. He seemed to have most of his mobility back.

It was a long ninety seconds before Doc called out to Six. "We're good here. Let's get this over with," said Doc.

The team commander looked over and said, "We have no idea

what's down there. Whatever it is, we kill it. Hopefully, the master vamp is down here. Watch your targets and watch the ricochets."

He reached out and pushed a button. The elevator descended again.

. The farther they ventured down the shaft, the darker it became. Even though there were lights on around them, they somehow seemed dimmer. The normally brilliant lights turned to a low twilight as they descended. It was as if the very air surrounding them was dark and oppressive.

As the elevator dropped past the edge of the seventh level towards the bottom, there was a loud, terrifying roar from below. Moments later, it was followed by an answering call. The team gripped their weapons tighter, and Doc's vestments lit up and glowed blue.

Warned by her vestments, Doc looked up and watched as a vampire threw itself at the platform. It flailed in the air as it realized its momentum would take it near the priest. Doc raised the staked end of her cross and waited for the vampire to land. A loud thunder of gunfire disintegrated the head and upper torso of the vampire. Doc looked at the explosives expert and Boomer lowered her shotgun. The explosives expert smiled and swung back to face toward the walls of the elevator shaft while the glow faded on Doc's vestments.

The elevator stopped at the bottom of level eight a few seconds later. Here, the distance between the floor and the ceiling averaged about fifty feet instead of the usual twenty. Several clusters of old storage tanks that previously housed liquid missile propellants such as liquid oxygen and hydrogen and a large mountain of crates surrounded the elevator platform. An inky blackness seemed to ooze from behind the crates, edging into the light and swallowing what it touched.

Out of the darkness stepped a large creature that none of the team had ever seen before. Standing eight or nine feet tall the massive creature made Heavy look like a small man. The bipedal creature stood upright and had dark gray and blue mottled skin. The large sloping forehead led down to an oversized mouth with two large canine tusks sprouting from the lower jaw. The creature wore a strange type of cloth for its clothing; the garments seemed to be made of a modern fabric, but both the top and bottoms were seamless and hung loosely, draping over the creature.

This creature was not carrying anything that remotely resembled a firearm. Instead, it held a large warhammer that looked like it weighed several hundred pounds. With short spikes on its face, the hammer looked more like a meat tenderizer than a weapon, if you discounted the three-foot-long blade that was opposite the hammer face. Holding this massive hammer in hands that spanned a foot and a half, the creature raised the weapon to parade rest, as if waiting to see what the team would do. As the creature stepped fully into the light, the inky darkness quickly curled in on itself and vanished with an audible "pop." The creature and the team stood as they stared at each other.

Six studied the creature for a moment and asked a simple question: "Doc? Ghost? What the hell is that thing?"

Doc and Ghost both shrugged.

"I don't know," Doc replied. "It is like nothing I ever studied in the Vatican."

The veteran monster hunter chimed in, "I've got nothing, boss. Some kind of troll, maybe? It's nothing like I've seen before."

The creature in front of them snarled in a bass rumble that the warriors felt in the soles of their shoes.

"How dare you call me a troll! I am Thoktaller, a warrior of clan Urkantos, mightiest of all the Chikara," the thick, gravelly voice rumbled from the creature. "I was prepared to accept your surrender, but now I shall destroy you."

"Where do you come from, and how do you speak English?" Doc demanded.

The creature's chuckle dislodged some of the loose debris scattered around the team. "Ignorant human. I do not speak this 'English' that you prattle on about. The nexus translates for me as it does for all travelers." The creature then growled. "Enough stalling. It is a good day for you to die. Let us get on with it."

All of the team members already had their weapons drawn and pointed at the creature. Six squeezed the trigger and let loose two short bursts of fire. The team leader watched as most of his rounds impacted with the upper chest of the creature, but not one of them even penetrated the creature's clothing. The creature staggered slightly under the assault, but it never went down.

A fraction of a second after their commander had opened fire, the rest of the team followed. Heavy and Boomer each unleashed a long string of automatic shotgun fire. The rattle of their shotguns was punctuated by the crack of Ghost's rifle. The combination of multiple hits from the automatic shotguns and the hunter's rifle was enough to make the creature reel and stumble.

Roaring in agony, the creature looked down and saw its thick purple blood running down and pooling on the floor. It took a huge step forward and swung the massive warhammer at the team. The team members scattered like bowling pins as they tried to get out of the way of the enraged monster.

Six and Ghost dove to the creature's left, and both of the agents ended up tumbled among the small crates and dross that surrounded the bottom of the silo. Six landed on top of a partially eaten animal carcass. Ghost landed a couple of feet away, ramming his still-painful shoulder into a small wooden crate that splintered on impact. The shipping materials in the crate spilled out and covered his face momentarily.

Boomer and Doc dove to the creature's right. They landed in a small pile of crates, and the impact jarred the cross from the priest's hands. As she reached for her sidearm, Doc realized that it, too, had fallen out during her dive. She quickly looked around the debris. Boomer landed and rolled onto her back about five feet away from Doc. She was somehow able to keep her hands on her shotgun. As she sat up to take aim at the creature, she realized she was sitting in a small pool of liquid. She really hoped that it was water.

Heavy leapt straight at the creature as he hoped to get inside the creature's reach. Dropping his AA-12, he rolled over and drew his blades. As they cleared the sheaths, he could see that they were again glowing their reassuring green. He crouched in front of the large creature and swung his blades. Hoping that the legs of this creature shared some of the same weak points that plagued human legs, he tried to swipe at the leg. The machine gunner's backhanded slash caught one of the giant creature's heels and bit deep, causing the crea-ture to crash down on one knee as that leg gave out. Heavy rolled to the left and out of the way as he tried to stay out of the range of those massive arms and giant fists.

Thoktaller had never felt such pain. His left leg refused to work, and he was angry that the insignificant humans had so far bested him. His rage was building inside him and threatened to tear itself out. But even with his rising rage, he realized that he could not take them all on in this condition.

"Matokar!" the creature roared.

The large stack of wooden crates directly behind Doc and Boomer exploded toward the team as another creature swung through the obstacles. Pieces of broken crates flew around the room. One of them struck Six in the head and shoulder and stunned him.

This new foe was of the same type and look as the first creature, but it was slightly larger and more muscular.

"My brother!" the creature roared back.

Matokar whirled his large warhammer above his head as he looked for his first target.

Doc scrambled to get out of the creature's way by backing toward the outer wall of the silo on her hands and knees. Here she was out of her element and out of the fight—her training never covered extra-dimensional beings.

Although Doc was fast, the movement caught Matokar's eye. Matokar looked at the small human nearly at his feet. Recognizing easy prey, he stepped toward her and prepared to strike. The giant creature grinned, its lips split showing rotting teeth and large yellowed tusks.

Doc began to pray.

Boomer had pivoted when the second creature burst through the stack of crates. Boomer quickly realized that this creature was targeting the priest, and the explosives expert dropped the drum from her shotgun and slammed a shorter magazine back into the receiver. She cycled the bolt, brought the automatic shotgun to her shoulder, and pulled the trigger. Twice.

The creature was about twelve feet away when Boomer's shotgun roared two short bursts of fire and the bolt locked back on an empty magazine. The first burst hit the creature in its right shoulder, and the miniature FRAG-12 grenade rounds detonated. Designed to explode and penetrate up to a half-inch steel plate, the miniature grenades detonated and tore apart the creature's shoulder; the damage severed the arm at the joint, causing the mangled remains of the massive limb to crash to the floor. The giant monster was only beginning to realize that it was in pain when the second burst hit the center of its chest. All four rounds impacted in a dinner-plate-sized area.

Matokar stood still for a second. As he looked down, it occurred to him that there was a hole where his chest and lungs were supposed to be. Even the natural bone plating that protected the heart of every member of his race was splintered and missing. He fell to his knees and then gave in to the embrace of death.

After seeing his brother killed so violently, Thoktaller roared in rage and grief. He ignored the human at his side and scrambled forward, dragging his wounded leg as he reached for the one who had just slaughtered his kin. He was brought up short when a human stood in front of him and drew a sword that glowed white in the dim light.

Angry that this insignificant human would dare challenge a warrior such as him, he struck at the human. The man dodged the creature's feeble attack and countered with an attack of his own. The tip of his sword pierced the creature's chest, and Thoktaller felt it lodge into the bone structure that grew around his heart. His rage blocked his pain, and he swung again at this swordsman. The man barely dodged his attack, and the swordsman countered with a thrust that struck a bone. Each thrust injured the creature, drawing blood, and Thoktaller could feel his life-force ebbing away.

Ghost yanked his sword from the chest of the creature. He settled into his dueling stance as he prepared to dodge another attack from the massive creature. He was still perplexed that he seemed to be hitting some sort of boney substance inside the creature's chest. The creature feebly swung at him again. Ghost drove his blade into the creature's chest. This time, the creature seemed to give a final heave and collapsed, nearly trapping the hunter's ancestral blade under-neath its great bulk. On the back of the now-dead monster clung Heavy. Both of his blessed blades were buried to the hilt in the crea-ture's back.

"I thought I'd give you a hand. I wasn't sure this damn thing was ever going to die," Heavy said as he wearily smiled.

Ghost smiled and agreed, "I wonder what it is."

Six stood up and shook his head as he felt a gash on his forehead. "Everyone ok? Make sure there's nothing else hiding down here," the leader said.

The team slowly rose from the wreckage around them. Each team member brushed at the debris on their clothing and then scoured the level. They made sure that they were alone in the bottom of the silo. When they found no other creatures, the team leader gathered everyone together.

"Ok, Doc, Ghost. Either of you know anything about these crea-tures? Why didn't your robes light up, Doc?" questioned Six.

Doc shook her head. "They must not be vampires. My vestments only warn of hostile undead nearby, and these creatures were clearly living," she explained. "What did it say it was? Chikata? Chikara?"

Ghost clarified that the beast called itself a Chikara. "I have never heard of that type of monster," he added. "I wonder if Section 28 has any records."

"We'll have to ask later," said Six. "Everybody make sure they have everything with them. Make sure you didn't drop anything. If you did, ask for help to find it."

Six activated his mic as he attempted to contact Spooky. "Spooky, Six. What's your progress there?"

"I'm about wrapped up here, boss. Maybe ten more minutes," Spooky replied. "You should see some of the stuff this dude had. I think I know where he released this virus. And you are not going to like it."

"All right. We'll discuss it when we get up there. You have your ten minutes," Six said as he answered his electronics specialist. "Prep everything that we need to take with us. Anything left behind is going to be buried."

The team leader looked at his team to make sure they were ok. Doc had found and retrieved her cross, and everyone else was verifying that they still had all the gear they came in with.

"Ten minutes 'till we move out," said Six. "Doc, take some tissue samples of these critters, in case Agent Smith wants them. Ghost, take all the photos you can on your SSP. Take a video walk around as well. That should get us enough visual evidence. Heavy, I want to take one of the heads with us. You've got the blades; find a bag or box for transport. Boomer, bring this silo down, and don't let it be recoverable. I want to fill in this silo, the tunnel, and the command levels. Make your plans and start rigging. Set everything on a timer for, say, one hour."

Everyone acknowledged their assignments and got to work. Six walked around to see what exactly was in those crates that had been scattered about the silo. Most of them had contained necessities such as food, water, and clothing. A few of the crates had held what appeared to be items or knickknacks, whose manufacturer and style the agent had never seen before. Following a hunch, he grabbed several of the items to take them back to Section 28 for analysis.

Ten minutes later, everyone else had finished their duties, and they were waiting on Boomer to finish placing her last explosives. She walked toward the group and stared in shock at Heavy. The big machine gunner stood in the middle of the lift with a box under his arm and one of the large warhammers over his shoulder.

After Heavy had severed the head of one of the creatures, he had examined one of the dropped warhammers. Although he had expected to find it to be incredibly heavy, the massive hammer only weighed about eighty pounds. Because it was made of a metal he had never seen before, he figured that Agent Smith would probably like to have one of these as well. When he carted it over to the elevator, Six had glanced at him and raised an eyebrow. The big man laughed and said, "Souvenir." The team leader could only shake his head trying to stifle a laugh at the big man's choice.

When all of his team was ready, Six pressed the button marked "Level Two" on the control panel, and the elevator slowly ground its way upward toward the second level. Once the team had arrived at the second level, they all walked into the tunnel, pausing long enough to allow Boomer time to place another series of charges at the end of the tunnel nearest the silo.

The team walked toward the other end of the tunnel, and Six radioed ahead.

"We're coming up the tunnel now. Stand down," Six ordered.

"Copy," God replied. "We're all clear here. Come on in."

The silo team walked out of the tunnel and into the command level. The sniper and the former deputy both stared at their disheveled teammates, from their minor wounds to the torn jumpsuits all around. When Do-Right saw the warhammer Heavy was carrying, he could only stare with a gaped mouth.

Six waved off any questions. "I'll fill everyone in on the way," Six said. "Are we set here?"

Spooky appeared around the corner and placed a small box on top of a small pile of similar boxes. He said, "I've got everything I need boss. We're ready to blow this sucker sky high." The electronics specialist caught sight of the giant warhammer. "What the heck is that thing, Heavy?"

The big man made a show of looking at the warhammer, then looked at Spooky and gave the same answer he had given his boss, "Souvenir."

Spooky thought for a moment and replied, "Remind me to never really piss you off."

Six cleared his throat to get his team's attention and started to direct them.

"All right, let's haul all of this gear out. If you have a free hand, grab a bunch of stuff. If we have to make multiple trips, we stage everything in the entry corridor and then take everything out to the truck. God, you and Boomer have overwatch. Don't carry anything. Boomer will be laying charges behind us."

Boomer set several small explosives in the doorway and in the lab area of that command level. As the team carried all the equipment and boxes past the first level, she stopped briefly to plant even more charges. With enough hands and help, the team did not have to make more than one trip, and Boomer placed charges at specific intervals throughout the tunnel behind them. When the team had left the tunnels and had moved to the waiting War Wagon, Boomer had Heavy prop the blown entry door back up and wedge it into the opening.

While they were able to store everything else inside the storage compartments of the truck, Heavy's giant souvenir wouldn't quite fit. He reluctantly consented to wrapping the massive warhammer in a tarp and strapping it securely to the top of the MRAP. After sternly warning Boomer about the consequences of losing or damaging his prize, he finally was able to secure it to his satisfaction.

As they waited for Boomer's explosions to seal the site, Spooky uploaded a report to Agent Smith about the excursion and included a query about the strange monsters encountered. While the report was being transmitted, the electronics specialist gave his team leader some troubling news.

"I think I figured out where the creepy Doctor Kaine unleashed and tested his virus," Spooky said as he pulled up maps and charts on his terminal. "According to his notes, what he said about the virus spread appears true... only one in five typically contract the virus, and it takes a couple of days to incubate. He increased those odds dramatically, to fifty-fifty, when he used a series of direct injections. And according to this notation, the 'stability and manifest powers drop according to each generation of the host.' I think that means that every time a new vampire is created from a new breed, the powers that show up are a bit weaker than the generation before."

Doc leaned over Spooky's shoulders and read some of the technical areas of the document. "Spooky's correct. Each generation gets less powerful," Doc explained.

Spooky nodded his thanks and continued. "So where would you test this out? He needed someplace close, yet out of the way, and somewhere his subjects wouldn't be missed for weeks. I think he chose a youth summer camp."

Boomer swore, and Doc looked at Spooky in horror.

The electronics specialist continued, his voice flat and somber. "Every one of the new breed of vampires that you fought and killed was a young kid. I also confirmed that with the records. Two of the new breed that I saw both were wearing camp attire from this 'Blue Mountain Ranch.' It's a youth camp about sixteen miles from here. On his hard drive, I found a couple of letters to the camp, as well as an application for a youth to attend. That's the only proof I have at this point, but my gut says I'm right."

At that moment, the timer on Boomer's SSP went off. Boomer shook herself. "Thirty seconds until detonation."

While everyone found a porthole to look out, God reached up and shut the top hatch as a precaution. Seeing the move, Boomer reached over and toggled the switch to close the back ramp and sealed the vehicle.

As the rear hatch closed, a distinct rumble shook the MRAP on its massive springs. About a hundred yards away, the tunnel entrance collapsed with a shower of dust and debris.

Boomer looked at her team leader and said, "All right. So what's next?"

28

HUNTING

Blue Mountain Ranch, Florissant, Colorado

I t was late afternoon as the jet black MRAP marked with "Department of Homeland Security" rolled through the front gates of Blue Mountain Ranch. Thirty minutes earlier, the agent in charge of the team had contacted his boss in Langley. After a brief discussion, Six had received the approval to hit the youth camp hard, and with as much firepower as they needed.

With real-time satellite imagery to guide them, the team was able to form a rudimentary plan to assault the compact youth camp. Realizing that the age of the campers ranged from seven to sixteen, Six knew they had to take extra care in planning this raid. Agent Smith told the team leader that they could not shoot unless they had positive proof that the camp was infected. They had to get a reaction from the campers and staffers and prove, to their satisfaction, that the camp was overrun.

In the end, the simplest plan was to roll up in the War Wagon with the story of an escaped convict on the loose. After Boomer pulled the truck to the front of the office building, they would all deploy quickly, having already geared up, and Doc would only climb out when they were relatively certain of infection. God would be up in the turret as soon as they established the presence of vampires.

Boomer pulled to a halt in front of the main office building and turned off the engine. As the big diesel cooled down, she flipped the switch for the back hatch. Six jumped out of his side door and walked around the front of the truck to meet the camp staff member who was coming out of the office.

The older gentleman introduced himself as the camp director, Frank Gould.

"What are you guys doing here? Is there some kind of problem?" the director asked.

Six gave the established cover story.

"I am Special Agent Burt Holstein, Department of Homeland Security. I hate to say this, but there is an escaped killer on the loose. His GPS tag last put him near this area. You need to enact whatever safety protocols you have in place. Every camper needs to be in his or her cabin, and we'll take one of your people with us on a quick look around the area to make sure he's not hiding out here."

The older gentleman turned and quickly walked into the office area. A moment later, the team heard a feedback squeal from the PA system, and then the director's voice came on.

"Attention campers and staff. This is a safety recall announcement. All campers and staff to their assigned cabins. Again, this is a safety recall announcement. All campers and staff report to your assigned cabins. I will provide more detail shortly."

As the director made his announcement, Six leaned over and activated his own mic.

"Doc, stay in the War Wagon with Spooky until I tell you to come out. We may catch a break on this one," said Six.

The director walked out of his office and found a team of six DHS agents in a loose group, all facing different directions. The lead DHS agent introduced the rest of his team and asked the director if he had enough staff members not currently assigned to cabins to send one with each of his team members.

The camp director shook his head. "I can maybe rustle up three or four more but not enough."

"That's fine," Six said as he nodded. "The rest can find their way, and they can explain what they are doing to any cabin they meet. Can you get those people over here now?"

Gould reached for the walkie talkie radio on his hip. "Attention, auxiliary staff," he began. "I need you at the main office ASAP for briefing and assistance. Please come quickly."

The camp director looked up and saw three people already walking across the camp toward him. A fourth soon walked out of another outbuilding and jogged toward the growing group.

Six turned toward the truck and keyed his mic. In a low voice, he said, "Spooky, can you monitor their walkie channels? I want to know what they're saying."

He could hear the smile in Spooky's voice. "Way ahead of you, boss," Spooky explained. "I'm monitoring all CB band and digital 900Mz bands. If they say anything, we'll know about it."

Six keyed his radio to answer. "That's why you're the best. Six out," he said.

Frank introduced the agents to his staffers. "This is Cliff Legg; he's the rifle instructor. This is Lynn Powell. Lynn is our camp nurse. Yvette Shand is our arts director. And Dylan Blaney is our chef. Everyone else is either in town or with their assigned campers."

Six nodded and pointed to his team, pairing them off with the staffers. "Jesús, why don't you go with Mister Legg? Rebekah, you work with Miss Powell. Christian, why don't you accompany Miss Shand, and Art, why don't you help Mister Blaney."

The team commander paused as if pondering his last agent. "Jonas, you wander around and check on the outlying buildings. I'm going to stay here and coordinate with Frank. I'm waiting on the sheriff to call back, anyway."

"Each team take a different set of buildings and cabins. Verify the adults and kids, number and names. You each know what this guy looks like, so keep your eyes open. Any questions?" Six asked. After pausing momentarily, he continued, "Alright then, let's get this show rolling."

All the pairs split off. Boomer and the nurse headed toward the girls' cabins. Quickly moving across the grounds, the two women hurried across the tennis courts and approached the first cabin. The cabin was filled with the older girls. As the camp nurse explained why the DHS agents were there, the explosives expert carefully looked around, trying to determine if any of the girls were infected. The bunks and rooms were as neat as could be expected from young teenage girls. Almost every bed was filled, although there were a couple that stood empty or unmade dotted throughout the rooms.

Once the counselors in the cabin assured Ms. Powell and Boomer that everyone was accounted for, the two women and went to the cabin that housed the younger girls. After meeting the counselors there, the camp nurse and Boomer were told the same story, that everyone was accounted for and that there had been no signs of strangers around camp. A few more empty beds dotted the rooms here, but no mention was made of them. While Boomer did not notice any outward signs of infection, the explosives expert's intuition told her that something was very wrong. As they stepped out of the second cabin, the nurse told Boomer that she needed to take care of some items in her office and asked if Boomer needed her help any longer. Boomer assured the nurse she would be fine, and the nurse trotted across the expanse of grass and scrub that covered the grounds.

As she walked away, the nurse pulled out her walkie talkie and said, "This is Lynn. All of the girls are accounted for. Heading to my office next."

As Boomer explored the area around the cabins, an older teen girl, probably fifteen or sixteen years old, snuck out from behind a cabin. Boomer tensed and swung her rifle in the girl's direction. When she realized that the girl was not going to attack her, the explosives specialist asked, "What are you doing out here? It's not safe."

The young teen looked at her. "It isn't safe in there either," she whispered. "Last night, Tina was taken away. I think I'm next. I think I'm the only 'normal' one left." She emphasized "normal" with air quotes.

Boomer knelt down and softly said, "Tell me what you know. I'll help you."

And the girl began to talk in soft, hushed tones.

ABOUT TWO HUNDRED YARDS AWAY FROM BOOMER, HEAVY JOGGED WITH the camp cook toward one of the staff cabins and the mess hall. As he took a quick glance inside the staff cabin, the machine gunner noted that there were four made-up bunks in the men's side of the cabin. As he looked in the women's side, he noted that there were three made-up bunks and one that was completely bare.

He nodded at the chef, and they moved to the mess hall. The hall was cavernous, large enough to sit over a hundred campers and staff at the tables arranged in neat lines. Through an open doorway on the back wall, Heavy could see a large kitchen. As the pair walked around and through the large mess hall and kitchen, something seemed off. Heavy couldn't quite put his finger on what was wrong. He suddenly realized what was bothering him—everything was put away neatly. It was all very clean.

As they were ready to leave the expansive mess hall, he suddenly realized what was wrong. It was *too* quiet. The chef should have been preparing food for the next day, and he should have had at least one other person helping him either prepare a meal or clean up from a meal. There should have been meals being prepped; instead, the kitchen was spotless, and there was no one else in the building.

Turning to the chef, Heavy asked, "What time do you serve dinner here?"

The cook stammered an answer. After several moments, he finally blurted out his response. "Five o'clock. Why?"

Heavy glanced down at his watch and realized that it was just after five. "Just wondering," he cautiously responded.

An odd look crossed the cook's face, and he said, "Will you excuse me a moment. I need to make a phone call. My office is back through there. I'll be right back out." The cook walked into his office and then shut the door.

Heavy looked around, searching for evidence that the kitchen was actually being used. As he opened the refrigerators, the machine gunner found what seemed to be enough food to feed the entire camp. When he opened the walk-in cooler, he found a great deal of meat stacked on shelves as well as other cold storage food stacked away neatly. His cursory glance seemed enough, and he turned to go, but then he spotted something in the back of the meats area. The big man reached back on the shelf and grasped a piece of meat that seemed out of place. Realizing what it was, he shuddered as he drew it out of the pile.

DO-RIGHT FOLLOWED THE OLDER ARTS AND CRAFTS DIRECTOR AS THEY headed north out of the office area. They first visited the offices for the staffers, including the nurse's office. Verifying that there were no intruders present in those areas, the two walked over to the large building that was just north of those offices and past the pool. As they trekked across the field, the former deputy marveled at the complete lack of local wildlife and nature sounds.

The wooded area surrounding the camp should be teeming with life, full of the sounds of birds and animals, but this area seemed almost unnaturally quiet. His years of hunting in the Colorado mountains told him that this meant that there was a major predator in the area.

The two reached the doors of the recreation hall. As they walked through the large set of wooden double doors, the young deputy looked around and whistled softly. The large building was elaborately decorated in the rustic charm of the west. The wood plank flooring matched the vaulted ceiling and exposed beams. The large exposed beam ceiling led his eye to the opposite end of the room to the massive fireplace that stood as the focal point of the room. Several long community tables were scattered throughout the expansive open area and, on one side of the room, an empty ping pong table and a foosball table awaited their players. Along one wall stood large cabinets and shelves filled with art and craft supplies.

"What a beautiful facility. You guys must be proud," the deputy commented to Ms. Shand.

"Thank you so much," she replied. "It makes a great place for the kids to be creative."

After verifying that no one else was in the facility, they closed the doors again and walked back toward the main office. Do-Right looked to their left and noticed a large building next to the small stables. Pointing to the building, he asked the woman, "What's that building?"

"That's one of the original lodges," the arts and crafts director explained. "They're currently trying to gather enough donations so they can renovate the building and make it usable, again. Right now, it's closed off because the structure is unsafe."

The deputy pointed to a lonely house up a short hill. "And that one?"

Ms. Shand smiled, "That's the head handyman's cabin, but I don't know if he's back yet. He went to town earlier today to pick up supplies."

Do-Right walked toward the other buildings. "Let's go check those while we're out here," he said, not waiting for an argument.

The arts director nodded and grabbed her walkie talkie. "This is Yvette. Pavilion and offices are clear. We're heading up to Henry's cabin and the bunkhouse."

* * *

GOD AND THE RIFLE INSTRUCTOR WALKED TOWARD THE BOYS' CABINS AT the north end of the camp. The only building area further north was the archery and rifle range. Ghost wandered along with the two men and then the monster hunter left the two men to check out the outlying ranges.

The sniper and Mr. Legg approached the first of the boys' cabins, which the rifle instructor informed him was for the youngest of campers, ages seven to nine. The two walked up to the cabin door, and the camp staffer introduced the DHS agent to the boys' counselor. After explaining what the DHS team was doing there, God walked around the cabin. He looked at the kids and talked to those who wanted to talk. He noticed that there were several empty bunks here and there seemed to be no pattern or apparent reason for it.

After he verified that all the counselor's kids were present, he and the instructor left to check out the next cabin.

In both of the remaining boys' cabins, there were several empty bunks, much like the first. As God walked around the third cabin with the oldest boys, he noticed a small tear in one of the empty bunks, with a faint pinkish stain on the edges of the mattress. Feigning that he never saw the tear or stain, he kept his smile in place and walked right past it in stride.

The DHS sniper walked out the door with the camp rifle instructor, and God motioned to the bathroom and shower rooms that stood a short distance away.

"Let's check those out, then we can head back," said God.

The rifle instructor nodded and grabbed his walkie talkie off his belt. After keying the microphone, he said, "This is Cliff. All the boys are accounted for. We're on our way back soon."

———————

GHOST PASSED THE BOYS' CABINS AND HEADED TOWARD THE boathouses that sat on the banks of a small lake. After quickly glancing around the structures, the hunter realized that they offered no place to hide, and he moved on toward the rifle range just around the bend in the access road.

As he walked, he keyed his microphone. "Spooky, Ghost. Any signs of life around the rifle range? Hot or cold?"

Spooky quickly replied, "Wait one... yes. I have one heat source in the bushes on the north side of the range, about twenty yards north. Looks like adult size. No other info."

Ghost replied, "Thanks, Spooky. Ghost out."

The hunter continued to stroll casually toward the range. As he approached shooting stations, he looked all around the range, including near the backstop. He then stood and faced the bushes Spooky told him about and cradled his rifle. Without directly pointing the rifle at the bushes, Ghost readied it enough so he could bring it to bear before whatever was in the bushes had a chance to reach him.

"I know you're back there," he called out. "Come on out. I'm a Special Agent with the Department of Homeland Security. I will not harm you if you come out now."

A youthful sounding male voice rose from the bushes. "Don't shoot. I'm coming out. I'm unarmed."

Ghost watched as a young man in his mid-twenties stood slowly and raised his hands. He carefully stepped out of the brush and walked toward the agent.

Lowering the rifle a fraction, Ghost motioned for the man to come closer.

"Who are you, and what are you doing out here?" Ghost demanded.

The man nervously looked around them. Seemingly satisfied, he spoke.

"I'm Bill Buckhorn. I'm the archery instructor and assistant rifle instructor here. I'm so glad you guys are here. I've been hiding out here for two days. I think they've given up on finding me," the man explained.

Ghost looked the man over. "Why were you hiding out here?" he asked. "Who are you hiding from?"

The man looked around and gulped. He took a breath and began to explain. "I think they're killing some of the kids. I noticed a few of the kids disappear over the last couple of days. And I think it had something to do with that doctor that was out here a few days ago. The director and the nurse said something about having everyone inoculated against a particularly nasty bug going around. After that, something changed."

There seemed to be a hitch in the young man's voice. "Yesterday, I was in the kitchen to get a snack during my break. I opened the cooler for some food, and I found... an arm! I thought it was a joke at first, but on the wrist was a craft bracelet that I recognized as belonging to one of my campers. They told me that she left camp early because she was sick. I freaked out and ran into the woods, and I haven't been back since." Tears slowly coursed their way down the man's dusty face.

Ghost reached down and pulled his cross out of his pocket. The hunter long ago learned how powerful faith was as a weapon against the undead, and belief in the power of the symbol was a powerful force. The hunter looked down. The cross did not give any hint of light, nor did the man shy away from it. He decided to break a few protocols and trust his instincts.

"I know this is going to seem strange, but would you reach out and touch this cross for me?" Ghost asked. "Just touch it."

The young camp staffer reached out tentatively and touched the cross. It stayed dark, and he was not burned.

The man looked at Ghost and asked, "What's the big deal about that cross? I'm wearing one here." And he reached into his shirt and pulled out his own plain gold cross.

Ghost nodded and held up his hand to the man. He keyed his radio and then spoke.

"Spooky, Ghost. Made contact. Check camp records for Bill Buckhorn. Archery instructor. And can you send a photo of Kaine to my phone?"

"Sending picture now," Spooky replied. "Confirm William Buckhorn listed as staff. Specialty is archery. Running search now. Twenty-six years old. Five-eight. Just over two hundred. Brown hair, brown eyes. Looks like possibly Native American. Does that help?"

Ghost smiled. "Perfect," he replied. "Ghost out."

The hunter held up his phone with a picture of the late Dr. Bishop Kaine displayed on the screen. "Is this the doctor that was out here for the inoculations?"

"Yeah, that's the guy," Buckhorn said with a nod. "So who is he?"

Ghost frowned grimly. "Someone who keeps causing trouble. Even from the grave."

He held up his hand again to silence the archery instructor.

"Six, Ghost. Attention for all team. Confirmed sighting of Kaine here at the camp three days ago. Gave injections to staff and campers as 'viral inoculations'. Witness says kids are disappearing. Outbreak confirmed."

"This is Six. Copy report. Anyone else have confirmation?"

"Six, Boomer. Confirmed with another witness. Teen girl."

There was a long pause.

The team leader quickly thought and created a battle plan. With his team spread all over the camp, he needed to get them back to the office area as quickly as possible. As he was thinking, he left the director and stepped outside to the War Wagon so he could have some privacy from the camp director and his staff.

He made up his mind and let his team know. "This is Six. Everyone back to the main office to regroup. Meet at the Wagon. Ghost, Boomer, exercise caution. Keep your cargo safe."

Boomer grasped the hand of the teenager a little more tightly as she walked with her across the grass and toward the offices. The explosives expert constantly looked around, waiting and watching for an attack. She saw God and the staffer with him appear from behind the boys' cabins, traveling at a jog. The sniper altered his course slightly so he could meet with Boomer and walk with her the rest of the way back to the truck.

Do-Right loped back down the hill from the empty groundskeeper's cabin toward the offices. As he looked to his right, he saw Ghost emerge from the wooded trails, his trench coat flapping and hat threatening to fly off with his movement. Beside the hunter trotted a young man who looked to be just older than the deputy. Their paths converged near the main pavilion, and they walked the rest of the way to the offices together. It soon became obvious to Do-Right that the man with Ghost stayed as far away as possible from the arts director who accompanied Do-Right. The young deputy was being as vague as possible when the arts director asked why they were returning.

Heavy had just pulled the strange piece of meat out of the walk-in cooler in the main kitchen when Ghost called Six and confirmed the infestation. Looking at the child-sized human arm in his hands, with a sick feeling in the pit of his stomach, the big man realized that the cook had been turned as well.

The machine gunner looked up as the door to the cooler slowly opened. The cook stood in the doorway with a large cleaver in his hand. The man had a strange glint in his eye, and he flashed a grin filled with razor-sharp teeth.

"I see you found my secret ingredient," the cook said. "Hey, it saves on the budget, and none of the non-enlightened kids ever knew."

"But don't worry," the cook added. "Your friends won't last long enough to tell anybody."

The man stepped toward Heavy.

"Catch!" said Heavy, and he tossed the arm to the unsuspecting cook.

The momentary pause and flinch of the cook gave the agent enough time to draw his khukuri. The blades once again glowed a faint green.

The cook lunged forward, and Heavy swung with the blades.

As he swung, Heavy tripped over some meat that had fallen on the floor of the cooler, and he fell face first, wildly swinging the blades. One of the khukuri went skittering across the floor and under one of the wire racks. The other one bit deeply into the lower leg of the creature, almost cutting clean through.

The creature stumbled and was unable to swing its own blade at the agent. Sitting back on his backside, Heavy fumbled with the shotgun that hung at his side. Bringing it to bear, he could only hold it with one hand. He pulled the trigger for a long pull. The fully automatic shotgun roared, sending ten rounds of silver and wood twelve gauge slugs through the torso and head of the vampire. The creature shuddered and dropped to the floor.

And then all hell broke loose.

29

CAMP

Blue Mountain Ranch, Florissant, Colorado

Six watched as his team approached the War Wagon. Boomer was holding the hand of her young witness while the rifle instructor was keeping pace with God. Do-Right and Ghost jogged across the field with the arts director and an adult who Six did not recognize in step. The roar of a full-auto shotgun filled the air.

Six heard the rear hatch of the truck drop as he quickly keyed his mic and said, "Heavy, Six. What happened?"

The team heard the machine gunner's panting reply. "I'm good boss. The cook was a nightcrawler... must be the new kind."

Boomer raised her shotgun and pointed it at the arts director, but Boomer was hesitant to pull the trigger. The woman raised her hands and took a few steps back as she began to sob and nervously babble.

"What are you doing? Why are you pointing that big gun at me? I didn't do anything," the woman claimed.

Sensing something amiss, Doc stepped out of the truck, and her vestments began glowing a bright blue. As soon as she saw the priest, the arts director fell back and cowered as she hissed and spit at the priest. The team watched in fascination as the fangs extended from both the upper and lower jaws of the vampire. Her eyes turned totally black. She raised hands with long, sharp nails extruding from her fingers.

Doc stepped forward and began to speak in Latin. Before the first sentence was out of her mouth, Boomer pulled the trigger on her AA-12. The shotgun barked once, and the camp staffer collapsed. The top of the vampire's head was missing.

"No time for Latin. It's time to take out the predators," Boomer said as she looked at Doc.

The teen by Boomer's side crouched in fear and clung to her legs, hiding her face in the folds of the tactical BDUs. Boomer reached her left hand down and hugged the girl tightly. She knelt down, so she was eye-to-eye with the frightened girl.

"I'm going to put you somewhere safe until this is over," Boomer reassured the child. "I want you to sit in my big truck and wait for me to come get you."

The explosives expert led her gently around to the back of the War Wagon and up the steps.

"This is my friend, Spooky," Boomer said to the girl as she introduced her teammate. "He will make sure you're safe. Just don't touch any buttons or open any boxes. And don't look out the windows. It will be scary out there. Ok?"

The frightened girl nodded.

"Keep her safe. I'll be back for her," the explosives expert told Spooky.

Boomer reached in and grabbed several magazines of the FRAG-12 grenades, including a couple that Norbert had marked as "Experimental - Use Against Vampires." She then climbed down the steps, and Spooky keyed the switch to close and seal the hatch.

As she climbed out of the truck, Boomer saw that Heavy, who looked a little rattled, had re-joined the team. As she listened in on the conversation, she heard the big man exclaim, "And they were feeding the pieces to the rest of the camp, vamp and human! I found an honest-to-goodness arm—a child's arm—in the cooler."

Six cut in. "Estimates? Boomer, how many girls?"

"I saw forty-five or fifty girls. Unknown percentage not infected," the explosives expert said after quickly doing the math in her head.

Six pointed to God. "And you? Boys?"

The sniper paused and said, "About the same. Unknown number uninfected."

"Ok. God, up on the roof of the War Wagon," the team commander continued. "You are our long distance line of defense. Start taking them out as far away as possible. Boomer, Do-Right, and I will cover from the ground. Ghost, Heavy, and Doc have close-in support. Engage from a distance with your long guns but use your blades when they get close. Doc, anything you can drum up will help now."

"Call it eighty hostiles, with friendlies mixed in. Plus staff. My guess is the master is around here somewhere. Do not fire until you make sure of your target."

Six keyed his mic and said, "Spooky. If we go down, call in air support and level this camp. You cannot let any of these vampires get away."

Spooky placed the call directly to Agent Smith and provided him with Six's plan of action. Agent Smith asked his assistant where the closest air base was, and he was told that it was Ellsworth Air Force Base in South Dakota and that they flew the B1-B "Lancer" bombers. Agent Smith said he would call the base commander and request he launch two of the bombers equipped with sufficient firepower. Smith explained to Spooky that the bombers were supersonic and capable of arriving within a short timeframe. They would be on station over the camp until the operation was over, one way or another.

The radio on the arts director's belt squawked. It was the camp director calling for his staff to check in. One-by-one, the staff radioed in, except for the cook and the arts director. Deducing the meaning of the gunfire and the lack of a response from two of his staff, the camp director gave a final chilling message over the radio.

"DHS agents who are listening to this radio: We are coming to get you," warned the camp director.

God scrambled onto the roof of the War Wagon and dropped to his knees for more stability. The rest of the team fanned out around the front and sides of the truck. Boomer and Heavy each stood on a different side of the massive vehicle. Six stood right in front of the truck, about equidistant from his long-range support. Ghost slipped in between Boomer and Six while Heavy stepped between Six and Do-Right. Doc stood behind Six at the front of the truck, waiting to hold off vampires.

The doors to the main camp offices flung open and the camp director, the secretary, and the director's wife all came out the door in a rush. Boomer and Ghost immediately fired, sending shotgun slugs and rifle rounds through the body of the director's wife. As the creature fell under the fusillade of vampire rounds, the camp director howled in rage and launched himself at the two. Six turned slightly and placed the crosshairs over the man's chest. After a quick squeeze of the trigger, a trio of rounds ripped into the vampire's chest. Screaming in agony, the camp director crashed to a halt and reeled from the blows. Regaining his senses, the director scrambled to his feet and flew at Six.

Boomer switched targets to the camp secretary. The explosives expert methodically squeezed the trigger on her shotgun and put three rounds into the chest of the creature. As the vampire fell, Boomer paused to carefully put one more round into the head of each vamp on the ground in front of her.

Ghost realized that Boomer could handle the last vamp, and he turned to support his boss. The camp director had paused when being shot. As it again lunged for Six, the vampire found itself impaled on a silver blade that glowed white as it struck and then pierced through its chest. Surprise changed to pain, and the pain overwhelmed the motor functions of the monster. The creature watched in horror as the blade traveled up its body and pierce its heart. Then its neck. The vamp did not understand its own mortality until the pain engulfed the creature, only to be relieved by darkness.

Six nodded his thanks at the hunter.

They both looked up in disbelief as the campers, led by their staff counselors, poured out of their cabins and savagely ran toward them. Many of the children ran across the grass much faster than should have been humanly possible. Every member of the DHS team opened fire.

The swarm of vampires ran in waves across the open ground. Ranks of infected kids and staff quickly covering the distance between the creatures and the DHS team. Even as the smaller children fell, the larger creatures jumped or ran over them, eager to tear into the agents.

Boomer felt the tears course down her face as she fired her shotgun. Her large vampire-hunting rounds ripped through the bodies as she shifted her aim and pulled the trigger. Concentrating on one vampire at a time, she would put two or three rounds into a creature, then shift her aim slightly to target another vamp beside the last. She numbly shot child after child as they charged toward the team. The bolt on her shotgun slammed open as the last round fired from her magazine, and she thumbed the magazine release button.

Realizing that her attackers were fast approaching, and with no end in sight, she grabbed one of Norbert's special magazines of FRAG-12 ammunition and slammed it into the receiver. She toggled the switch to automatic and squeezed the trigger, emptying the magazine in under four seconds. In front of her, a line of explosions rippled across the front of the charging mob. Eight explosions ripped the vampire children and staffers into pieces. Boomer saw a fine, silvery haze envelope the area where the explosions occurred, and those creatures who were merely wounded began screaming and writhing in agony as the cloud of atomized silver nitrate descended and coated their open wounds. The explosives expert had to blink away tears as she saw the contorted faces and heard the screams of these children-turned-creatures.

Six was busy on Boomer's left with his own wave of attacking creatures. Firing short bursts, the team leader shifted targets between shots. As each vampire fell to the ground, Six would shift slightly, place the sights on a new target, and pull the trigger. His mind refused to see anything past targets on the battlefield. He realized that he would have to account for his actions later, but, until then, he would bury his feelings. As he switched magazines, he felt and heard the concussion as Boomer opened up with her mini grenades and watched as the mist of silver bit into the surviving monsters.

Slamming the bolt home to load a new round into the chamber, Six picked off more of the survivors of the initial rush. Concentrating on his wounded foes, who were slowly rising to their feet, he calmly and methodically chose his targets. If they recovered and stood, he would place a three-round burst into their head or chest. If the first burst did not kill the creature, a second one was usually enough to do so.

In between the Six and Boomer, Ghost held on to his sword with one hand. In his other, he drew the Webley revolver from his holster. Taking careful aim, the hunter pointed the revolver at a wounded vampire. He squeezed the trigger, sending the .38 caliber silver and wood slug through its brain. His next target took two shots before it fell; the vampire after that required three shots to put it down, leaving Ghost with an empty revolver. The hunter thumbed the lever to release the cylinder, and the entire cylinder and barrel rotated forward.

He dumped the spent shells on the ground and stuck the revolver under the crook of his sword arm. Ghost loaded six more shells into the revolver, grabbed his gun, and then flicked his wrist. The cylinder swung closed and latched. Ghost thumbed back the hammer again and set his sights on his next target. Two shots were required to put this creature down. Ghost moved on as he continued to shoot and reload, shoot and reload.

Heavy stood next to Six and waited as the first monsters came out of the cabins. He noticed that there was already blood on several of them. Narrowing his eyes, he began to methodically work the trigger on his shotgun, sending silver and wood slugs at the creatures. As the bolt locked back on the empty shotgun, the heavy gunner dropped the drum onto the ground. Palming one of Norbert's specialty FRAG-12 magazines, Heavy slammed it into the receiver and made the weapon ready. After moving the selector to single fire, Heavy walked the rounds across the front line of infected campers as they raced toward the DHS team.

The line of explosives tore up the monsters who were leading the attack. Those that weren't blown apart with a direct hit found themselves in agony as the clouds of silver nitrate filled the air. The grimace on Heavy's face exclaimed his pain in mowing down unarmed combatants, but he knew he had no choice. He dropped the spent magazine from the AA-12, slammed another just like it into the receiver, and released the bolt forward. He lined up on a part of the attacking force that had not felt the effects of the shotgun and let fly.

At Heavy's side, Do-Right was doing his best to ignore every instinct he had so that he could fire on these unarmed children and adult counselors. Even the fang-filled mouths, animal growls, and black eyes only slightly eased his troubled conscience. Pushing past his training, he raised his AR-15 and pulled the trigger. With every pull of his trigger, a monster staggered or fell. The former deputy had grown up hunting wild game, but his prey today was making the hunt a lot easier by running straight toward him.

The deputy dropped the empty magazine out of his rifle and replaced it, then he let the bolt slide forward on a fresh round. Picking out more targets, he was startled when the ground erupted in explosions in front of the advancing horde. As he watched the silvery mist settle, he saw the heavy machine gunner to his left slam another magazine into his shotgun. When Heavy raised his shotgun again and started firing the fragmentation grenades, the deputy stopped targeting monsters in the same area. Instead, he began to finish off the monsters that had survived the initial explosions by doling out well-aimed shots to the head and torso.

Kneeling on top of the War Wagon, God used his rifle with a precision that few could match. The sniper constantly looked in all directions, paying close attention to the areas where the team's field of fire left area uncovered. Any time a vampire popped into an area that the team could not fire on, God's 5.56mm silver and wood core round would put an immediate stop to the threat and the life of the creature.

Living up to the "One shot, one kill" motto of snipers everywhere, the former HRT sniper was focused on the task at hand. The minor explosions from Boomer and Heavy only served to distract the vampires attacking the team, but they provided God with plenty of opportunity to capitalize on the distraction. He noticed quick movement to his right and swung in that direction. As he watched the camp archery instructor who Ghost had found flee the safety of the truck and run toward the staff offices, God could barely refrain from pulling the trigger.

Standing behind the DHS team as the vampires came out of their cabins and offices had been a real shock to the system for William Buckhorn, the camp's archery instructor. The volume of firepower was impressive, and the disciplined control had been incredible to watch. Bill had wanted to help, but he didn't have any weapons that he could use. After realizing that these were actual vampires, and that there was something he could do that might help, the archery pro took advantage of a pause for reloading and broke for the staff offices. When he had almost reached the building, it dawned on him that this could be a very bad idea for him. He knew he would have to be very careful on his way back to the truck... he didn't want to get mistaken as one of the creatures.

As he reached the staff building, he threw open the door and ran toward his office. He opened the door, glancing at the wall behind his small desk. Two bows hung on the wall. The first was a beautiful modern recurved bow. Even unstrung, the bow exuded power and quality. This bow was the one that almost took Bill to the Olympics five years prior, but he had never had a chance to compete. The other bow was a smaller, older, almost crude-looking longbow. Although this bow lacked the aesthetic appeal of the other, this bow was the reason he had made the dangerous dash back to his office.

The bow was originally handmade, and any repairs had been made with the same craftsmanship. As a full-blooded Navajo, Bill's grandfather was a Shaman and had hand-crafted this bow specifically for his grandson, Bill, before he died. While not as beautiful as the Olympic bow, this one held special meaning, and, if his grandfather was to be believed, special power for his grandson.

Bill reached up and lifted his grandfather's bow from the hangers. He quickly strung the bow as his grandfather had drilled into him He quietly spoke the ritual Navajo words he had been taught and felt better as the string neatly fell into place. Bill looked at the two quivers full of arrows that hung on the wall. One was of a modern material, with modern fiberglass target arrows neatly waiting to be slung and deployed. The second was a crude leather sling with a long single cross-body strap. The quiver contained authentic wooden arrows with feather fletchings and flint arrowheads. It was this quiver that Bill chose.

Bill slung the quiver over his shoulder and drew one of the arrows from the quiver. Nocking the arrow in the string, he turned to leave his office and head back to the DHS truck but, instead, found the camp nurse, Lynn Powell, standing in the doorway and blocking his escape. Her coal-black eyes and mouthful of fangs told him that she had been infected. And his lack of vampire changes told her that he was her prey.

Before she could move toward him, he raised, drew, aimed, and fired in one smooth motion. One second the nurse was standing in the doorway looking hungrily at Bill; the next she was pinned to the wall behind her with an arrow jutting out from her forehead. The archery instructor looked down at the bow in his hands. He could barely make out a faint red glow as it faded quickly from the hieroglyphs carved into the shaft of the bow. Soon it was gone, and Bill didn't quite know if he had actually seen the glow.

As he stepped through the doorway, he could see that the DHS team was winning but that the battle was beginning to take its toll. Even with the tremendous firepower at their disposal, the team could not stop all of the vampires before they reached the truck. As Bill watched, the big mountain of a man they called "Heavy" drew two inward curved blades from the sheath on his back and began to attack those monsters that got too close for the others to shoot. Completely severing the arm of one vampire with a vicious backhand, the big man swung around as a follow-through and ran his khukuri through the neck of the creature and removed its head.

On the other side of the truck, Bill watched the tall agent who had earlier found him in the woods drive his glowing blade into the chest of an adult vampire. The creature screamed and writhed. The man they called "Ghost" withdrew the blade and made a swipe with the blade, severing the vampire's head from the body. Continuing that same movement, the hunter then stepped into another vampire that had gotten too close, drawing the blade across the creature's abdomen and chest. Moments later this creature was dispatched again by the blade.

As he stood next to Heavy, Six was startled as an infected staffer was able to slip past their defense. Six could not fire in time to stop the vampire from getting to him. Both Heavy and Ghost were engaged, and this one got inside the team leader's defenses. Six jammed his rifle sideways across the chest of the creature that was trying to eat his face. He could feel the hot, fetid breath of the vampire and see the gleaming of the razor-sharp teeth. As he struggled to get the creature away from him, the commander felt the monster shudder as he watched an arrow with feather fletchings appear, sticking out of the temple of the monster's head.

The commander looked to his right and saw the archery instructor nocking another arrow in the string of an old bow. The bow was engraved or marked with some sort of writing or symbols on it, and they appeared to be faintly glowing red. Six watched as Bill took aim again and let fly another arrow, piercing the head of another vampire that was about to attack Do-Right. Six watched as the instructor drew and nocked another arrow before the archer ran back across to the truck.

The team could not kill every vampire before they came into close range. Those that were not killed from further away were dispatched by the blades of the hunter or the big man, or they were executed with a short-range shot by Bill. In a few minutes that seemed like hours, the fight was over, and the silence was overwhelming. Blood and ichor soaked the grass all around the center of camp, and the small yard looked like a charnel house. After making sure that there were no more vampires in the vicinity, the team stopped to take stock of their condition.

Six wearily said, "Before we clear the remaining buildings, let's refresh our ammo and bandage up any wounds. Anyone get hurt?"

Heavy muttered a soft, "Damn." The big man looked at his team leader. "Looks like you caught a little piece yourself, boss," he said.

The team leader looked down at his shredded armor carrier and saw a small wound in his stomach. Shaking his head, he muttered a few curses.

"Well. Looks like I get to play the waiting game with Boomer and Heavy," Six reported. "Anyone else?"

Everyone else shook their head.

"All right then, let's clear this place out," Six continued. "Non-vampires are screened for scratches. Vampires are killed. Questions?"

A deep, smooth voice emanated from around the corner of the staff office building. "I have one."

A monstrous figure, with its face obscured by the sunlight, presented itself to the team. Drawing closer, the figure inquired, "What will you do when you have to fight a real vampire?"

30

SHOWDOWN

Blue Mountain Ranch, Florissant, Colorado

Six did as best as he could to look unimpressed.

"Zachariah, I presume?" Six said to the creature.

The monster chuckled, his voice deep. "I am. And you must be Smith's latest team? How is Agent Smith getting along?" he asked. "I assume he told you that this was somewhat personal for him?"

The team leader nodded and said, "Yes. And that's why it ends today."

The vampire shook his head with an amused smile on his face. "Many before you have tried, and they have all failed," the monster said. "What makes you so special?"

Anticipating a fight, the team took their positions. God stayed perched on the War Wagon for his vantage point, but the rest of the DHS team spread out around the vampire. Boomer fanned out to the vampire's left and raised her shotgun. Ghost moved with her, making sure to stay in between the explosives expert and Six. The monster hunter held his now glowing sword at ready. Do-Right split off to the creature's right, and he raised his rifle and centered the sights on the vampire's forehead. After abandoning his shotgun for the green-glowing khukuri blades, Heavy positioned himself to the left of the former deputy. Doc stepped up next to Six and stood in the middle of the group as her vestments glowed blue.

"How are you out in the sunlight?" Ghost questioned. "You're a vampire."

The monster looked at the monster hunter. "So, the hunter speaks. You are the last of your line, correct? Too bad your line ends with you here."

"Alas, I *was* a proper vampire before the good Doctor Kaine was able to cure me of my terrible allergy. His virus made it possible for me to stand before you today. And I cannot wait to share this with my brethren."

Zachariah looked at the team spread around him. Raising his hands in mock surrender, he smiled. His fangs glistened with saliva in hungry anticipation.

"Now is the last chance I will give to let you walk away from here," he said. "I have killed every team that dear Agent Smith has ever sent, and you will follow in their footsteps. It is your choice."

Even as Six pulled the trigger on his rifle to take his first shot, the vampire moved. Faster than any other vampire they had engaged, the creature danced to the side away from the reach of the team leader's rifle. Moving fluidly, and almost faster than the eye could follow, Zachariah struck at Boomer, knocking the shotgun from her grasp and spinning her around. She collapsed to the ground with a groan and cradled her arm.

Ghost was ready for the attack and struck, scoring a line across the vampire's chest. Howling in agony, the creature struck back at the hunter. The blow landed solidly on Ghost's ribs. Even through the protection of the blessed duster, Ghost felt a rib break as he flew backwards. The hunter landed hard on his back; he landed so hard that he felt as of the wind had been knocked out of his lungs. Ghost lay in agony, gasping as he tried to breathe.

As Six shifted the aim of his rifle, he aimed at the vampire. He pulled the trigger and fired off another three-round burst. One of the rounds struck the vampire in the shoulder, spinning him slightly, and it caused the creature to howl and swear. The monster leapt past Six and Doc and ducked under the blades in Heavy's hands. The vampire caught the big man's wrists in his hands and threw the machine gunner over his shoulder. The big man tumbled in the air until he crashed into one of the parked cars near them. Heavy dropped to the ground and lay still.

Do-Right stepped backwards as the vampire lunged at him. The creature grabbed the rifle and yanked, pulling the deputy off balance and whipping him around. Do-Right pulled the trigger on his rifle and sent a round through the hand of the vampire. The impact of the shot caused the vampire to let go. The deputy's momentum carried him toward the side of the War Wagon, and he bounced off the side of the truck and tumbled to the ground. Do-Right shook his head and tried to stand up.

A three-round burst hit Zachariah in the chest as he turned toward Six and Doc. The vampire looked up and seemed to notice God on the roof of the truck. The creature growled as he leapt for the sniper. In the same moment the creature left the ground, Six snapped his rifle up and pulled the trigger, sending another burst into the master vampire's torso.

The creature landed on the truck, and a thick black ichor dripped from the gunshot wounds on its chest and shoulder. Before the sniper could shoot again, the vampire grabbed the rifle barrel and dragged it and the agent off the roof and threw them to the ground. God felt a snap as his right leg hit the ground, and pure agony blackened his vision. He passed out.

With bloodlust in its eyes, the vampire turned and looked straight at Six and Doc.

"I'm going to enjoy killing you, priest," the vamp said in a harsh growl.

Doc closed her eyes and pulled her hands together. Chanting a high Latin liturgy, her hands glowed with a blue light. Hoping to get to her before she finished her prayer, the vampire sprang at the priest.

Six leapt in front of the vampire. The agent collided with the monster and grabbed on, knocking it away from Doc as she finished her incantation. The two crashed to the ground, with Six hanging on and attempting to keep the vampire busy. Six hoped his mangled armor would protect him.

Zachariah shoved Six with all of his might and broke the hold that the DHS agent had on the creature. Incensed that this human would dare physically attack him, the vampire quickly leaned down and opened his jaws. The razor sharp fangs pierced the throat of the team leader. Six went stiff when he felt the teeth take hold, but then all he felt was pain. Zachariah lifted his head, taking a large chunk of Six's throat in his mouth. Blood surrounded the vampire's mouth and dripped down his chin as the agent's life spilled out onto the ground. Zachariah grinned as the light left Six's eyes.

When the vampire looked up, his growled threat died in his throat as Doc opened her eyes and pointed at the vampire. Her eyes glowed with a blue light as she thundered, "*Creatura autem nox. Tu exterminantur. REVERTERE AD INFERNUM!*"

A blinding light seemed to envelope the master vampire. His screams and howls of agony reverberated throughout the camp. The vampire felt his body burning, and he looked down. Zachariah felt the heat rising from his body as flames appeared across his body. His skin began to blacken and peel away with flames filling the cracks.

Zachariah stood and took a desperate step toward the priest, but his agony drove him back to his knees. He stretched out a hand toward Doc as he tried desperately to reach her. The priest's hand was still outstretched, and she still glowed with righteous power. He gave one last effort to stand but collapsed back to his hands and knees. The flames were rising faster now, and his agony burned brighter.

The monster looked in horror as a red, scaled claw reached out of the ground around him and grabbed him by the throat. Zachariah's screams were cut off abruptly as the massive hand wrapped around the vampire's throat and head and dragged the creature down into the earth. The last of the vampire's battered frame passed through the earth, and a small charred spot was the only evidence it had been there.

The former camp archery instructor had watched the whole fight in horror. When the vampire had been dragged into the earth, he had watched as the priest let her hand drop and as the glow left her eyes and vestments. She sank wearily to the ground once more looking like the middle-aged woman she was. The archery instructor rushed to Doc's side.

As Bill reached her side, he heard moans and groans from the rest of the team. He knelt down and asked if she was ok. She looked back up at him and offered a weary smile.

"That was worse than I thought. I'm ok," Doc responded. "I need to check on the rest of the team. We also need to make sure that we got them all. And check for other human survivors."

Bill looked at her with a no-nonsense look upon his face. "First things, first," he said. "I've got first aid training. I'll help you check on the others."

Doc nodded and stood to her feet.

The medic went to check on Six first. As soon as she saw that his throat had been ripped out, she blinked back tears and gave him last rites. Stepping back, she next walked over to Heavy who was unconscious and in a heap against a crumpled car. With the help of Doc's smelling salts, he woke with a start and groggily shook his head. Quickly checking him over, Doc realized the big man was probably lucky enough to walk away with a few simple bruises. Although he'd be sore for a while, he'd recover.

Next, she went to check on the former deputy that had joined their party in Trinidad. As she knelt next to him, she realized that he was groggy and that he couldn't focus on what she was saying. A few more field tests showed that he was possibly suffering a concussion and would need medical care.

She then went to check on the sniper. By this time, Bill had already gotten around to him and was splinting his lower leg with supplies from the truck. As Doc checked the former camp staffer's work, the efficiency and scope of his work impressed her. The leg would be set temporarily—long enough to get him to a decent hospital in Colorado Springs.

Doc also checked over Bill's work on the other two team members. Bill had correctly diagnosed a fractured arm for Boomer and had applied another splint to the injured limb. He had also checked a possibly broken rib on Ghost and told the hunter he would need to have it checked out at the hospital. As Doc examined Ghost, she told him the somber news about Six.

After resting for several minutes, Heavy was fully recovered and offered to check the rest of camp to make sure that there weren't any other survivors. Bill volunteered to go with him, just in case they came across a frightened camper. The two went south to start with the girls' cabins and work their way north.

As they walked off, Ghost pulled out his SSP and dialed Agent Smith's office. When Timothy answered, Ghost said in a flat, weary voice, "Timothy, it's Ghost. Is Smith in? I need to talk to him ASAP."

"Wait one," Timothy said as he placed the agent's call on hold.

"Agent Smith."

Ghost began, "Agent Smith, it's Ghost. This was a complete cluster. Zachariah is dead, but so is Six. There were at least eighty of the new vampires at the camp. It was an ugly battle. Only two known camp survivors, although Heavy is looking for more." Ghost paused to catch his breath.

The pause lasted a few seconds as Agent Smith absorbed the news. The supervising agent finally spoke, "Mr. Holstein was killed in action?"

Ghost nodded subconsciously. "Yes, sir. He sacrificed himself so that Doc had enough time to do her thing. She was the one who finally put the master down."

Agent Smith thought through the rest of the initial statement. "Was anyone else hurt? Does anyone need medical attention?"

Ghost ran down the list of the wounded. "It looks like Boomer has a broken arm. God broke his leg. Doc thinks Do-Right has a concussion, and I probably have at least one broken rib. Heavy's going to be sore in the morning, but he seems to be ok."

"The best hospital for the team is Evans Army Hospital just off base at Cheyenne Mountain Air Station. They'll be able to handle your wounds, and your ranks and credentials should keep them from asking too many questions. I'll have Timothy clear the way for you." Agent Smith paused some more as he looked at his notes.

"You found over eighty new vampires? Is there any chance that any got away?" Smith questioned.

Ghost thought for a moment. "It's not likely, sir," he responded. "They all seemed to have come to attack us. But Heavy is sweeping the camp with the help of the camp's former archery instructor."

"Who is this 'instructor,' Agent Vanhof?" asked Agent Smith.

Ghost backtracked a little. "Sir, I found him on our initial sweep. He seemed to be the only surviving adult staff that was not turned. He was hiding in the woods, but Spooky directed me to him. According to Spooky, he's a former world-class archer, almost made the last Olympics. He has an older, carved bow. And he took out several of the vampires during the final attack. I'll have Spooky forward his dossier."

Agent Smith paused and then said, "I'll trust your judgement. You said there was one other survivor. Who is it?"

Ghost recalled Boomer's tagalong. "Teen girl, fifteen or sixteen. She was not infected. Boomer found her and got her to us before the vamps attacked. I don't know if there are any other survivors yet, but I doubt it. These vamps were systematically slaughtering and eating those who weren't infected."

Agent Smith suddenly asked a very poignant question. "Has anyone on the team been infected?"

Ghost closed his eyes. He was wondering when that question would pop up. "Possibly, sir. Boomer and Heavy were both scratched in the silo. According to the doctor's paperwork, they each have a one-in-five chance of turning from the contact. The change takes several days, three to five, according to the doctor's notes."

Ghost heard a soft, "Damn," come from his boss. Ghost couldn't agree more.

The monster hunter asked his own question next. "Sir. What's next? As much ruckus as we raised, we're bound to get law enforcement out here, eventually. And at some point, parents will want to come get their kids. These are new vamps. They don't dissolve in smoke. DHS just mowed down over eighty unarmed kids and adults. How do we cover this one up?"

Agent Smith was already thinking about the problem. He pulled up satellite maps of the area and saw that the camp area was actually a fairly small area. He made a snap decision.

"Agent Vanhof, your team has thirty minutes to vacate the camp. I'll have Timothy send the local law enforcement to the other end of the county. You are to get everyone clear. In precisely thirty minutes, an Air Force fuel tanker will crash into the hillside, precisely where you are sitting. It will, of course, have help from us. DHS will investigate. And the Air Force will compensate the families. There is nothing else we can do. Thirty minutes. Time starts now."

Ghost looked at his watch as he broke the connection. He keyed his mic and said, "Heavy, Ghost. We are leaving in twenty-five minutes. That is two-five minutes. No exceptions. Move your butt."

As each team member heard those words, they looked to the hunter for an explanation. They realized that no explanation was forthcoming.

Ghost quickly organized the team. Doc found a body bag in the truck's supplies, and she and Ghost carefully placed Six's body inside. They strapped the body to the roof of the truck so that it was mostly flat and would not show while they were driving. They cleared out other boxes and stacked them on the top of the MRAP, hiding the body even more.

Despite the pain, Boomer sat down to talk to the teenager she had rescued.

"I don't know what's going to happen," she confided. "I can't have you talk to your parents right now, not until my boss gives me permission. Confidentially, I don't think he knows what to do with you. Until then, I'll keep you safe. I promise."

The teenager hugged Boomer, and slowly her tears dried up. After a few minutes, she wiped her eyes and thanked Boomer.

Boomer smiled and kept her arm around the girl's shoulder. "I don't think I ever caught your name, hon. Mine is Rebekah, but everyone calls me 'Boomer.'"

The girl smiled and replied, "Boomer? I like that. My name is Hannah."

After twenty-three minutes, Heavy and Bill jogged up to the truck.

"Nothing living out there, sir," Heavy reported to Ghost. "No other survivors. It looks like they slaughtered those who weren't infected before they came after us. Each cabin is a slaughterhouse. We checked out the old lodge, and it looks like Zachariah was living there. Found all kinds of crap from him... I grabbed a few journals and items and tossed them in my pack."

"Thanks, Heavy," Ghost said. "Bill, our thanks for helping. Unfortunately, it looks like you might be with us for a little while. At least until we can sort it out with our boss. You need to come with us. Anything you need to get from your office, or bunk?"

Bill shook his head and raised the bow still gripped tightly in his hand. "Honestly, this is the only thing I want to take with me. My grandfather carved it for me."

"All right. Everyone mount up," Ghost said. "We're going to sit at the end of the camp driveway for a couple minutes and then we are leaving. This area won't exist in about three minutes."

A pained look crossed Boomer's face as she climbed into the passenger's chair—pained that she was too hurt to drive the Wagon. Ghost climbed up into the driver's seat and fired up the engine. He slowly moved the truck to the end of the drive, blocking any entrance to the camp. After two minutes, with just under a minute to spare, he put the truck in gear and drove back out toward town. As they were pulling around a curve, they all heard a very low roar and watched as a large Air Force jet trailing smoke dropped below the tree line. Moments later, the ground shook the truck violently, and a wave of wind and heat rocked the War Wagon.

Spooky was monitoring real-time satellite access and watched as an Air Force KC-135 Stratotanker flew with smoke pouring out of three engines. It pancaked into the ground right where the camp's driveway started and then fireballed, sending burning JP-8 throughout the camp and the surrounding forest. Spooky shuddered. There was no way anything would survive that inferno.

The resulting fire would incinerate everything within a quarter-mile of the crash site to ash and would leave a burn area that covered ten square miles before finally going out. It would soon be named the worst military and civilian accident in the history of the United States.

31

AFTERMATH

The War Wagon pulled into the Pueblo Memorial Airport the following afternoon. The evening before, the team had stayed at a hotel close to the base while Boomer, God, and Do-Right had their battle wounds treated at the base hospital.

God and Boomer both had their fractured bones set and were both told that they were lucky that they did not have to have surgery. Do-Right was put through a battery of tests, and the hospital staff agreed with Doc that he had suffered a concussion. The team was also able to store the body of their leader in the hospital morgue for the night, and they made arrangements to get him to the airfield the next afternoon.

The next morning, a weary, bruised, and battered team set out for the small town of Trinidad in the War Wagon. Bill, the former archery instructor for the camp, and Hannah, the camper who Boomer rescued, both refused to stay and wait on base. Instead, they rode inside the cramped MRAP with the rest of the team. When they arrived, the team immediately went to the county jail to check on their prisoners. As Doc had predicted, the former acting mayor and the former coroner were little more than gibbering fools. They were shouting about monsters and blood and fire to any who would listen. A quick call to the Colorado Springs U.S. Attorney's Office yielded an involuntary commitment to a psychiatric facility for both of them.

At the urging of Ghost, Christian Folsom officially resigned from the Las Animas County Sheriff Department. Turning in his uniforms and service weapon, he walked out of the building with his head high. Do-Right's smile was bittersweet as he climbed up into the War Wagon, turning his back on his youth and his hometown. The memorial service for his wife and children, as well as all the other victims of the monsters, would take place in a week, and he promised that he would be back for the services.

The town of Trinidad had already started recovering and rebuilding from the tragedies of the recent monster scourge. The paranormal and conspiracy websites were working overtime because of the incoherent reports of monsters and secret government teams. The new acting mayor and sheriff were quick to stop any rumors that contradicted the official story of a deep ISIS cell buried in the small town. And they never, officially, deviated from those statements.

The team had one last stop to make before they could leave town. They traveled out to the old pharmacist's residence to make sure that the mouth of the hellgate was sealed. As they arrived at the top of the driveway, all but three of the team's passengers got out of the vehicle and wandered around the property. They individually kicked through the charred and scattered ruins of the house, making sure that there was nothing to link DHS to the house or to any monsters.

Heavy walked up to the big cellar doors that led down to the caverns. He gave several good tugs to make sure that the welds were solid and that the chains would hold. He jumped back when the doors rattled from the other side. As he stepped back and drew his sidearm, he yelled for his teammates.

As the others drew around, the large doors bulged and creaked outward, as if some immense force was pushing from the other side. Those who were armed quickly drew their sidearms, and Ghost drew his sword. The team took a collective step back as the doors groaned under the weight of the force. Suddenly, a weld seam ripped, and the doors crashed open as the chains that bound the doors shattered.

A roiling darkness waited just below the ledge of the doorway. Doc recognized that it was the same material that pooled in the pit from the caverns and the bottom of the silo. Her vestments glowed a bright yellow as a form emerged from the inky blackness. As it rose smoothly, the darkness acted like liquid, as it dripped and ran in rivulets down the emerging figure.

The humanoid figure stood about five feet tall and was thin and dressed in all black. Its pale gray skin was visible on its hands as the figure held a small staff or cane while the rest remained hidden beneath a voluminous robe with a cowl and hood that obscured the face. The figure threw back its cowl, revealing a pale gray face that was all at once terrifying and beautiful. Its blood red mouth was unadorned with fangs, however the creature's coal-black eyes were lit with a faint red glow. Long violet hair was pulled back in a simple knot and revealed slightly pointed ears.

The figure smiled and spoke in a voice that was beautiful but cold. "You must be the humans causing me so much trouble. Not much to look at, are you?"

Ghost stepped forward and leveled his blade at the figure. "Who are you, and what do you want?" he asked.

The figure moved his hands and held them in a placating gesture. "Please, human. We will meet later, rest assured. I never forget an insult. As for who I am? Tell your Agent Smith that Demius Sayevuud sends his greetings."

With a small gesture, the inky darkness began enveloping the figure before them. In seconds, the figure was fully engulfed, and the darkness spread back down into the doorway. It then spiraled and folded in on itself until it vanished completely.

Heavy took the first step forward with his flashlight. The stairwell down was darker and a bit rougher after the Boomer's first explosion, but the corridor still angled out of sight at the bottom.

Boomer walked back over to the War Wagon and opened her kit. Working one-handed, it took her a bit longer than was usual, but she came back to the hole holding a rather large chunk of plastic explosive fixed to a timer. She raised her eyebrow at Ghost, and he simply nodded.

Setting the time for ten minutes, she carefully double-checked her setup. Boomer walked down the stairs and leaned around the corner. The light filtering down showed her that the first cavern was still largely intact. The explosives expert calmly walked over to the center of the cavern and set the explosive package down. Looking around once more, she reached down and hit the start button to begin the countdown timer.

The War Wagon was parked at the bottom of the driveway when the explosive package detonated ten minutes later. The twenty-seven-ton truck rocked on its massive shocks as the top of the hill erupted in a geyser of rock and mud.

Heavy looked at the geyser and said, "I guess we call that Mount Saint Hellgate?"

The tension broke as laughter rolled throughout the truck. The team was still laughing minutes later as the fire trucks arrived on scene. Ghost wiped the tears from his eyes and stepped out of the truck. He waved his badge at the first responding truck and then at the fire chief when he arrived. By the time Ghost let the trucks through, there was nothing to clean up, except for a few small brush fires. Ghost put the War Wagon in gear and headed north to Pueblo Airport.

———

WHEN THE WAR WAGON PULLED ONTO THE AIRPORT PARKING LOT, THE team saw the waiting C-17 Globemaster. A small ambulance, surrounded by an armed troop of DHS agents, was parked next to the Air Force jet. Ghost parked the MRAP next to the waiting ambulance, and the team began to unload.

As the agents climbed out of the truck, the stairs to the passenger compartment came down, and Gretchen and Agent Smith walked slowly down the stairs. The supervising agent solemnly went to each team member and shook his or her hand as he offered his thanks and condolences. When he got to the two civilians, Ghost introduced them.

"Agent Smith, this is Hannah Cresswell. She was one of the senior girls at the camp. And this is Bill Buckhorn, former archery instructor at Blue Mountain."

Smith shook hands with both of them. "Miss Cresswell. I'm sorry that we haven't been able to let you contact your parents yet. We have several questions that we need to answer before we can do so. Don't worry. I want to return you to your parents if at all possible."

"Mister Buckhorn. I understand you were instrumental in helping save my team. For that, I am grateful. We need to talk a little later about possible employment opportunities, now that your prior position is no longer available."

Smith looked at his team. "As Ghost requested, Mister Holstein's body is still waiting to load onto the plane. There is a special storage compartment for his remains, but I thought you would want to carry him aboard yourselves."

As one, the team moved to the back door of the ambulance. The paramedics brought out the body, still in the body bag they had originally used, on a stretcher. Every team member took a handle, save for Doc and God. The sniper could not carry the body with his broken leg, and the priest stood behind the body and read last rites and funeral liturgies as the rest of the team carried the body solemnly up the ramp and into the waiting storage. They would again perform the somber duty when the plane touched down outside Langley.

The team grabbed their gear from the War Wagon and allowed one of the waiting cargo masters to drive the truck up the ramp and secure it in the plane. One-by-one, the team, their passengers, and the Section 28 staff filed up the stairs and into the waiting lounge. Unlike standard Globemaster aircraft, this one had been designed so that the passenger portion of the cargo bay was well appointed and comfortable to be in. Thick soundproofing muted the dull roar of the spooling engines, and comfortable chairs and tables were available, and fold-down bunks lined the back wall. The team settled in, and Agent Smith lifted a handset attached to his chair.

"Tell the pilot we're ready to go when he is. Have him get clearance for a direct flight. Make this one as short as possible. Thank you."

The huge engines roared outside, and the passengers felt the plane taxi and then take off. They would touchdown in Virginia in just under four hours.

Back at the headquarters for Section 28, the team apartments somehow felt empty. Six's gear had already been collected and sent to storage. Agent Smith let the team know that memorial services would be held the following afternoon and that anyone needing a suit or other clothing should let him know so that the quarter-master could locate proper attire for them. The service would be a small memorial with only current on-site staff attending, and they would inter Six in a plot consecrated specifically for Section 28 Agents.

The cold and dreary day fit the somber mood of those who attended the memorial. The light drizzle masked the tears of Boomer and Doc as they watched their fallen team leader lowered into the ground. The service was short with a few words from Agent Smith and final rites from Doc. The procession of black SUVs back to head-quarters was silent as the other agents reflected on their own mortality.

The following day, Christian Folsom and William Buckhorn were both sworn in as the newest members of team Knightmare. Do-Right had earned his new callsign in the field, and it became official. Buck-horn's experience and his Navajo heritage gave Agent Smith the perfect callsign for the new agent: "Scout."

That same day, Ghost was officially recognized as the new team leader for Knightmare.

Agent Smith talked with the new team leader. "You will need to pick a second, and soon," Smith advised. "I have full confidence in your leadership. Your skills with handling people will be a major asset as we move forward."

Do-Right flew back to Pueblo for the trip to Trinidad four days later. While he expected to make the journey alone, Agent Smith released the entire Knightmare team to attend with him for support. The Agency's Citation X flew the team to Colorado in style, and the multiple black SUVs waiting for the team at the airport added the perfect touch.

Instead of their tactical BDUs, all members of the team, except for Ghost and Doc, wore gray or black business suits the following day. Looking every inch the federal agents that they were, each member wore their suit well, while the team's sniper leaned on a cane with his leg in an air cast. Ghost showed up in a shirt and tie with dress pants instead of his normal jeans. Instead of a suit jacket and dress shoes, the new team leader wore cowboy boots, his blessed leather duster, and his hat, which he removed and held for the ceremony. Doc wore her full vestments and stole for the ceremony.

Once the memorial service was over with, Do-Right needed to see his family's home one more time. The former deputy entered through the front door, ducking under the police tape that was stretched all around. He went throughout the house and gathered some pictures and a few knickknacks that were of sentimental value to him. The new DHS agent wandered around his house for thirty minutes as he remembered his family and dried the tears from his eyes.

Do-right spent the rest of the next day sorting through his personal life and arranging for his departure from town. He met with a broker and put his house on the market. Agent Smith sent a discreet moving truck with additional help to clean out his house. Those possessions the former deputy no longer wanted were cleaned and set aside for an estate sale.

While Do-Right sorted through his life prior to Section 28, the rest of the team split up and ran several errands. Doc led a team comprising God, Heavy, and Spooky back to the recently nicknamed Mount Saint Hellgate. When they were there, they placed a small electronics package on the site. Burying the main box console about three feet deep, they extended two small antennas up through the ground so that they could sample the air and electromagnetic field emissions from the surrounding area. This specially designed instrument package was engineered to monitor the site for any incursion-related activity and to relay the activity to Section 28.

Boomer drove Ghost and Scout out of town the same afternoon. As they drove up to the former site of Blue Mountain Ranch, the agents were anxious to see the area firsthand. Two hours later, the government SUV arrived at the burnt-out wreckage that was the Ranch. Every building and most of the trees in the area directly surrounding the camp were flattened from the concussive blast and burned from the resulting fires.

The team was amazed at the destructive power that the tanker had unleashed when it crashed onto the field. They had read the reports of the mangled bodies and shredded remains, but they had not imagined what it would look, and smell, like in person. Ghost showed his credentials to the sheriff's deputy that was guarding the road. Moving forward, the team's SUV was forced to stop about a hundred yards from the actual site. After they exited their SUV, the team walked toward the main staging area for the National Transportation Safety Board and DHS teams charged with handling the crash.

Ghost walked up to the DHS agent in charge, Special Agent Hart, from the Denver office. Agent Hart recognized Ghost and Boomer, and her demeanor chilled. "Agent Vanhof, and Agent... Callahan. To what do I owe the pleasure? And who is this with you?"

"Special Agent Hart, this is Agent William Buckhorn," Ghost said as he turned to Scout and introduced him to the agent. "He recently joined our deployment team." Turning to Bill, Ghost continued, "This is Special Agent Sonja Hart. She's the SAC from Denver. If we're in this area, we're stomping on her backyard."

Scout reached out to shake Agent Hart's hand, and, as she took it, she paused. A look passed through her eyes as if she was putting pieces together. She suddenly rounded on Ghost and unleashed a torrent of questions.

"Isn't there a 'William Buckhorn' that's missing from this site? Is he of any relation?" she questioned.

Ghost smiled and replied, "It is possible that he shares a name with a former employee of the camp. He's now one of ours."

The light dawned behind the senior agent's eyes. She let out an expletive, and her voice grew quiet and cold. "This was one of your operations? What happened? Did the little kids insult Agent Smith?"

Ghost's eyes narrowed. "Cheap shots don't become you, Agent Hart. You know the drill. 'I can neither confirm, nor deny, that we were here.' If you need any further answers, you might want to contact Agent Smith's office."

"To that end, I do need a favor from you," Ghost said and then smiled his most disarming smile.

Hart spoke through gritted teeth. "What do you need?" she demanded.

Ghost set a small bag down on the table in the command center and drew an incursion detection unit from the bag. Ghost set about showing Agent Hart how to bury and activate the device, a twin of the unit just placed in Trinidad.

At the end, the new team leader said, "Hopefully, this instrument package will help us make sure that there is not another incident like this in the future."

Hart looked at the device and then back at Ghost. "I'll make sure it gets done properly. Anything to get you out of my hair faster."

AT SECTION 28 HEADQUARTERS, OUTSIDE LANGLEY, VIRGINIA, AGENT Smith sat down to have a conversation with a sixteen-year-old survivor of Blue Mountain Ranch. The meeting was in the team's lounge area, outside the room where she was temporarily assigned.

A sixteen-year-old Latina girl with black hair and deep hazel eyes sat slouched in an overstuffed chair across from the prim and proper figure of Agent Smith. He had just sat down with the girl after bringing her a carbonated beverage. He paused a few moments to look over the girl. Satisfied, he began.

"Miss Cresswell. I sincerely apologize for making you wait this long to talk to your parents. I had to make sure we had all the options sorted out before I could talk to you."

Hannah looked up, eagerly waiting to hear when she could call her folks. They must be going out of their minds. She leaned forward a little as she waited for the federal agent to go on.

"As I see it, we have two options for you. If we take the first option, you could return to your parents' house almost immediately. With a little makeup and special effects, we can easily make it look like you were wandering in the woods for a long time." Smith saw the gleam in the girl's eyes. "Before you get all excited, this option requires certain... assurances."

"First, you will never be allowed to talk about what really happened at camp. You will have to forget that Section 28 even exists. This condition is absolutely required. What we do is a secret, and it has to stay that way. Other than a few crazy conspiracy theorists who might have seen our name somewhere, we don't really exist. We cannot officially exist."

"Second. If you ever do speak about what happened there, or who we are, there will be some unimaginable consequences. You'll be crucified in the media. We will sow the seeds of disbelief in your story. In the end, only the crackpot conspiracy theorists will believe you. Outside of them, you'll be a laughingstock." Smith saw he had Hannah's attention.

"Not only will your reputation and presence be thoroughly trashed, but we'll go after your folks, too. Financially, we'll bankrupt them. Socially, we'll have them outcast. When they continue to believe you after your statements, they will grow to resent the effect you had on their life. Do not think we won't do this. I crashed a multi-million dollar jet filled with jet fuel to cover for one of my teams. Crashing someone's financial future would be child's play."

Team Knightmare's supervising agent let the potential dire consequences sink in. "Of course, there is always the other option," he continued. "For this one, you stay here and eventually work for Section 28. I have a plan in place to form a new team, and I believe you would fit in very well. To stay here, you will officially die at Blue Mountain Ranch. We will provide you with a new identity and everything you need to live.

"Your marks in school were exceptional. You were also a track star and a rather formidable IDPA and three-gun competitor. We will continue your schooling at a local school we can trust for the next two years. We'll also train you in hand-to-hand combat and monster fighting. When you graduate, you will be ready to fulfill our mission."

Hannah brightened a little. She asked a question, "So, I'd kinda be like that chick vampire slayer. Muffy? Betty? What was her name?"

Smith smiled a little knowing smile, "Ah... I think the name you are looking for is 'Buffy.' And while you would attend school and train like the so-called 'slayer,' I am not British and you will probably not be killing vampires at your own school."

He paused and studied her, making sure the teen understood the implications. "What do you want to do? Once you decide, there are no do-overs."

Hannah thought for a moment. She realized that she could eventually become like the woman who rescued her, Boomer. She thought about how great it would be to learn how to kill monsters, but she also thought about her family. She would be dead to them. Forever. She would, could, never see her friends again. Her life would be gone, and her parents would be devastated.

The sixteen-year-old girl took a huge breath, looked Smith right in the eye, and told him her decision.

EPILOGUE

I t was 5:32am. The cool of the night was waning as the day prepared to spring forth. As was his routine, Garrett Malley pulled his gray BMW into the parking spot closest to the track. Climbing out of the car, he slipped his wallet and spare car key into his waist pouch, along with his cell phone. The rest of his keys, as well as the clothes he would change into, went into the trunk of the luxury vehicle.

The man stretched through his normal routine. Jogging in place for a few minutes, he limbered up, his mind drifting as he began his routine. He stepped onto the running track that circled the baseball fields at the Williamsburg Recreational Center, in Kingstree, South Carolina. Setting off at his normal pace, his long strides ate up the distance. Garrett wanted to run a marathon in the fall, and he was training diligently.

As he rounded the final bend on his first, of many, laps, he noticed a form lying in the children's play area that was next to the track. Garrett slowed, and he looked closer at the form. It looked to be a man, and it seemed to be lying face down in the sand. His pace faltered, and he slowed to a walk, moving off the track and toward the body at the playground.

Hoping that the guy was decent when awakened, Garrett reach

into his pouch and grabbed his cellphone. With his phone in hand, the jogger leaned down and gently poked then pushed the person as he tried to wake him.

Pushes turned into shoves, and eventually, the jogger gently rolled over the person. Wide, open eyes stared out into the early morning air. The man's face was frozen in his last terror. Looking up and down the body, the jogger noticed that the front of the shirt was soaked with blood. Startled, Garrett quickly stood up, and called 911 to report the body.

IN THE KINGSTREE, SOUTH CAROLINA, POLICE DEPARTMENT, DETECTIVE Melissa Chambers finished typing the report into the computer. This was the second body dumped in the last three weeks. Each body had a single puncture wound. The coroner's report showed a wide, triangular blade to the chest that was forced through to the heart. Each time, the body was at least a mile from where he or she was last seen.

The police department withheld one fact from the reporters: each body had strange markings drawn on the skin of their foreheads and chests. The detective shuddered. Although it seemed illogical, these bodies looked like they had been some part of a ritual sacrifice.

In a department with only fourteen full-time officers, Detective Chambers didn't think she had the right resources to handle this case. She looked up at the clock. It was too late now, but she'd call her friend over at the county sheriff's office to see if he could help her. This was going to take more than her small department had to offer.

IN THE LAW ENFORCEMENT INFORMATION NETWORK (LEIN), A TINY data worm was scrounging through all the materials being fed into the system, a country's worth of information and statistics. The data worm picked up on several characteristics of the case from Kingstree, South Carolina, and filed it in memory. It then snooped through the data for that city and the surrounding county. Finding another report with the same characteristics, it compiled its findings. When it had enough information to trigger a response, the small program quietly transmitted the compiled report to its master.

The data worm bounced its findings to a server in Houston, Texas. From there, the report travelled to Los Angeles, New York, Detroit, and finally back to a small building outside Langley, Virginia. Once the program sent out its report, it then resumed mining for more documentation.

AT A DESK LOCATED IN SECTION 28 HEADQUARTERS, AGENT TIMOTHY Wilson of the Department of Homeland Security received a small report from his worm in LEIN. Sifting through the compiled report and the raw data, Timothy made the same connections that the worm did.

Timothy keyed a very specific sequence on his computer. This, in turn, signaled Agent Smith's planning and analysis team and transmitted a copy of the report file with the raw data. This signal also informed each member that there was a potential incursion and that they needed to perform a quick analysis and assemble in the conference room within one hour.

Timothy then placed a call to his boss, Agent Smith.

The agent answered the phone immediately.

"Sir, we have a potential incursion event," Timothy informed his superior. "The planning team is assembling in the conference room as we speak."

Supervising Agent James Smith concluded the phone call with his assistant, and then he wrote the last few sentences of the report he was working on regarding the newest young field agent. Smith smiled and saved the paperwork. He grabbed his SSP and began the short walk to the conference room.

IT HAD BEEN TWO WEEKS, AND BOOMER WAS CONFUSED. ACCORDING TO the data from Dr. Kaine, the gestation period from exposure is about five days. Neither Boomer nor Heavy had turned to vampires because of the scratches they sustained while battling that new type of vampire. Earlier this evening at dinner, she couldn't tolerate much of the food. She normally had a healthy appetite, but her stomach was aching, and she was doubled over in pain. When Boomer looked at her reflection in her bathroom mirror, she could see how gaunt and hollow her cheeks had become.

Suddenly her fingers started to ache. The explosives expert cursed as her knuckles and fingertips were suddenly on fire. She was in agony. Her bones felt fragile. Boomer looked down and watched as claws extruded from her left hand. She stared in horror at the newly formed claws.

Boomer felt tremendous pain and pressure behind her eyes. It was almost as if she was having the most intense migraine of her life. She opened her eyes. Each eye turned a solid black, both the pupils and the whites. Suddenly, details became sharper and her vision shifted from color to black and white. Boomer noticed details on things she had never been able to see before. She squeezed her eyes shut. Slowly, she blinked her eyes open, and the explosives expert found that she could concentrate and filter out some of the more garish sights.

While she was looking her new eyes, she felt a new, terrible pain in her jaw. She opened her mouth and examined her teeth and gums. She was watching when they first elongated and then sharpened. Through the mouthful of sudden fangs, she muttered a candidate for the Understatement of the Year, "Damn."

GRAND RAPIDS, MICHIGAN. SATURDAY, 4/18/2015.

Thank You!

Thank you so much for reading *INCURSION: Knightmare*, the first book in the Knight's Bane Trilogy, and my first venture into writing fiction. I appreciate your time, and I hope you enjoyed the story.

If you enjoyed this book, please take the time to add a review on the website of the retailer where you purchased this book.

This book is the first in a trilogy chronicling the adventures of Team Knightmare as they fight monsters and try to protect the world. The trilogy is part of the larger series exploring the Hidden Worlds, called Incursion Legends. More information about the Incursion Legends series and the Hidden Worlds can be found online and on Facebook.

Online: IncursionLegends.com
Facebook: facebook.com/incursionlegends

Sign up for my World of Incursion newsletter and receive an exclusive short story about a mysterious delivery that threatens Section 28.

Go to: https://bookhip.com/PPJKFG

As a special bonus, we've included a special preview of *INCURSION: Faeblade*. Continue reading…

PREVIEW OF INCURSION: FAEBLADE

Prologue

A roiling mass of inky blackness rose from the worn concrete floor. To those in the room, the black seemed to writhe and move organically, as if it was a living thing. After a few seconds, the liquid darkness formed into the rough shape of a doorway anchored to the ground. As it finished forming the portal, a tall, well-groomed man appeared, stepping through the darkness. As he walked into reality, the liquid black appeared to run off of him, leaving no sign that the heavy darkness ever existed.

The man stood over six feet tall, had dark, almost a coal-black skin, and dark hair that was brushed back. His jet-black mane had scattered gray throughout, and his carefully groomed beard was short, almost a van dyke style, and it showed a great deal more of the salt and pepper look. His thin, angular face spoke of nobility, and his bright green eyes almost glowed with intelligence.

An expensive, tailored suit accented his fit and trim body, the dark suit offset by the pale blue shirt and royal blue tie. Anchoring the tie was a dazzling sapphire-crusted tie tack that matched the large sapphire in the ornate ring on his right hand. From his perfectly cut shoulders to the razor-sharp creases that brushed his black leather shoes, there was not a seam or crease out of place on his suit.

Plucking an imaginary piece of lint from his suit jacket, the man looked around the large warehouse floor. Nodding to those present, the man gave a slight grin. As his lips curled, the man standing in front of him could see a hint of a sharp, white tooth. The tall man spoke with a deep, warm voice that seemed to cover a harsh metallic undertone, "Mister Hammond. Report."

The man in front of him nervously adjusted his tie before he spoke. "Everything is as you commanded, my liege. Your court is waiting for your presence in the hall. I have personally verified the attendees, and even your Knight is waiting for your arrival."

The gentleman in the custom business suit nodded curtly and spoke. "And the other matter?" His voice was flat and cold.

The man called Mr. Hammond turned and looked at the woman to his right. She bowed her head slightly and purred, "The preparations have been laid, my lord. When you so order, my people will cause chaos for the other side. We'll keep them off balance while you strike them down. It will be your finest victory. They'll never see this coming."

The gentleman looked at the woman. Her ethereal beauty and diminutive size belied her warrior prowess. The ginger-haired woman had silver eyes, and was lithe, powerful without being heavily muscled. Her royal blue cocktail dress sparkled and shimmered. The effect was almost hypnotic as the dress clung to every curve on her perfect body. If there was any word that applied to this beautiful woman it was "sensual".

The gentleman's eyes glowed a deep red for a brief second, before returning to their natural green color. He turned back towards the liquid dark portal and made a small dismissive gesture with his hand. At the wave, the blackness started to fold in and consume itself, sinking to the floor, and quickly disappearing. Turning back around, the gentleman began walking towards the door on the opposite wall of the warehouse.

Around him, the men and women fell in step behind him. One of the larger men in a tailored suit had an earpiece in his ear. He raised his hand to his mouth and keyed the radio microphone he held in his hand. "This is Galen." The man spoke softly, "The King has arrived. We are en route to the Hall."

IN A LARGE CONTROL ROOM JUST OUTSIDE LANGLEY, VIRGINIA, AN alarm was sounding, and one of the on-duty technicians was trying to silence it. After he figured out which alarm was sounding, a few simple keystrokes silenced the audible alarm.

Frederick Tremblay had worked for the agency for less than six months. After an intensive training period, this was his first shift without his trainer leaning over his shoulder. And this was the first time he had ever seen this alarm section come to life. Grabbing the action binder, he cross-referenced the alarm code, and found the proper response sequence. He keyed the sequence into the terminal in front of him and watched as the alarm location and activation type scrolled in front of him. At the bottom of the screen, a reference code flashed insistently.

Looking over his notes, Fred paled. He signaled the watch commander and told him about the alarm. The watch commander walked over to Fred's desk as he tapped out a series of messages on his mobile phone. The watch commander leaned down and read the summary of the alarm. Noticing the flashing code, he patted Fred on the shoulder and said, "Good catch. You did everything by the book. I'll note that in the after-action reports."

The commander's phone rang. Looking at the screen, he nodded and answered, "Yes, Agent Smith. This is Donaldson, I'm the watch commander tonight. We just got a new alarm that was code 'Zulu-Three.'" There was a pause, and Donaldson continued, "Yes, sir. The Incursion alarm triggered for the Unseelie Court, sir." Another brief pause, and Donaldson began nodding absently to the person on the other end of the line. He assured the caller, "Yes, sir. I'll start the data collection. I'll have it ready for you by oh-eight-hundred. I'll have the new kid, Tremblay work with me. It'll give him some good experience. Yes, sir. I'll see you in the morning."

Donaldson looked down at the young rookie smiled. "Lucky break, Fred. You just caught a full-on Incursion alarm. You get to help me begin gathering data and then present it to Agent Smith and the planning team in the morning."

The color that had been returning to Fred's complexion was again lost as he realized that he was expected to present their findings to THE boss. Donaldson peered down at the screens in front of his young analyst, ignoring the look of horror on Fred's face.

The watch commander began muttering to himself, "Let's see where this alarm was located. Hmm. Looks like a city in western Michigan. Now, what the heck are the Unseelie doing in Grand Rapids?"

WE HOPE THAT YOU HAVE ENJOYED THIS preview of Book Two of The Knight's Bane Trilogy–*INCURSION: Faeblade*. If you want to find out what happens to Section 28 and Team Knightmare, the book is available wherever print and ebooks are sold.

ALSO BY BRYAN DONIHUE

INCURSION: Faeblade

The Knight's Bane Trilogy–Book 2

A massacre at a fae nightclub drives the Seelie Court to blame humans. Team Knightmare is sent to Michigan to investigate the horrors, and their job is about to get very difficult. With skepticism from the fae on one side and a group of human monster hunters on the other, Knightmare is trying to stop a war between the fae courts and humanity.

INCURSION: Dragonfire

The Knight's Bane Trilogy–Book 3

Section 28 is the secret agency that is tasked with hunting monsters and with controlling mystical forces that live on our plane. The agency is under attack from forces from Smith's past and from within the United States Government. Can Section 28 survive the attacks? Can Smith?

Pick up ebooks and signed copies of the books at:

IncursionLegends.com/shop

or at Amazon, iBooks, and your favorite retailer.

You can read short stories from the World of Incursion at:

IncursionLegends.com

ABOUT THE AUTHOR

Early in his life, Bryan decided that he would try as many different jobs as possible. Well, it was his high curiosity and low attention span that decided for him. He started in fast food and has worked in sales (retail, used car, business-to-business, door-to-door, credit card processing, vacuum cleaner, and firearms). Bryan has also been a security guard, police officer, and armored car vault manager. And he was a youth pastor.

Eventually, he decided he'd take the "easy path" and become a writer. He was an idiot. Writing is not easy, but it turned out, he was pretty good at it. People seemed to like his stories, so he kept telling them.

Bryan is a published author (fiction and non-fiction), game designer, graphic artist, web designer, consultant, trainer, ministry leader, and multiple-business owner. He is also happily married to his wife of over 20 years, Christina, and father to six or seven kids, depending on the day. He even sleeps occasionally.

Bryan is currently writing from a hidden bunker in Grand Rapids, Michigan. At least that's what he claims. We know he sits in a home office with a brass plaque that reads "Dungeon" affixed over the door.

To read more of the World of Incursion:
IncursionLegends.com
bryan@incursionlegends.com

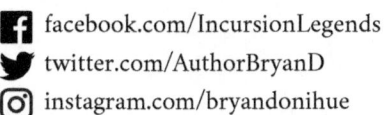

facebook.com/IncursionLegends
twitter.com/AuthorBryanD
instagram.com/bryandonihue

ABOUT SECTION 28 PUBLISHING

Helping Authors Find Their Voice...

Section 28 Publishing is a small, independent press created by author Bryan Donihue to publish his dark paranormal fiction. The fiction published by Section 28 is typically urban fantasy. Currently, Section 28 only publishes works from Bryan, but we are looking forward to working with other authors.

Why "Section 28"?

Originally, the name "Section 28" was created by Troye Gerard, and he graciously allowed Bryan to use the name as a secret government agency in the world that Bryan was creating. The first book set in that world was INCURSION: Knightmare. In that book, "Section 28" is the name of the secret division of Homeland Security that is charged with monitoring and controlling the paranormal in the United States. Bryan chose to use the name as his publishing imprint in homage to that organization, and his first published fiction.

The Mission of Section 28 Publishing

Section 28 Publishing's mission is to help authors figure out the labyrinth that can be independent publishing. From cover design and layout to marketing and sales, Bryan loves to help authors go from a manuscript to a published book that readers want to buy. For an author, nothing is better than having that first fan approach them at a venue, and Bryan wants every author to get that chance.